THE ICE KILLER

A DI BARTON INVESTIGATION

ROSS GREENWOOD

Boldwood

First published in Great Britain in 2020 by Boldwood Books Ltd.

This paperback edition first published in 2021.

1

A CIP catalogue record for this book is available from the British Library.

Paperback ISBN: 978-1-80280-356-3

Ebook ISBN: 978-1-83889-555-6

Kindle ISBN: 978-1-83889-556-3

Audio CD ISBN: 978-1-83889-548-8

Digital audio download ISBN: 978-1-83889-550-1

Large Print ISBN: 978-1-83889-554-9

Boldwood Books Ltd.

23 Bowerdean Street, London, SW6 3TN

www.boldwoodbooks.com

'Only the dead know the truth.'

— LEONID ANDREYEV

DOUBLE JEOPARDY

The double jeopardy rule is an important protection for individuals against the abuse of state power. It prevents police and prosecutors from repeatedly investigating and prosecuting the same person for the same crime, without good reason. The rule demands the authorities get their case right on the first occasion as it will be the only chance they get, and then accept the court's verdict. Equally, when a person is found not guilty in court, they know that the result is final. Being the subject of a criminal charge can be a difficult and distressing experience and has substantial consequences for the accused – who may be innocent.

1

THE ICE KILLER

It's Valentine's Day. A day I love and hate in equal measure. A rising sense of panic begins in the weeks beforehand, which forces me to make poor choices. The fear of missing out deafens the voice of reason. Who wants to be at home alone on that night when everybody else is out having fun?

Christmas without a partner I can handle. I always visit my mother's house then, although it will only be Mum and me this year. My annoying sister, Lucy, said she would only come up on Boxing Day now as the children are at university and want to do their own thing. It's a shame they won't be with us, because it's a time for family. And, if I'm honest with myself, I like the fact that their energy distracts me from thinking about my own failings.

Valentine's Day is different. It's a time for couples; for love and magic and the start of something wonderful. Glossy magazines tell you to snag a man, have kids, be happy, but as time passes I wonder whether I'm pursuing the impossible. Do these perfect men exist? If they do, then is it me? I admit that, while I enter relationships with enthusiasm, especially leading up to Valentine's Day, it soon wanes to inertia.

I believe my obsession with 14th February stems from school. In my final junior year, when us kids were about eleven years old, we had a new fresh-faced supply teacher. She wasn't like any teacher we'd had before. Young and smartly dressed, with full make-up and high heels, she resembled a famous actress to us impressionable children.

Her idea was to have a postbox where we could put our secret cards. I suppose, if you were naïve, it might have seemed like a marvellous idea. She enthused about great romances – Romeo and Juliet, Caesar and Cleopatra. I absorbed every word. Us girls talked of little else. We tried to pretend we weren't watching when the boys posted their red envelopes, even though I had decided not to get my hopes up. Kids ignored me, or, worse, noticed me and deliberately kept their distance.

When the big day came, Miss Diamond took the box to the front of the class and opened it with great fanfare. I could barely breathe. It was by far the worst moment of my life, and there was some serious competition. She read the first name out.

'Scarlett Starr.'

A tiny piece of me died, despite knowing it was irrational. Scarlett was the dream girl in school. She was all the things you could imagine: swimming team captain, the girl with the longest hair, the brightest smile, and so confident, despite living in a children's home. Even at that age, I could see her life would be different from mine. I was never sure if I thought her name was beautiful or crap. Regardless, the girls basked in her shadow. That was the year the lads realised they wanted to be in that spot, too. Ironically, it's her house that I'm driving to now.

Back then, Scarlett was on the table of four opposite me. The teacher skipped over and placed the big red envelope on her desk with an indulgent smile. Scarlett beamed as if someone had presented her with an award for a lifetime's commitment to charity. Miss Diamond picked the next one out and grinned. It was covered in small gold love hearts.

'Danny Stanton.'

The rugged striker from the football team received his card without interest. A wasted effort, I thought. I think he plays football in Spain now. We met first at playschool, and I don't think we ever said more than hello to each other over the following decade. The next card came out.

'Scarlett Starr.'

And the others followed a similar pattern.

'Scarlett Starr.'

'Danny Stanton.'

'Jim Jones.' Danny's best friend. Now works as a paediatrician.

'Scarlett Starr.'

'Amy Wicklow.' Later became a runway model and died in a Paris apartment from a heroin overdose.

'Carl Quantrill.'

That was my card. Even then, I knew not to aim high. I was a five-out-of-ten, maybe a six if I tamed my black hair, and I was bright enough to know that Danny Stanton wouldn't have been able to pick me out in a line-up of llamas. At that moment, my expression resembled one.

Carl Quantrill was the mysterious guy at school with slightly too long greasy hair, which covered his eyes. He only responded to his surname as he thought it was cooler than Carl. A suggestion of body odour added to his allure. He drawled and mumbled. I'd had a few conversations with him but often failed to catch what he'd said. I'd be too nervous to ask for clarification and so would smile instead. He would be my first, but that was many years later.

I was crazy about him. I'd worn away Damon Albarn's face on my Blur poster with kissing practice. As Carl opened the card that day, flames threatened to burst from my cheeks. All I'd written was, 'To my Valentine'. He couldn't have known I sent it, yet he immediately turned around and stared my way. He ripped the card to pieces and threw it in the air. The girls gasped, most of them, anyway, while the boys cheered.

Miss Diamond's mouth opened and closed. She should have stopped there and then but something made her plough on; each new name another dagger driven into my unloved heart.

'Sally Dawning.' My best friend, sitting next to me.

'Scarlett Starr.'

'Danny Stanton.'

'Jim Jones.'

And so on, with escalating cheers and boos echoing around the room. But the last letter was for me. 'Ellen Toole.'

I couldn't believe my good fortune, even though it was the smallest one by far. I turned to Sally, whose pudgy fingers were pressing her card to the desk as if it might float away. She smiled at me with genuine happiness. I suspected mine was from Sally, because I'd secretly sent hers. The room stilled while I opened my flimsy envelope with trembling fingers. The card had a single white rose on the cover, and I looked inside.

There was only one word in capitals. UGLY.

2

THE ICE KILLER

I am not ugly, but neither am I beautiful. If someone described me, the word they would probably use is tall, even though I'm only five feet nine. It's because I have slim, toned arms and legs but no bottom or breasts to speak of. Quantrill once said I had the arse of an old man, which I've tried hard to forget. Strong teeth and thick hair can't make up for my normal aloof expression, which Scarlett calls my resting witch face.

I park outside Scarlett's house in the lovely, peaceful village of Stilton and wait for the electronic gates to open. It must be nice to live here. Imagine being able to come and go as you please without speaking to anyone if you don't want to. Although Scarlett says the isolation drives her mad.

It's hard to say if we're friends. If you looked the word up in a dictionary, it wouldn't be a close match to what we have. That said, we attended the same senior school as well, and she was never outwardly unfriendly like some of her group. I never really fitted into any specific clique, and certainly not hers. I preferred the company of a rag-tag bunch who stayed together because we didn't suit anyone else. I'm not in touch with any of them now. It's as if, when school finished, we fled from each other in the hope of something better.

Scarlett and I flitted in and out of each other's lives over the years. We bumped into each other in a nightclub a few years after sixth form finished and occasionally went out together or met for coffee. The acquaintance would gradually peter out, then we'd pick up months down the line. I suspect we don't particularly like each other, but I have few other options.

I used to keep a diary for events such as tonight. I began doing this after my first Valentine's date twenty years ago. I recall filling it in and thinking how we'd be able to look back at it and smile when we were married and retired. It was date four when I realised how crazy that was. This evening will be my twelfth Valentine's date. I hope he doesn't bring twelve red roses, although that might be a sign.

I've slept with more people than twelve, though. I made some mistakes when I was younger so will never know the true figure. Besides, if you give your body away for next to nothing, counting seems pointless. How many is a lot nowadays, anyway? With Tinder and Bumble, and the rest of those dating websites, women don't need to be lonely any time of the year, as long as they aren't too fussy.

Valentine's night, though, is special. It's not a night for blind dates. I'm ever the optimist, even though Scarlett got me a card this week saying '*The definition of insanity is doing the same thing over and over and expecting different results.*' Is that mean of her, or is it her way of managing my expectations?

I wonder sometimes if she keeps me around so she has someone to remind her of when she was the best and had it all. She has no other friends now, either. We both sacrificed all of our female relationships at the altar of men. Even fat Sally, who stuck by me despite my desperate behaviour, eventually escaped. Sally and I had resigned from our jobs and booked tickets to India, then Australia, when we were twenty-five years old. Girls together and to hell with love. She hadn't even had sex by that point. Well, other than a vague, flimsy tale from a party into which I never probed too deeply.

Shortly before our flight, I got back together with my previous boyfriend, despite his violent behaviour, and let her down. I think he was around number twenty of those I remember. To her credit, she went on her own.

She picked up a terrible stomach bug in Delhi, which she struggled to shake off for the following three months, but still made it to Sydney. An Aussie property developer trod on her foot during the New Year's Eve fireworks show and couldn't believe nobody had snapped up this funny, slim, pretty, innocent girl. We used to be friends on Facebook, but it was tough to watch her smiling, young family grow up, so I blocked her.

A few months after she'd gone, when the hospital had discharged me and the courts had imprisoned him, the only job I could get was in a call centre. I've been in one ever since. My ex was inside for seven months, then he was deported, whereas my chosen career seems an open ended sentence with no light at the end of the tunnel.

One of the perils of call centre work is that you are regularly made redundant. Five years ago, I started another mind numbing role and Scarlett was on the same induction training course. Her beauty was fading, and she'd actually been left at the altar. Life was breaking her.

We were about thirty then, and amongst the oldest there by a decade. Yet again, I found myself out of the in-crowd. It was worse for Scarlett, because she knew what it felt like to belong.

A damaged Scarlett was a much nicer person. I helped build her back up, and at least we both had a friend again. Obviously, Scarlett did to me what I'd probably have done to her given the chance, and she settled down with the next rich guy she found. The surprise pregnancy forced his hand, and I got to wear an amazing dress on her big day. She kept her surname, so she must have liked it, although Tim's surname is Ovett, which doesn't go well at all with Scarlett. The best man became number thirty something. He was lovely, but didn't last the course.

Sadly, Scarlett and Tim suffered a cot death at six months, which they never mention. Tim's wealth means Scarlett doesn't need to earn, but she came back to work anyway, saying being alone was dangerous for her health.

I check my watch. It's seven o'clock on a Wednesday night, and I drum my fingers on the steering wheel until the gate finally opens. I shouldn't think like this, but I'm sure she makes me wait so I can admire her big house all lit up. I park next to her husband's white Audi A5 Coupé. He keeps it so clean you need sunglasses to stare at it. Tim and his car are a match made in heaven. But he and Scarlett are a union from hell. She is too pretty for him, and he has too much money for her.

It's him who greets me. He kisses me on both cheeks; as ever, he's overly keen to see me, lingers too long and presses too hard. He caught me coming out of the bathroom at their annual barbecue last year with the immortal line, 'I've always worried about you.' I told him that his flies were undone and slipped by as he checked them.

Scarlett is behind him, wearing designer jeans and a fitted shirt. Hers are air kisses with a hint of Chardonnay. She smells like a million dollars with immaculate, smooth skin. He has his pyjamas on. The I'm-living-the-perfect-life lie is laughable, but she has no other hand to play.

'Come in out of the cold. Right, upstairs. I've got a few options for you.'

'Thanks, Scarlett. You didn't have to bother. I could have thrown an outfit together.'

'Power up, Ellen! It's been how many years since you had a decent date on Valentine's? You need to pull out all the stops.'

She guides me past their eleven year old man-child, Dwayne. Now, that is a shit name. He's a boy from a Greek holiday fling that Tim had long before he met Scarlett. To his credit, Tim took the boy in when he was a toddler and his mother wanted to return to her job as a holiday rep. Dwayne gives me the finger with a cheeky expression. He's a lively lad.

Scarlett has her own dressing room, and there are three outfits on display. I can see straight away two of them wouldn't reach my navel because I'm over half a foot taller than her. Is she drunk or does she just not care?

I slide the blue one off its hanger. 'This looks nice.'

'That old thing. It's a bit dowdy and doesn't have the oomph factor. I want my assets seen.'

I haven't got time to consider her words, so I ignore her and strip off. Scarlett has never said anything about my physique. I'm what they call up-and-down. Food has only ever been fuel to me, so I've never had to worry about my weight. I stare in the mirror and beam. It's as if they made the dress with me in mind. Just above the knee, with a split up the side to show off my long legs. There's even a ruffled top to disguise my lack of cleavage.

'I hope you're doing something with your hair.'

'Yes, I'll do it at home.' It's a lie. I've already done it. I put my woolly hat back on while giving her my most winning smile. She scowls in mock disgust.

'Here, try these. They're Louboutin's, very expensive. I spilt oil on the toe, so I was going to throw them out, but they'll do for tonight.'

'You're too kind.' Weirdly, we have the same size feet, but she rarely lends me her shoes. She reckons she once caught a verruca from shoe swapping. I think she doesn't like to acknowledge we both take size sevens. That must be why she was so good at swimming.

I see my reflection and catch my breath. Admittedly, I'm too tall for her mirror and the image finishes at my unmade-up chin. I notice a spot on it. It's rubbish having bad skin at my age. My medication doesn't help. She stands next to me with tears in her eyes and lifts my hat off my head.

'Wow. You look lovely. Sit, and I'll do your make-up.'

That's why I keep at our friendship. Sometimes she forgets who she's trying to be.

She's brilliant at the layers and shading. I have a slightly thick nose, but with her contouring it shifts focus up to my grey-green eyes. Afterwards, I air kiss her. She sits on her little stool in front of the mirror as I wave goodbye. The tears are back, but they are for her.

I'll have to put my trainers on to drive home, but I shimmy down the stairs as if I'm the belle of the ball. Her husband opens the front door for me with his jaw on the floor. I give *him* the finger on the way out.

3

DI BARTON

Barton closed his eyes after DCI Cox walked away from his hospital bed, but his mind churned over her words. When he'd joined up, there had been no plan. It had been a wage slip and a job he'd found interesting. His career had progressed naturally. Uniform had suited his nearly six and a half feet frame, then becoming a detective had been a natural progression when he'd searched for new challenges. Passing the exams had been hard work, but he'd got there. He'd assumed DI was as far as he would go, and that was fine.

Now he had the chance to move up to the next level, he worried if it was what he wanted. His last two DCIs had ridden their desks hard. They had usually been in their offices before he'd arrived and still there when he left. Detective Inspectors tended to have bouts of crazy hours during major investigations, but other times he'd attended the kids' sports days and concerts with no problems. Barton didn't like the idea of giving that up. He'd never met anybody who wished they'd missed more of their children's youth.

Yet, it was a fantastic opportunity to cover Cox's role while she was on maternity leave, and she'd mentioned that she might not return. Part of him needed to be stretched. There was always a bigger picture in policing, and he wanted to see it. But there would be a price to pay in family time, and he was unsure if the cost was worth it. Life seemed easier when you only had yourself to think about. Now every choice carried a risk of regret.

Barton smiled. Holly would know what to do. He had great confidence in his wife's common sense. If they made the decision together with the family in mind, then it'd be the right one.

With that, his eyelids drooped from the pain medication that they had given him for his wounds. It had only been a few days since The Soul Killer's actions had left him with a painful scar on his chest. Barton drifted off to the rhythmic beat of the heart monitor. But he still sensed the swoosh of the door and the giggles as people neared his bed. He recognised Strange's, 'Shhh,' but kept his eyes closed.

'Is he alive?' asked Zander.

There was a brief pause.

'It doesn't smell like it,' said Strange.

'What does the beeping mean?'

'It sounds every time he farts.'

'What does it mean if it stops?'

'You need to press the red button for the laundry room.'

Barton laughed and gasped in agony with the same breath. 'Very amusing, you pair.'

Zander's black skin didn't show the bruising in the same shocking way as Barton's chest, but the eye above his injured jawbone was a ball of fire. They'd taken The Soul Killer down, but it had been a close-run thing. Only Strange had escaped serious injury. A short blonde, she had transferred from the Met over a year ago, and proven hard-hitting and likeable.

Zander, on the other hand, had been policing Peterborough almost as long as Barton and was a similar size. Zander rested a large box of Milk Tray on the bed. He and Strange sat in the two seats on either side of Barton.

'Good to see you both. Are you going to be all right, Zander?' asked Barton.

'Yep. I was lucky to escape with a mild concussion. Kept me in to be safe but now I can go home and rest.'

'Cox said to have the afternoon off.'

Zander chuckled. 'She's gone soft.'

'It's her maternal side coming through,' replied Barton. He explained about Cox's maternity and grinned at his two sergeants' faces as they processed the fact that if Barton got promoted, he'd leave a vacancy, and they were each other's competition.

Zander attempted to play it cool but couldn't help himself. 'There'll be some staff moves, then.'

'Who knows? This is the police, remember. They'll probably give me a mop and tell me to keep on top of the cells at the same time.'

'Yeah. I recall the good old days when they paid you for the job you did,' said Zander.

'I bet you both miss cycling around the neighbourhood too,' said Strange.

'With all your jokes, you'd think there were thirty years' difference between us, not ten,' replied Zander. He turned back to Barton. 'What's your prognosis?'

'The operation went great and the rib break was clean. I should be back at work in about six weeks.'

'They might want someone to cover as DI until you return,' said Strange.

'Yes. I mentioned to DCI Cox that Huntingdon Station had a really promising sergeant.'

Zander grabbed his box of chocolates and ambled to the door.

'It's been nice chatting, John. We'll see you in a couple of months.'

'Just kidding, guys. Cox said she'll visit me when I'm discharged. Hopefully, they'll offer both of you the opportunity to gain some experience.'

Zander slid the Milk Tray back on the bed. 'Call if you need anything. Text me with any news, and we'll collect you when you're ready to leave. Holly can focus on the kids.' He smiled. 'We'd better let you rest.'

Barton guessed they were heading to the pub to discuss matters. He overheard their comments as the door closed.

'Perhaps we'll have to arm wrestle for promotion,' said Zander.

'More likely they'll just give it to me for saving both of your lives.'

'We had it under control.'

'Bullshit.'

Grinning, Barton picked up the Milk Tray box. He opened it up to find most of the contents and all of his favourites had gone.

4

THE ICE KILLER

Scarlett and Tim's driveway slopes down to the house and I over-rev the engine of my blue Ford Focus pulling out. I daren't stall the car because it probably won't start again. On the road, I tut as there's a delay before it responds to my instructions to speed up. A sense of impending financial doom hits.

It's a desperate time of the year if you're already feeling gloomy. A thick layer of cold-looking mist lies over the land, lending it a haunted feel. BBC weather said a polar vortex may be approaching. Scarlett's been calling it the polar express after the animated film, but it's no joke as they cause extreme conditions, which is dire news for my heating bill.

My place is ten minutes from Scarlett's country mansion, but the neighbourhood is different. I live where you end up if you've made mistakes. It's a small, functional, top floor flat in a block of six at Monument Square. My insurance customer service agent job means I can just afford the mortgage. I had a plan that when I got married, I could keep the flat and rent it out while I moved into a family place with my husband. That was seven years ago and there's still no husband.

I'm pleased the tramp who has been languishing near the entrance of the car park has gone. The stone gates curve, giving him shelter from the wind and some cover from the rain. It's not a night to be out in the open. I took him some warm soup a few evenings ago. I think he slurred thank you, but the soup was half frozen in the bowl the next morning. When I got home from work that night, I had to clear up the broken pieces of porcelain. Judging by the bits of carrot on his sleeping bag, he'd rolled in it. It was annoying as it was from the matching set my mother bought me last birthday. My fault for not using plastic, but I thought he'd enjoy it more out of a real bowl.

Trent Anderson, the arsehole from the bottom flat underneath, has parked in my space again. He was Valentine number eleven. I'm sure he parks there so I have to ask him to move. I drive into his space instead, although in the morning, he'll wait for me to leave for the office and come out at the same moment even though he works from home. For about the fiftieth time he'll point at our cars and say, 'What does it mean, what does it mean?' He's the only person I've ever met who's more stalkerish than I am.

His behaviour is only just on the border of acceptability. When I told him to stop annoying me, he said he was just being neighbourly. He steadily chips away at any happiness in my life. There's little for him to go at. I keep my head down as his curtain twitches.

Letting myself in, I see I have fifteen minutes before date time. I take a moment to stare out of the lounge window. I viewed this place once before buying it. They had the blinds drawn. What kind of person spends all that money and only sees the building the one time? I even looked at my car twice and that's shit. When I moved in and pulled the blinds, I found my view was directly into the cemetery. I knew it was there, so it wasn't a complete surprise, but I'm so close I can read a few of the residents' names on their gravestones.

My dad's in there at the far corner. He doesn't have a grave, but my mum said he asked for his ashes to be scattered in the memorial garden. I often sit on the bench and wonder what could have been if he hadn't left us. Sometimes I go through a gap in the fence behind the flats and sit in the dark with him. There's a statue of an angel nearby which always catches my eye. It feels as if she's looking over him.

Scarlett reckons it's creepy to live that close to a cemetery, but that's not what I think. I've never seen any ghosts. I have spotted our car park sleeper sitting on the benches with his friends with a different kind of spirit. The caretakers usher the drunks out at nightfall and lock the gates, leaving it pitch black, but I like the idea of my dad nearby even if I don't remember loads about him.

I was more positive back when I first moved in. I used to look out at the graves when I was getting ready for work and think, I'm going to have a better day than you lot, no matter how bad it is. But that isn't always true. Nowadays, I occasionally think they wouldn't have far to drag me if I hurled myself from my window. I put the radio on to drown out the *Friends* episode that is actually coming from the deranged woman two flats underneath me, and remove my hat.

I brush my hair slowly but still more comes out. My mood drops further. When I've been down in the past, I've often thought at least I have good locks. The only thing I can do is add water, put mousse on, and blow-dry it up to create volume. I find a YouTube video on the best method and copy it by creating bangs to hide my high temples. I hope the Chinese restaurant is dimly lit or I'll dazzle him.

Saying that, it's more likely that I'll need shades. Number twelve, tonight's date, Brad Averescu, has a similar hair loss problem. His is beyond help as well, and he hides it similarly. Perhaps we can compare techniques.

He's one of those blokes in their mid-thirties who has never grown up, but I'm still excited. For him, football is for watching on a Saturday, playing on a Sunday and discussing all week. He'd better not arrive wearing a Manchester United shirt. Saying that, I can forgive him most things just for his name. He could be an Italian gigolo, when he actually comes from Burnley. Although Ellen Averescu sounds like something you catch from mosquitos.

Still, Brad's in great shape and could pass for a young Jude Law. He's worked in our department for years. I've always thought he was a bit of a player with women as well as sport, but Scarlett said he's been keen on me for a long time. The fact she wants me to date someone she calls Boring Brad says it all. Apparently, she'd heard he was great in bed. It wouldn't surprise me if she knew first-hand.

Scarlett has a nickname for most people. Once she called me Crazy Ellen, but I gave her such a look that she never mentioned it again.

I open the fridge and remove a bottle of white wine. I had a glass earlier to calm my nerves. What was I worrying about? He'll either like me, or he won't. I take a big gulp from the bottle. It's cheaper to preload. Wine in restaurants is so expensive. I learned that to my cost when Valentine date number nine left the swanky pizza place we were in to get some money out of the bank and never came back.

I think the man should pay for the first meal, especially if he did the asking. My beau tonight was the instigator even though he communicated by text, which isn't super-romantic. Especially as he only sits about twenty metres from me at work.

A beep informs me I have a new message. Never a good sign ten minutes before the arrival of your date. My mobile is in the bedroom. I stand in front of my own full length mirror where I can see my eyes. They look sad. They know the dress, shoes, immaculate eye shadow and expectation have been a waste of time. I take a bigger glug from the bottle and enter the code on my phone.

Running a little late, should be there in fifteen.

That's unexpected. I skip to the fridge in the lounge-diner and put the wine back. Pacing myself is important if I don't want to fall over in Scarlett's shoes. I slide the high heels on. Damn, they make me feel good.

I decide to nip out for more booze in case he's a no-show. This end of Eastfield Road is a rough place at night. There's still plenty of people hanging around in doorways and sitting on car bonnets despite the cool wind and swirling mist. I smile at the guy behind the counter of the off-licence. I'd hate his job. It must be a constant battle against the shoplifters, but I feel safe inside the shop with all the security cameras, and it's warmer than my flat.

After perusing most of the range, I purchase my usual cheap bottle. It tastes fine if it's freezing cold, otherwise it makes me gag. I step outside and pet the shivering wee spaniel tied against the bin. It's called Pebbles or Peebles. The elderly owner is Scottish and talks fast. As I step away, a group of young lads appear around the corner with an enormous dog, whose heavy breath steams in the air. It pads along, muscles rippling under the damp fur. It's immediately clear who's taking whom for a walk.

I step back and look at the vulnerable Pebbles, who's seen the threat. There's nothing he can do. He whimpers and accepts his fate. I'm not shocked either. It's the way it is around here. Survival of the fittest and law of the jungle, although usually the violence is between men. The boy holding the lead has sensed the danger. I pray for the Scotsman to leave the shop.

'Woah, Ace. Stop, stop. Shit!' panics the dog walker.

The rottweiler easily pulls himself over to the bin and stares down at a crouched-in-submission Pebbles, and opens his mouth. Butting in around here doesn't pay. Ace isn't hungry, he's showing his strength. I don't want to be his focus or attract the attention of the gang, but as Ace's head lowers, I whistle. He stops and turns his huge head in the direction of the sharp sound. Empty eyes study me for a few seconds while he considers if I have anything of interest.

I can almost sense his brain processing centuries of breeding, which tell him humans are his friend. He returns his gaze to Pebbles, who is not human. Sensing Ace's body tensing to strike, I whistle again, but this time Ace only blinks in reply.

'Help me, you twats,' the desperate boy shouts at his mates as he tries to pull the beast back. At that moment, the Scotsman steps out of the shop, unclips Pebbles and whisks him away, carrying him down the street. He doesn't look around and his expression doesn't change. He's lived here long enough to know the rules. I leave swiftly, too, and quickly forget.

Back home, I sit on one of the stools at the kitchen pull-out table. This is the part I enjoy most: the anticipation of the date. At this point, it's all excitement and nervousness, although as the years have passed, I've felt less of both.

Nevertheless, I find myself humming the song about going to the chapel, and going to get married, when the doorbell sounds. A deep breath, then I let him in. When I open the door, I actually bark the beginnings of a howl of laughter before I prevent the rest of it falling out.

He doesn't notice because he breezes past me with a bag containing clinking bottles and another that leaves a waft of Chinese food in its wake. He spots the kitchen, takes three bottles out of the bag and puts them in the fridge, despite two of them being red wine.

'Come on, get the plates out.'

He kisses me on the cheek, and I'm relieved to say he smells of aftershave rather than alcohol. Three bottles don't bode well. Either he's got a problem, or he thinks I have.

I pull a chair back. 'Do you want to eat at the table?'

'No, we can have it on our laps. I brought a movie you'll know. *Shawshank Redemption*.' He waggles the DVD at me. 'It's a modern classic, and I thought we could kind of watch it and natter at the same time as I bet you've seen it loads, too.'

He must have asked Scarlett what my favourite film was. Smooth move, I like it! While I get two plates and the cutlery, I sneakily check my phone to reread the message where he asked me out. It says;

How do you fancy a Chinese meal on Valentine's?

Trust me to think I was getting the nine course tasting menu at the Jade Emperor instead of a greasy bag of pork balls on my own sofa.

But I choose to enjoy the night and go with the flow. Brad chats away to me while the movie plays. His humour is not bad: a little childish, perhaps. First dates aren't the time for burps, whatever he might have eaten. We end up drinking the dregs from my wine bottle as well. He tells me he's parked around the corner. That's a sign if ever there was one.

I tidy up as the film finishes and consider my options. He appears at my side and helps with the washing up.

'You look great in that dress.'

And that's it. We're kissing, and soon we're shagging. It's okay. I'm stuffed and bloated, and he isn't particularly gentle. It's too porn-like for a first time, and I even catch him looking at himself in the mirror. I suspect he has a routine of positions. My phone rings during the act and I ignore it, leaving voicemail to answer. There hasn't been much romance at my place, so I don't interrupt his performance. It's nice to be desired, though. Afterwards, he rolls behind me for a cuddle. His hands are soft and gentle. There's potential here. I feel cosy and drowsy, and we're asleep in seconds.

I forget about the missed call.

5

THE ICE KILLER

It's a car backfiring that wakes me. I sense I'm alone. Two bottles of wine thud in my brain, as you'd expect. I hear someone – I assume Brad – brushing their teeth. I cringe as I don't recall him bringing his toiletries. My dressing gown found its way into the wash at the weekend, which is a relief because it was minging, and I pull it out of the pile on the chair in the corner. At the toilet doorway, I'm relieved and shocked to see he brought his own toothbrush with him. Talk about confident, or do lots of them do that nowadays?

'Do you want a coffee?'

He looks at his watch. 'Sure, quick though. Black, please.'

He wanders past me and begins picking his clothes up off the floor. He's in better shape than I remember, although he also has a really hairy back. You'd think I would have noticed that last night.

He comes out of the bedroom and takes his DVD out of the player. I receive a smile when I pass him his cup.

'How did you know *The Shawshank Redemption* was my favourite film?'

'Isn't it everyone's?'

He slops the top third of his drink down the sink and fills it back up with cold water. I had already put some cold in. He downs it in one go and grimaces.

'Right, I'd better go.'

'Sure.' I shouldn't say anything else, but I can't help myself. 'I had a nice night.'

He stops at the door. 'I'll text you.' That's it, he's gone. He'll see me in the office in three hours. I decide I'm not going to over-analyse last night's conversations, although it's partly because they're a bit hazy.

I pick up my phone to check the time and remember the missed call. It's from my mum. She's been needier of late. I suppose that's understandable with her advancing years and declining health, especially living alone.

I dial the voicemail and listen in.

'Hi, pet. It's me here. Could you give us a ring, only I'm not feeling so good? Nothing in particular. I just have a bad sensation, like something terrible is going to happen. A friendly voice will perk me up. I'll get an early night, so if you don't hear this soon, we can chat tomorrow.'

I immediately call her back, even though it's only 6 a.m. No answer. Grabbing my car keys, I realise I am way over the limit and can't risk losing my licence. She's only about half a mile away. I will have to run.

6

DI BARTON

Zander was as good as his word and came to pick Barton up a few days later when the hospital doctors had agreed he could go home. Zander rushed in, grabbed Barton's case, and stood next to the door.

'Is the hospital on fire?' asked Barton.

'No, Kelly is parked in one of the ambulance bays.'

Barton raised his eyebrows.

'Just kidding. She's circling the car park so she doesn't have to pay for parking. Let's get outside. You know how snippy she can get.'

Barton stepped to the door. He gave the room a last look, smiled, and walked gingerly down the corridor.

'Are you scared of her?' asked Barton.

'No more than is necessary.'

Outside, Barton half expected Strange to be waiting in a joke vehicle like an ice-cream van, but he recognised her car as she swung round the corner. Barton lowered himself into the front seat, which had been pushed right back.

'How you feeling, boss?' asked Strange.

'Tender, but pleased to be going home.'

Peterborough looked the same as she drove through the morning rush-hour traffic, but he realised that he looked at the streets nowadays as scenes where crimes had taken place. Whereas once, he'd looked at them as places he'd frequented as he grew up. Leaving hospital with a healthy prognosis, though, was a happy day, so he smiled and cracked the window to let in some non-hospital air.

'Did they say how long you'd be at home for?' asked Strange.

'Four to six weeks.'

'Nice,' said Zander. 'I didn't realise all you had to do to get extra holiday was nearly die.'

'I wouldn't recommend it. How's work?' he asked.

'Cox is pushing hard to get us all into shape for when she's on maternity leave. She keeps asking if we're ready to put in for our inspector exams.'

'Are you?'

'Getting there,' they both chimed.

Even through the fog of his pain medication, his suspicions were raised. They pulled up outside Barton's house. The three children and his wife were all frantically waving at the lounge window.

'Coming in?' he asked his sergeants as he got out.

'No. Crime doesn't sit at home and watch boxsets. We have jobs to do,' said Strange with a scowl as she took his case out of the boot and put it next to him. 'And we'd already planned to go for a fry-up before work. Enjoy every minute, John. We'll see you soon.'

Barton waved them off as his family came running out of his house to greet him. It was good to be home.

7

THE ICE KILLER

It's a grey morning. A thick fog has blanketed the streets, bringing visibility down to twenty metres. Orange streetlamps are the only sign that I'm not about to disappear into the middle of nowhere. It feels like 2 a.m. as opposed to a little after six. My mother doesn't live far away, but I'm no runner, and the streets are slippery, which causes me to slow down.

Halfway there, as my tongue searches for moisture in the chilly air, I curse my choice of footwear. The driver of a car that's creeping along the road gives me a strange glance as he studies my old-lady-shuffling technique in my flat shoes. What's waiting for me at my mum's house? Should I worry?

I'm light-headed and stumbling by the time I arrive. A milkman next door gives me the look he probably reserves for when he sees a suspected burglar. The lounge curtains are drawn but I can tell the light is on, which is unusual. My mother's only flaw is a determined tightness over electricity consumption. She'll give food to the homeless and put cash in collection tins, but the thermostat doesn't go over twenty-one, and leaving a room without flicking the light switch off is a crime worthy of a firing squad.

My concern ratchets up a notch, and my legs wobble as I stagger to the rear of the house. That could be from the run, the alcohol, or worry. I take the key from under the watering can and let myself in.

'Mum! Mum, where are you?' Silence.

It's been a quiet house for many years. Apparently, my dad was a noisy man with a deep laugh and a love of rock music, even first thing in the morning. I recall him in the kitchen rapping his hands on the work surfaces when a song reached its climax. Well, I think I remember that, because I was only five when he died. Are my recollections of him my own, or my mother's? Whatever, I miss him, or at least the idea of him.

He went to the doctors with a mild complaint and discovered he was riddled with cancer. Three weeks from diagnosis to death. If I try to recall that time, all I have are memories of anger. I guess that's normal. Dad was one of the good guys. I suppose most people think of their father in that way, because fathers hide who they really are from their kids until they're no longer children.

Thank God I still have my mum. She's been my anchor to sanity throughout my turbulent life. Even though she couldn't do anything for me after the incident, she gave her fragile daughter a safe place after they fixed me.

A few hours of moping at her house and listening to sound advice gave me a fresh perspective on many occasions. You need love to survive in this world. I've always had enough from her to sustain me. There are no secrets between us. I become a child again when I'm here and the future disappears from my mind.

Obviously, losing him affected her the most. She lives a simple life and rarely leaves the house. It's a relief to find her in the lounge. I stare at her in the armchair and notice how old she looks. Her phone is in her lap and she's still. Yet, I can see her cardigan rising slightly. I release a long breath.

'Mum, wake up.' I squeeze her hand, and it's freezing. She's deaf, so I shout. Nothing, then her eyes open a little. They struggle to focus.

'My chest hurts,' she whispers.

My mobile isn't in my pocket, so I grab hers, ring 999 and tell them heart attack. The first-aid course I did five years ago lurks in my knowledge. I consider putting her in the recovery position, but she seems comfortable in the chair even though her breathing is shallow.

How long does it take for an ambulance to arrive? I check her pulse using her wrist. The beats are slow and erratic. What to do? I stroke her arm, and the words fall over each other.

'Don't leave me, Mum. You're all I have and I love you so much. I don't know what I'd do if I lost you. I've tried to be a decent daughter, and I'm sorry about not giving you more grandchildren, and the stuff at school, and costing you money.'

I ramble on, apologising and begging. Sirens sound in the distance and rapidly become louder. I feel pressure on my hand and see her eyes have opened again. I can just make out the words as she says them. 'Don't worry. Your sister will help.'

I open the door and the paramedics stride in. They are brilliant: polite, efficient and competent. After checking her signs, they stretcher her to the ambulance and we're tearing through the streets. They take her away when we arrive at the hospital and I'm left in a waiting area next to a nurses' station with a cup of coffee between my feet.

A nurse comes over to say my mother is poorly but stable. She offers me a sandwich, but I only manage a single bite. It's late morning before a doctor appears to speak to me.

'Hi, I'm Dr Olafemi.' She sits next to me and rests her hand on my arm. 'Your mother has been taken to Intensive Care.'

'Is she going to be okay? Can I see her?'

I've seen kind smiles like the one she gives me all my life. I know when I'm about to be let down gently.

'Your mother is very ill. I've read her notes on the database. There's a whole catalogue of problems, many of which involve her circulation.'

'What do you mean? She's healthy.'

'She was diagnosed with faulty, leaking valves last year, and her heart is enlarged.'

'Can't you fix them?'

'We could, if she was younger. There are other circulatory issues present, too. I would give her a zero chance of surviving the operation.'

'What can you do?'

She takes my hand. 'We'll make her comfortable but I'm afraid we'll have to accept that she's dying. It's just old age. Her kidneys are failing as well. She could go at any time.'

'But that's not fair.'

It's a stupid thing to say. Her kind eyes remind me my mother is seventy-five next year. It's not a bad age. Many never get anywhere near that. I'm not surprised to realise that, yet again, Mum has tried to protect me and kept the diagnosis to herself. It's kind but stupid. I didn't want to lose the chance to spend time with her. I think of the nights I've lain on my sofa and got pissed watching pointless quiz shows, while my poor mum was sitting at home on her own coping with all manner of horrific news.

'Is there anyone you'd like to tell?'

'How long does she have?'

'It's hard to say. Maybe just a few minutes, or a couple of days at most. Come, I'll take you up there.'

We wander through a maze of corridors. We clean our hands at the entrance to the ICU. It's quiet inside after the hubbub of the nurses' station, just whispers and beeps. I sit in the seat next to the bed, but it's too low to see her face. The ICU nurse tells me she'll be at her desk if I need anything.

There's so much tubing helping her breathe that I struggle to recognise her.

'Mum, it's me.'

I stop talking. When we rode in the ambulance, I sensed my mum was still there. The body in front of me seems empty even though the slow, constant beeps indicate otherwise. What will I do without her? Her texts every morning were often the highlight of my day.

I ring my only remaining relative, my sister, Lucy. She never picks up her phone to me. Not after my bad spell. She's seven years older and we've never been close. She moved to London very young and never came back. Well, perhaps twice a year. My mum proudly shows me pictures of her house next to a stream and the odd article about her genius. It's funny because I used to joke about becoming a lawyer, and she's now a solicitor. I do love her kids, though, but that's all we have. I leave a message on her mobile.

I consider who else to ring. There's no one. Scarlett has never formally met my family. My mother's friends don't need to know right now. It will only be the two of us until the machines are quiet. Then it will be just me. I rest my head on the bed and sob.

8

THE ICE KILLER

In the end it took thirty-seven hours for my mother to die. I was there for each one of them, even though she never regained consciousness. My sister, Lucy, blustered in on the second day and stayed for an hour. She asked the right things, but we didn't touch the entire visit. When she left, she kissed Mum on the forehead and said to keep her updated. She blew me a kiss as she went out of the room.

Nevertheless, my heart shrank over those hours at my mum's bedside, until it felt as if I weren't human any more. I foolishly checked my phone for messages from Brad. There weren't any. The only person I rang was Scarlett. I asked if she could bring me some spare clothes because I stank. She said she was really busy but would pop in that night. When she didn't arrive, I called again. It went to voicemail.

When I spoke to Lucy to tell her the news afterwards, she said her husband had someone who would sort out the arrangements for the funeral. Delegating that seemed cold, but they did a good job when my mum's crazy sister, Aunt Dora, died a while back. Anyway, what do I know about that kind of thing?

The funeral was a very small affair. People attend the funerals of those who've mattered to them. They've touched them in some way. My mum must have preferred her own company most of the time.

A friend of my mother's arrived after the service and hugged me. She said my mother was always talking about her family, and that I was a wonderful daughter. I wept again.

Today is my first shift back at work. I haven't seen a soul since I left the hospital other than at the funeral. My only communications have been through Instagram and Facebook. The only human contact I had was HR ringing to offer me a week off for compassionate leave. It doesn't seem much time for something so life-altering. Not that I've done anything but lie in bed or on the sofa; not even get drunk. I'm just so lonely.

I sneak a glance at Brad as he walks in with his friends. They talk animatedly. No prizes for guessing what the topic is. I try to drag my eyes from him with my last remaining gram of self-respect, but fail. To my surprise, he looks over and waves. I watch him say something to his mates, who all laugh, and he swaggers over.

There's a radiator next to my desk, and he leans against it.

'Hi. I heard what happened and just wanted to tell you I'm sorry for your loss. I'm close to my mum and would really struggle if she died. When you're ready, we'll have a drink or something.'

'I thought you'd be in touch.'

'I assumed you'd want to be with your family.'

'I could do with some company. How about tonight?'

He looks pained. 'Erm...'

'Or tomorrow?'

What have I become? He doesn't care about me, and still I clutch at him.

'Look, I had an enjoyable time but I'm not in the market for a relationship. I've got a lot on at the moment, with the team and stuff. If you want to hook up like last week then that's cool. I'd better go and log on. Catch you later.'

I watch his snug trousers as they weave between the chairs back to his desk. How sweet. He'll pop around, get lashed, and shag me if I like. Fucking bastard.

I sense a presence next to me. It's Scarlett.

'Hey, sorry I didn't come to the hospital last week. My idiot husband got drunk and hid the car keys. We had a big row, but I couldn't escape. I hope you're all right. Do you fancy going out at lunchtime? I need to buy a frock for the races at the weekend.'

She leaves without waiting for an answer, safe in the knowledge she is more important than me.

My phone beeps and I take a call from a furious person. She's mid-rant about the loss adjustor turning up late to assess her burglary when I notice it's the third claim for stolen goods she's made in the last two years. Something stirs inside me and I slide my headset off, retrieve my coat from the back of my seat, and stride out of the building.

Even though I drive home, I arrive back remembering so little of the journey that it scares me. I stare through the window into the graveyard. It looks cold, damp and sinister out there.

I turn on the CD player and flick through my collection. I wonder if I'll lose my job. The firm I work for can be ruthless, whatever the circumstances. My dreams of owning an iPad in the future will have to remain just that. 'Tears in Heaven' by Eric Clapton will be perfect. It's such a beautiful song, and I'm glad he made his way through his grief, but I'm not sure I can.

The deep, hot bath is ready. I drop in a bath bomb and climb in with a carving knife. I have a moment's worry about being found naked but decide I'll be beyond caring. As I relax into the warmth, I gasp at how good it feels. The smells fire up my brain. I check the packaging and realise the bomb contains invigorating eucalyptus. Maybe that's why the thoughts that bubble up aren't suicidal. They are angry and vengeful.

I place the knife on the side and sink beneath the surface.

I've always been the victim. Why should I be the one to die?

9

DI BARTON

As Barton left his house, he grinned at the 'get well soon' cards. The cards surrounded the mirror he was using to check for toothpaste from kissing the children goodbye. Luke had insisted they have them up until he went back to work, or he reckoned it would be unlucky. Barton felt fortunate. He'd survived The Soul Killer when many others hadn't, and even the police had lost one of their own.

Six weeks at home after being discharged by the hospital had been lovely once the pain had subsided. Especially when the children were at school. He and Holly had reconnected in every way, and it was nice to spend relaxed time with the kids when they came home from school.

However, he was getting bored. Retiring wasn't for him just yet. He missed the team and couldn't wait to start learning the DCI role. He'd popped into work a few times to re-acclimatise himself and he had a meeting with DCI Cox first thing.

Holly had said she'd take the cards down tonight, so he had a last look at his three favourites. The first was from his six-year-old, Luke, although he guessed twelve-year-old Layla had written the words. It said, 'Get better because I want you to take me to McDonald's', above a picture of a demented clown. Lawrence, who was seventeen, had drawn him an impressive picture of a fat Robocop, with the caption, 'Come quietly or there will be... trifle'.

The third was from Mortis, the pathologist for the city, and had a teddy bear with a sling on the front. Inside, Mortis had written, 'Chin up, or chin down,' and there was a handmade voucher for a free postmortem.

Barton pulled his coat on and left the house, chuckling. He fired up his Land Rover and drove down The Village road. He loved Peterborough, perhaps because it was so familiar, but large parts were altering fast. He'd read in the local paper that Peterborough was the UK's fastest-growing city by population through a combination of immigration and births.

The rougher areas of the city were getting rougher. Crimes were changing. Violent incidents, which would have raised both eyebrows years ago, were accepted as commonplace now. The world had become an angrier place. Peterborough was no exception.

He knew the moment he stepped back inside the station and put his coat on the back of a chair, he would be right back in it. A smile crept on his face as he wandered through the desks. The only detectives present were DS Zander and a recently trained detective, DC Leicester. It sounded like the latter was on the phone to his mum.

'Where is everyone?' Barton asked Zander.

'A few are at court. Strange is on a long weekend break with Sirena. Ewing and Zelensky had a date last night, and Ewing dropped a bowling ball on his foot. She took him to A & E this morning for an X-ray as last night's waiting time was six hours.'

'I didn't know they were dating.'

'I think he's keen. She's like a mini-Strange; very focused on her work. Cox said to go right in when you arrive.'

'She must be keen to pass on her wisdom.'

'I wouldn't be too sure about that.'

'Eh?'

'Looks like she's packing.'

Barton strode to her office and found the door open. Sure enough,

Cox whistled a jaunty tune while throwing things haphazardly into a big cardboard box. She had a proper bump now, whereas previously she'd just looked as if she'd eaten a big dinner.

'Don't tell me it's your last day,' he said.

'It seems that you'll be getting the same induction training as I did.'

'Which is?'

'A handshake.'

'Perfect.'

'Did you expect more?'

Barton pondered the question. Naively, he had.

'I'll leave you the chair.'

Barton spun the seat a full turn and slumped in it. He glanced around the room, then out of the window. Stark office blocks loomed opposite. Still, it would be nice not to hot-desk any more. Cox removed the top drawer from her desk, emptied it into the cardboard box, and slid it back. She removed a picture from the wall and put it on top of the other items. Barton made a mental note to bring a family photo in.

Barton leaned back. 'Looks like you don't expect to return.'

'Who knows how I'll feel? What I do know is that I can't leave anything drinkable, edible or useable behind, as it'll be gone before I've driven out of the car park.'

Barton held his hands up in mock surrender, even though he already had his eye on her fan.

'Don't be glum, John. You know what you're doing. Be yourself. The super is a good man. He'll help all he can.'

'If I can find him.'

She chuckled. 'You'll see him when some shit needs shovelling downwards.'

'What about a DI to cover my role? Or are the sergeants acting up?'

'You know the budget for extra staff is non-existent until next year, or you will do when you start doing my job in five minutes.'

'Strange and Zander are hungry for promotion.'

'Not that hungry.' She gave him a cryptic smile and shook his hand. 'Good luck.'

'Before you leave, what's the first thing I should do?'

'Finish up your paperwork on The Soul Killer. He's in a semi-vegetative state now and out of ICU. We may have a trial yet.'

She took one last look around, grinned at him, and carried the box from the room. Barton steepled his fingers and called Zander's number in the office. When Zander arrived, Barton was spinning around in the large office chair.

'Cool, can I have a go?' asked Zander.

Barton shot him a disappointed look, then relented and smiled. 'Sure.'

'Congratulations. Does this make you a bigger cheese now?'

'I'm only acting as a medium Cheddar. In true police fashion, it looks like I'll be doing this job and my old one until she comes back.'

'It's always the way, but you know how it works. Show them you can do the job and it's yours. I take it you'll be in Huntingdon at HQ a fair bit.'

'Yes. I'll be counting on my supermotivated sergeant team, who have been focused on passing their inspector exams.'

Zander stopped the chair. 'Ah! About that. I can't get motivated. If we pass the board, they'll probably move us back to uniform as inspector. Neither of us want to do that.'

'I assume it's you and Strange you're talking about. Pass the exams and go from there. You don't have to do anything you don't want to. You could revise together. I'm sure you'd enjoy that.'

Zander raised an eyebrow but said nothing. He joined Barton at the window and they looked out.

'We've come a long way. Hard to believe it's twenty years,' said Zander.

'Can you remember the nervous excitement when we first started? You'd receive the call from control and grin as you hurtled towards the unknown.'

'I don't feel like that any more.' Zander's head drooped. 'I miss it.'

'That's because we've seen it all, and we know as a team we can handle it all. If you feel like that in your role, it's time to move on. I'll be nervous in senior meetings, and that's going to make me feel alive.' Barton put his hand on Zander's shoulder. 'Study for your exams. I'll give you the experience needed for the next step.'

Zander took a deep breath. 'Agreed. We'll be running the force before you know it. All we need is a huge case that covers us in glory.'

DC Leicester interrupted them.

'Sorry, sir. There's been an incident at the bottom of Padholme Road near where it meets Eastfield Road.'

'What kind of incident?'

'A kidnapping.'

'Of a child?'

'No, a postwoman.'

10

Barton checked his watch. That hadn't taken long. He smiled at Leicester.

'Find out the details and ring me. You can hold the fort.'

He nodded at Zander. 'I'll drive.'

Barton took his own car as he had promised Holly he'd try to be back for lunch. Peterborough's road system used to be fantastic, but the influx of people – unofficially fifty thousand in the last twenty years – and all the construction work meant that the town centre was slowing. It seemed they were building everywhere. Barton drove around the parkways instead. It was twice as far as the direct route, but at seventy miles an hour, he'd arrive sooner.

Zander put the phone down from Leicester's call giving them the latest as they arrived in the Eastfield area. The police did a lot of business in these streets. Barton could remember two hold-ups at the bookmakers in the last year. Zander gave him the address on Padholme Road. Details were sketchy, but it seemed a man had pulled a postwoman into his house and wouldn't let her out. A passing driver noticed and rang the police.

The traffic was already backed up along Eastfield Road, letting Barton guess that the road ahead had been closed. Instead, he drove up

Whalley Street, through Charles Street, where they could see the flashing lights of the emergency vehicles.

Barton parked up, and they got out.

'Haven't we been to this address before?' he asked Zander.

'I thought it sounded familiar. What was that ex-squaddie's name, Sixtrees or something?'

'Twelvetrees!'

They exchanged a curled lip as they simultaneously remembered the case. Twelvetrees was a troubled man. He'd returned from active service with PTSD. The armoured vehicle he'd been driving had over-turned after a landslide, not his fault, but one passenger had died and another had ended up in a wheelchair. Barton knew Twelvetrees would have seen terrible things in the Middle East because the Royal Marines had been in the worst of it. Maybe the accident had been the final straw as they'd discharged Twelvetrees within a year.

He'd returned to Peterborough with his wife, but the man who'd left had never really come home. What had returned was a shadow, and a dangerous one at that. His wife had taken the brunt of his illness. Despite him refusing help, she'd stuck by him for years, always declining to give evidence against him. Then something had happened two years back, and she'd asked for a divorce. Twelvetrees had smashed up the Prince of Wales' Feathers pub after hearing the news. Barton had got involved due to the seriousness of the crimes alleged against the ex-soldier, which included racially aggravated threats to kill the Asian owners of the establishment, criminal damage of twenty thousand pounds, numerous common assaults, and a few others besides. Zander and Barton automatically thought of other similar cases as they neared the scene and knew the dangers.

They arrived, negotiated the barriers, and found the officer in charge, Chief Inspector Brabbins. He'd been involved in the case of The Soul Killer too.

'Greetings, John. I see you're inching up the slippery pole.'

'Not a phrase I expected to hear this early in the morning, sir.'

Brabbins smiled. 'Just Frank now, seeing as we're sitting on the same perch. Are you here to take over?'

Barton laughed. 'No, this is your show for the moment. This is my first full day back, so I thought I'd come and help. Is it Twelvetrees?'

'Yes, you know him?'

'Yeah, I got called when he wrecked that pub a few years back.'

'I've heard about his past but haven't met him in the flesh. We had a brief chat through the letter box. He reckons the postwoman, a lady named Sue, is working for the High Court. Apparently, she's answering his questions now, and he won't hurt her or anyone else as long as we don't force entry. We've got a negotiator on the way as well as the armed response, ETA thirty minutes. We'll sit tight until both of them arrive unless it escalates. What do you reckon? Is he likely to harm her?'

Barton thought back to the case. Twelvetrees had calmed down by the time Barton had become involved. He'd pleaded guilty to every-thing at the first opportunity, even when his solicitor was telling him to be quiet. When his many years of exemplary military service had become known, some charges had been dropped and a few of the witnesses had disappeared. A kindly judge had accepted the dimin-ished responsibility plea at sentencing, but he'd still committed serious crimes.

The fact he'd told the judge he wouldn't attend any courses or submit to a community order was surely proof of his poor mental health, but there was such a shortage of beds on psychiatric wards in the UK that to be sectioned you needed to be frothing mad and naked. Twelvetrees hadn't been, and the judge had felt only a custodial sentence would suffice. He'd sentenced Twelvetrees to two years. When Twelvetrees had been released at the halfway point, he'd returned to this house, thereby breaching the restraining order, and got sent back to prison to serve the other half. He must have only been out a few months.

'I don't know, Frank. He was messed up, and two years in jail won't have helped his mental state,' said Barton.

'Bloody typical. I'm on holiday tomorrow.'

'You're all heart.' Barton rubbed his chin as he thought. The main risk here was to the woman. Getting her out was the primary goal. Barton had connected to Twelvetrees in the custody suite two years ago. He knew how to talk to men his own age.

'He's not armed or agitated at the moment?'

'We don't think so, and, no, pretty calm.'

'Now might be the best time to speak to him, then. He might be steaming mad in thirty minutes. I reckon he'll let her go now with the right persuasion.'

Brabbins stared at him for a few moments, seeing a quick end to proceedings, but he was a professional, loath to cut corners.

'You're going to swap yourself for her.'

'Correct. Then he'll walk shortly after, and we can cuff him the moment he gets outside. Be careful though, he is trained to kill. I'll judge his responses at the door first. If he's lost it, we wait for the negotiator and the shooters. Otherwise, I'll calm him down.'

Brabbins looked away as he ran through the options. Getting the woman out would defuse the situation, and Barton knew what he was doing. Everyone on the force understood that.

'Okay, no hero stuff. We'll be ready.'

11

ACTING DCI BARTON

Barton and Zander walked to the door. A fierce wind whipped at their suits. Barton regretted not taking his coat in the rush to leave. He pushed the letter box open.

'Mr Twelvetrees. It's Inspector Barton. You remember me?'

Barton's ears strained for sounds of crying, but all he could detect was heavy breathing. Twelvetrees must be right behind the door.

'No, who are you?'

'I'm John Barton. I was the one who questioned you two years ago after the pub incident.'

There was a pause. 'Tall, fat, white guy?'

Zander smiled next to Barton, who replied, 'That's right. Although I prefer the term big-boned.'

'Yes, I remember. What do you want?'

Barton shook his head in disbelief. 'Let Sue go, Tom. You're getting yourself into a lot of trouble.'

'She's lying to me. Reckons she doesn't know anything about a repossession.'

'Why would she lie to you?'

Another few seconds of silence followed. 'I'm not sure. My wife always paid the bills on time.'

'Maybe she had money worries.'

Barton listened as the man whispered the word 'fuck' repeatedly under his breath.

'Let me in, Tom. I'm experienced in these matters. I can see if there's anything I can do to put the eviction off, but every minute that Sue is in your house means more time in prison. Release Sue now, and things will look much better for you.'

His reply was almost a sob. 'I don't know what to do.'

'Open the door, please.'

Twenty seconds passed, and Barton heard the key turn and a bolt slide across. Barton still spoke through the letter box.

'I'm coming in. DS Zander is with me, is that okay?'

'Is he the big black one?'

'Yes.'

'No, only you.'

Barton and Zander had worked together so often that they didn't need to talk. Zander edged out of view, and Barton opened the door. He stepped inside and closed the door quickly, hoping Twelvetrees would forget to lock it again.

'Where's Sue?'

Twelvetrees's sallow, haunted face seemed almost doll-like. He scratched the side of his face hard under a surprisingly thick head of blond hair and drew blood. He pointed into the messy lounge where a fleshy middle-aged woman in a Post Office uniform sat on a sofa, visibly shaking, surrounded by ripped paper. Twelvetrees remained standing next to him. He looked so weak that Barton's concern dropped a notch, especially because Twelvetrees was unarmed and wearing nothing more than jogging bottoms.

'I need to stay here in case my wife comes back,' said Twelvetrees.

'I know, but Sue doesn't have anything to do with it. We have to let her go.'

Twelvetrees stared at the ceiling, head wobbling from side to side. Barton pressed his advantage.

'Once she's gone, I'll look at the paperwork.'

Twelvetrees's head shot back. 'I have to stay in the house.'

Barton beckoned Sue to walk out of the house behind him. She hesitantly rose from the seat with her eyes on Twelvetrees, but he only had eyes on Barton, and she scuttled out of the door.

'Help me,' begged Twelvetrees.

Barton had spoken to the wife after Twelvetrees had been recalled to prison. She'd asked him to confirm his release date and she'd had no intention of being anywhere near the family home when her husband was released next time. Looked as if she'd been true to her word.

'Okay, show me the correspondence.'

Twelvetrees frantically scrabbled around in the piles of letters. He managed to find the enforcement notice a few seconds later and thrust it under Barton's nose. Barton read it without saying anything. After no response to any previous correspondence and the non-payment of accrued rent, the High Court had authorised eviction. It was for today's date.

'I'm sorry, Tom. This has gone too far. They're coming today.'

Twelvetrees snarled his reply.

'There will need to be a lot of them to get me out of here.'

Barton heard Zander talking in a low voice outside, even though he couldn't quite make out the words. Brabbins might look to storm in now the woman was safe, but Zander would be telling him to wait. It was a dangerous moment, but Barton suspected honesty was the best route out of this.

'Look, you need to get some things together. Personal items and important documents. We have no choice but to take you to the station. What you've done with Sue is extremely serious.'

'They'll change the locks while I'm away. All my stuff will be here.'

'You can't change that now. The bailiffs aren't allowed to throw anything away, so you can come and get it later, but take your valuables. I'll give you a few minutes.'

Twelvetrees rubbed tears from his eyes. Then he ran up the stairs and Barton heard crashing and banging for a while. Twelvetrees returned holding a full rucksack and wearing a thick jumper. He looked around the place, as if for the final time. It reminded Barton of Cox as she'd stared around her office before leaving.

'I just want my wife and child back,' said Twelvetrees.

'I understand. Let's go back to the station and sort this out.'

Barton put his arm around Twelvetrees's shoulders and guided him out of the room. The front door was open and Barton could see hordes of police and flashing lights at the edge of the front garden, but Twelvetrees's eyes were down. When they got to the doorway, Barton hustled the man onto the front step. Twelvetrees leaned back when he noticed the welcoming committee.

A tensed Twelvetrees glanced round at Barton. His expression shifted and Barton saw a flash of the marine Twelvetrees once was, then it was gone. Zander stepped into view, and grabbed Twelvetrees's right arm and Barton took his left, while removing the rucksack from his grip. They moved his hands behind his hips and Zander slipped some cuffs on. Twelvetrees sank to his knees and sobbed.

After uniform led him away, Zander and Barton exchanged another glance without words needing to be spoken. They might charge him with false imprisonment. A postal worker was classed as a public servant, which aggravated the crime, but it would be a waste of time. CPS were unlikely to want to take this to court.

It was the worst aspect of policing. Many served their country and returned changed. Twelvetrees would get away with a caution. They'd keep him in the station until this evening, so he couldn't return to attack the bailiffs, but he'd be free. The authorities didn't like to focus on the fact he desperately needed help, because there was none available. People like Twelvetrees deteriorated in prison, and they couldn't cope outside, despite wanting to lead a normal life. It wasn't beyond the realm of possibility that eventually someone would get killed.

12

THE ICE KILLER

I blamed my impromptu exit from work on grief when they called me to hear why I'd left the office without telling anyone. I suppose it wasn't a lie. Sweetly, and surprisingly, they told me to take as long as I needed. That took the sting out of my anger, and any feelings of revenge faded as the weekend approached.

I used to spend Sundays at my mum's but there will be no more of them to look forward to, and tomorrow looms large as a lonely pitfall. I'll return to work next week, even though my job sucks, because I'll go mad on my own. That obviously makes me pathetic. How can I moan about work when I can't think of anything I'd rather do than go in? At least keeping busy might stop me considering my forlorn existence. In the meantime, I hope weekend TV will fulfil the same task.

I rattle around my flat until lunchtime. I clean in the afternoon and the place has never been so spotless. The azure dress Scarlett gave me hangs on the back of my bedroom door. I stroke the sheer material often as I do my housework. It feels wonderful, and that's how I felt wearing it. Brad hasn't rung or texted all week, but I'm fine with that. The woman who wanted him unconditionally has gone. I'll be a doormat no more.

Looking back, from the start of school, I was eager to please – the teachers and other pupils. I've always been motivated by that. Back in junior school I can even remember being called onto the stage and being confident enough to give a speech. Where has that girl gone? How has she turned into me? My mum used to introduce me back then as her whip-smart daughter. Now I'm what the Aussie's call a drongo.

But the fact people take advantage is my fault. I've let myself become drab and weak. Would I want a date with me? There were two men who sent me hurtling into the destructive lifestyle in which I find myself, and a couple of others who haven't helped since. I have to return to how I was. I want my confidence back. No one else can do it for me.

But I also need to understand so I don't make the same mistakes. Why did those men hurt me? What did they see in me that made me worthless?

I decide to attack my wardrobe and cupboards. There are loads of items I haven't worn in years. Other items of clothing make me wonder what I was thinking. And I'd need to be in a coma for six months to fit in the rest. Instead, I've been rotating a few boring baggy browns and shapeless greys.

I fill a huge bin liner with clothes. I'm brutal. To my surprise, some things I had, which I thought were crazy, suit my present mood. They aren't so different from Scarlett's dress. I'll drop the rest at the charity shop and see if they've got any other stuff that might suit this new upbeat me. At their prices, it won't hurt to try them out.

I haul the bag to the car and drive to my favourite charity shop on Oundle Road. It's a local one called Sweet Millie's. They aren't a national chain, so they focus on turning the donations over. Everything's a pound. I recall I've bought a lot of grey and brown stuff from there. The bin liner splits when I get to the till. An elderly lady laughs from behind the counter, which causes her chins to wobble.

'That was good timing,' she says.

'You don't know what I've brought.'

'Chuck it over here for me, please. I'm getting weak in my old age.'

She looks as if she could lift me, never mind carry them. I gather the items and wait as she opens a door behind her. There are twenty similar bags in a storeroom.

She shrugs. 'I'm too busy to sort it all out. Even though this is a working-class area, people are generous.' Her eyes linger on me a little longer than is normal.

'You've been here before, haven't you?'

'Yes. I've picked up some lovely things over the years.'

'If you find anything out the back here, you can have it for donating your own stuff.'

A tinkle sounds at the door and she leaves me. I rummage through a few bags. One smells as if it contains the contents of the donor's dog's basket. I blow my cheeks out. I need to empty everything on the floor and be methodical. She returns from serving a customer.

'It's a big job, isn't it? And we shut in a few minutes.'

I glance up at her kind face. She reminds me of my long-gone nana.

'Yes, but I could do with some new clothes. There's bound to be something nice here.'

'Do you fancy helping? It's not paid or anything. Every Thursday night at six for two hours, I do a stock check. If you want to drop by and help whenever you're free, do so. I could do with the company, and maybe you could, too. You can take what you like afterwards.'

I seize the offer, immediately grasping I'm doing it for interaction as well as clothes.

'It's a deal. I'll come to one soon.'

As I step past her, she reaches under the counter and hands me a plastic bag.

'I found this a while ago. My daughter is a similar shape to you. She said she'd visit this week, but didn't. She doesn't want for much, not even my company. You have it instead. Get yourself out tonight and enjoy being young. I'll hopefully see you next Thursday. It's my shop, so you know my name.'

I'm tempted to kiss and hug her, like I used to with Nana, but I manage to resist. I walk to my car feeling a little giddy. Impulsive, unexpected acts of kindness turn your day around like nothing else. They should teach the benefits of them at school.

Trent, my ever-present neighbour, washes his car every Saturday afternoon. He takes forever over it. It's a feat of modern engineering that the bonnet still has any paint left. Fair enough, you might think, but he only has a Vauxhall Corsa. He leans against it with a James Dean frown.

'Hi, Ellen. Getting chilly. Fancy coming in for a hot chocolate?'

I shake my head. Ten out of ten for persistence, but eleven for annoyance.

'Tempting, Trent. However, I've just bought some self-massage oil and I'm keen to get started.'

I step inside my flat, laughing. If any more blood had flowed to his face, it would have ruptured like a water balloon. But when I shut my door, my shoulders droop. It's no use being on form on your own. I quite fancy a frothy hot chocolate. The new me takes control and I return outside, but he's gone. The peeling front door of his flat makes me chuckle as I knock on it. Scarlett reckons a dirty front door is evidence of a nasty back door.

'Hi, Trent. Have you got marshmallows?'

He stammers a few unintelligible words and backs away into the kitchen. The lounge isn't too terrible, but I smile at the frantic sounds of moving crockery and cutlery. He's a systems analyst for a top supermarket. They would be freaked if they realised what an oddbod he is.

I realise I'm still holding the bag from the shop. It contains a white lace tunic dress, which I remove. I can't wait to put it on. Trent returns and gives me a chipped mug containing a suspicious viscous mahogany liquid. He grins and wipes his hands down the front of his trousers. He seems to be trying to think. Staring at the dress in my hand, his brain engages.

'Pretty outfit.'

'Isn't it? A lovely lady gave it to me.' I know I shouldn't but it's a day for impulsivity. 'Shall I try it on?'

His eyes bulge, but I decide what the heck. Whoever said that the kitchen contains the most germs in a house hasn't been in Trent's bathroom. Nevertheless, I'm only in there a minute. The mirror isn't big enough, so I sneak into his bedroom. You'd think Trent would have satin sheets on an airbed, but it's remarkably normal apart from all the computer equipment, which includes a keyboard on one of the pillows. When we did the dirty deed a year ago, it was at mine.

After a few spins, it's me that has the rush of blood. With a pair of cowboy boots, I will look awesome.

When I return to the room, Trent has removed his shirt. I tut.

'What are you doing?'

'I don't know. I just thought...'

'You're a strange boy. I'll let myself out.'

'What about your drink?'

'Varnish your door with it.'

13

THE ICE KILLER

I was right. In my boots and 'outfit', as freak boy called it, I feel almost as good as I did in Scarlett's dress. Different though, sassier. I wouldn't be able to control myself if 'Cotton Eye Joe' was played. A depressing evening of TV quiz shows doesn't appeal. I pace from the lounge to the bedroom and back again. My thoughts return to the men who helped create the victim I've become. The first one was Carl Quantrill, who stole my virginity when I was eighteen.

It was the Valentine's Ball during my final year of sixth form. Nobody asked me to go as their date. Instead, a group of us misfits went to The Hartley pub in town. Everyone had too much to drink and arrived loaded at the school hall. I had a denim skirt on, which kept riding up my stomach, and I spent the whole evening pulling it down on the edge of the dance floor. Quantrill was friendlier than he'd ever been, popping over to chat more than once and even bringing me a strange-tasting apple drink. I appreciated it as no one else wanted to talk to me. Later, he didn't want to dance but suggested we go outside even though it was a grim night.

I can still recall the heavy drops of rain on my arms and face. He gave me his coat as we slipped out of the hall. It began nicely enough, with gentle kissing, but soon I was steered behind the maintenance shed. His coat came off and up went my skirt. I lost my virginity the same way an animal does. When he'd finished, he took his coat back and left me kneeling in the mud.

I've tried not to think about that night over the years. It doesn't make me feel good even now, but what was worse was the worthlessness that followed when he ignored me in The Hartley over the next few Saturdays. I gave him something important and got nothing in return.

I wonder what he's doing now. He didn't go to university. I know that as I bumped into one of his thick mates, Trevor Ash, a few years later. He said they were working together at Hotpoint. So much for being a rock star.

I have a flash of inspiration. If I want to rediscover myself, I should start at the beginning. I'll see if I can make myself up as Scarlett did, and I'll go and have a few drinks at that pub. It's still there and open. It used to be banging. Well, that was Quantrill's description, not mine. To be fair, you often couldn't move in there. Smoke stung your eyes, and the general volume made your ears ring. No one will know I'm on my own. If Quantrill's still in Peterborough, it's possible he'll be in there. If he isn't, who knows what the night might bring?

It's a shame to put a coat on over my dress, but I don't want to pay for a taxi. I get a text from Scarlett saying she's bored. I reply, and, after a few seconds with no response, give her a ring. She's hammered and not making much sense but I chat to her as I walk, which distracts me from my cold knees. Town is empty despite it being nearly 9 p.m. I suppose the horizontal rain would deter many. Of the bars I pass, only the Wetherspoons has more than a few people in. Perhaps they're all at The Hartley!

My steps shorten as I approach. Taking a deep breath outside, I shove open the heavy black door. There are two further doors, left and right with glass panels. They've split the place into a bar and a lounge since I was last here. I turn to the left, push open the bar door and force myself towards the counter even though I can only see four old men in the long, narrow room. I stand in front of the barman. We both look as surprised as each other.

'All right, love. You lost?'

'Half a lager, please.'

A man on a barstool unashamedly leers at me as I wait. Perhaps he's never seen a woman this close in living memory. I turn with my glass and realise that The Hartley has become the type of establishment frequented by people after forty years in prison. It's a place to drink alone with your memories, whatever they may be.

There are two booths in the middle of the room. I can hide in one and finish my drink. But both have single old fellows in them bent over newspapers, so I attempt to coolly stroll to the far end near the toilets, which still has an open fireplace. There's only a solitary log burning, but it warms my hands. It's quiet and secluded up here. Two men in heavy-metal T-shirts, who were out of sight behind the booths, are the only other people present.

They also stare at me as if I've materialised out of thin air. They are an unusual pair who are dressed similarly. One has a grungy deadbeat look about him, which suits his clothing, but the other could have stepped from a fitness magazine. He has a New York Metz black baseball cap pulled low. Hard eyes sit under it.

I remove my coat and notice their expressions change, but I hide my grin. Nevertheless, I chug half my drink back. There's something familiar about Mr Muscles. It's only as the men's toilet door opens and Quantrill appears that I realise it's his friend, Trevor Ash, with the impressive physique. We used to pull his leg by calling him Treevor at school, but I wouldn't want to upset him now. He's twice the size, and I only saw him a couple of years ago. Quantrill gives me an appreciative once-over as he passes with no flicker of recognition. I'm not sure if I should feel good or bad about that.

I can't believe he's really here. It's a long way from Wembley or Glastonbury or wherever he reckoned he'd be headlining.

My confidence drains away with the last of my drink. Rarely does anything good come from reopening old wounds. I stand, pull on my coat and head for the door.

'Don't you want to say hello before you leave, Ellen?'

I'm glad my back is to him. He won't have seen my wide smile.

'Quantrill? Is that you?'

'Yes, it took me a few moments to recognise you. I don't remember you looking like that at school. You know Trevor, and this hairy creature is Graham Duncan, or Drunken, as we call him. The boys out on the beers as usual.'

'Wow, you've all changed.'

It's not true. Ash has, probably through a love of steroids, but Quantrill could have been in stasis. That is until I see his teeth. They've time-travelled back to the Middle Ages.

'I'll get you a drink,' he says. 'I know what you like.'

Ash stares at my knees after Quantrill heads to the bar, while Duncan drinks an entire pint in three huge gulps. Quantrill returns with half a cider for me. That was what he bought me the night he took what he wanted behind the shed and I haven't been able to drink it since. It makes my teeth itch. Still, I'll make the effort seeing as he's trying.

'What you up to now, Quantrill?'

'Kicking back. Work are hinting at promotion. The band are finally coming together. We're going to make some moves this year.'

'Do you remember your old band, The Craven Crew? Remember everyone laughing that time you played at assembly?'

His face falls. 'The Brazen Crew. That's who I'm talking about. People respect us now. Hotpoint sponsor us and give me time off for gigs.'

As we chat, Ash and Duncan join in more. Ash has been out of work for six months, and Duncan, who apparently was in the year above us, seems never to have had a job, which he seems very proud of. I buy myself another half a lager in a pint glass and pour the cider in.

The evening passes quickly. It's fantastic to have living proof in front of me that there are those who've made more of a mess of their lives than I have. It's good to reminisce, even if there's a blurring of the truths that come with time. I'm steaming when the bell rings for last orders. We have a shot for the road and the night takes a downward shift. Ash goes to the toilet and leaves his hand on my shoulder for a few uncomfortable seconds. A Chinese guy comes in selling plastic roses. Duncan and Quantrill go halves on one.

'You should come back to ours,' says Quantrill.

I compare my options. Is the right decision to walk away to an empty flat? They've been competing for my attention. For a few hours, I've known what popular feels like. I came looking for answers about why he treated me as he did but it's not the type of discussion to have in front of his mates. Perhaps I can get him alone and ask him. With that in mind, I stand and make my choice.

'Okay, but not for too long.'

My voice slurs and I have to put my hand on the wall to steady myself.

'Let's go,' says Ash.

It seems they're in a rush to leave.

'Shall we catch a taxi?' I ask.

'No, Drunken's van is over there,' says Ash with a smile.

I assume that Trevor will drive as he hasn't drunk much and Duncan can barely keep upright. I walk next to Ash, who has mentioned numerous times he's training for something. For what, he's never said, but he rambles on about diet and supplements. I hear Quantrill behind me saying London's beckoning. It's all a load of vague BS from a trio of losers, but it's better than being alone.

'We'll get in the back. There's a bed for when he's really drunk,' says Quantrill.

'He'll lose his licence,' I say.

They chuckle at that.

'You can't lose what you've already lost,' states Ash, who sniggers. The others laugh at that, too.

Duncan drops the keys next to a large white Transit van which makes them laugh even harder. I shut my eyes and steel myself to leave.

Quantrill climbs in the back, says my name, holds out his hand and I find myself taking it and he pulls me up. We sit on the bed. He doesn't let go of my fingers and I daren't look too close at the sheet underneath me. I'm holding the plastic rose as though it's a magic wand. If only. Duncan swings the van out of the car park and I almost slide onto the floor. Quantrill puts his arm around me.

A few minutes later, we pull up outside a dilapidated terrace in the roughest part of Millfield. It's not far from my own house. Alarm bells ring a little louder as I notice the dark, quiet street with many broken streetlamps, but the warnings are dulled by the buzz from the alcohol. We walk to the door in silence, my limp hand still seized by Quantrill. I hope I haven't made a mistake in coming here. I focus on them being old school friends. I've enjoyed catching up. If the mood changes after I ask my questions, I can just leave and run home.

14

ACTING DCI BARTON

It was 8 p.m. when Barton arrived home. Luckily, he had remembered to ring Holly, or he'd have been safer sleeping up the road at the Holiday Inn. There was an obvious smell of perfume when he walked through the front door. He was just pondering whether it might be air freshener when Holly strode into sight. She wore a white polo neck above tight jeans and high heels, and her hair was up. It was his favourite look on her. Her made-up eyes sparkled with mischief.

'I heard your car arrive.'

She handed him a glass of something bubbly, while his mind raced into overdrive at what special date he might have forgotten. He had one sip, then she took the drink from his hand and placed the glass on the window sill. Grabbing his tie, she pulled him up the stairs. At their bedroom, Barton asked about Luke.

'In bed,' whispered Holly.

'And the other two?'

'Both out, but Layla is due back at half eight. I've just slipped the shoes on, but I've been wearing the rest since lunchtime. I had planned to surprise you then. I told the kids I had a date with my friends later, so they didn't vomit at the truth. Now, you've got ten minutes.'

Five minutes later, Barton snuggled up to his wife, but she slid from the sheets and started pulling on her scruffs.

'Hey, where are you going?'

'I've got two more loads of washing to put on.'

He laughed. 'Not that I'm complaining, but that's not how I'm usually greeted at the door.'

'Don't get used to it. It's been nice having you here recuperating, especially the last few weeks. It seems regular sex can become a habit.'

'Shall I jack my job in?'

'Hell, no. Six weeks of you cluttering up the house and having to tidy up around you and behind you is quite enough, thank you. That's not to mention your ability to strip a fridge in a matter of minutes like an enormous ravenous woodpecker. Tonight was a reward for getting through a tough experience and returning to work with enthusiasm. But from now on, it's back to normal.'

Barton found his mind wandering to the events earlier.

'What's wrong?' asked Holly.

'Nothing really. We had a sad case today. A mental-health thing where there isn't the right support out there when people need it. People end up isolated and alone.'

'I'd jump at the chance to be alone,' said Holly. 'I haven't browsed the aisles in Primani for something to catch my eye in years. Sometimes I dream I'm in a cosy chair with a large glass of white wine and a thick book. Instead, I have someone yanking my chain every two minutes.'

Barton pulled the covers over his head, then Holly dragged them down.

'Get downstairs and stop that bloody kitchen door squeaking. You said you'd fix it when I was last pregnant.'

Barton climbed out of bed and grabbed an old pair of jeans. He knew Holly wouldn't trade the madness of family life for anything. Wasn't that what Twelvetrees was desperately trying to reclaim? Loneliness could be a dangerous thing.

15

THE ICE KILLER

There are huge split bin liners at the front door spilling out rotting waste. I can't make out if it's a shadow or a rat that disappears underneath them. If possible, the inside is worse.

'Is this a squat?' I ask.

No one replies, and the bonhomie of earlier vanishes the moment the door is locked.

Duncan barges past me. 'Let's have a drink.'

'I'll get my whisky,' says Ash.

That leaves Quantrill and me in the lounge. Although another mattress lies behind the sofa, meaning it must double up as someone's bedroom.

'Sorry it's a bit messy. We had a party last night. You know, band stuff.'

'Sorry, but I think I'm going to go.'

'Just stay for one drink. I'll ring for a taxi after.'

He smiles mischievously. It's the same expression that I fell in love with at school. A mix between geek and pop star. Sadly for him, it's too much of the former these days and he'll never be famous. It's been nearly twenty years since we last met. I don't know who he is, and I realise that I didn't even all those years ago. I decide to ask him.

'Why did you have sex with me and ignore me afterwards?'

'Oh, yeah, I remember that. We were young. It was just some fun.'

'Being cold-shouldered after wasn't enjoyable. You told everyone as well. I gave you something of value and you didn't appreciate it.'

His face drops. He is hard to read. Is it shame or regret that I see? I detect a flash of anger in his flint eyes. It's pity, but not for me. His life is pathetic. Deep down he knows that. Their lives are as squalid as the room we stand in. They cling to this embarrassing existence because admitting the truth would break them.

They are too far along the track to turn back, even though it leads nowhere.

'Come on, Ellen. It was only a shag. You should be pleased. Loads of girls were after me.'

Ash returns, drinking straight from a bottle of Bell's. He sweeps a pizza box and a dirty tea towel off the sofa and sits down on one end. Quantrill takes the other end. There's a shiny place between them that they've left for me. Ash uncorks a bottle labelled Red Wine and pours me a glass. I grimace at its foulness. Quantrill pulls me into the space between them.

'Put our promo video on, Drunken. You'll love it, Ellen,' he says.

Duncan grabs a DVD from on top of a table with a wink. Watching it is obviously a regular occurrence. He presses play, then takes a seat on a battered recliner next to the sofa.

Ash sits with his legs unnaturally wide and I can't keep a gap between us. I shift my bum forward in the seat, pretending to focus on the old TV. The DVD of their band starts. It's clearly been filmed on a phone in a sparsely populated pub. The juddering images and poor sound can't blunt out the pathetic lunges and sneers of Quantrill as he crucifies 'Paradise City'. I'd laugh if my situation weren't so precarious.

'I bumped into someone you know,' says Quantrill with a leer.

I say nothing, but I can't help being curious.

He grins and sings his name. 'Vickerman.' After a few nods, he continues. 'He told me a lot of interesting stories about you. Tales about what you like to do.'

'Oh? I'd hoped he died.'

'Alive and well, actually. Now that man is squatting, and only ten doors up from here. So perhaps not that well. He said you were a fun girl to know.'

I jump to my feet and rush to the door, forgetting it's locked. I turn around. Quantrill and Duncan sit quietly in their seats. Ash gets up and steps towards me with a key in his hand. I let out the breath I'm holding. After sliding the key onto the window sill, he stands in front of me and lays his big hands on my shoulders. Whisky fumes pour over me.

'It's not going home time.'

I regain consciousness but know to keep my eyes closed and not move. It's quiet; the only sounds reverberating around the room are deep drunken snores. Last night's events assault my mind like camera flashes. Ash, standing naked, with a large flaccid penis. Quantrill undressing his lower half but putting his shoes back on. I remember thinking the carpet can't have known the caress of a hoover for many years. Duncan watched, sweating despite the cold, with his hand down his trousers.

A draught from somewhere chills the exposed skin on my back where my dress used to be. Ash's raging hands had ripped my dress off and forced my mouth open while Quantrill assumed the position I experienced years before with him. Resistance was futile.

Now I move each part of my body and find little external soreness. I pull a piece of shattered crockery out of my knee. I'll live if I can get out of here. I swing my still-booted feet off the clammy mattress and stand. Duncan sags to the side in the recliner, drool running from his mouth. One of his hands clutches my knickers, the other hand part of my ripped dress. Ash is clothed again and lying along the sofa breathing abnormally fast; probably another symptom of the steroids that dented his performance.

The floor is an obstacle course of broken glass, newspapers and even the ashtray has been upended. No wonder Quantrill kept his shoes on. What does that tell you? It resembles a scene from a violent orgy but that wasn't what happened here.

I slide my coat on as quietly as I can. I'm almost at the door when a loud crunch echoes from under my foot. Glancing behind, I see Ash's eyes flicker open, and a large hand shoots out and seizes my calf. He yanks me towards him, and I drop to my knees and gasp with pain. He exhales heavily, eyes blinking.

'Ready for round two?' he asks.

As I push back, I feel an object under my hand. I seize it and thrust it at his leering face. His right eyeball comes away with the tip of the withdrawing corkscrew. His remaining eye blinks twice. I ram my weapon back and forth, time and time again, hard, knowing my life is on the line now. I focus on his neck. Warm liquid squirts over my hand and arm and sprays my legs. The glaring eye dilates and closes.

'Jesus.'

I spin around to see Duncan staring open-mouthed at me. The only other thing nearby is the wine bottle from earlier. He puts a weak hand up, which I hit first. Aiming for his head then, I count to ten with my teeth bared until he stops moving. Then a floorboard creaks above me. I tiptoe through the litter on the filthy brown carpet into the kitchen, spotting a knife block on the work surface. I slide the remaining blade out of it and check its keenness. It'll do.

Heavy feet plod down the stairs. I stand out of sight and follow Quantrill after he turns and walks towards the lounge. He stops dead at the gruesome scene. I imagine his stunned expression.

'Quantrill.'

The moment he faces me, I ram the blade into his stomach and upwards. There's a brief glimpse of the bitterness I recognised earlier, but, as the handle hits his chest, his eyes empty like a TV having its plug pulled. He crumples to the ground and is still. Nothing feels real. I sit on the bottom step with my brain throbbing. What have I done?

17

THE ICE KILLER

After a while, the cold drives me to move. I stand in the doorway of the lounge and gasp. The scene hasn't improved with time and smells far worse. I should ring the police, although it will take some explaining. Would they believe me?

I read a newspaper article where a husband raped and beat his wife for years and she eventually snapped and stabbed him twenty times while he slept. The judge said that even though there were extenuating circumstances, she could have just left the house. He sent her to prison for fifteen years.

I won't do a day inside for these losers if I can help it. The realisation of my predicament stirs me and self-preservation kicks in. Nobody knows I was here. I don't know anything about genetic material or fingerprints except what I've seen on TV, but I assume mine will be everywhere. With modern techniques, I suspect I could clean this place from top to bottom and still leave traces. I should focus on the most important parts. After all, incredibly after what happened, I'm not on any database. Evidence of my being here will be present, but it won't lead the police anywhere.

I glance up and even see red liquid on the ceiling. I pull open my coat and look in the cracked lounge mirror at my small bruised breasts splattered with blood. I look like I've staggered from a high-speed train wreck. There's no way I can walk home in this state.

My phone is still sticking out of my coat pocket. Wiping blood off the screen, I can see a text has arrived. It's from Brad Averescu.

Hey. Been thinking about you. I could pop around.

It was sent at 3:06 just after the nightclubs must have closed. It's been a while since I had a booty call. Depressingly, a small part of me is pleased to have received it, even after what's happened, although a bigger part is happy that I wasn't able to respond. Let's see how he enjoys being ignored.

I need to act before my brittle control shatters and I fold in on myself. Using some oven mitts and a shirt from the back of a chair in the kitchen, both of which smell like they've been used to wash the deceased already, I wipe clean the corkscrew, wine bottle and knife. I then place each item in the hand of one of the dead men. Only Graham is alive. His gargling breaths are shallow but regular, despite the blood oozing from his head. What do I do?

My phone tells me it's nearly 5 a.m. I should escape before the world awakes but leaving an eye witness doesn't make sense. But there's lashing out in the heat of battle, and there's killing in cold blood, and I'm not sure I can do the latter.

Giving myself time to think, I climb the stairs to the bathroom, wincing at the pain in my groin. The filthy mildewed shower reminds me of the pod they found Ripley in at the start of *Aliens*. Blasting freezing water sparks me to life. The stubborn dried blood forces me to remain until my bones are numb. I'm the same height as Quantrill, so I take some jeans and a jacket from his wardrobe and pull them on over one of his band T-shirts.

I shake my head at the drum kit in the corner of his room. People must love living in the same street as these idiots. I put my foot through the bass. I reckon the neighbours will be ecstatic when they find out what I've done until I realise the drummers are dead.

Strangely, there's a pair of women's slip-ons amongst a huge pile of shoes on the other side of the bed. I think of my cowboy boots and their distinctive soles. Most of the place is carpeted, but I'd better check. I grab a rucksack and stuff in my clothes, including my boots. Downstairs, I walk around in the woman's shoes, then put on an old pair of trainers I find in the corner of the lounge and smudge any incriminating prints I can see.

It's time to go. I find a small sharp knife in a kitchen drawer and stand in front of Duncan.

'I'm sorry,' I whisper. 'I don't have a choice.'

His neck would be the deadliest target. I place the blade against his Adam's apple and prepare to shove. This isn't me. I imagine myself staring down from the ceiling, watching. Stepping back, I bite my lip. I return the point to the soft spot and notice his breathing has stopped. There's a greying pallor to his face that wasn't there before, and I let out the breath I've been holding as he's clearly died. Would I have found the strength to do it otherwise?

One last look at the scene has me removing Ash's baseball cap. He won't need that where he's going; his horns will be in the way. My white rose, spattered with blood, lies on the coffee table. I place it in my bag, recalling that Valentine's card all those years ago. Who'd have thought it would end like this?

Blowing out my cheeks, I open the door with the key holding some tissue paper. I step outside, briskly walk up the road, but suddenly stop. My purse fell under the table during the attack. I'll have to go back.

I keep my head down as a car door slams nearby. I sneak back inside and crunch my way through more glass. It takes a few minutes, but I finally find the purse under a cushion. I'm beginning to shiver, through cold and shock, draining the energy from my legs. I must get home before daylight. There's no time for feelings.

I stride into the salt-and-pepper dawn morning. The blood-speckled white rose appears in my mind as I focus only on walking fast. I use the image as a beacon, and stagger through the empty streets a different person. I've been many things but, as of tonight, I will always be a killer.

18

ACTING DCI BARTON

Barton leaned back in his chair. The new role was challenging him, but he found that, after twenty years in the police, most answers lurked in his past somewhere. Meanwhile, Zander and Strange had restarted their studies for their inspector exams. There was a healthy competition between them. He smiled as they approached his office and each tried to enter before the other. Zander won.

'Take a seat, you two. Both are the same, before you try to decide which one is bigger or better.'

'He pulled my hair,' said Strange.

Barton opened a packet of digestives and slid them across the desk. The easiest way to quieten children was to fill their mouths.

'Thanks for coming. We'll have this meeting at midday every Wednesday from now on, roles permitting. It's your half-hour. We can discuss whatever you like. I suggest you talk together beforehand to get the best use of it. This is for your development. You're studying for your exams but on-the-job learning never stops. Zander?'

'I'm busy with quite a few cases, but it's humdrum stuff. That brawl outside the pub had hundreds of witnesses and entering statements has been so time-consuming. I'm doing long hours and find I have little energy left for revising at the weekend.'

'Is that the same for you, Kelly?'

'Affirmative. I appreciate you giving us some of your paperwork to do as training...'

Barton chuckled, but he'd barely given them the frost from the tip of his iceberg.

'You know the saying.'

'Shit rolls downhill?' asked Zander.

'I was thinking more along the lines of no pain, no gain. But trust me, there's plenty of both to spare. Look, guys. When you're in situations, even doing the mundane stuff, think about what you're doing and compare it to the DI role. What might a DI consider that a sergeant might not? What do they have to do that you don't?'

A knock on the door interrupted them.

'Come in.'

DC Zelensky entered. Barton thought for a minute she was going to salute.

'Sir, they've found some bodies at a house in Millfield.'

Strange and Zander leapt to their feet.

'Who's on scene and is it protected?' asked Strange.

'What's the address?' asked Zander.

Zelensky retreated towards the doorway.

'Hold your horses, you two. Great questions, but you're missing the most pertinent one,' said Barton.

Zander responded first. 'Thank you, Maria. How recent were the deaths?'

'The bodies have been there a while. Days. That's all I know.'

'There's no imminent danger to the public?' asked Zander.

'No, Sergeant.'

Barton cleared his throat.

'Thank you, Constable. Sergeant Zander will be with you shortly. Please shut the door as you leave.' Barton paused while she left. 'Take your seats. Always best to find out if there's a human killing machine marching down Lincoln Road with an Uzi. Zander, you're going to be acting SIO. What do you do first?'

'Contact whoever's at the location. Make sure the scene is protected. Go from there.'

'See? It's not hard. The remains could be historic. It might be old people, or carbon monoxide...' Barton's eye widened as he realised his faux pas. Zander had lost his son to CO poisoning.

'Don't worry, John. I can cope,' said Zander.

'Good. And what's one of the first things you learn at training college?'

'First officer attending duties,' said Strange.

'Correct. Trust in your fellow officers. The scene should already be secure. They'll have notified Control. CSI and the pathologist will be present or en route if required. It's only ten minutes' drive, so I wouldn't even call anyone. Grab a couple of DCs and get down there. Off you go and relax. You can do this.'

Strange and Zander stood.

'Not you, Strange. We don't need both of you there at this point. If the Terminator isn't on the rampage, then we have some time. You said you had something on your mind.'

19

ACTING DCI BARTON

Strange gave out a big sigh when Zander had gone.

'The DI role involves more responsibility than I imagined. How do you know when you're ready for such a jump?'

Barton considered her question. 'Part of it is a maturity thing. You notice that newer detectives naturally ask for your advice and experience. They also stop including you in their youthful gossip and banter.'

Barton's phone rang.

'Barton.'

Strange stared as her superior listened. He winked at Strange.

'Fine. See what you can do. Involve the other parties and decide on a way forward. They need to understand that further incidents of similar antisocial behaviour will have meaningful repercussions. These events easily escalate to serious violence. I'll leave it in your capable hands.'

Strange grinned as he disconnected the call. 'I get what you mean about promotion being a natural progression.'

'Actually, that was my wife. Allegedly, Luke and another boy bit each other at school. My comments were just an in-family joke that she'll sort it without involving the police. Now, was it DC Zelensky you wanted to talk about?'

Strange leaned back. 'How did you know?'

'Call it intuition. What's the problem?'

'Zelensky's one of our up-and-coming DCs. She's motivated, conscientious and reliable.'

'And now?'

'She's had two Mondays off sick recently. I had a word with her, and she said it wouldn't happen again. But she was late this Monday. DC Leicester called her Sicknote in the locker room. DC Ewing stuck up for Zelensky, who shouted at him that she could look after herself. Zander got in the middle before it overheated.'

'Mondays, eh? What are you thinking?'

'Usually it's people pulling sickies after a heavy weekend. I did smell alcohol on her one morning but haven't since. She doesn't seem the type though. I wouldn't want to report her, but it can't continue.'

'What will you do, then?'

'I'm not completely sure. Talk to her again, but she didn't tell me much last time. I'd hate Professional Standards to get involved.'

Barton held up his hands in submission. 'I don't think we should call for the Spanish Inquisition just yet. If we sacked people for smelling of drink on the odd occasion, we'd spend all our time recruiting new staff. It sounds like you've had a nice chat. Now for the nasty one, but be supportive.'

Strange nodded but didn't comment.

'Send her in. I've got a good idea what the issue is. We should be able to give her some helpful advice.'

Strange returned a few moments later. 'She went with Zander.'

Barton's mobile beeped. The message from Zander was brief.

'Get over here!'

20

ACTING DCI BARTON

Strange and Barton left the building in her car and continued to discuss Zelensky as they drove. She raised an eyebrow at him as they arrived near the location in Millfield. They'd had investigations there many times before. Narrow Victorian houses without driveways meant cars had been seemingly deserted in every available space. A couple of times a year, the police would turn up with low loaders and haul away the untaxed and unroadworthy vehicles, and Barton suspected half of the city's illegal landlords operated in these streets.

Strange had worked in Peterborough long enough not to attempt to park nearby. She drove onto a disused garage forecourt, and they walked the rest of the way. Barton glanced around for CCTV cameras without hope. It was a miserable day with heavy, swirling, grey clouds. Rain had threatened all morning but never arrived. With the gusting wind, the deluge would be biblical when it fell.

Barton tutted at the small outer cordon that had been created. They found a constable surrounded by people in the middle of the road. The small crowd were shouting at each other in a variety of foreign languages. The emergency vehicles' flashing lights lit up the animated faces in the gloom, while honking horns jarred Barton's brain. He strode to the young officer.

'Everything okay, PC Brown?'

Normally Barton would address him by his first name, but he hoped to remind the edgy crowd of the officer's authority as his wild eyes gave away his lack of control.

'Neither of these men want to give way in the street. It's caused more congestion. This gentleman seems furious but doesn't speak English.'

Barton glanced along the road at the line of traffic and clapped his hands. When all faces had turned to him, he announced the news.

'There's been a murder. We're about to close the whole road and start questioning everyone here. Several of you will need to come to the station. The vehicles that are present will have their registration documents checked on the police database.'

Strange smirked as the men quickly retreated to their cars and began to vanish. Anyone actually involved in the incident would have long since disappeared.

'I'll help Brown get the area clear,' she said. 'We'll cordon off the bottom of the road and take this end a further twenty metres up. Brown, where's everyone else?'

'There's a big domestic occurring two streets away. Someone's set fire to a bin behind the Royal Mail club, some eight-year-olds have climbed through a hole in their school fence in Woodston and are nowhere to be seen, and there's a three-car pile-up on Fletton Parkway.'

Barton left Strange and Brown to it. They'd earn their money today. Zander stood next to a rickety gate with the Crime Scene Entry Control Log in his hand. Barton noticed the terrible state of the front garden. There were at least three different companies' pizza boxes strewn amongst the spilled refuse.

'All hands to the pumps?' asked Barton.

'Yes. I've got Zelensky escorting people to and from the houses. Sirena and her team were at the station and came straight away. Mortis has just arrived. They told me not to enter, but that's fine. I had a look and no one would choose to be in there.'

A pungent waft of decaying flesh blanketed them when the door to the property opened and the pathologist, Mortis, stepped out in protective overalls. Multiple flashes went off behind him. Zander and Barton blanched at the smell as Mortis pulled his mask down to reveal a rictus grin.

'Now that's what I call a crime scene.'

Mortis was close to retirement but had a love of his job that made Barton suspect he'd never leave. That was a good thing because his diligence regularly led to rapid progress in an investigation.

'You were here quick,' said Barton.

Mortis smiled. 'For the first time in thirty years, I didn't have a post-mortem lined up. I was walking out of the department for a Costa coffee when I received the call. That's the beauty of our line of business. There's always fresh work.'

'Quite. Can I have a look?' asked Barton.

'Sirena wants the door closed and as few people as possible in there for the moment. It's a rubbish tip, and this wind is moving things around. One of the technicians will be out with a video to show you the scene.'

'There's no urgency?'

'No. I've only had time to check the condition of the three bodies and make superficial judgements. My guess, with the putrefaction, is they've been dead for three days.'

'All three are murders?' asked Barton.

'Most definitely. One's still got a knife in his chest, another has a bludgeoned skull, and the third one is missing quite a bit of his Adam's apple and an eye.'

'First thoughts?' asked Barton to Zander.

'As I said on the phone, it's a mess. If this isn't a squat, then whoever lives here doesn't believe in wasting time on cleaning. The lounge looks like a scene where kids have a party when their parents leave town. Only it goes viral and two hundred people turn up and trash the place.'

'Apart from the dead bodies?' said Barton.

'Well,' replied Zander. 'They do look a little like remnants from a hedonistic party. They're slumped as if they've passed out as opposed to having been murdered. The two in the lounge don't seem to have put up a struggle.'

'Who were the first officers attending?'

'PC Rivendon and PC Brown. I sent Rivendon to the domestic. He said that the neighbour here rang in saying he could smell dead bodies and the house was weird.'

'How does he know what a dead body smells like, and what does he mean by weird?'

Zander shrugged and pointed next door. A curtain moved at the window.

'He lives there, but I told him to go back inside. There's no damage to the door or windows of the crime scene, but the front door was unlocked. My initial guess is they let in whoever it was who murdered them. That narrows it down a little.'

'Mortis?' asked Barton.

'It's an intriguing scene. There's a lot of debris on the floor, which could show signs of a struggle, but the two victims in the lounge almost look like they were killed as they slept. That's purely conjecture, of course. It might be that the third victim attacked them and got knifed. He made it to the kitchen before he died. Or there could be any number of other perpetrators. The post-mortem and scene investigation will tell us more but, I fear, not everything.'

Sirena, the Crime Scene Manager, had appeared with a male technician and shut the door behind them.

'Hi, John. You well? Here's the recording of the scene.'

Barton winced through sixty seconds of close-up footage.

'Brutal. Is that an eyeball under the table?'

'I agree, and yes,' said Sirena. 'All I can hazard at this stage is guesswork. I would say a disagreement led to the killings, and a deadly brawl ensued. The perpetrator is unlikely to be a woman due to the extreme violence used. We've found a bank card on one victim and a wallet on another. There are pictures of the three of them on the wall in some kind of music group, so identifying them should hopefully be easy enough.'

'Do you think anyone else is involved?'

'It's a mess. You could probably find the DNA of half of Peterborough in there somewhere. I agree with Mortis though. There's something unnatural about the way the bodies are situated.'

'People who live down here and exist like this are likely to have been put on the Police National Computer at some point,' said Zander.

Barton took a deep breath. 'We can't do much at this stage until we know who they are and exactly how they died. How long for PMs, Mortis?'

'Late tomorrow at the earliest for all three.'

'How long here, Sirena?'

'Probably the same timescale to bag this up. I don't even want to think about what's in the bins.'

They all chuckled. It was the only way to handle events such as these.

'We'll question the neighbours now to see if anyone saw anything, or at least can give us a picture of the type of people who've been killed,' said Barton. 'I'd just like to know if there was definitely another person involved.'

'My professional hunch would be yes,' said Sirena. 'It certainly doesn't look like a hit though. The fingerprint guy's having a field day. There are full prints over everything. He was on his game, though, and checked the handle of the door to leave the property before we rubbed anything off as we left.'

'There's a clear print on it?' asked Zander.

'You'd expect it to be covered in them. Everyone who leaves the house would have touched it, but there's nothing on the inside handle at all.'

Barton understood straight away. That meant someone had wiped it clean.

21

ACTING DCI BARTON

Mortis and the CSI team went back inside. PC Rivendon had returned from the domestic, which had been resolved by taking both parties to the police station, separately. He took over the cordon. Barton smiled at the empty street in front of him. Small crowds gathered at the outer cordons, but the onlookers were too far away to bother him. He knew they'd soon get bored. Two traffic motorcyclists pulled up – the modern equivalent of the cavalry arriving.

'Okay, Zander. What next?'

'I thought you were taking over.'

'It's still your scene. Have I done anything you couldn't?'

'No, I realised that as you were talking. I panicked a bit when I didn't have enough officers.'

'It's rare for that to happen, especially with potential murders, but, as I said before, you revert to the basics.'

'I get it. The scene was secure. There was no need to put out an all stations call as they died days ago, and we had no suspects. I couldn't have done much more until you guys arrived.'

'Spot on. We're often temporarily short-staffed, but back-up is always on the way. Now what?'

'Strange can take charge here. Seeing as we're light on bodies, you and I can take the statement from the 999 caller while the CSI team crack on.'

'Any other thoughts?'

Zander squinted as he concentrated. 'While we wait for the PMs and the CSI report, we speak to the victims' friends and their next of kin. If we can discover the deceaseds' movements, we might learn who else they were with, or, better yet, who didn't like them.'

Barton nodded and was about to open his mouth.

Zander continued. 'The most important thing is the scene and evidence. We only get one chance at this. No mistakes and we take our time.' He smiled. 'I remember what you once said: Calm down. There were dramatic events here, but they've finished now. All that's left are people with jobs to do.'

Barton grinned appreciatively. 'Lead on.'

They strolled up next door's path and marvelled at its tidiness compared to the crime scene. A small, tanned man with an enormous moustache opened the door before Zander knocked a second time.

'Come in, come in.' He ushered them into an immaculate room filled with what seemed a thousand pictures of his family. The place smelled heavenly in contrast to the hell next door.

'Sal Fratelli? We're here to take a statement.'

'Yes, that's me. Now, let me get you a coffee. I put fresh on. My wife makes beautiful cake, so take a seat.'

Zander and Barton exchanged a glance and a grin. Zander sat while Barton perused the photos. The grey-haired man returned a few moments later with a tray containing biscuits and their drinks. A stooped lady shuffled in with two of the biggest slices of cake Barton had ever seen, and he considered himself an authority on the subject. Zander's grin widened as she passed him a plate. He took a huge bite, and his eyes bulged.

'Wow, so moist,' he mumbled.

Fratelli's wife beamed and blushed as if she'd unexpectedly won *The Great British Bake Off*. Bowing, she left the room. Barton opened his mouth to speak, but Fratelli sternly gestured for them to finish eating. With their mouths full, the detectives listened.

'So, something terrible next door, eh? Only a matter of time. They call themselves the three amigos. Three *bastardos* more like. Forty years I live here. Sure, it's a little rough, but I come from the streets of Milan. I enjoy the edge.' He leaned towards them and clicked his fingers. 'But only if there is respect. These chooches don't understand the meaning. They party all the time. I hear bloody drums all day and night. Which one is dead?'

Barton's and Zander's mouths were incapable of speech.

'It's not surprising. The big one wants to fight everyone, and the other two are rude. I don't wish anyone dead, but I wouldn't shed a tear. Understand?'

Barton observed Zander as he considered the Italian's words. Fratelli might be a suspect, but the news would be out soon anyway, and it would give them a chance to see how he took the news.

'All of them are dead,' said Zander.

Barton disguised his smile at his sergeant's perception by eating more cake. He got his notepad out and listened. It clearly wasn't devastating news to Fratelli.

'Sad to hear, but they annoy everyone. They play music and shout at all hours. Incredible. It's lucky my hearing isn't as good as it used to be. Throw their rubbish in gardens. One of them is always drunk. He pisses against my car at least once a week. I tell him if he does it again, I cut his dick off. They just laugh. The big idiot shoved me a couple of times. What can I do?'

'Did you call the police?' asked Zander.

'Pfff!'

Only an Italian could disrespect an entire nationwide organisation so thoroughly with one expression, thought Barton.

Zander put his plate down and sipped his coffee appreciatively. 'We suspect it occurred last weekend. Did you see anything untoward then?'

'No, they were quiet on Saturday night, which meant they were probably out. I heard them come back about midnight, and then there was the usual. TV too loud, terrible songs being played. I wake to breaking glass and cheering at two in the morning.'

'Like a window breaking?'

'No, like someone threw something at a wall.'

'How do you know it was 2 a.m.?'

Fratelli raised his shoulders at Barton and showed his hands. 'I may be old, but I can still see a clock. Well, if the numbers are big enough.'

Barton didn't bother to hide his laugh. 'So, you are a light sleeper? Did you hear anything else after two?'

Fratelli paused to recall. 'Maybe around five. Our family owned a café, and that's when you get up. It's my favourite time of the day, providing they aren't partying next door. You know, very peaceful. I tend to look out the window first thing to make sure my car's still in one piece and noticed someone at the door of the house.'

'Can you describe them?'

'Tall man, scruffy, loose clothes. Black baseball cap. Nothing more, sorry.'

'Was he running from the scene?'

'No, but he left quickly, so maybe he was up to no good.'

'Anything else you want to tell us? I hear you rang the police because you could smell dead bodies. Not covering your tracks, eh?'

Fratelli chuckled, but it tailed off into a grimace. They waited for him to continue.

'I did national service for my country. There were occasional deaths. You only have to sniff one once, and you never forget it.'

Fratelli agreed to attend the station for a full statement later. At the door, Barton shook the hands of the Italian couple and it dawned on him how small they were. He had a thought.

'You said the man leaving was tall.'

'That's right.'

'How would you describe me?'

'A giant.'

Barton and Zander stepped back outside, sluggishly. The Italians waved them away as if they were emigrating as opposed to going ten metres. Strange stood in front of the door to the murders with Rivendon.

'Any news?' she asked Barton.

He shook his head. 'This case is only a few hours old and already it appears tricky and confusing. Anything obvious inside?'

'Sirena said to knock when you returned.'

Barton did so, and Sirena and Mortis appeared. They pulled the hoods back from their suits and took off their masks.

'Afternoon, guys,' Sirena said. 'Anything from next door?'

'He said he saw an unidentified man leaving the house around the time of the murders, but he gave us nothing concrete.'

'Fleeing the scene?'

'Maybe. He might have just knocked or posted something, or they were still alive. Whatever, all we have is that he's tall and scruffy.'

Sirena ran a hand through her hair. 'Some of these wounds would have caused pools or at least bigger drops and sprays of blood, but there aren't any, or they're missing. This scene was trampled before we got here, and it looks like it's been partially cleaned up. That person could be the key to your investigation. Here's what I'm thinking. We'll have a search in the streets and gardens until this evening, then you might as well bring the cordon in to the immediate area outside the house and open the road.'

'Good. We'll need to organise an enquiry team to complete the house-to-house, but there won't be any point if they're parked up elsewhere.'

'The murder weapons appear to be inside,' she continued. 'We'll need the remainder of today and at least all of tomorrow to get this done. This rubbish needs bagging, and the rest of the property is in some ways worse than the lounge. Mortis and I will meet you here tomorrow at 5 p.m. if that's okay? We might have an idea of what's occurred by then, but my initial thoughts are not encouraging.'

'What do you mean?'

'Three dead bodies usually tell you a lot. I've been here hours and I have no idea who killed who. There could be someone else involved, or there may not. If that person did kill these people, I would guess it's a strong male who knows them. However, if you don't get a confession, we might never know what happened here that night.'

'Music to my ears,' muttered Barton.

Mortis chuckled. 'Do not fear, John. This will be an investigation that they'll speak of when we're long retired. So let's not mess it up. These bodies are already talking. The battered zone on that head indicates a right-handed assailant, probably the big guy opposite him. He's abnormally huge. Only the most dedicated and genetically gifted could hope for such musculature. He has a spotty body though, most likely from injecting steroids. Testosterone impacts the way that the sebaceous glands function, leading to acne – especially on the back and shoulders.

'Also, the elasticity in the skin isn't always equipped to accommodate for unnatural sudden gains, leaving this man with stretch marks on his biceps where the skin failed to adjust in time. I'll need a good look at his balls. You obviously know they are responsible for testosterone production, but the human body is amazing. If you inject testosterone, it will cease its own production, which causes testicular shrinkage.'

Barton's mind scrambled as he struggled to process a large quantity of unusual information. 'Steroids often lead to roid rage. There's a possible explanation of how it may have begun.' He braced himself for further complex conclusions.

'That's just the beginning,' said Mortis. 'The time the potentially fleeing person was seen leaving the scene fits as a time of death. Rigor mortis has finished and this aroma, scientifically known as putrescine and cadaverine, comes from decaying flesh. I said around three days, which means Saturday: a fine night for fighting. I'll see you here tomorrow, or you can come to the mortuary earlier and we'll examine his genitalia together.'

Zander nudged Barton in the side. 'Would you call that a date?'

Sirena gave him a list with three names on it: the deceased. She smiled and then beckoned to two technicians. After a quick chat, they began peering in the neighbours' front gardens and looking under the cars and along nearby kerbs. Barton took a deep breath, then realised something surprising. His role had changed. As acting DCI, knocking on doors was way below his paygrade. He needed to return to the station and set up the incident room, inform the chain of command and ensure Major Crimes was set up to deal with a triple murder.

He watched Zander pointing at doors for people to knock on. Strange was briefing an officer on the new cordon. Barton relieved Strange of her car keys and made his way back to the car, confident in the ability of his team. He had to admit he enjoyed the beginning of a murder investigation. If they were lucky, they would catch the killer and solve the puzzle in the first few days to much adulation. But he also knew that if they didn't, it could take years.

The most important thing now was to contact the victims' families. He looked at the list of names. They could then build up a picture of each person's background. Victims were killed for many reasons, including revenge, power, the thrill to kill, rage and madness, but usually it came down to money or sex. Which one would this be?

23

ACTING DCI BARTON

Two days later, Barton pushed open the door to the incident room and strolled inside. He stopped at the three boards where photos of each of the victims hung. Information spread out from each of them. None of it hinted in the direction of a killer. Barton's boss, Detective Superintendent Troughton, was stricken with the norovirus, which was a great relief to Barton because they had made little progress.

As with many such investigations, there was a sense of excitement and enthusiasm from those present. He shook hands with a lady from the new investigative support team. That team had been set up to help give the detectives time to focus on solving the cases instead of dealing with the masses of admin a murder enquiry created.

Zander and Strange, both wearing black suits and white shirts, chuckled in a corner over a comment that Strange had made. Barton made a mental note to mention the film *Men in Black* to them. The rest of the room consisted of DCs. Barton was struck by how young and keen they looked, even though most were pushing thirty. They had all dressed professionally and quietened as they realised who had arrived. Many leaned forwards in their seats as he stood in front of them. Ewing and Zelensky, the EZ Crew as Zander had named them over a year ago, were now two of the more experienced staff. He thought of the terrible investigations of late and knew that nothing hardened and aged you like murder.

'Thank you, everyone. This meeting is to summarise the progress we have made so far on The Millfield Murders. Zander and I attended the property last night and had a thorough look at the scene. The location is still secure, so I suggest you take a look now CSI have finished. Walking it helps. Zander will run the investigation under my oversight. Zander.'

Zander strode to the front with purpose.

'Right, team. The three deceased, Carl Quantrill, Trevor Ash and Graham Duncan, were a group of friends who lived together. Much of this information came from a neighbour three doors down who came forward and worked at Hotpoint in the same department as Quantrill. He described the three men as sad losers. PNC gave us the rest.

'The house was in Quantrill's name. His only living relative is his mother, who has dementia and lives in a care home. He is known to us after an allegation of sexual assault a few years back. The CPS dropped the case due to lack of evidence.

'Ash used to work on the production line at Hotpoint and regularly had lunch there with Quantrill. Ash was adopted and has no family. He's got a couple of public order convictions, one of which was affray. He was involved in another group fight two years before, leading to a conditional discharge.

'Duncan was unemployed. His family live in Stanground. They have little to do with him as he is, according to them, a raging alcoholic. That's confirmed by his criminal record, which lists a string of driving convictions, including ones for excess alcohol. He is currently disqualified, but the white van outside the property is apparently his although it's in Quantrill's name.

'The details were released to the national news and feature heavily this morning. We've had some phone calls already around it, but nothing of interest. One person asked if it was Carl Quantrill of The Brazen Crew. Anyone heard of them?'

Zelensky raised her hand. 'They're a local band. They had a bit of fame about ten years ago. I saw them once.'

'Any good?'

'It was in the Cherry Tree pub and was too shouty for my liking, but they had a few fans. I assumed they'd split up.'

'Excellent. There's an angle to investigate because we don't have many lines of enquiry. The CSI information is being loaded onto the system. In summary, Quantrill was stabbed to death. The knife wound to the stomach helps to prove that.' Zander glanced up to find only Strange and Barton were chuckling, while the rest took notes. He continued. 'It looks like the tip missed the heart despite the trajectory but it would have been incapacitating and rapidly fatal.

'Ash also died through loss of blood from various lacerations to his throat possibly by the bloody bottle opener found in the hand of Quantrill. Duncan died from complications from multiple traumas to his brain, we think from the wine bottle at the feet of Ash.'

Zander waited for them to catch up. 'Any thoughts? Yes, Ewing.'

Ewing resembled a thin Elvis. He had the same half-smile and love of his hair. 'Could they have had a fight with each other and died?'

Zander smiled as his trap was sprung. 'That was our initial guess. Ash beats Duncan to death. Quantrill stabs his neck with the corkscrew and as he dies, Ash sticks the knife in Quantrill's belly, who makes it to the stairs and expires. The plot thickens, though. Finger-prints, most full, some partial, from all the victims were found on all the weapons. Other than that, they were fairly clean, as if they'd been wiped clear beforehand. If you've seen inside the house, you'd know that was unlikely. What does that imply, Zelensky?'

'It's been staged to look like a fight but the perpetrator has escaped.'

'Correct. Also, Mortis confirmed that Ash was indeed on steroids. I read an in-depth, and in my opinion unnecessary, description of the man's shrunken plums.' Zander paused for the laughing to stop. 'Mortis has examined Mr Duncan's head wounds. He seems to think the skull was pounded many times.'

'Didn't he say the guy on steroids was likely to have done that?' asked Strange.

'That's what he thought, but, judging by the size and strength of that man, the damage would have been much worse. He thinks someone weaker did it as the skull was more or less intact. The swelling killed him, not trauma to the brain.'

'It could be any of them then, or a person we don't even know about,' said Ewing.

Zander nodded. 'Correct. The violence indicates a male because these are ruthless close-up kills. It might even be someone who's been trained to kill. A man was seen leaving the scene, but he might not have been the first to leave that house. He could have arrived after or before the event. There are no other fingerprints on the weapons apart from those present, and no prints on the front door handle, which backs up the idea of a fourth party covering their tracks.'

Ewing put his hand up. 'There could have been a fifth party or even a sixth.'

Zander smiled. 'That's certainly possible. It's a bit of a nightmare at this point. All we have is a poor description of a man rapidly leaving the property. He could have come to chat, or to score or sell drugs, but there is no evidence of substance abuse. No one in their right mind would hang around if they opened a door to that. It's possible they wouldn't report it either.

'The last piece of muddle stems from the scene. CSI have picked up multiple footprints in the house which don't match any of the victims. Before you say it was the man leaving the scene, these seem to be from a smaller shoe. Perhaps some kind of woman's loafer.'

Again, Zander waited for the chatter to stop. 'There's also the print from a boot that appears to have left the odd bloody mark throughout the house.'

'John, how did the neighbour describe the man fleeing the scene?'

'Tall.'

'Sirena guessed, and she reiterated that it was only an estimate, the shoesize of that boot would be approximately a six or seven. Few tall men take a six.' Zander rose to his feet and crossed his arms. 'The HOLMES manager has allocated roles. You'll work in pairs. Each couple gets a victim. We'll meet each afternoon, assuming we don't get a break that changes our direction of focus. I want to know everything about these guys. How long they've worked where they did, who their friends are, the places they drink, current girlfriends, ex-girlfriends, look at their records, you name it. These people were killed for a reason. Someone out there knows what it was. Maybe more than one person does. Any thoughts or questions?'

Barton watched the confused faces and felt much the same way. Zander had performed well, but Barton wanted to ram home the severity of what had occurred. Zander had also failed to focus on the importance of the dress that had been found, which Barton believed might solve the case. He gave Zander an appreciative nod and turned to the room.

'The post-mortem turned up one final clue. Quantrill and Ash both had skin under their fingernails. That's a common occurrence in a desperate fight. Remember, CSI found parts of a ripped dress with blood on it. I'm going to guess that when we get the DNA results back from those fingernails, they will show it was the skin of a female. It will be an exact match to the blood on the dress.'

Barton waited for that to sink in.

'We need to get in touch with every A & E and night shelter to see if anyone fits the bill, or hope that CCTV from the surrounding routes gives us something. An abused, scared, injured woman left that house. We need to find her.'

24

My eyes itch through lack of sleep as I stare through the cracks of the blinds and wait for Scarlett to arrive. It will be a long time until I dare peek through the slats and not expect to see the police. I've existed this last week as though in a waking coma. I had to get out of the house, but I can't remember a call or conversation I've had at work all week. No one mentioned my distant state. It's as if I'm invisible. For a few days, all I could eat was soup and cereal, then just bread and butter, and finally nothing. It feels as though everything sits in my stomach, as if it's waiting for a sign to carry on.

I'd started to think they'd never find them. In the dark hours before dawn each morning, I even imagined that I'd made it up. Yet the scars remain, both physical and mental. I took pictures of the scratches on my back and thighs. My entire chest was a range of blues by Monday and livid finger marks appeared on my neck, which I hid with a roll-neck jumper. I'm glad I remember so little.

After printing the images out on my PC, I placed them in an old Quality Street tin that my mum used to bring cakes around in. My ripped underwear went in there, too. As did what was left of my dress. My container of shame lives under my bed. I know that if bad things happen to you, it's best to lock them away and ignore them. Time doesn't heal, but you can forget eventually. Especially if more horrible events occur. On this occasion though, it's me that's also done something terrible.

I don't feel particularly distressed by the attack. I've been raped before. Is it possible to get used to things like that if they occur often enough? I just feel lucky to have survived the experience, and I'm pleased that those responsible didn't.

If I'm being sincere, over the years, part of me has quite enjoyed playing the victim. If I can blame life for being unfair, then I don't have to shoulder total responsibility for my pointless existence. But now, for whatever reason, I can look back with clarity. I'm at fault. I've wasted my life. Am I worse now, or better, after what I've done? I'm a murderer. I've killed three people, vile rapists admittedly, but humans all the same. It's a lot to take in.

I pored over the newspaper each morning while holding my breath, and waited dry-mouthed for my picture to appear on the TV screen. It wasn't until Thursday that there was any mention of my crime. Details were sketchy. The bodies had only been found the day before and the victims had been dead for days. It was the lead story yesterday. The police were asking for witnesses or any information that could help their investigation. In particular, they wanted to speak to a guy in a baseball cap who was seen leaving the scene around the time of the murders.

Scarlett's SUV pulls into the forecourt of my block of flats. As I lock my front door and patter down the stairs, I allow myself a slight grin. It seems the authorities know nothing. That man they are searching for is me.

I slide into Scarlett's Nissan Qashqai. She calls it her old car despite only getting it new three years ago. The smooth ride soothes me. It always feels as if I'm in a steamroller when I get back in my Focus. She says nothing and I detect tension, so I attempt some small talk.

'Morning. Sorry I couldn't drive, but my battery died. I had to accept a lift to work yesterday from my weird neighbour.'

'No worries, sweetie. Did he miss the gear stick by mistake and touch your knee?'

'I stabbed him with a pen, so he only did it once.'

'Men, eh? They're all scumbags.'

Scarlett's always slagging men off, especially her husband, who she calls Terrible Tim. She reckons he stops her going out and doesn't let her have any money. Seems to me with two cars and a black credit card, she doesn't need any cash. Apparently, he checks her spending and gives her grief for anything he deems unsuitable.

'Nice to see you've put make-up on.'

I check in the mirror. Apart from lipstick, I haven't. I'm just ghost-white. Weirdly, my skin has cleared up though. Perhaps murder agrees with me, although more likely it's to do with not boozing as much.

'Thanks for taking me out, Scarlett. I need the distraction. Did you say on the phone we were going shooting?'

'Yes. Clay pigeon. What a pointless way to ruin a bright Saturday.'

Scarlett says her husband is new money, so he's always trying to look like old money. Hence the country pursuits. She often takes me along; I think to show off to me. But I'd never get to do anything interesting like this otherwise, so I don't mind at all. We went go-karting once. I loved it, and there was a superb BBQ afterwards.

We trundle down miles of quiet lanes and arrive at Bourne Shooting Lodge. The gravel parking space must hold a million pounds' worth of cars, despite there only being eight vehicles. Ours is the worst of the lot, so perhaps Scarlett was right.

'You should have brought the Evoque.'

'I didn't want to get it dirty.' Her narrowed eyes indicate regret. Scarlett has a posh car, which she keeps for best. I've only ever seen her in it a few times. It's a tough life.

I plod after her to the reception desk, mostly with my head down. There are about ten men chatting good-naturedly next to the counter. Some women chat together in the corner of the room. I expect scathing glances to come our way, but they don't seem interested in our arrival. Scarlett grabs two bottles of water from a table.

'We'll wait outside,' she says to me.

Through some double doors, her husband waves to us from a group of laughing men holding shotguns as casually as if they were books. He doesn't come over. The view of rolling countryside is incredible. It's freezing cold, yet clear and windless. I detect the first snowdrop tips poking out of the manicured beds. The trees and even the grass have a sharp edge to them. A perfect day for shooting, I would guess. It's so peaceful that I relax further and begin to forget my worries.

'What are you grinning at, Ellen? You look simple.'

'It's beautiful here.'

Scarlett grunts in reply.

'Scarlett, why do you bother coming to these things?'

'He makes me.'

'Why do you bring me?' The question slips out before I realise I've said it. Perhaps it was a combination of relaxation and exhaustion. But I already know. I'm here for support. She doesn't fit in here any more than I do. A woman in a waitress outfit hands some small glasses from a tray to the men. Scarlett's husband says something I can't hear, but all the men laugh.

The waitress walks over to us, rolling her eyes. I smile and take a glass. Scarlett does too. We clink them and down the contents. I expected sherry, not whisky, and almost spray it back into Scarlett's face. Judging by the expression on her face, she almost did the same. We giggle. Maybe it's the instant warmth of the alcohol, but I'm glad I'm here. In a way, Scarlett and I only have each other now.

A bald man called Peter arrives and runs through a safety talk. He stares at me throughout, so I assume the rest have heard it before. I catch the odd appraising glance from the others present, but they aren't unkind. They're dressed similarly. There must be an outfitter where they all go.

We wander to a field, and the shooting begins. A cloud comes overhead, which darkens Scarlett's mood.

'Are you happy?' she asks.

'I never expected life to be like this, if that's what you mean.'

I'm not sure she's listening until I see a cheek twitch.

'Nor me,' she says.

'I thought I'd have more friends.'

We both laugh, but tail off as she says, 'Me too.'

I turn to her. 'It's crazy, but I kept thinking that once I sorted a man out, you know, got married, then the rest would come. I'd build my social life around us as a couple. With that mad thought in mind, I desperately threw myself into destructive relationships and ditched anyone who was boring, even if they were kind. I should have built my life around myself and my friends. Then the men could come to me. I've been a fool.'

A tear trickles down Scarlett's face. 'Me, too.'

Scarlett removes a hip flask from her pocket and takes a glug. She offers it to me, but I shake my head. My brain's still fizzing from the nip we had earlier. Scarlett has my ration. Looks like I'll be driving home. The instructor points at us to let us know we're next.

'Ready, ladies?'

'Sure,' Scarlett says, knocking another mouthful back. 'Come on, let's show these pansies the art of warfare.'

We approach the metal frame that people are shooting out of and watch. Tim is inside one. An orange disc rises from behind a tree and arcs through the air. It disappears intact, then another safely follows it, despite the sound of gunshot.

'Aren't they supposed to be trying to hit them?' I ask.

'You made me nervous,' jokes Tim.

'Perhaps you're firing blanks,' says Scarlett.

We giggle as he misses again, but then he gets six in a row.

'It's funny,' I say. 'I knew they weren't real pigeons, but I thought they'd at least look like them.' The giggles become open-mouthed guffaws.

Tim steps back with a raised eyebrow. 'Think you ladies can do better?'

'Too right, come on, Ellen. You go first.'

'Have you done this before, Ellen?' asks Tim.

'I've played Space Invaders. Surely it's the same idea.'

He smiles. It's an oddly warm smile, without the leer I sometimes observe. For the next few minutes, Tim shows us what to do, starting with our dominant eye, and then following the target in an arc before pulling the trigger. Tim is a trained instructor. Even so, it's bloody confusing. As he holds my arms and moves the gun through the motion, I detect a firm thing pushing against my arse. Typical. I turn around with a scowl.

'Is your little friend pointing me in the right direction?'

He reddens, looks down, and raises his binocular case. I blush and jokingly grimace at him.

'Scarlett, you kind of know what you're doing. Go first. We'll do ten in a row for a bit of fun. I'll release the clays when you say either *ready* or *pull*. Choice is yours.'

I whisper a comment to Scarlett as Tim steps to the side and picks up a box with three buttons on it. 'He's in a pleasant mood.'

Scarlett tuts. 'He's showing off to his friends. Last night, he wanted sex and half-strangled me during it. Bastard.' She grabs the shotgun from me and steps towards Tim, who passes her two cartridges. She takes aim. 'Ready!'

A target comes flying out from the same place behind the trees. The trap must be in that spot. I wait for the bang, but there's an eerie quiet. Scarlett rubs her eyes and turns back to me.

'I could see three of them.'

'You remember what Uncle Paulie said in *Rocky*? Hit the one in the middle.'

She hits two of her ten. She stands to the side and watches Tim load the gun for me.

'Did you see three blokes got murdered?' she asks me.

'I saw some of it on the news. Do they know what happened?'

'They don't appear to have much idea, but they named the victims.'

Tim interrupts. 'Try to remember what I said, Ellen. Don't aim, just look. Follow the flight of it and try to hit the bottom right edge. Chin closer on the stock and relax. Ready?'

'Ready!' I trace the arc, close my left eye and squeeze. I lower the gun to see a cloud of dispersing dust and cracked clay in the air.'

'Shot!' says Tim.

'Nice!' says Scarlett. 'One of the dead was Carl Quantrill. Didn't he take your cherry?'

I clench my teeth. Why ask this now? Is she trying to distract me?

'Ready!' I raise the barrel too fast and jerk the trigger. I miss by miles.

'If I'm honest, I was a willing victim of his, too,' she says. 'I fell for his I'm-going-to-be-a-star patter, although he was very considerate, if you get what I mean.'

Tim reloads the gun while giving Scarlett a dirty look. 'Talk to her afterwards or she won't be able to concentrate. I don't want to hear it, either. Relax, Ellen. That first one wasn't a fluke. Follow the clay and squeeze the trigger.'

'Ready.' I unclench my jaw, steady my breathing, and blast the target to smithereens. It's a thrill, and I smile. I turn to Scarlett, who's ignoring Tim. She's staring at the sky with a sneer.

'Quantrill wasn't nice to me afterwards though,' I say.

'Well, most men are arseholes. Feel free to accidentally miss and hit Tim instead. Aim for his binocular case.'

I laugh so hard I pull the trigger before the clay pigeon is in sight. Tim tuts next to me but takes it in good humour. Scarlett stays quiet, and I finish my ten. I slip into a zone and find it straightforward.

'Well done, Ellen. Six out of ten for your first time is amazing. Come and meet the guys in the tent. They don't get to meet many Lara Croft types.'

'Actually, we're off, hubby,' says Scarlett. 'Ellen's going to try women from now on.'

She grabs my elbow and steers me away after I give Tim the shot-gun. The men and women are in a group as we walk past. One of them waves, and I see some of the men look shy and bashful as they nod in our direction. A woman who looks a bit like Joanna Lumley gives me a thumbs up. Nice people, I think, and rather wish I weren't leaving.

Scarlett falls into a drunken stupor when we get back in the car. I suspect she must have had a drink before she picked me up. Is being lonely worse than being stuck in an abusive marriage? I drive her home where she plants a slobbery kiss on my cheek before she gets out.

'Keep the car, Ells. Bring it back when yours is fixed.'

She wobbles away, dropping her handbag at the door. I can't help but smile until she slumps to the floor. Her shoulders shudder and she places her head in her hands. I run over and put my arm around her.

'Hey, it's okay. Don't cry.'

Her tear-stained face turns to me. 'I'm not sorry that Quantrill got killed. He used me like every other man I've ever met. I wish the rest would get what they deserve, too.'

I pull her in close to me. What she's said could have come from my own mouth. I've no doubt I'm on borrowed time. The police will eventually find me. It's up to me what I do with the weeks or maybe even days that I have left. What should I do with my remaining freedom?

25

ACTING DCI BARTON

Barton and Zander stood outside The Hartley Almshouses in Westgate and stared up at the creaking sign. Zander had been assigned DC Ewing as his partner, and they'd been looking into Carl Quantrill's background. Zander had found out the day before from talking to Quantrill's work colleagues that he drank regularly in The Hartley.

Barton had offered to check it out with him that evening since Ewing had a previous commitment. He thought it'd be nice to have a few beers and catch up at the same time. They had dressed casually and decided not to approach anyone when they first arrived to suss out what kind of place it was.

'It's been a while since I was out in town on a Saturday night,' said Barton, blowing into his hands.

'The young women will be pleased,' replied Zander, whose huge parka made him look as if he was going ice fishing.

Barton pushed the front door of the pub open and paused when he saw they had split it into two bars. The last time he had come in here was when he arrested a bail absconder nearly fifteen years ago. He chose left as he recalled the toilets being that side. Barton surveyed the scene. Only tumbleweed was missing.

The few hardened drinkers were slumped at the bar on stools. It seemed the pub catered for the older end of the market. If this was rush hour, the place was in trouble.

The landlord wiped his hands on a tea towel and stared over the pumps at them. 'What do you want?'

'Two pints of OB, please,' said Zander after checking the range.

The man smirked and poured them their drinks. An elderly gentleman next to them with no teeth grinned their way. As they left, the barman hummed the theme to *Magnum P.I.* Barton and Zander sat opposite each other in a booth.

Barton took a sip. 'Nice to see we've still got it.'

'Yes, Secret Squirrel has nothing on us.'

'Lively place.'

'I can't wait to dance.' Zander laughed. 'Didn't you recognise the barman? I can't remember his name. We sent him down for dealing, must be six or seven years ago.'

Barton leaned out of his seat and peered at the bar. The humming man gave him the V-sign. Barton slumped back. 'I recall now he's waved at me. Irish guy. Four years for possession with intent. He'll give us nothing and I suspect he'll tell everyone else not to either.'

'Good pint though.' Zander took another appreciative swig.

'Tell me what you and Ewing learned at Quantrill's work.'

'Ewing agreed to do the talking, and he did a cracking job. Quantrill's team leader was an attractive, frosty woman aged around thirty and Ewing had her eating out of his hand. She confirmed a picture of him that we already suspected. Quantrill was a failed rocker who never grew up, and he still took advantage of groupies.'

'And The Hartley connection?'

'She said he played here for a couple of years. I'm guessing she may have fallen under Quantrill's spell while dating and got hurt because she seemed pleased nobody wanted the band any more. She had also warned him lately for being rude to people at work. He drank a lot, used women, but he wasn't violent with her, just uncaring and obnoxious.'

'What did she say about Trevor Ash?'

'She didn't know him well, but said he was trouble.'

Barton raised his eyebrows. 'Did you get hold of the woman who accused Quantrill of sexual assault?'

'She's disappeared, as a lot of them do when no one's interested.'

'Damn. Did Malik make any progress with Graham what's-his-name?'

'Duncan. Yep. He's a drunk, but not an angry one. Malik visited his parents' house and said it was sad. It sounded like his parents had given him every chance, but he was quite happy to sit about on benefits and drink cheap alcohol. He used to have a "man-with-a-van" business, helping people move house or get rid of things for extra cash. That finished when he got caught under the influence.'

'Quantrill and Duncan don't seem the type to instigate a violent brawl. This other guy, Ash, must be the one who started it. Any news on the fingernail scrapings and bloody dress?'

'No, the lab results aren't back yet. Sirena said too much time had passed for them to be 100% about the date of the blood, so the dress could have been there before, but that's unlikely, and it'll be a surprise if the two DNAs don't match.'

'Maybe it was Quantrill's girlfriend and Ash wanted a piece. They fought and ended up stabbing or beating each other.'

'It's possible. She leaves somehow, and the bloke who arrives does a runner when he sees the scene. What else do we know about Ash?'

'Strange and Zelensky have gone to his gym to ask questions.' Zander exhaled deeply, puffing his cheeks out. 'Jeez, all we've got is guesswork. There was zero evidence on CCTV. The nearest camera had been vandalised. None of the neighbours knows anything apart from our star witness, the short-sighted, slightly-deaf Italian next door. He spotted a man in a cap leaving, but that man has disappeared into the wind.'

The toothless guy from the bar stumbled past them to the toilets. Barton cleared his throat.

'Can we have a quick word, please?'

He stopped and tapped his veiny nose. 'You'll be here about those three murders in the paper.'

Barton nodded. 'Is this your local?'

'I've been coming here on and off for thirty years. The three that died were in here regular.'

'Were you in Saturday night?'

'A drink would loosen my memory.'

Zander stood. 'What'll you have?'

'Two pints of Alpine.'

'Why two?'

'Save my old legs going back and forth.'

Barton chuckled as the man swung himself into Zander's vacated seat.

'Were they in here on Saturday?' asked Barton.

After a scratch of his grey stubble, his eyes brightened. 'They were, you know. Normally I couldn't tell you one night from the next, but it was quieter than usual in here. I remember because they had someone else with them.'

Barton tensed. 'A bloke in a baseball cap?'

'Hardly. She was a looker. You know, a dolly-bird. She had a lovely dress on, legs up to here.' His hand shot up in a salute.

Barton deduced that she'd be about eight feet tall if that were true.

'What was she like? Young, old, fat, thin, white or black?'

'Everyone's young and thin to me, son. She was English with black hair, longish in a strange style at the front. Short white dress. Nice girl, even had a joke with us old fellas. That's why I remember her so clearly.'

Zander returned and put the two drinks down. Barton updated him. Zander squinted as he thought what to ask. 'It has to be her, then. Would you recognise her if you saw a photo?'

'Her legs, yes. Not sure about her face. Why? She's not dead as well, is she?'

Zander shrugged. 'We haven't found her and it's important we do. Do you know anything else we might be interested in?'

'She smelled nice.'

'Did they leave together?'

The witness waged an internal battle before answering. 'I don't usually get involved in other people's business, but that Ash was a horrible piece of work who jumped queues and never said please or thank you.'

Barton tried to drag the man back on track. 'What time did they leave?'

'No idea, because I left to buy chips from MegaBite. The cheeky idiots in there asked if I was going clubbing. You know, today's young-sters really piss me off. I've got no pity for those fools. Perhaps it was their day of reckoning, but I hope the girl's all right.'

With that, he hauled himself to his feet and grabbed his drinks. He winked at Barton.

'I'll take them to the bar. I don't want to be seen drinking with your lot.'

Zander glanced at Barton. 'Do we let him finish his drinks?'

'No, two more pints and his statement will be one long word. Hope-fully we can get someone out on call to do an artist's impression.'

'Of her legs?'

Barton smiled, finished his drink and stood to leave. Both knew every little piece of information would help. The key was to build a picture before something else unpleasant happened.

26

THE ICE KILLER

The manager smiles at me as I rush to my desk with three seconds to spare. Scarlett's car drove beautifully on the way here compared to my own. It was a real treat, one which I'd guess she has long stopped appreciating. I usually hate Mondays, but I'm in a chipper mood. I feel eyes on me and spot Brad staring from behind his PC. He waves, not caring who notices, which is a first. I nod back and look away.

I sit down and almost remove the scarf from my head. My positivity vanishes when I remember the state of my hair. Approximately a tenth of it came out this morning and is in my bin at home. It's no wonder I'm all over the place at the moment. I'll leave the scarf on. Perhaps no one will comment if I keep my head down. Some Muslims cover up, as does a Jehovah's Witness girl who works in business support. I take call after call on autopilot and try not to think about anything.

At my break time, I log out of my phone and wander to the toilet. With a deep breath, I stare at myself in the mirror and drag off the scarf. I put my hand to my mouth. There's a monk-like quality to what's left of my hair. When I comb it now, chunks come out, which means only one immediate option remains.

A tear wells but doesn't trickle down my cheek. I knew this day was coming and mourned the loss some time back. My doctor spoke plainly after running tests. Many women suffer alopecia. Considering the stress I've been under recently and over the years, it's not a huge surprise. The medication can make things worse. I realise I might not have taken my meds this morning and, worryingly, I can't remember taking yesterday's. My mum used to remind me in her daily text.

The toilet door slams open. It's too late to replace the scarf. I stand rigid and wait for whoever it is.

'My God, time goes so slow here. How long do you reckon I can get away with having a nap in the bog?'

Scarlett stops next to me and our eyes meet in the mirror. Her gaze drifts around my head. She gives me a tiny smile.

'Ah, Ellen. I'm sorry.' She pulls me into an enormous hug, the like of which I've rarely experienced from anyone, never mind her, and I return it with interest.

'I knew it was inevitable. I'll just have to shave it off and get a wig.' A little giggle escapes. 'Those weren't words I ever expected to say. Who the hell's going to want me now?'

'Some men prefer short hair on women.'

'Gallows humour, eh? What would we do without it? I could put on red make-up, glue little horns to my head, and look like Darth Maul.'

'Kinky, now you're talking.' Scarlett holds my hands. 'I've never told anyone this, but I wore a wig for a few years.'

I examine her perfectly coiffured blonde bob. 'No way, when?'

'Years ago. You know how I was after getting left at the altar. I barely functioned. I drank to forget, and couldn't see the point in it all. Work got even more stressful because I was hungover every day. My hair started coming out when I brushed it. Not as much as yours, admittedly, but it was horrible, really thin and greasy.'

'Did you get a wig on the NHS?'

'Yes, it was okay actually, bit sweaty, but then I got with Tim. He bought me one shortly after we met that was made specifically for my exact head size. Nobody ever noticed.'

'Was it expensive?'

'Fifteen hundred pounds.'

'Wow, so much. That was lovely of him. Did he mind you wearing it?'

Scarlett looks oddly confused, as though she doesn't want to tell me the truth.

'You know what men are like. Every hole's a goal, even if it's a bald one.'

'Yuck. You've got such a dirty mouth sometimes. It was nice that he paid for it though, and that he still fancied you.'

'Terrible Tim probably caused some of the hair loss.'

I decide that's not true, especially seeing as he shelled out that much for it after just meeting her, but there's no point arguing. Does it make it less of a gesture if you're rich, or is that being unfair?

I run my hands through my hair and more comes out. Now that is unfair. Many people live such privileged existences and breeze through the years, whereas I'm going to end up looking like an extra from *Star Trek*. At least Scarlett cares, but it makes me miss my mum more than anything. What I'd give right now to be able to go to her house. Everything was plain and of another era there. Even half the food was out of date, and it smelled a little odd, but all that was reassuring. And you can't replace the trust and comfort that your own mother provides. In a way, I'm lucky, because I knew that a long time ago when she helped me rebuild my life. I always cherished every moment with her. But that leaves a gaping hole now and doesn't seem much of a comfort.

It's strange, but the night of the deaths already seems distant and vague; almost as if that evening occurred in a film I watched. It's as though the desolation of today has washed away my guilt. The more I think about it, the more I believe they deserved it. Who would defend their actions?

Quantrill also told me where to find Vickerman, who appeared in my life not long after Quantrill used me. Vickerman was the one who really broke me. What he did was worse than the rest put together. Perhaps he should pay for his actions as well. I search my feelings and realise that I would look forward to seeing him again, and not just for revenge. If he answers my questions honestly, I might even leave him be.

But only if he feels guilty. He needs to see what he created. It's a strange thing to consider killing someone, even if you're not really going to do it. But somehow my thoughts keep returning to how to do it if necessary, and, perhaps more importantly, how not to get caught.

I must just be confused and lost. I watch enough police shows to know it's only a matter of time before the game is up. It's possible I have got away with the men I killed in self-defence, but if I took more lives and was careless, I would spend the rest of my life behind bars. Imagine knowing you'd never be free again. It'd be a prison in your mind as well as your body.

'You all right? You're grinding your teeth,' says Scarlett.

'Sorry, I was thinking about my mum.'

She shakes my headscarf out and fixes it in place. 'Come around this evening. Tim often brings Thai food home at the start of the week, although the git usually says I've eaten too much of it. We'll order in otherwise. I'll shave your head afterwards.'

'Very kind.'

'Sorry, honey, but yours is too far gone. I've still got that wig and it won't be forever. My hair grew back when I returned to the gym, took hold of the alcohol problem, and then there was the pregnancy too.'

That seems an extremely air-brushed version of events, but I appreciate her kindness. Would it be better if I did it alone? Cutting my hair off might make me feel vulnerable, but if I want to be strong and in control, I should take responsibility. I change my mind.

'No, it's okay. I think that's something I need to do myself. Could you bring the wig in tomorrow and I'll cut it then?'

'Sure. Here, you heard the latest on those murders? Apparently, they were brutal. Blood everywhere! I can't wait to watch the news tonight. It's a shame they took our work Internet access away because it's not the same on a phone screen.'

Scarlett is obsessed with watching the news on TV. She says her life is so uninteresting that she loves the drama and tragedy of it all.

'Do you think they deserved to die, Scarlett?' I ask.

'Too right.'

27

ACTING DCI BARTON

Barton had arrived at work on Monday with enthusiasm, but they still had little to go on. Strange knocked and entered his office looking demotivated.

'Sorry, John. The manager of the gym rang me this morning, and we learned nothing new. Ash was a known steroid abuser and all-round numpty, but it seems most people steered clear of him. The manager said Quantrill attended for a while but cancelled his membership. Other than that, Ash worked out alone. I've talked to Zander and neither of us know what to do next.'

Barton rubbed the sides of his head as he stared at her.

'Do you need to ask the master for his opinion?' he said.

'That's right, but yours will do instead.'

He grinned. 'Sum it up for me.'

'We have three unexplained deaths. The crime scene has been compromised by persons unknown. We have an unidentified male who should be able to help, but we can't locate him. There's also an unidentified woman involved who is probably the one they were drinking with at a pub earlier. Intel gives us nothing. Media appeals led to the usual nutcases calling in. CSI have revealed they think the semen was fresh on the dress.'

Strange took a deep breath. 'The most likely explanation is that the three men had a drunken fight and killed each other, but the wiping of prints suggests something more sinister. A ripped dress indicates rape. The woman could have attacked them, but more likely defended herself. There might even be two female footprints, which could mean another female was involved. Or the man seen leaving the scene could have been a boyfriend and murdered one or more as some kind of retaliation for rape. In fact, it could have been any combination of those things.'

Barton nodded. 'What do we have that's concrete?'

Strange frowned at the ceiling as she thought. 'Nothing, really. Just three stiffs.'

'Is there anything else we can do?'

'I've got Zelensky still chasing phone records and bank accounts. A & E records have been reviewed, and no women were admitted with injuries that match. There are a few people who we haven't got in touch with, so she'll chase them. I double checked with the owner of The Hartley that the CCTV hasn't worked in months, and he confirmed it. We did catch Graham Duncan in his van on CCTV. We have an image of him and a large man, clearly Ash, driving in the direction of their house at 23:30 on Saturday night.'

'Just the two of them?' asked Barton.

'Yes, but we'd impounded the vehicle, and I had a look inside. It contains a bed in the rear.'

'Maybe Quantrill and the girl were making out in the back.'

'Or they could have gone for a kebab and went to hers.'

'True, but this is dodgy. Someone's trying to hide something. Have you checked the bed for DNA?'

'Waiting for the results.'

Barton stared into the distance, tapping his finger on his table, wishing the results came back as fast as they did in the movies.

'What are you expecting from those results?'

'That the DNA from the bed will match Quantrill and the bloody dress.'

'Anything else you should check?'

Strange rolled her eyes. 'Check where they were sitting in The Hartley? CSI might be able to find a match and at least we know it's the same person.'

'That's a bit of a longshot and doesn't really help our case.'

'I give up.'

Barton smiled. 'Don't be afraid of doing nothing for a few days while you wait for results to come in. This isn't TV where we solve a crime each week. Lab results may break this case. Meanwhile, we work in a revolving world with new cases every day. I've just received reports of six overdoses from fentanyl in the Ortons.'

'Someone finally moving into the Chapman sisters' old area?'

'Perhaps. It's been quiet over there. The Snow Killer left a warning for those who break the law. It might be an up-and-coming entrepreneur buying chemicals from the dark web, some Chinese lab maybe, and knocking them out. The real problem is this drug is incredibly strong. Two of the victims flatlined, luckily when they were already in hospital, and the medics got them back. You and Zander leave the Millfield murders for the moment and work on catching whoever's responsible for the drugs, hopefully before the weekend and party time. A couple of the overdoses were kids. They roll over straight away when they've almost died, and the parents will be looking for someone to blame.'

Strange rose from her seat. 'Great, I'll leave Ewing and Zelensky chasing any loose ends and wait for the test results. With any luck we'll get a break or someone will have a brainwave over the next few days.'

'Correct. Good job, Kelly, you've done all you can at this point. Somebody knows something out there. My guess is that the three victims fought, probably over the girl, and she somehow survived. Maybe she was the last one alive and left. I think the man arriving and leaving came in, saw the horrors, and just vanished. People who've seen or done such gruesome acts will struggle to process it all. We could get a confession or further information. They may be considering coming to the station to talk right now. Guilt and shock do strange things to people.'

'Unless they fit the worst scenario.'

'Which is?'

'The perpetrator murdered those three in cold blood. They don't feel guilty, and, at some point in the future, they'll kill again.'

28

ACTING DCI BARTON

Barton tried to get home early one evening a week, so he could eat with Holly and the kids. He entered the house on Wednesday night to a scene from a Dolmio advert. His wife was placing a huge bowl of spaghetti bolognese on the kitchen table. Layla, Lawrence and Luke sat around it with expectant faces.

'Hi, Daddy.' Little Luke was the only one who rose from his seat to give him a hug.

'This is a nice surprise. We can be like a real family. You know, ones that talk and eat together as opposed to food-shovelling TV-watching zombies.'

Layla tutted. 'Don't get your hopes up. This is a one-off. Mum said we needed to have a family discussion and we've agreed.'

Lawrence rolled his eyes.

'Hey, I saw that,' said Holly.

Barton grimaced.

'And that!'

Family discussions usually involved a demand for a fairer distribution of housework. Holly would be the only person who benefitted and not for long. Barton flopped into a seat at the end of the table.

'Tough day?' Holly asked him.

'I never realised how much time the DCI spent with meetings and phone calls. Sometimes both combined. It's interesting work, and I'm enjoying it, but I feel sedentary. Unless something really serious happens, it's basically a desk job. Even though dramatic things are happening, it doesn't seem that way when you're so distant from them.'

'I understand completely. What you need is an exciting holiday.'

Loud bells clamoured in his head. It was a four-pronged attack. His brain screamed retreat as Holly ladled a huge portion of pasta onto his plate and passed him the Parmesan. He was tempted to push it away, so he wasn't outmanoeuvred, but his belly won, and he started wolfing it down.

'I vote for Australia,' he spluttered as he burned his mouth.

He'd wanted to go Down Under for years. Many of his school friends had travelled after they finished their education, but he'd worked from an early age. Escaping the British winter to a Sydney summer sounded brilliant. Opera House, Harbour Bridge, beaches, barbecues: it all appealed. Perhaps he could visit the *Neighbours* set, or was that Melbourne?

'We could hire a campervan and drive the Great Ocean Road. Miles and miles of nothing except kangaroos and sandy snoozes,' he added between mouthfuls.

'No way,' said Lawrence. 'I don't want to sit on a plane for twenty-four hours and beaches are boring.'

'What's it to you? Didn't you say no more lame family holidays?'

'It depends.'

Barton eyed his stepson suspiciously. Barton had been Lawrence's father for all intents and purposes for years, so, now he'd just turned seventeen, Barton could read him like a book. In fact, the four of them were looking sheepish.

'What about you, Layla?' he asked. 'You're always saying how cool visiting Australia would be.'

'I want to go backpacking there with my friends, not see the sights stuck in a cannister full of your farts.'

'We're going skiing, Daddy,' said Luke.

'What? People my size don't ski. I'd never be able to stop.'

Holly came around to hug him from behind. 'It'll be great. The kids can learn a skill and do something healthy. There'll be amazing views and you can just chill if you don't want to ski. We might even find a hot tub big enough for you. You don't need a flight to the other side of the world after your operation and think of the fondue.'

Barton ignored the grinning faces of his elder children. 'This is what you wanted to discuss? It doesn't feel like a discussion, more a statement of facts.'

'No,' said Holly. 'We decided on skiing before you got home. It's your mum we need to discuss. She's called me twenty-seven times today.'

With that, Holly's phone rang. She checked the screen, picked up a pen and marked another line on the shopping list whiteboard attached to the fridge.

Barton put his fork down. He understood what that meant. His mother had acted oddly at Christmas. While he was recuperating from his injuries, Holly had taken his mother to her GP and she'd been referred to a clinic to confirm Alzheimer's. Holly had listened during the tests and knew it was a foregone conclusion. His mum seemed to be deteriorating fast with her short-term memory being appalling, and she lived too far away for them to visit easily. Holly squeezed his shoulder.

'Kids,' she said, 'your nanny is getting old and confused. She has dementia. It's a normal process of ageing, but soon she won't be capable of living on her own.'

The children looked at each other.

'What's *demonshire*?' asked Luke.

'It's when ancient people go mad and behave like toddlers,' said Lawrence.

'No, it's not. Elderly people just get frail and forgetful and need looking after more,' said Layla.

'What do we do?' asked Luke. 'Do we have to give *her* pocket money now? She can have some of mine.'

Barton smiled at the workings of a young boy's brain. Barton and Holly had already chatted about the topic and were of the same mind.

'We aren't close by,' said Barton. 'So, we need to look at getting people to visit her each day, or maybe choose to move her into a care-home.'

Layla stood. 'That's not fair. Why can't she live here?'

'Yes,' said Lawrence, also standing. 'Although she's not having my room. We can turn your office into a bedroom.'

Luke rose too. 'That was easy to fix. I thought I was going to have to give up my room.'

With that, the three kids picked up their plates and headed towards the lounge.

'Hey,' said Barton. 'What are you lot doing?'

'Meeting's over,' said Lawrence. 'There's an Avengers movie on.'

Holly sat on Barton's lap, and they smiled at each other.

'We have fabulous kids,' she said.

'Skiing, eh?'

'Yes, and soon. I'm taking your mum to her GP tomorrow to talk about options. If she moves in, it will be tough for all of us, her included. There'll be no more holidays for a while, and there'll be no happy ending.'

Barton gave his wife a kiss. He thought of the unsolved murders and feared the same could be said for them.

29

When work has finished for the day, I stride from the building with a purpose. I've spent the whole afternoon ruminating over how I've ended up working in a call centre, living alone, and going bald. I planned to cut my hair off last night, but I didn't feel strong enough as I examined myself in the mirror. Tonight, I've decided to be proactive.

Quantrill told me that the man who is largely responsibility for my predicament lives ten doors up from him. The traffic is light as I drive through the streets. Rush hour in Peterborough is pretty much over by 6 p.m. I slow Scarlett's car as I pass the property where Quantrill died. There's tape on the door, but no sign of the police. I count the houses to the right and stop. A young Asian family are leaving the tenth house. The houses either side, judging by the curtains of one and a pram outside the other, also contain children. I pray that Vickerman never had kids.

After a three-point turn, which is tricky in the narrow road, I return and count the other way. The tenth house is plain. It doesn't resemble what Joe Public would think a junkie's home would look like, but heroin addiction is misunderstood. I should know. It's his house, I'm sure of it. There's no space to park, so I stop at the end of the street and walk.

My mind wanders back to those first few months after I finished my A levels. I was already adrift from life. Everyone had left school and started university or apprenticeships, and I sat at home. My mum didn't push me to do anything. I thought she didn't care, but she knew enough not to heap pressure on me. Later she told me she'd known something was wrong, but getting me to talk had proven impossible. Six months passed by and I struggled to get out of bed before midday, even if I went to bed early.

I met Vickerman walking past the Old Guild Hall a few days before Valentine's Day, funnily enough, on my way to sign on. He was smoking cannabis openly while sunbathing on the steps of the building. He was five years older than me, skinny and tanned; heroin chic in the summer. I thought he was so cool, even though I declined his offer of a smoke, but we got chatting. He joked that I could be his Valentine if I didn't have one. A few days later, we were a couple.

He looked a little Jaggeresque with big features, but he wasn't unattractive. His long hair was his crowning glory. He'd have a ponytail at the back and a fringe hanging over his eyes. Then he'd push the fringe to one side, his dopey expression would smile my way, and my stomach would flip.

I'd smoked weed while at school. It had taken the edge off everything and left me unthinking. I could focus on schoolwork then to a reasonable level, whereas before I hadn't been able to concentrate or see the point in anything. After a while, though, the paranoia had outweighed the relaxation and I'd quit. Vickerman got me back on it.

A short while later, his parents had gone out, and we sat bored in his lounge.

'Fancy trying something different?' he asked with a wave of his hand.

'I told you I'm not into weird stuff.'

'It's called brown. We can smoke it.'

'Then what?'

'It's amazing.'

I couldn't remember the last time I did anything that could be described as amazing.

'Do we have to go and get it?'

'No, I've got some here.'

'Well then, why not?'

And that was it. Heroin is something else. Not a dragon that you chase, more a beautiful snake. Once it bites and infects you, you fall into an all-consuming love story. The aroma was familiar. I realised too late that it was a scent that already clung to him. A kind of burnt-brown-sugar aroma. I'd thought he smelled of cheap washing powder. My descent was rapid. Vickerman was well down the slide. He wouldn't have rushed if he knew what was at the bottom.

It meant we disappeared from our homes before anyone realised something had changed. Turns out you don't even have to smoke the drug. There's a faster way.

Addiction costs money though. He stole for us at the beginning, while I tidied the dosshouse we were living in. You see, if you're cluck-ing, you need to distract yourself and housework can help. When you're high, some, like Vickerman, go on the nod and slip into a monged-out state. I enjoyed doing little innocent things such as dusting or even painting. There was just you and the joy of the job in hand. It pulls at me still, that contentedness, despite looking back from so far away.

But habits escalate. His thieving couldn't keep up, and he sold the only thing we had of any value, and it wasn't his to sell. I'm breathing heavily as I stamp along his street with my head down, remembering what he did. I knock at the door and wait. When it opens, it isn't Vick-erman, it's one of his old drug dealers, Quinn. That's weird.

'Yes?'

'Is Vickerman there?'

'Yeah, he's reading. Is that you, Ellen?'

I nod.

'What do you want?'

'Does it matter?'

He steps back. 'I guess not.'

The house is clean and empty. The walls are clear, as is the TV stand when I arrive in the lounge. Vickerman is sitting on the sofa and doesn't register my arrival. He has so many layers of tatty clothing on that it makes his head look too small. Even the beanie looks oversized. He's turned into Beetlejuice, with his once beautiful long hair now lank and thinning. Quinn has a thick duffel coat on that looks so filthy I wouldn't wash my floor with it.

'What are you reading?' I ask Vickerman.

Blank eyes flicker up. He unconsciously picks at a scab on the back of his right hand. '*1984*.'

'Again? Has it improved?'

His gaze focuses on me and a half-smile rises on his face. 'Ready to be turned, Ellen?'

He was always complaining about the power of the state. Although, he was one of the ones who genuinely believed what he said, as opposed to using it as an excuse to avoid getting a job. Quinn sits next to him. He also looks ill and shivers. The energy companies disconnect the electricity and gas when nobody pays the bill, but these two would have sold the pipes and the boiler ages before that happened. The TV and microwave were usually the first things to go.

'You two get married, then?'

Vickerman grins, but Quinn's head jerks up. The sadistic look that ran his business is a mere spark now, and the wide muscled body that protected it is long gone.

'We both live here. Moved in a year ago. We made it nice,' says Quinn.

Nice and bare, perhaps. 'I heard you lived here from a friend. There were some questions that I wanted to ask you.'

'Like what?' asked Vickerman.

'About how you treated me.'

Vickerman looks serious.

'I treated you good, and I didn't make you do anything you didn't want to, if that's what you're thinking. When did I ever threaten you or be violent?'

It's nice to see him, but any compassion abandons my heart. An icy focus compels me to lay out why I'm here.

'You turned me into a whore.'

Vickerman returns his gaze to the scab. I step closer to him.

'You made me have sex with strangers, so you could get high.'

'You got yours, too.'

'You pimped me out when I was nineteen. And you got me hooked on heroin. I was a silly young girl and you should have known better.'

Vickerman frowns at me. He has no answer to that.

'Clear off, Ellen. I'm not interested in dragging up the past, however you remember it.'

Quinn gets to his feet, eyes twitching, and lurches towards me. He grabs me hard on the upper arm, as he did once before.

'I remember it different, too,' he says.

'I nearly died,' I reply.

Quinn lets go but leans into me. 'We thought you were dead. We searched for you because we missed your company, but you'd vanished.'

It seems the drugs have ruined their minds as well as their bodies. I look to see if Vickerman has anything else to say, but he coughs and coughs. It starts Quinn off. He slumps back next to Vickerman on the sofa. I shake my head.

'It's a shame we lost touch, what with you two doing so wonderfully for yourselves.'

I'm surprised by my boldness in risking Quinn's anger, but he's not the force of old.

Vickerman wipes his mouth with his sleeve. 'We're getting clean. Have you got some cash? Only we're waiting on a cheque to clear and haven't any food.'

It's the biggest lie since Adam and Eve said, *'What apple?'* My arm aches where Quinn grabbed me. 'My money and cards are at home, so no.'

'Come back at the weekend, we'll have some fun like old times,' says Quinn.

They sit there nodding and smiling at that. It's the exact image of when they told me what I had to do all those years ago. I knew I didn't have a choice. The next few months were a rabbit hole I never want to end up down again. I plumbed new depths, and they held my hand and forced me to carry on. There's no regret from these two, and there never will be. These men are spent and worthless, and I need to hurt them.

'I'll come back Saturday night with some money. It'll be like old times.' I wink at them. Quinn's face is hard to fathom, but Vickerman returns my gesture.

'Hey,' he says. 'Did you hear about what happened down the street?'

I feel myself tense. 'Yeah, wasn't you two, was it?'

Quinn sneers. 'Bunch of dicks deserved it.'

'I never knew their names, but Quantrill sounds familiar. I can't remember where I know the name from.' Vickerman smiles as he seems to look at me properly for the first time. 'What's with the scarf?'

'My hair's falling out.'

He removes his beanie. 'Mine, too.'

I leave quietly laughing to myself, but stop outside. I wouldn't normally chuckle at someone else's misfortune, even if he did resemble that guy in the wheelchair from *Little Britain*. Screw them, anyway, they're only after what they can get out of me. I walk back to the car and slam the door shut. Those itching, gurning peckerheads will climb the walls when I don't turn up on Saturday night. There's nothing worse than waiting for drugs that don't arrive. They deserve to suffer.

I put Scarlett's car through its paces on the way home, and I'm grinning when I pull into the car park for my flat. My grin fades when a man in a suit steps towards my vehicle. Trent, standing beside him, waves and disappears inside. There's something familiar about this tall man's face and walk, yet I'm pretty sure I don't know him. I'd suspect a debt collector, but he's nervous. His mismatched grey trousers and brown jacket could have been chosen for anonymity.

'Ellen?'

'Who are you?' I smile, which puts the man at ease, because he stops fiddling with the trilby hat that he holds.

'I came when I heard about your mother. I'm sorry I missed the funeral, but I've been ill for a long time.'

'She wouldn't have minded.'

'No, perhaps not, but I should have been there, for your sister and you.'

Close up, he's taller than I realised. His facial features remind me of my sister. He has her nose and the same dark-green eyes.

'Who are you?'

'I'm your dad.'

I step back in stunned surprise, then stare into his eyes for signs of deceit. They implore me to believe him, yet they seem shaded. He drops his gaze to the floor. Is it weakness I detect, or shame?

'Do you mean stepfather?'

'No, I was there at your birth. I held you while they cleaned up your mother. I hated the name Sue Ellen because it morphed into Swellen. Eventually it became just Ellen. Your mum was the only one who kept calling you Sue Ellen, and in the end only when you were naughty. Don't you remember being called Swellen? I suppose you were pretty young.'

'Anyone could know that story.'

Despite my words, Swellen registers deep inside my brain even though I've been Ellen for as long as I can recall. His deep voice is familiar, too.

'Forgive me for doubting you, but my father died decades ago.'

I glare at him, and now it's him who backs away. He stops and stands straighter.

'Please, give me ten minutes. I should have been here for the funeral, but I choked at the last minute. Did it go well?'

'As well as those things go. You could say it was a nice one.'

I look him up and down. He seems scared of his own shadow. I don't feel as if I'm in any danger. In fact, after the time I've had recently, it's him who should be worried.

'Are you for real?'

He nods once, firmly. I shrug and beckon him to follow me. He keeps a respectful distance between us as we reach the top floor. I usher him in and watch as his eyes flash over my pictures, photographs and ornaments. I wonder if he's scoping the joint until he turns and smiles. 'May I?'

He stops at a picture of my mother and frowns.

'Pamela was a beautiful woman.'

I stand next to him, needing to peer up into his face, and for the first time I sense a wiry strength. My sister's nearly six feet tall and we were both the tallest in our classes for a long time until a few of the boys overtook us. My sister and I towered over my mother. She was a quiet, consistent type, who wanted a peaceful life. I search my mum's expression in the photo for signs of sadness, but there are none. It's strange to think of her as a young mother with the man standing by my side.

'Do you want a coffee?'

'No, it's okay. I won't take much of your time and then I'll get going.'

My mouth drops open again.

'The least you can do is stay for a drink. You're not turning up here, saying you're my father, checking out the photos, and clearing off. It doesn't work like that. Where the hell have you been?'

He sits at my small kitchen table and covers his face with his hands. I'm not sure if he's crying. I fill the kettle and get two cups out. The water boils and I make us two milky coffees, which I place on the table. I decide I don't care if he likes his with sugar or not. I scrape the chair back opposite and sit down.

'Well?'

His eyes are red. 'I was sick. Suppose I've always been a little that way. I have serious depression, and I hear voices sometimes. They tell me to do unpleasant things, but I don't. I just have to concentrate really hard to stop myself, and I can end up in a kind of trance. The doctors call it a catatonic state. I can be in it for ages, months once.'

'What are you saying – that you've been in an institution all this time?'

He smiles and his eyes shine in the same way as Lucy's. 'We like to call them psychiatric hospitals, but some of it, yes.' I detect a glimpse of my sister's dry humour there, too.

'Why didn't Mum tell me? Mental illness affects most families. I needed a father, even if he wasn't there all the time.'

He struggles with what he has to say. He spits it out. 'I did bad things.'

I lean away. 'You hit us, hit Mum?'

'No, never!'

'What, then?'

'I would sink into a black rage and no one could talk to me. I'd stomp around the house and frighten everyone. Your mum threw me out. I had to live with strangers, and my grip on reality slipped. They sectioned me. I didn't know what was going on.'

His answer seems contrived. My mum wasn't the type to throw anyone out.

'You could have written, paid the odd visit. Just knowing you cared would have helped.'

'I spent ten years in one place. They wouldn't let me go. Said I was too sick. I did come back home once though. It took me a while to find you after so long as you'd moved house. I chose a dreadful moment because when I turned up it was the morning your sister was getting married. Your mum pushed me out of the door. Shouted how dare I turn up on her special day.'

I also missed my sister's wedding, which wasn't fair of me. Vickerman had me hooked on drugs and living a desperate life by then. I have consoled myself with the fact that I would only have ruined it, and I was sick, but isn't this what my dad is saying?

'Did you speak to my sister?'

'No, she was getting her hair done at a neighbour's.'

'Did you ask after me?'

'Of course. Your mum cried. They didn't know where you were. You'd gone missing six months earlier. They'd looked all over, put posters up and been on the radio, but nothing. She begged me to leave you alone. Pamela said she told you that I was dead, and it was best to keep it that way.'

'Surely my sister wanted you in her life?'

The shame I detected earlier surfaces. He whispers, 'She was older than you. She remembers my...' he searches for the right word '... behaviour.'

It's a lot to take in. We sip our drinks in silence. I hate to think what his behaviour might have been, but my mother's dead and my sister is a stuck-up judgemental type whom I never see. We all act differently when we're not in our normal mind. I've been in one of those hospitals myself. Maybe he and I could build something together, yet I can't help lashing out.

'Well, you missed the wake. What do you want to do now? Take me to McDonald's? Do some jobs around the flat for me? I've had no offers for Christmas this year.'

And there's the guilt again as he rises from his seat.

'I should go. Look, I'm not a good person to know. I'm still not completely better. Finding out one of your daughters was missing and the other one was going to walk down the aisle on her own was too much to bear. I lost control again, and they sent me back to the hospital. You're better off without me in your life.'

'Why did you come to my flat, then? How do you know I live here?'

'The people at Pamela's old house had this place as a forwarding address. I always wanted to hear how you and your sister were. Pamela used to keep me updated occasionally, but obviously the letters stopped when she died. I suppose I have no right to know about your lives.'

'No, you don't. I can't believe this. My mum told me you were dead, yet she was still in touch with you. Did you never consider what my life was like?'

He moves quickly and pulls the front door open. I think he's going to flee down the stairs, but he stops. He grimaces as though in pain. The words when they come are spoken slowly.

'You're right. I'm a selfish man. It was a mistake to come, I understand that now, but I have little in my life. It's a poor existence. I sometimes consider ending it but, honestly, I can't be bothered. Dying seems too dramatic. I kind of hoped that perhaps we could send birthday cards to each other and the like, keep in touch a bit. Maybe pictures of grandkids, or holidays. Apart from my children, my existence will have been for nothing.'

Unbelievable. He needs to get out before I throw him out.

'Brilliant. You rock up after all this time, then say goodbye, because it's too much trouble to be a proper part of my life.' Suddenly, I'm exhausted. 'Just go.'

He places his hat on his head and shuffles backwards out of the door, seemingly also wearied, and I hear his slow footsteps on each step. I don't know why, but I follow him down the stairs. I stop at the entrance and watch as he hobbles across the car park.

'Dad! Wait.'

He turns with hope.

'Christmas and birthdays. You write first.'

He beams, and the years drop away. Perhaps he grinned like that as he named me Ellen. He tilts his trilby and there's a definite spring in his step as he departs from view.

I shake my head. Can today get any weirder? It would help to chat to someone. I hear the TV blaring from Trent's flat and can't think of anyone else. He rarely locks his door because he never goes anywhere.

When he doesn't reply, I assume the TV is too loud and walk in. Trent is sitting on the sofa, manhood in hand, trousers next to him, intently staring at the TV, and furiously pleasuring himself. He rolls off the sofa in a vain attempt to turn the TV off as opposed to covering himself up. Nothing could shock me further today. I approach his struggling body and check out what was so enticing on the box.

'Have you been watching *Dempsey and Makepeace* again?'

'I was thinking of you. You remind me of her.'

'Rubbish, I look more like him. Put your trousers on and fetch your hair clippers.'

He walks naked to his bathroom, returns with his clippers and passes them to me, still with no trousers. It's lucky the clippers need to be plugged in or I'd be tempted to turn him into Action Man. I walk out of his flat, shaking my head, and leave his door wide open. Hopefully a neighbour will look in and call the police. Or maybe not.

Back on the top floor, I close my flat door and look in the cutlery drawer. I have the sharpest bacon scissors on the planet. It doesn't take long to trim my hair down to stubs. It looks weird in the mirror, as though I have male pattern baldness as the crown is so thin. With an understanding of why men shave their heads, I do the same. I look so much younger, almost innocent. Without the hair, it's hard not to focus on my eyes, which have a cool glare to them. I suppose that's not surprising, but it's unnerving. I'm not sure I like what I see.

From the side, my head resembles a near perfect egg. I hope that's apt. Today, and all its strangeness, can be a new beginning.

ACTING DCI BARTON

Barton observed DC Zelensky through the blinds as she flew into the office towards her seat. Checking his clock, he saw she was three minutes late. Winter hadn't loosened its grip, but the forecast snow hadn't arrived, so she'd need a better excuse than traffic. Strange sat steely-eyed at her desk. Zelensky perched on a chair at a corner table and exhaled long and slow. Even from his office, he could detect the sheen of moisture on her forehead. He picked up his phone and rang Strange.

Strange, on the other hand, entered his room with a spring in her step. He commented as such. She beamed at him.

'We're cracking the drug case. I received a call this morning from one of the parents of the kids who overdosed. His daughter nearly died. She's told him everything, who she got them off, who he got them off, and so on. Zander extracted something similar last night from a known user in Werrington. Sounds as if Zander crossed a few lines, but if the info matches, we're closing in.'

'I saw from the analysis that it wasn't a Chinese lab.'

'No, they think there's an Indian lab in Birmingham. I've got a call booked with Balsall Heath station at eleven. They've had three deaths over there and nearly twenty ODs, but they think they're close as well.'

'Excellent. I noticed your bouquet arriving. I picked them from my own garden.'

'Very funny. It was a making-up gesture from Sirena. We had our first row.'

'That's good. Holly and I are only communicating when we're shouting.'

Strange didn't even smile. 'We've been getting on well, small steps, but we got onto the topic of marriage and children. She's not interested in either.'

Barton raised an eyebrow. 'Ah, the dreaded questions that come to most relationships, often after around six months, so you're early. It's the point where you jockey for position, some even call it a power struggle, and decide if what you have could be forever.'

'You've been married for years. How do you make it work?'

'Wanting the same things is important. Then it's often about not giving up.'

Strange's face dropped. Sirena and she had a big hurdle approaching. He wondered if they could jump it together.

Strange changed the subject. 'I take it you want a chat with Zelensky.'

'Almost. I want you to speak to her. I'll be here to help.'

Strange rang Zelensky's desk phone. She arrived with a pinched face and brief eye contact. She attempted a smile, which showed lipstick on her front teeth.

'How are things, Maria?' asked Strange.

'Fine.'

'Everything okay at home?'

'Yes.'

'Do you know why we've asked you to come in for a chat?'

Zelensky glanced up, close to tears. 'My timekeeping? I was barely late. This job is my world, so please don't give me a warning.'

'How would you describe your performance at work recently?'

'Not bad. As good as most.'

Strange gently rested her hand on Zelensky's arm. 'But you could be better than most.'

Zelensky crumpled, and she sobbed with her head bowed, shoulders heaving. Barton nodded to Strange as she held Zelensky's hand. Nothing like a compliment to undermine a determined defence. At that moment, it was hard to believe there were only six years between the two women in front of him.

When Zelensky had pulled herself together, she spoke as if relieved to get it off her chest.

'I reckoned I'd seen it all as a PC, but I hadn't. I saw The Snow Killer's victims and thought I could handle it, but as a detective you're around the bodies longer and need to keep looking at the images. They stay with you. The Soul Killer appeared in my dreams. Post-mortem faces remained in my head when I woke up. Sleeping became something out of reach, and I started having a few drinks to drop off, which helped at first. I was busy during the day, worked long hours, and then passed out at night. Now nothing helps.'

'You won't be the first or last officer to use alcohol to forget.'

'How do you guys cope?'

'DCI Barton spends every spare minute practising t'ai chi.'

Barton did his finest spiritual pose from behind the desk. Zelensky gave a little smile, and some colour returned to her cheeks.

'Exercise will help,' continued Strange. 'But the best way is to talk about it with others. You can always speak to either of us, or Occupational Health if you want someone out of the department.'

Barton noticed a slight eye-roll from Zelensky. Many worried that signs of weakness would go on their permanent record.

'You get on with DC Ewing, don't you?' asked Strange.

Vivid red blossomed in Zelensky's cheeks. 'Yes, we joined on the same day. We've had a few dates over the years, but I'm focusing on my career. I want to be like you, Sergeant.'

Strange also blushed. 'I struggle as well with the things I see. Everyone does because it's a tough job. The bodies won't stop coming, but alcohol is a short-term solution. Eventually it becomes a bigger problem than the sleepless nights. Stick with Ewing, just as close friends if that's all you need. Your colleagues understand and might need the same support from you. It really does help to know you aren't going through this alone and your feelings and thoughts are normal.'

'I understand, but Ewing's not suitable boyfriend material.'

Strange smiled. 'What man is? And remember, you must have a life outside this job, or you'll become a clichéd statistic and burn out.'

Barton had detected a barb in Zelensky's last comment.

'Focus on doing healthy things like regular jogs, walks or family visits,' he said. 'A planned holiday to look forward to is how many cope, including me. I hear skiing is fun. DC Malik is at the gym most nights. I've retired from that injured, but he's always looking for workout buddies. You need to do simple things with friends, or you just spend your life dealing with criminals. Most people in the city are grounded, helpful, friendly, law-abiding and nice. If they weren't, it would be total carnage out there, and we'd have to police a war zone.'

Zelensky leaned back in her seat and relaxed. 'I'm not getting a warning?'

'No, we think you have a promising future,' said Barton. 'But take this chat seriously. Remember, if you're not at your best, it's not just you who could be in danger.'

'I understand. Thank you, I won't let you down.'

Barton shook Zelensky's hand as she left, but he shared another look with Strange after she'd gone. They both knew not everyone survived a career in the police.

I'm going to see Quinn and Vickerman on Saturday night after all. I want them to know what happened to me. Maybe they can give me some answers about that lost time. They need to understand what they did, even though I bet they don't care. I've also had a horrible thought. Back then, I complained to Vickerman about how Quantrill took my virginity. Vickerman's addled mind hasn't clicked, but it might. I need to know if he's recalled that information. If he does, it's a worry.

It's not like me to be this purposeful. Normally, I struggle to decide what to have for breakfast and end up having toast for the fifth day in a row. I feel more alive somehow, yet also a little out of control. I'm not used to being so upbeat.

I tossed and turned last night thinking about my father. It doesn't seem right that he has a life and I'm not part of it, even after what he did to us. I'll meet him again and try to persuade him to be closer to me. Like my dad, I had long ago decided I was better off on my own and gradually cut myself off, even when my therapist had said that it was hazardous for me. Perhaps I should start my sessions again, but I genuinely thought I could cope.

Scarlett, the scatter-brained cow, forgot to bring the wig in on Tuesday, so I'm driving to collect it now. I don't mind as I have little else to do and it's a reason to drive her Qashqai. The psychiatrists encouraged me to spend more time with other people. However, I'm pretty sure they didn't mean someone as morally corrupt as Scarlett.

There are tyre tracks across their lawn and through a flower bed. I half expect to find Scarlett's Evoque upside down in the pond, but it's in front of the garage. Tim answers the door and has a big grin for me.

'Come in, come in. How's things? It's good to see you. Scarlett looks forward to your visits. She struggles out here with all her friends living in the city.'

What friends? I smile and bite back the comment. 'Why don't you move, then?'

'We love it out here. The Little Man has so much space.'

Little Man Dwayne has more than outgrown his nickname. 'Where is the terror?'

'He's returned to boarding school. Didn't Scarlett tell you that he started last September? She was keen for him to get a good education.'

I detect his lack of enthusiasm for the idea. He also looks perturbed that Scarlett hasn't told me.

'Do you have a boyfriend?' he asks.

Here we go. 'Why?'

'A few of the guys at the clay-pigeon shoot took a shine to you and asked.'

'No, thanks.'

'These are decent men. Bankers, lawyers, accountants.'

'They sound smashing. Where's Scarlett?'

'In the garage.'

I raise my eyebrows.

'Don't ask.' He smiles, though.

When most people say garage, they are usually talking about a thin building that the family car won't fit in and is therefore full of crap awaiting a trip to the tip. Scarlett and Tim's, however, could accommodate a couple of buses. The raised area in the corner even contains a gym. I assume she's there. Instead, I find her cursing at the washing machine.

'I didn't realise you knew how to work one of those,' I say.

'Bloody thing. I couldn't open the door and thought I would have to take a crowbar to it. I unscrewed something at the bottom and a load of water poured out. There are so many programmes. Which do I choose?'

'Doesn't your – now, what is it you call her? – housekeeper do that?'

'Maid, she was our maid, and yes, she did. She's left.'

'Wow, another one. You've been through more servants than the Queen. What this time, stealing again?'

'She shouted in my face that she wasn't a slave and stormed off. Next thing I know, she's driven through the flower bed and disappeared. Nothing was missing, so I wasn't too bothered. She left an enormous pile of washing on the floor, but it smells funny.'

'Eh?'

'Yep, I reckon she pissed over it.'

I can't help laughing. 'Sorry to hear that, but can I distract you from your terrible rich-person problems? My dad showed up.'

'No way. I thought he was dead. That is juicy news. Come on, let's get out of here. Men like playing with machines, so Tim can sort this out.'

As we are about to leave, I spot the shotguns hanging against the far wall.

'Aren't they supposed to be locked away?'

'God knows. I reckon Tim enjoys looking at them. They're unloaded. He keeps the cartridges hidden under the sofa in his office, thinking I don't know where they are. Maybe he's worried I'll grab the gun when he's being an arsehole.'

'Things aren't that bad, are they?'

She ponders that for a second, which is worrying. 'Sometimes.'

I suspect Tim wouldn't be familiar with the washing machine either, so before we leave I pick a sock off the pile and give it a cautious sniff. It smells more like lavender to me. I wonder briefly why people like Scarlett always assume the worst. We walk through the rear door and into the kitchen, where she listens to my news in amazement.

'Let me get this right. Your mum and your sister lied to you all these years about him being dead when in fact he was in a loony bin.'

'Yes, it's hard to believe.'

'Why didn't he visit or write? He can't have been in one all that time.'

'He reckons he was really ill and they wouldn't release him for ten years. Although he said that my mother was in touch with him.'

'That's mental. And now he doesn't want any contact because he's not worth knowing?'

'Correct.'

Scarlett plays with her fringe for a few moments. 'That doesn't ring true. Tell me exactly what he said.'

I repeat his words as close to how I remember them. She clicks her fingers.

'You're not being suspicious enough. Those places can't keep you in if you want to leave, not for that amount of time, I'm sure. You checked out of your hospital when you felt ready, even though they said you should stay longer.'

'What if he was proper bonkers, and the courts sent him?'

'That's more likely, but not for exactly ten years. That sounds like a sentence. Maybe he's not worth knowing because he did something terrible.'

To my horror, and for obvious reasons, that makes sense. We turn and stare at her laptop.

'What's his full name?'

'Ted Deacon.'

'Not the same surname as yours?'

'No, my mum said they were never married. I had her last name growing up. That's a bit odd, too. Don't they usually use the father's surname for the children, in the expectation that marriage will follow?'

She shrugs and enters her password. I pause while she taps away. I have a sinking feeling my life is about to change.

'No, nothing.'

'Phew.'

'Wait, what does Ted stand for?'

'Theodore.'

Scarlett hits the keys again. She lets out a little gasp.

'Holy shit, your dad was a bad man.'

She spins the laptop so I can read the screen. The letters are large and bold.

DOUBLE KILLER, THEODORE DEACON, SENT BACK TO RAMPTON PSYCHIATRIC HOSPITAL.

Scarlett reads the rest of the article. She shakes her head.

'Wow, he was scary. It says here that Theodore Deacon stabbed a woman in the homeless hostel he was staying in after she spat in his face and attacked him with the knife which he ended up using on her. When they entered his room afterwards, his cupboards had defaced photos of her on them. They'd been dating but recently split up. During questioning by the prosecution, he had a complete psychotic episode, and the judge declared him unfit for trial. He was released after ten years, seemingly well again.

'Some time later, a burglar broke into your dad's apartment through an open window. He woke up, disturbed him, chased him down the street, and strangled him to death. Apparently, two neighbours tried to pull him off but were unable to do so. Deacon only let go when the police sprayed CS gas in his eyes. Again, while on trial, he displayed manic mood swings and hallucinations.'

'It appears my dad didn't take kindly to being hassled.'

Scarlett almost lets something slip but manages to prevent the words from forming. Just as well – that will be about the other thing we agreed never to mention again.

'Got anything to drink?' I ask to change the subject.

'Of course! We had a delivery from Naked Wines, so take your pick.'

We settle in front of the TV in her snug. We never go in the lounge because Tim's always watching sport in there. She leaves it on the news. After a load of political rubbish, there's a report on the local bulletin about a deadly batch of fentanyl that's doing the rounds. The police are appealing for information. A raid in Birmingham recovered over ten thousand pills. They believe a similar amount is in the Peterborough area.

'I should slip a few of those in Tim's Horlicks. I checked the will, and I'll be more than fine.'

I glance over to see if she's joking, but she's expressionless. She tops her glass up for the second time. I've had one sip of mine. I'm not in the mood for her drunken bellyaching about what a git Tim is, so I make my excuses. She's still in the happy stage, so I endure another sloppy kiss through the window and I'm told not to worry about returning the car to them in any hurry. She'll use the Evoque. Somehow she remembers the wig and leaves me pondering her words as she goes to fetch it.

When she returns with a victorious smile, I decide to warn her against any crazy drunken behaviour, especially now I've heard where the ammunition is for those guns.

'If you killed Tim, you'd go to prison. It would be very different from this,' I say through the car window, while waving my hand around at the house and grounds.

'I think I'd like it.'

'How so?'

'More sex. Admittedly, non-consensual from the prison bullies.'

'Ah, I see. You're harbouring lesbian jail fantasies.'

'Don't we all?'

I smile and decline to answer. I had an experience when I was receiving my treatment. It was fun, but the thing I missed most was hanging onto broad shoulders.

'I prefer men,' I reply. 'If I got sent to jail, I'd have to get a butch partner. Tell her to fart and burp a lot and keep messing the cell up after I'd tidied it.'

She snorts, another sign of impending drunkenness. I'm surprised I've said such a thing out loud. That's not the kind of comment I'd make usually. Besides, maybe it wouldn't be too terrible behind bars. Maybe I'd have more friends inside. There'd be no more money worries, and no more endless days in that godawful call centre. I drive off and toot my horn at the gates.

On my own, though, my mood darkens. Everything that's occurred suddenly becomes real. During the drive back, I realise I'm different since Mum died. The person I created after my breakdown all those years ago has crumbled away now I'm completely on my own. I used that person as a shell of respectability to protect me from the world, and the world from me. My mother was part of that cocoon, and she's gone. I had hoped to be something new and shiny, but what's emerged is unstable and angry.

I felt invincible earlier, and I liked it, but that seems a distant memory now. Instead I feel an approaching storm inside. The temperature has dropped, the wind has changed, the day has darkened and the first squall has arrived, but the hurricane isn't here yet. Let's hope it passes me by.

As I approach home, I drive past Sweet Millie's, the charity shop. It's Thursday, the night of her stock check. The angel on my shoulder wins, and I pull up outside and park. The door's locked, but I can see a light on in the back. After a brief wait, she smiles broadly and opens up.

'Hi, you came.'

'Yes, sorry I'm a bit late, but I hated the thought of you tackling that room on your own.'

'You're too kind. I've mostly been staring in awe at it because it's grown since you were previously here.'

I catch her looking at the scarf on my head. Last time, I had hair. Like my manager, she doesn't mention it though.

'Shall we have a coffee first? I could do with a boost,' she says.

I give her a thumbs up. It's a phrase my nana used. I'm so reminded of her – they even look similar – that a lump has formed in my throat.

Soon, we're ripping open bin bags and laughing our heads off at the unusual contents. She swings the biggest bra I've ever seen in my life around her head as if it were a sling. It'd be some weapon with a ten-pin bowling ball in it. She has a great eye though and pulls garments out that should fit me and look nice. An hour flies by, and the powerful emotions that threatened to swamp me fade away. Talking to her is like chatting to a counsellor.

We walk through the shop at the end, having carried on until past 9 p.m., both carrying bags with a smile.

'Hang on,' she says, and walks back to the counter to remove a box under the till. 'Do you want these?'

I open the flaps and think for a moment it contains guinea pigs.

'Take them home, try them on. You already know people give everything you could imagine. Some will be cheap dressing-up stuff, but we get expensive ones, too. Cancer is the end for many of us. My sister had a lovely wig before she died.'

I'm not sure what to say, but don't feel like talking about it. I bob my head.

'Ellen, things will improve, trust me. One of my friends had an awful pregnancy. Most of her hair and some of her teeth fell out, but she lived a full and happy life.'

'Did they grow back?'

She chuckles. 'No, neither of them did, but she had a cracking set of falsies.'

I smile. 'Thanks. I do appreciate it.'

She puts an arm around my shoulder. 'Thank you. Clearing that room is usually a terrible job, but I had fun tonight. You know, loneliness is a killer as well.'

As I lean into her, I think how right she is.

34

ACTING DCI BARTON

Zander and Strange barged into Barton's office without knocking. He was debating if it would make him look like a dictator if he made them go back outside when Strange spoke.

'The DNA test for the semen on the dress matches Quantrill. They picked it up off the bed in the van, too. The DNA of the blood which we assume is from the owner of the dress doesn't give us a name.'

'Right. So what's with the wide-eyed enthusiasm?'

'But that DNA matches a case from years ago, and that murder has similarities.'

Barton squinted. 'Eh?'

'A man was murdered over fifteen years ago, but the case was never solved. There was blood and skin cells under the victim's fingernails. The detective on the case never located the woman they belonged to, nor the murderer, assuming it wasn't the same person. We've had a flick through the notes. It seems they made little progress.'

Barton steepled his fingers. Fifteen years was long before his time as a detective. 'Who was the victim?'

'An Alan Mason, aged forty-six,' said Strange.

Barton shook his head.

Zander grinned. 'Also known as Wee Jock.'

'No way,' said Barton. 'How many times did we arrest him over the years?'

'At least twenty. I recalled he'd died, and I remember us discussing it. We were still in uniform and not involved. We assumed it was over drugs. From the file, they pulled the usual suspects in, but nobody talked.'

'Who ran the investigation?'

'Our old boss, DCI Naeem. Mortis did the post-mortem.'

Barton continued to fight to get his head around it.

'Study the case files further. Look for anything that might help.'

When they'd left his office, he picked up the phone to the hospital mortuary and smiled as the assistant said she would fetch Mr Menteith. Everyone had called him Mortis for years due to his fascination with the stages of death.

'Inviting me out for cream tea, John?'

'Of course, but first, can you remember Alan "Wee Jock" Mason?'

'Gosh, that is going back. Asphyxiation, I think, and never solved.'

Mortis had great recall of all the murder cases he'd had involvement in.

'That's it. You found DNA when you scraped under the fingernails. They never matched anyone on our database and the murder remained unsolved.'

Mortis's end stayed silent for a few moments while he tried to remember the details.

'I assumed that he was raping a woman and got disturbed by the victim's boyfriend and killed. It was strange that we found neither person.'

'Well, get your head around this. The ripped dress from the Millfield killings scene has been tested. The sample recovered matched that of the one from under Wee Jock's fingernails. Are you following?'

'Let me try to summarise. A woman was assaulted by Wee Jock, fifteen years ago, and vanished. She may have killed him. That same woman was raped by Quantrill, Ash, and Duncan, and disappeared again. The men are also deceased. That's one unlucky woman.'

'Not as unfortunate as the men who are dead.'

'Ah, I see. You're wondering whether the woman was responsible for their deaths, as well as Wee Jock's. That would make her rather deadly.'

'That's right. They attacked her and, in self-defence, she killed them.'

'Hmm. This last case involved three violent, drunken men. Was Wee Jock a known rapist?'

'Not that we know about, but he was a bully and exploited vulnerable types. There's violence on his record.'

'I don't like a woman for these deaths, especially with Wee Jock's death.'

'Why's that?'

'I'd guess whoever committed that crime was a strong, angry and determined man. He didn't just strangle Wee Jock. He crushed his throat.'

35

THE ICE KILLER

I wake up on the floor of my bedroom on Saturday morning. A dry mouth hints at a hangover, but I didn't drink anything last night despite it being a Friday. My head isn't pounding either. I climb back into my bed and pull the sheets over me. They are cold and clammy. When I close my eyes, my mind returns to the dream.

In it, I'm stuck inside a billowing cloud, neither rising nor sinking. There's so much noise and anger, shouting and screaming outside the cloud, but the whiteness muffles it away. Time means nothing, yet I'm aware it passes. Hands arrive through the cotton wool, poking, probing, wanting. Those fingers are over me, inside me, holding me. And there are tears, from my eyes? Is that touch my own? Those hands are familiar and then I feel wet tears on my cheeks. There are gasps, from abusers maybe, but there's rapture too, so maybe those sounds are my own.

I jerk upright, swing my legs from the bed, and leave the room. Hot water showers the memories away. As I dress, I recall the gradual emergence from that cotton wool nothingness. I remember knowing it was time to leave that place. The hospital staff had concerns but I wasn't a prisoner. They waved me off with advice and prescriptions and sorry glances. I left with no thoughts of shame or feelings of false imprisonment. They'd made me better. I was much improved from the wretched animal that had arrived there.

When I left that day and reached the road, I turned and stared at the whitewashed building. I believed the sickness remained behind those high walls. I was grateful: one of the lucky ones. A girl who I'd become close to inside had lived there for five years. It was clear many of the other inhabitants would never leave. Even so, the group discussions we'd shared made me see I wasn't alone. I heard worse stories than mine and wondered how much trauma the human brain could take before it changed forever.

The past is gone and can't be changed. Was it a doctor who said that, or my mother? Or was it neither? Maybe it's a rule I imposed on myself. Usually I can shove away thoughts of years gone by, but it seems that lately they are more persistent. I stare at my alarm clock in a daze. It's a shock to see it's already the afternoon. Can I really have been in bed for twelve hours?

I have plans and skip breakfast, or maybe that should be lunch. For once, Trent isn't hanging around outside. I drive fast through the streets to an area called West Town, stopping once for the cash machine, putting myself near my overdraft limit, and once at Waitrose for some beers. The guy I'm after lives on Mayor's Walk. He could have moved away, but I have a feeling he won't have.

Shortly before I bought my flat, I had a wobble and visited my old dealer, JC, to score some weed. He grinned when he opened the door and was pleased that I wasn't after the hard stuff. The dope was too strong after so long without it, and I only had one spliff and threw the rest away.

JC was one of those drug dealers that liked to say he's only providing a service. Without his wares, addicts would be forced to trade with hardened crooks selling substandard products.

Obviously, that's a load of rubbish. He was in it for the money. As a business plan though, it made sense, because abstinence made him reliable, which was a rarity in that line of work. Quinn was the opposite. The rule was if you grassed, JC would know and cut you off, so nobody did. That's why I hoped he might still be around. Those who sampled their own goods often had their life expectancy measured in months rather than years.

I knock on the door. It's a plain semi-detached property. You would imagine the owner worked a couple of manual jobs and had little time or money for home improvements. The doorbell is one of those gadgets where the resident can see who's outside on their mobile phone. I smile into the eye. After an entire minute, a man in just a towel opens the door. Moisture pours down his smooth skin. He must be pushing fifty, but he's in good nick.

'Hi, Ellen.'

'Hi.' I don't know his name, never have. I follow him into his front room. That's always been as far as I'm allowed. He locks the door behind him and pulls a heavy bar into position. It resembles a doctor's waiting room with a few chairs and blank walls.

'How can I help?'

'I'm looking for some fentanyl and a little bit of heroin. I heard there's some good stuff in town.'

'I see.' He runs his hand through his straggly wet hair. He always made me think of an anglicised version of Jesus when I scored off him before. Maybe it was his gentle ways and quiet voice, but it was probably the drugs. We nicknamed him JC but never called him that to his face. He's one of those people who command respect.

He pauses while he processes my last sentence. He doesn't care about what drug he sells; everything has its price, but he expects his customers to understand the risks.

'And who told you that?'

'The news. There are middle-class kids overdosing at the moment, and you know how that upsets the politicians. Strong is good as long as you know what you're doing.'

He tells me the price and leaves the room. Vickerman used to say he had a police radio, so they couldn't surprise him. We used to see JC a lot. One occasion, I asked him what he did with his spare time. He said he did a lot of yoga.

I loved that, thinking it was trippy. I reckon the original JC enjoyed a bit of spiritual stretching too. Vickerman laughed his head off and said he was taking the wazz. He said all dealers slept with whores, and that was a proven fact. I didn't know who was taking the wazz most, but I recall them now as good times. I may have been at the bottom of society, but I wasn't alone.

Vickerman was good to me then. He'd surprise me with the odd gift like a dog-eared paperback. We'd discuss some of his left-wing beliefs, and he'd think he was converting me. I'd then wind him up by standing to attention for the National Anthem and using the covers of his precious books for roach paper. I respected his mind, though. Vickerman said there were enough words in the English language without resorting to swearing.

The relationship was never particularly physical, especially when we were addicts. But I do recall feeling as though I was part of a team, and that's why I'm now Ellen Vickerman. He wanted to get married but we couldn't afford it. So I changed my name instead. He loved that, but my main motivation was that I hated Toole. Life's hard enough without a surname like that.

We were happy, until he sold me like a piece of meat.

JC returns and hands me a small bag filled with white tablets and one of powder. 'Careful with the pills. You're playing with recreational dynamite. One mistake can be fatal.' He scratches the stubble on his chin. 'You don't look like you've been partaking of late.'

He tried to dissuade me from buying the weed last time. Does he ask through good motives, or does he know there's no changing your mind at this point in the proceedings? You can't sell Slimming World products in the queue at McDonald's.

'I'll see you next time.' Smiling, I stand to leave.

Again, he considers my answer. 'I wouldn't recommend anyone using this product. I was about to dispose of it and disappear. I wouldn't have let many people in today. There's heat from the police over these overdoses. Whoever supplied them could get a life sentence. You know what you're doing though, just be extra careful.'

I nod. 'I would say you need to be careful, too.'

A minute later, I'm a hundred pounds lighter in the pocket and he's closing the door in my face. As always, it's been a weird experience. He seems to think his non-committal answers will protect him as he never says anything obvious. Who knows? He's still here when most aren't. The dealing business is a strange one. If you strip it down, dealers are peddling death and disease, but they expect to be treated as if they're doing you a favour. He gives me a final warning about the perils of mixing fentanyl with anything else.

I smile sweetly back at him. 'Don't worry. The pills aren't for me.'

36

I decided to drive to see Vickerman and Quinn tonight. It was tempting to wear the dress Scarlett gave me. I could have worn her shoes and wig, too. That way, if anything went wrong, she'd be the prime suspect. I only considered it for a second though. That really would be unfair. Instead I settle for the tightest jeans I have and a slim-fit shirt. I take my time with my make-up and I look nothing like me. The red wig will knock them dead. I smile at my choice of phrase.

I crush the pills and mix them with the heroin. My phone beeps as I'm leaving. I return to the table and there's a message from Brad asking if I want to go to the Paul Pry pub tonight. There's a few from work going to have a couple of quiet drinks. No doubt it's a load of his mates and they're looking for someone to take the brunt of their jokes. I almost put my mobile in my pocket, but throw it on the sofa, as I don't want that being tracked.

I drive fast, still unable to get enough of Scarlett's car. I'll be gutted when I have to hand it back. This must be how rich people live. I thought one car was much the same as another but I buzz with adrenaline every time I drive it. I park a few streets away to be safe and take a few deep breaths to calm myself. A chill settles over me, and I leave the beers in the car.

The walk there cools me further. It's got to be below freezing, and the pavement is slippery. A man whistles as I pass him in a street near their house. It drags a memory up of being whistled at before with this colour hair. I shuffle away as fast as my wedges will allow. It feels as if I'm gliding to my destination. There's a lightness in my head that rests at the edge of insanity.

I knock and wait for them to answer. My little internal voice begs me to go home but too late as Quinn answers the door.

'Ellen, come in. We weren't sure you'd turn up.'

Vickerman and Quinn have attempted to make the place look more homely, and they've even put on semi-decent clothes. There are a few night-lights burning around the sides of the room in saucers. One of them contains jasmine, I recognise the relaxing aroma as soon as I walk in. We sit down, and Quinn pours the wine. The candles' flames show the smudges in the glasses. There's a more cautious edge to him I didn't sense a few days ago. He can't sit still, but it's Vickerman who stands and disappears out the back without explanation.

Quinn rambles on about music and other stuff that I have no interest in. It's clear he's nervous. The alcohol mellows me out as he talks.

'Seeing you looking like that has made me come over funny. You've hardly changed after all these years. Do you remember dyeing your hair red before? It ended up a wild pink colour. I found it sexy.'

My mood changes fast. The memory of the whistle was from a passing car on a street corner. Kids messing about, but I was working. Quinn remembers our relationship as though we were friends. Vickerman comes back looking shifty and smelling of smoke.

'Where have you been?' I ask.

'Outside for a fag.'

'Really? Are you worried that your squat will smell?'

They both frown. 'The council gave us this and told us to look after it,' says Quinn. 'We'd been in supported accommodation together on Oundle Road, and this is so much better. We don't want to lose it.'

I'm not sure if they're lying or not. Everything feels false. Vickerman scratches his leg, then his foot. Has he gone outside and shot up?

'What have you got for us, then?' asks Quinn.

'I thought we were having a drink.'

'You wouldn't come empty-handed.'

Veins pound and twitch under the tight skin on his head. What a world they live in still. I came here for answers and there're only inevitabilities. Even so, do I want revenge? Vickerman clicks his fingers.

'I remembered where I knew the name Quantrill. It was through you. Wasn't he your first boyfriend? You hated him. Sure it wasn't you that killed him?'

He and Quinn laugh, and I do too, but I'm the first to stop.

'I'm off if you two aren't going to be friendly.'

Quinn is up and edging around the table as though he's circling a loose chicken.

'Don't go,' he begs.

'Just kidding. I got you a present.'

They stare at the plastic bag in my hand, slow smiles rising. They mutter insincere thanks.

'Sweet.'

'Nice one, Ellen. Powder, too.'

'If you fetch your works, I'll sort you out.'

As I expected, Vickerman sprints out of the room and comes back with a tobacco tin. Quinn reaches under the sofa and pulls out what looks like a pencil case. I watch him sneakily remove his own pouch of drugs and put it in his top pocket. I say nothing and get to work.

For some addicts, preparation is half of the pleasure. I can't really remember that period in my life, but I know my habit took over. Pure luck kept me from contracting a serious disease. For many, though, it's time that does the damage. Heroin is highly addictive and withdrawal extremely painful. It quickly breaks down the immune system, and it's that which leaves you sick, bony, empty and, ultimately, dead.

Fentanyl is fifty times stronger. The amount I suck into their two syringes would stun a brontosaurus, never mind a human heart. Vickerman takes his sock off and hunts for a vein. Quinn's habit must be more recent as he examines his arms. I can't watch.

'I'm just nipping to the toilet.'

When I return, Quinn looks asleep in his chair. Vickerman is still on the hunt for a suitable injection point.

'You were always a wild one. You not having any?' he says.

I sit up and lean forward, forcing the words out. 'You got me hooked.'

'What? You were as bad as we were. I reckon it was you that kept me on it. Then you disappeared. They tried to pin the murder of that Scots bloke on me.'

Another flashback shows me an image of a small Scottish man with terrible skin.

'Wee Jock,' I say, not having thought of the name for years.

'That's it. You'd started hanging around with him a bit. He was a right prick. Luckily I had an alibi from my sister's funeral.' He grins. 'The police didn't have a clue. We were pleased as he was stealing from everyone. Quinn reckoned you killed him, but then he was the one who found Wee Jock and took his stash before the police turned up.'

All of a sudden, I'm lying on cold concrete on a rear-garden patio. Wee Jock is on top of me, holding me down with one hand, removing my clothes with the other. Then a flash of pure burning white, but I don't remember killing him. I didn't even know he was dead. Vickerman snaps his fingers in my face, then sits back down.

'You okay, Ellen? You were in a trance. Look, nobody mentioned you were spending time with him to the police. We were just glad he was gone.' He places the empty syringe on the table.

His gaze wanders to his friend, who coughs and gurgles. Vickerman shrugs and slowly turns his focus to me through drooping eyelids.

'You still have your gloves on. Aren't you staying?' He waggles his fingers at me.

For a moment, I wonder what he's referring to. 'I have eczema. The gloves stop my skin getting irritated.'

'No worries,' he whispers.

'Vickerman, why did you and Quinn put me on the game?'

He attempts to pull himself up from his slumped position, but it's beyond him. His voice is slurred, but clear enough.

'What are you on about? It was your idea.'

I spray my wine over the table. 'What?'

But I'm too late, nobody's listening here any more. The whole evening has made no sense. I hoped to resolve the past, not hear made-up stories. Events are in motion, though, and they'll either live or die. I'd prefer the latter, or they might mention my involvement with Quantrill or Wee Jock to someone in authority.

I've got to get out of here. Vickerman has froth at the side of his mouth and is twitching, whereas Quinn hasn't moved in a while.

I try to think logically. If they survive, who'd believe them about me trying to OD them? If they die, it won't be too much of a surprise. But it's better there's no trace of me to be found. I put my wine glass in my handbag.

Popping my head out of the door, I see an empty street. I stride away, searching my brain for answers around my past. It doesn't help. Chunks are missing. I slide into the car and smile at the still-warm seat. I turn in the direction of the Paul Pry and grin, imagining Brad not expecting me. He's going to get the time of his life, and I speed up in anticipation. Vickerman was full of shit. I curse as I'm forced to stop at every single red light on Lincoln Road.

It's as if fate is forcing me to analyse tonight's events. Vickerman can't be right, or what the hell kind of person was I? With creeping unease, I understand Quinn's reaction to my arrival tonight and the other night. He wasn't nervous, he was scared of me. He always was.

Three days have passed since I met up with Brad at the Paul Pry. I had to force myself to take slow, deep breaths when I reached the entrance of the pub that night. It's mostly a food place now, so the bar was empty except for four of my work colleagues and a few of their partners. I shouldn't have worried. The expression on Brad's face was similar to someone who'd spotted a long-lost friend.

Usually, in such social circumstances, I worry about what to say. By the time I've analysed my contribution, the chatter has moved on, and I'm left an observer. That night however, I wanted to distract myself from my earlier actions. Anything that came into my head, I released, unless alcohol was going down my throat.

I received a few strange looks, but then often chuckles followed. Some of the others said weird things, and I joined in with the laughter. I felt a different kind of drunk that I'm not sure I knew existed: happy, carefree, silly even. And, just at the point when it could have got messy, it was 'time, please, ladies and gentlemen'. We all hugged at the door like old friends.

Brad drove me home. I'd failed to notice he'd kept sober, but I could tell he had from his lingering kiss, which smelled of peanuts and cola. I was ready to ask him in when he explained that he had football in the morning and wanted a clear head and a relatively early night. I watched from the car-park entrance as his rear lights disappeared from view, thinking how normal and sensible that was. I could do with more of that in my life. Trent's curtains flickered as I sauntered past.

Before he left, Brad offered to follow me to Scarlett's house when it was time to return her car. Unfortunately, the garage rang this morning to say mine was repaired, so that time has arrived. The bill for my car will have to go on my credit card, which may push the balance over its max. I know they won't lend me any more so I'll need to ask for help.

My sister can be nosey, but she has helped me out in the past with loans when I've been short. She checks in once a month and asks how I am. Sometimes I wish she'd visit or invite me to theirs. We're all the family each other has left now, if you don't include our elusive father.

Scarlett didn't appear at work today. Brad said she was AWOL, having failed to ring in. Her phone went straight to answer machine when I rang to tell her I'd drop her car off, but I decided to go tonight anyway. I can always just leave it if she isn't there. Brad came around on time and we're on the way. Glancing in the rear-view mirror, I smile at him singing.

He pulls up behind me while we wait for the gates at Scarlett's place. They open quickly for a change, and we park outside the front door and get out.

'Wow,' says Brad.

'I know. It's quite something. They've got eight acres.'

I'm not sure why I say that, not knowing what an acre is really, but Scarlett is always proud of that fact. After a few minutes of pressing the buzzer, no one appears. I try her mobile again to no avail.

'She must be in because she opened the gates,' says Brad.

I shrug, suspecting she'll be in a drunken mess and won't want Brad seeing her like that. 'Let's go. I'll put the car keys under the seat.'

The door finally opens just as we're going to leave. I've seen Scarlett in some states over the years, but her face is so puffy, it looks as though she's contracted myxomatosis. Red eyes glare at Brad, then back to me.

'What's he doing here? You gave me a fright. I thought it was someone else.'

'He came to take me home after I've left the car.'

She tuts and wanders away towards the kitchen, so we follow her inside.

'Who did you think it was?' I ask.

She ignores the question. I'm distracted by Brad's wide eyes at the spiral staircase. When we catch up with her, she's rummaging in the fridge.

'Glass of wine?' she offers.

We both decline. I place her keys on the table. 'Are you all right?'

She sniffs as her trembling hand attempts to fill her glass. I step close to her and notice that even though her eyes are puffy, they aren't unfocused as they often are when I see her.

'What's wrong?'

'Everything. Tim and I had a big row and he's steamed off in a huff. He told me I wasn't allowed to go to work any more.'

'No way. You said getting out of the house was the only thing that keeps you sane.'

'Yep.' Her eyes harden. 'I wish he were dead. My life's a misery.'

I look away from Brad, knowing he will be amused at the thought of her luxurious hell. It's true what they say – money doesn't buy you happiness. I doubt I'll ever know, but in many ways Scarlett's life is as hard as mine, only her towels are softer.

'Hey, it's Peterborough on the television!'

Obviously, Scarlett has been watching the news again. She grabs the remote and turns up the volume. The reporter is live at a street in Millfield. My face burns with recognition and guilt. I know the location well, after the things I've done there.

'Earlier today, two bodies were discovered at this property by someone from the council. It seems they may have been dead for at least two days.'

The camera pans to Vickerman and Quinn's closed front door. A uniformed policeman stands in the way.

'The police have stated that at this point all lines of investigation remain open, and anyone who has any information is to contact Thorpe Wood Police Station directly. A neighbour who asked not to be named said that "junkies", his words, frequented the property.'

The programme returned to the news desk.

'In other, perhaps related news, the police raided multiple locations in the city in what they hope will signal the end of the fentanyl overdoses and deaths that have blighted parts of Peterborough in recent weeks.'

The images show another police officer at the door of the semi in Mayor's Walk where I purchased the drugs. I pour myself a glass of water from the sink with my back to them and try to remain calm. I needn't have bothered as both of them are staring uneasily at each other as opposed to the TV. Regardless, it's time to leave.

'I'll ring you, Scarlett. We'll get out of your hair.'

She glowers at us in a way I've seen previously and which only means trouble. I grab Brad's hand and leave before she has anything else to say. He's silent for most of the journey. I almost daren't ask.

'What're you thinking about?'

'You.'

'Very smooth, but I can't have sex with you because I'm getting my nails done in the morning and need a quiet night.'

He laughs while sneaking a glance at me as we approach a roundabout.

'See, that's what I mean. You're different lately, kind of lively and exciting, and hard to pin down.'

'Was I dreary before?'

He grimaces. 'A little. Look, I've always fancied you. You're beautiful and sexy.'

'Right, don't overdo it now.'

'Seriously, and you seem like a nice girl. I've wandered over to your desk to ask you out in the past, but sometimes you came across as disinterested. Other times, you'd be chatty and pleasant, but I'd think I want someone more...'

'Stimulating?'

'I guess.'

'I'm afraid I can be a bit up and down.'

His face softens.

'I can't stop thinking about you.'

'Yeah, right.'

'Scarlett said you'd had other interest. I hope I'm not too late?'

I don't answer, just shake my head. As we hit the parkway, he reaches over and places his hand on my leg. A brief chuckle slips out of me.

'Typical bloke. I should have known that treating you mean would get you keen.'

'I have a shot, then?'

I tut. 'Are you sure you aren't just jealous?'

I was starting to soften, but I tense and a wall comes down between us. He senses it too and removes his hand.

'Do you want to go out again soon?' he asks.

'Look, I've been hoping to make some changes in my life. Focus on myself a bit more. So I wasn't bothered about seeing anyone, but then you've got under my skin and I think we could be good together.'

'That's how I feel.'

'I've got a few things to sort out first. There's a person I have to speak to so I can get to the bottom of what happened in the past.'

He doesn't say anything, but I'm sure I detect a little frown. Screw him, though. I don't need his bullshit. We pull up outside my block of flats and he slowly drives in and stops.

I'm out of his car without giving him chance to comment.

'Thanks for the lift. I really appreciate it.'

Before I slam the door, I spin and blow him a kiss, noting his grin at the unexpected gesture. Who knew Tuesday nights could be such fun? I clump upstairs and yank the case from under my bed. My school diaries sit inside. I haven't read them for years and can't remember why not. Who you were is surely who you are?

I open the last one. I skim through the pages from a few months before I finished school. It's mostly moaning about how boring my life is. But, there's an entry with a line in bold red.

I felt like killing someone today.

38

Barton rubbed the bridge of his nose. Twelve hours had passed since he arrived at 7 a.m. Yesterday's deaths had had him fielding questions from a variety of sources. He grabbed his coat and traipsed to the front of the building. Zander wanted to chat about the interviews resulting from the drug busts and was waiting in his vehicle outside. Strange had called and said that the victims clearly overdosed. Barton didn't need his twenty years' experience to guess they were linked to the fentanyl cases. He opened the door to Zander's car and climbed in.

'Evening, John. You sure you want to attend the scene? You look all-in.'

'Would you believe me if I told you sitting on your arse was more tiring than chasing around town?'

'Erm, no.'

'Well, it is.'

'I'll remind you of that in the middle of winter. Right, I'll bring you up to speed. The first bust we did in Paston hit the bullseye. It was a proper distribution centre. We recovered drugs, scales, bags, mixing agents, you name it. We were lucky. A Syrian was there paying back a trafficking debt. He was relieved to get caught, because he had a colleague who'd died of an overdose a few days earlier. He realised it was from trying the product himself. Anyway, he gave us his contact, and he'll talk, too, I reckon.'

'Definitely the fentanyl?'

'We won't know for sure until we test the samples, but we think so. The Syrian guy had been stuck here six months. He said they told him to use the special heroin sparingly when mixing.'

'Excellent. And the Mayor's Walk place?'

'It looks like poor intel. The property is clean, although maybe too empty. Bloke who owns it was a bit of a hippy and his security was full-on, which seemed odd, but there wasn't anything incriminating. He said he works for charities and is a bit of a painter, doing commissions for people. There was some decent art on the walls and a studio. I was going to check with you and let him go.'

'Damn. Does he own the place?'

'No, he's been renting it for decades. Looked like he was planning to move out, which makes me suspicious. Perhaps he got warned.'

'And there are no priors?'

'Nope. Not even traffic.'

'CSI took samples and did a sweep?'

'Yes. Quick tests showed nothing, so if he cleaned up, he knew what he was doing. Further, finer tests will show if there was fentanyl or other drugs about.'

'Okay, let him go and let's hope he doesn't vanish. Hopefully this rocket-poison will disappear from the streets now. If we get a sniff that he's involved, he'll find himself under a microscope with my beady eye on his secrets.'

'Rather his than mine.'

Barton nodded, too tired to laugh. 'Strange asked earlier whether we should bother with full CSI for the two bodies we found. What do you think?'

Zander pursed his lips as he thought. 'You're always saying that we should keep costs down, so I guess it's an option with it looking cut and dried.'

Barton put his best *Who Wants to Be a Millionaire?* voice on.

'I'm going to need your final answer.'

Zander squirmed in his seat, knowing Barton had him beat. 'Maybe do some CSI but not a complete sweep.'

Barton laughed. 'You mean just do one body, or one of the rooms? Come on, Zander. Save the department some cash.'

Zander. 'Okay, no CSI yet, secure the building. We wait for the post-mortem and go from there.'

'Not bad, my friend. But wrong. Think about the situation as a whole. We know why they died, but this might be a manslaughter case. We need every angle covered for a watertight conviction. No mistakes or criminals walk.'

'I thought it was really hard to convict for manslaughter from supplying drugs. After all, the victims were all addicts. They knew what they were doing, and they probably understood the risks more than anyone else.'

'Almost correct. Your reasoning is that if the victims freely inject themselves, it breaks the chain of causation, so the dealer can't be held responsible. However, fentanyl's new. It's deadly and cheap. If these guys wanted heroin and were therefore lied to, they wouldn't have been aware of the danger they were in. Manslaughter or even murder are possible charges.'

'Right. So full crime scene investigation.'

'Correct. It's in progress, and don't forget this occurred a few doors from a potential triple murder.'

'You think they were connected?'

'All we're doing at this point is counting bodies. God knows what might come out of it.'

Zander pulled up behind the CSI van on the street in Millfield and they hopped out. Zander rested his hands on the roof of the car.

'Wait. You kept saying remember costs and expenses. You set me up.'

'Sergeants and trainee inspectors don't need to worry about police cuts. Until you are 100 per cent sure, you always ask for everything. Let someone else who gets paid more money than you make those kinds of decisions. You've worked here long enough to understand that we don't just operate a detecting business, it's an arse-covering one, too.'

39

JC

The drug dealer stepped down the police-station steps and ran his hand through his hair. It was a little damp with sweat, but he always kept his cool under questioning. He'd spent years preparing his answers. Ellen's visit had been the tipping point to engage the plans he'd put together over the last decade. Looked as if she'd saved his arse.

He decided to walk home. It would only take half an hour, and he could use the time to get his head straight. He'd led a strange life, always under the radar. Money had ceased to be any kind of problem years ago. In fact, he wasn't sure what had kept him here. Girlfriends had come and gone, but still JC stayed. Perhaps he was as addicted to his position in society as the addicts were to theirs.

He'd loved it when he'd started out. Being thin, nondescript, and generally a nobody, he'd enjoyed the instant status that his new career had provided. That young, disillusioned boy was long gone, and it was time for a change. Bizarrely, the painting that his lifestyle had afforded him time to develop was now bearing fruit.

At first, he'd spent the money he made, thinking it was only a matter of time before he got caught. But he'd had a few near misses with the police and changed into a man who dealt only in cash, never on tick, always on the quiet, and he'd saved for the future.

He smiled at the thought of Ellen. She'd been so young and wild when he'd met her all those years ago. Pretty, too. The room had fizzed when she'd entered it back then. He'd considered asking her out for a drink at the start, but she'd been too untamed and someone like her burned bright and high for all to see. Ellen and those idiot mates had shown no caution with what they must surely have known was a dangerous pastime. So, he'd kept his distance and admired her carefree lifestyle from afar, wondering whether it was fun to be so reckless, or if they lived with a sense of impending ruin, with one eye on their graves and the other behind them.

He'd made sure the drugs he gave her were the best he had and was always pleasantly surprised when she showed up again. He'd found himself hoping each knock on his door was her. There had been a developing sadness to her with time, as though her spirit was gradually being crushed, but she'd appeared back in form the last time she'd come. He pitied and envied whoever had that tigress by the tail.

The moment she'd left with the fentanyl, he'd known that he'd been blinded by his affection for her. But he had realised with a jolt that at least she'd been honest with him, even if it had been cryptically. People were going to die and he hoped they deserved it, but the game was over. JC hoped Ellen realised that too. He smiled at passers-by, even stroked the neighbour's dog, and, for the first time in a long time, he breathed the air.

When he arrived at his address, the house he'd lived in for so long seemed different. There was little of his stuff there now. It was all in storage. He'd grab the last few bits and bobs, his easels, and pack a bag. He had money secreted all over the world. His life in the UK was over now, and he would never be back.

South America beckoned first, and he realised he couldn't wait, because he was finally free.

40

ACTING DCI BARTON

Barton spoke to the scene guard when he arrived at the house where the overdoses had occurred and knocked on the door. Strange opened it in full CSI outfit and stepped outside. Before the view disappeared, he observed two investigators, also in full suits, picking over a coffee table with tweezers. He imagined that they would have been doing the same thing to the human remains at the mortuary. A pool of dried blood caught his eye on the frayed carpet.

'Checking up on me, boss?' asked Strange.

'That's right. We've had reports of laughter on the job. You know nobody's allowed to enjoy themselves. I take it Mortis was all over the bodies.'

'Actually, he didn't come yesterday.'

Barton raised his eyebrows.

'I know,' said Strange. 'He said he was on his way. Then I got a text from him saying he wouldn't make it and to take the bodies to the mortuary. I've had a look around and we might not find much. There's little more than a few bits of furniture, some clothes and a couple of mattresses.'

Barton thought of the pathologist with concern. He couldn't remember Mortis missing something like this ever.

'Have we identified them, and do we know them?'

'Yes, and yes. James Vickerman, addict with multiple custodial stays for shoplifting and commercial burglary. Magnus Quinney, AKA Quinn, known addict and occasional dealer, record as long as your arm, the worst of which is GBH, for which he received five years.'

Barton knew them both. Vickerman and Quinn sounded like a firm of solicitors, but they were on the wrong side of the law. He'd arrested Quinn for the GBH. It was still sad, though. At one point in their lives, they would have been innocent children. It was no way to end up.

'Wait. That's the second time I've heard the name Vickerman recently.' He clicked his fingers. 'I read the case file last night for Wee Jock's death and Vickerman was questioned.'

Zander shrugged. 'Most of the addicts know each other and would have hung out at some point.'

'Yes, but it's another link. I'm getting a nasty feeling in my stomach about this.'

'Well, try to keep it together. You wouldn't want to use the toilet here,' joked Strange, but Barton was wracking his brain for the connections.

'No signs of a struggle?' he asked.

'Nothing. Looks like they sat down for dinner, and by that I mean a nice syringe-full of drugs each, then conked out. That blood pool drooled out of Quinn's mouth, but there were other spots of blood elsewhere. Could have been from poorly addicts coughing, or maybe another person was here. Perhaps one who left the scene.'

'Nasty way to go,' said Barton. He had a thought. 'How tall are these two?'

'Both around five feet seven unfortunately,' replied Strange.

'Damn.' He paused for a moment. 'So Vickerman could be linked to Wee Jock's demise. The missing woman links to Wee Jock and the murders up the road. Maybe the woman is connected to this incident as well. Could she have been here?'

'I had a thought about that,' said Zander. 'Let's say Wee Jock raped her, and he was killed. Then there was a gang rape by those three further down the street, and they were all killed. Perhaps she's a prostitute with a ruthless pimp. He strangled Jock, then went Quentin Tarantino on the others. He's this tall guy seen fleeing the scene.'

'Not bad, but it doesn't help us locate either of them, and there's a massive time gap between the incidents,' replied Barton.

'Precisely, that's what I reckoned,' said Zander with a wink. 'These events happened over fifteen years apart. What's the chance of the same pimp or boyfriend being around?'

Zander hummed to himself while they caught up.

'Shit, that is brilliant,' said Strange. 'People kill for love, but it's not just partners, it's family. What about a brother, then?'

'You've got it,' said Zander.

'But how does that help with locating them?' asked Strange.

Barton grinned at Zander's fine work and explained it for Strange.

'The DNA matched the two scenes but gave us no identities. These are vicious crimes. It doesn't get more brutal than stabbing, bludgeoning and throttling. Whoever killed Quantrill and his mates was an extremely violent person, and it's unlikely this was his first crime. It's possible that person was responsible here, too, protecting a sister, perhaps. Zander here is guessing we might have this brother on our records. It's certainly worth a look.'

'I read about that,' said Strange.

'Yes, software now allows us to compare one forensic profile to everyone on our database to generate a list of those offenders already in the system that are most likely to be a close relative. It's called familial DNA searching. With a bit of luck, in a week or two, assuming our man's been in trouble, we'll know who our person of interest's brother is, or maybe even her father.'

41

ACTING DCI BARTON

Barton and Zander returned to the car after surveying the scene. It had told them little they didn't already know.

'Fancy a beer?' asked Zander. 'This new technology makes your head spin. It won't be long until we scan the body, touch a few options on the screen, and the name and address of the perpetrator will pop up.'

'Probably with a 20 per cent off voucher for Deliveroo. Actually, that sounds pretty good.'

'Shooting fish in a barrel is boring.'

'Great for crime stats?'

Zander grinned. 'Terrible for waistlines.'

'I wouldn't worry too much about being made redundant. Take cyber-crime. The criminal methods develop faster than our solutions. Devious ways of using new technology appear daily. For every Sherlock Holmes, there's always a Moriarty.'

'At least we have an angle now.'

'Let's hope we get lucky. Not everyone has a relative on the system. I'm more concerned by the fact that most of the people who know anything are dead. And folk like that can't confess or answer questions.'

Zander was frowning. 'In other news, it's not like Mortis to miss a crime scene.'

Barton had been thinking the same thing. He pulled his phone out of his pocket. Mortis picked up.

'John, what is it now?'

'I just fancied hearing your voice. Is everything okay?'

'Yes, I'm in the mortuary. I've had a glance over the bodies, and they have all the signs of overdoses.'

'I don't suppose you can tell from what drug?'

'Not at this point. It's nearly always heroin combined with something else.'

'Could it be fentanyl?'

'Easily. I did a girl's post-mortem not so long back. She had surprisingly little in her system.'

Barton had an unusual thought. 'With an overdose, how quick is it? Could someone get help if they suspected they'd had too much?'

'No, I wouldn't have thought so. It's rare for a person to die immediately from an overdose. But when people survive, it's usually because somebody else was there to respond.'

Barton strained his ears. He could definitely hear what sounded like sobbing.

'Mortis, what's wrong?'

Barton heard sniffs and wipes.

'Talk to me.'

After a few moments, Mortis came back on. 'Just life, John. My wife's ill. We found out today that it's cancer and quite a nasty one. I'm a doctor and I'm all too aware of what happens next. At least in her case it will be quick if we don't beat it.'

Barton let out a gasp of shock. He didn't know what to say, not having met Mortis' wife, or even knowing her name. But he had real affection for the pathologist.

'Why are you at work, then?' he asked.

'She wanted to rest and said I was unsettling the peace in the house. That's her all over. I'm coping. I've seen enough of Death's indiscriminate ways not to be completely shocked, although I have no idea how I'll cope if she doesn't make it. I'll speak to you tomorrow after I've examined the bodies. Put the phone down and spend time with your young family. Cherish every moment because things can change so fast.'

Mortis cut the call off as Barton arrived at his house.

'Is he okay?' asked Zander, with the engine idling.

Barton knew that Mortis wouldn't want anyone knowing.

'He'll tell you when he sees you. Come on, have a beer inside. The kids will still be up.'

They stepped through the doorway and shock lit up their faces.

There in front of them was a masked gunman pointing two pistols their way. He had a mean sneer on his face. Eyes narrowed. Both index fingers twitched menacingly on the triggers.

'Freeze, fools, now hands up,' said the villain.

Barton and Zander put their hands in the air. Luke pushed the brim of his cowboy hat up with the barrel of the pistol in his right hand. The other pistol flicked between the two men.

'Which one of you two's been rustling sheep?'

Zander was too fast. 'Your dad's always been partial to a pretty sheep.'

'Zip it, dummy. I tell the jokes,' said Luke.

With a crazed grin, Luke pulled both triggers repeatedly. Caps fired off with loud bangs, and filled the varmints with imaginary lead. He ran away hollering and whooping.

Barton ambled towards the kitchen where his wife was waiting with a smile.

'May I die with a beer, ma'am?'

Holly laughed and opened the fridge.

'Luke's been doing that all day. He called me prissy knickers earlier and shot me in the back. What have you been watching with him?'

'I think he finds stuff on Netflix, but that's my boy. Chip off the old block.'

She kissed Zander on the cheek and hugged him.

'Good to see you, Shawn. Hungry? I grabbed fresh bread from the supermarket.'

They settled in the kitchen. Lawrence was out, but Layla came in and chatted for a while. Barton and Zander had a beer and a sandwich each, the latter being as wide as encyclopaedias. The three of them talked about Barton's mother's dementia.

'We're going to ask her to move in with us,' Holly explained to Zander. 'Assuming *he* isn't working every day!'

'Don't worry, I can get time off for that,' said Barton. 'I've just been snowed under.'

Zander pushed his empty beer bottle across to the middle of the table.

'I've got loads of free time. Now I'm doing John's job, I see that he's been pulling our legs about how much work he has to do.'

'I'm going to borrow Luke's guns,' said Barton.

'Is it because you're unfamiliar with the position, or will you always be this busy?' Holly asked Barton.

'I haven't even taken on the whole role yet. There'll be disciplinaries and training, community relations, resource planning, and expenditure reviews amongst other things. They've organised some training for me, which is much-needed.'

'Oh, dear, you look knackered already.'

Barton pulled himself to his feet and grabbed another drink. 'I've got no time for tired. Who knows what's around the corner?'

'He'd be livelier if he were at less crime scenes,' said Zander.

Barton lowered his bottle, guiltily. 'I know I should stick to the office, but we're short-staffed. Another beer?'

Zander stood and stretched. 'No, I've got an exciting book on the go, and I can't be bothered to walk home.'

Holly followed him to the door. 'It's always nice to see you, Shawn. You look well. Do you have a new lady friend keeping you happy?'

'I'm free and single, getting to the gym, eating healthy, life's good. Although I am a bit worried that John's caught TBV. That's probably why he's so tired.'

Holly's face dropped. 'What's TBV?'

'It stands for The Bear Virus.'

She raised an eyebrow. 'I've never heard of it.'

'It's pretty prevalent in men when they pass forty-five. The symptoms are generally the same. Once infected, the patient tends to get heavier and clumsier. Even though hair falls out on the head, it sprouts feverishly over the rest of the body, almost like fur. Libido will lessen to a degree where it's barely present, much the same as with giant pandas, and, like them, eating becomes the focal point of their day. Irritability is common, as is terrible flatulence. The weight gain can accelerate at an incredible rate.'

'Is there a cure?' Holly laughed.

'Few cases have a successful conclusion. It's as though the victim is going to hibernate for the winter. John is one of the worst instances I've seen. Most of those subjects explode.'

Meanwhile, in the kitchen, Barton swiped the mushrooms and peppers out of the way, so he could get to the good stuff at the back of the fridge. He heard Zander chuckling as he left, and Holly laughing her head off as she ran up the stairs.

A growl rumbled from within while he continued to forage.

42

THE ICE KILLER

I stay up all night and read my diaries. It's hard to believe what's inside them. I must have written down dreams and other things I imagined. Paranoia seems to have plagued my final years at school. There are gaps after I leave. The biggest in them was when I was with Vickerman and heading off the rails. I kept a diary when I was in hospital, but stopped when I got out. The therapist told me to stop reading them; it was time to move on.

I'm not surprised she said that, as it still makes me furious to think of the three men who messed me up. Quantrill, Vickerman, and the other, a man called Hofstadt. There's a policeman who can also join the list, but for slightly different reasons. Once Hofstadt's image appears in my brain, I can't shake it out, and prowl the flat thinking of how he cruelly dismissed me from his life. It's been over ten years now. Even so, I think it's time we caught up.

He hurt me in the coldest way. I did everything he desired, like having sex in car parks and public toilets with no concern for anyone else who might be around. We were together for years, but he was slippery when I asked where it was going. Even though I lived at home, I spent a lot of time at his place. He made me feel like his housekeeper, yet he gave me just enough love to keep me there. Near the end, I paid for us to go on a romantic holiday with a hot tub. It was only a week at Center Parcs – I bought a daily newspaper for two weeks just to get the vouchers – but I hoped it would lead somewhere.

He cut me off dead a month before we were due to leave. A disconnected phone, an unopened door, and no response to my texts, emails and finally letters wore me down and unsettled my equilibrium. The final occasion I arrived at his house, he stared impassively at me from an upstairs window and shook his head. I don't recall what I did afterwards. Did I lose control again? My past seems distant and unimportant since my mum died, but it's what made me who I am.

My phone rings after I spent most of my day off in bed, and my sister's name appears on the screen. Our monthly chat must be due. We have a strange relationship. Sometimes she genuinely seems worried for me and quite a caring person, but she never invites me to her house. In fact, I can't even recall where she lives. I think it's Harrow, but it might be Harlow. I don't feel like talking to her, but I'm skint and sometimes she offers to help if I've had an unexpected bill. Occasionally, I don't even need to repay her. I press answer.

'Hi, Lucy.'

'Hi, Ellen.'

She always pauses at this point. She expects me to start the conversation, even though it's her who rang.

'How's things?' she eventually asks.

'I'm lovely. The job's great. My flat's tidy.'

She mentions the weather and her kids. It's banal stuff and I comment in the appropriate places. I realise I'm meandering through the call. There doesn't appear to be any substance to it, nothing for me to cling onto. It dawns on me that I haven't challenged her about my father. With everything that's been going on, I've forgotten the terrible deceit my mother and Lucy maintained for all those years. It has to have been him, as he knew too many intimate details, although my birth certificate has a space where the father should be. I cut her off mid-sentence.

'Lucy. Can you tell me about our dad?'

This time the silence is deafening. Seconds draw out, each one damning confirmation of her treachery.

'What do you want to know?'

'The normal. What was he like? I remember being sad in a corridor, which I assume must have been the hospital. What are your memories of him?'

'I can't recall much. I was only young...'

'When he died?'

'That's right.'

'You were practically a teenager. You must be able to remember loads.'

Another pause. I can almost hear her brain frantically trying to unscramble the years of lies.

'He wasn't around much,' she finally says. 'You'd only just started school when he moved out. I think he had a few mental-health problems.'

'Mental issues like mine?'

'Similar. I don't know for sure. We didn't live with him by the time he passed away.'

I can't help laughing. She may be an interfering mare with a holier-than-thou attitude, but lying is mostly against her nature. This must be killing her. My chuckle tails off as my teeth grind and I focus on the depth of the deception perpetrated by the pair of them. My mother said I could always trust her, and she would be in my corner forever. Well, I can't tell her what I think of her dishonesty, but Lucy is still here. My words rise in intensity, and I roar the final syllable.

'You lying bitch!'

'Ellen, stop it.'

I swipe away my cereal bowl which has been on the table all day and watch it smash against the wall. I snarl down the phone. 'Screw you. Tell me the truth.'

'About what? Please, calm down, I only want the best for you. I wish you could see that.'

'Our dad is alive.'

My eyes squint as I strain to hear down the line.

'How? How could you possibly know that?'

'Because he came to my flat.'

'Oh.'

'Oh? Oh? That's all you have to say after nearly thirty years of treachery.'

Her voice changes. She talks softly, almost tenderly.

'Did he say where he'd been?'

'He told me he was in a hospital of some kind.'

'Did he say why?'

'Only that he'd been ill.'

'Right. Well, that's true. He needed help and had become dangerous to others.'

'I'll say.'

A final pause. 'What do you mean by that?'

'This isn't the 1960s. I Googled him. What the hell is this? Some type of sneaky little family secret? Shush, don't mention the double murderer in the family. You deceived me for decades.' I start to shout again. 'Lies and more lies. Is it any wonder I feel like I'm going crazy myself?'

'Ellen, sweetie. Have you been taking your medicine?'

'How dare you? If you cared for my well-being, you would treat me with respect.'

'We tried to protect you, Ellen. He was unstable, even he knew it. Look, I'll come and explain. I can be there on Friday around six.'

'I never want to see you ever again.'

We are both stunned to silence by my words. I imagine them vanishing down the line, but I want them back. I'm lonely already. I don't want to be more alone. I never have. Can't someone just hug me? Isn't there a person out there that can do that for me without wanting something else in return? Please say something, Lucy. Don't hang up.

'How are you for money?' she asks.

I exhale. 'Struggling, as usual. The alternator killed the battery.'

'How much was it?'

'Four hundred pounds. I put it on my credit card.' I stare at a variety of unopened red reminders on the kitchen worktop.

'I'll come over and take you for dinner. Somewhere nice, and I'll bring you the cash.'

A tear slides down my cheek. I roughly brush it off with my sleeve. I've had enough of weakness. I want answers, and I will make sure she gives them to me.

'All right.'

'Good. I'll look forward to it.'

'I should go. There's a man I need to catch up with.'

'Ellen. Don't go looking for confrontation with our father, just take it easy. I can hear your anger. Have a bath and try to relax. You'll understand when I explain.'

For once, she's right. I don't feel stable right now, but how dare she make demands? Perhaps a bath will help, but I'll see my father and Hofstadt soon, and they will answer my questions too. It's not vengeance that I seek. Only knowledge.

43

ACTING DCI BARTON

Barton stared at the piles of paperwork on his office desk. He heard the rapid pinging of his computer as more emails arrived. Organisation had never been his strong point. His way was to ignore the to-do pile, sit down before it fell over and hammer away until it was gone. Then let it build up again. Simples. He had a brilliant knack for holding the information of a case in his mind while it was under investigation, but the details raced out when it was over.

Barton's door opened and a mature Asian lady with a tight smile stared at him. That smirk turned into a full-on beam as she saw the state of his desk. Barton recognised her as Superintendent Troughton's secretary.

'Chief Inspector Barton. How are you getting on?'

Barton leaned back in his chair and gestured with both hands to his covered desk.

'Peachy.'

'Well, I'm yours for the day. Use me as you wish.'

'Well, Mrs Chan, I was about to have a bonfire, but I can be distracted.'

She chuckled. 'Including Troughton, you'll be the fourth Chief

Inspector I've mentored. My first one was DCI Naeem, over ten years ago.'

'Really? How come the secretary does that?'

Barton regretted the words, but Chan smiled. 'Who do you think really runs the show?' She dragged an enormous diary out of her briefcase. 'Only kidding, but I'm an organised person, and that's what you need to learn.'

'I can see why anyone would struggle. It's quite a transition,' he said as she pulled up a chair.

'You're ahead of the game if you understand that already. Are you ready for some words of advice?'

'If it means I don't have to work twenty hours a day, I am.'

'Excellent. Here's the first thing. Doing this job, you are no longer a detective inspector. That's a different role. Some of you accept that quicker than others. I know you're only acting up and there isn't a replacement in your old job, but you'll still want to get involved in things that don't need you any more. Trust your team, or you'll drown under the workload.'

'Right.'

'You have confidence in the staff under you?'

'Absolutely.'

'Perfect. Then what's the easiest way to reduce what you have to do?'

'Give it to someone else.'

'Correct.' She beamed at him. 'I knew you weren't just good for scaring villains.'

Barton raised an eyebrow at that comment.

'Don't lose your sense of humour now you're behind a desk. And relax. Being a great DI is an excellent start to being a fabulous DCI, but that's all it is. You still need to adapt to a new position, and you can't do it in one day. It's a tough job. You'll make complicated decisions, which will affect many other people. Sometimes those choices may be the lesser of two evils. Safety of the public and those under you becomes paramount. Innocent until proven guilty may look different in this role.' She glanced kindly at him. 'Everyone has faith in you, John, or you wouldn't be sitting here.'

Barton imagined himself shackled to the desk. 'It's hard to let go.'

'Of course, it is. You'll know when the time is right. Remember when you were in uniform and buzzing as you raced to an incident. That was the life you craved, and you enjoyed it. However, eventually you sought new challenges and went for promotion to sergeant and so on. People tend to stop where they're happiest. Maybe being a DI is who you are and where you should stay.'

He opened his mouth, but closed it without replying.

She nudged his elbow. 'I'm here to help you find out.'

The day progressed rapidly. He realised much of his job was now a filtering role. Crimes, tasks and queries came down the line and it was his job to allocate resources to them. There were a lot of people counting on him. Chan helped him sort his files out, digital and physical, and rattled through his emails without mercy. He was briskly tapping the keyboard at 4 p.m. when she stood to leave. She opened the door and turned to Barton.

'Happier?'

'You know what? In time, I think I can do this.'

'That's the spirit. I expect, if you fill the role permanently, you'll get a bigger team. Then there'd be further training for appraisals, performance reviews, budget-planning, community collaboration policies, and crisis management. The glory days are over.'

Barton failed to hide a grimace.

'Do you know what I mean by that?'

'Not really.'

'Last piece of advice is that if there's a buzz of adrenaline to any task, it's probably best that you get someone else to do it. Your role is management.'

Zander knocked on the door she had opened and stepped out of her way. She studied him with a slight smile and left.

'She scares me. It's like she can read my mind. Did she tell you off?' said Zander.

'No, but it felt a little like that. What's up?'

'We've received the information from the familial DNA search. There were multiple matches, but one was close. It's got to be a family member.'

Zander was almost hopping from foot to foot.

'I assume we know the person,' said Barton.

'Yes, it's Theodore Deacon.'

Barton stared blankly at him for a few moments, then his mouth fell open.

'No way. Ted Deacon, the double killer?'

'The very same. I checked, and he was released from prison quite a few years ago. Obviously, he's on probation for a long time after what he did, so we have a current address. Strange and I were about to pay him a visit.'

Barton thought back to what Chan had told him and shook his head. 'Hold on. Not just the two of you?'

Zander nodded. 'He's an old man in his early sixties.'

'Yes, but he might have been involved in a triple murder in the last few weeks. Have you spoken to Probation?'

'I couldn't get through to his handler. You know how the probation changes have doubled their workload.'

'Where's the handler based?'

'Huntingdon.'

Barton moved his mouse and clicked on the contact folder Chan had set up earlier for him. He found the number of Huntingdon Probation in seconds and dialled. After a few loops, it arrived at their reception. There was a confusing array of options after the offender supervision changes. Barton knew they were seriously struggling in what was already a stressful line of work. He finally got through to a manager.

'This is Detective Chief Inspector Barton investigating a live murder enquiry.'

After a five-minute conversation, he replaced the receiver in its cradle. Zander had an amused air about him.

'Didn't you used to laugh at DCIs who threw their name and rank around to get faster results?'

Barton took his coat from the stand that had somehow survived the previous DCI's departure.

'I don't recall that. Let's go. Deacon's offender manager is on holiday today, but her boss has agreed to look through the file. We'll drive down there and have a chat. We can decide how we deal with Mr Deacon after that.'

'I thought you were taking a less hands-on approach.'

'I will be, but right now my in-box is empty.'

44

Zander and Barton arrived in quick time with only a twenty-mile stretch of three-lane motorway separating Peterborough and Huntingdon. They were told to wait in Reception. Strange had stayed back at the station after discovering the many tasks delegated to her. Barton grinned at the whistling Zander, who, unbeknownst to him, had the same waiting for him.

A middle-aged man in a crumpled suit opened a door, introduced himself as Al, the probation manager, and took them to his office.

'Thanks for coming,' he said without gusto once they were seated, letting Barton know he didn't appreciate the lack of notice.

'Pleasure. As I explained over the phone, we need to talk to Theodore Deacon with some urgency. I wanted some background first,' said Barton.

Al flicked through the thick file in front of him while he came to a decision. 'I gather from that you're asking if it's safe to visit his house?'

'Yes. I don't want to make a big deal of it because at this point all we have is conjecture. But I'd rather be informed beforehand of his risk levels.'

'Good call, because I've checked the dates you supplied and I can confirm that he was categorically not involved with the first murder, that of Alan "Wee Jock" Mason.'

Barton sighed. 'Where was he?'

'Enjoying the facilities at a psychiatric hospital and had been doing so for some time.'

Barton gave Zander a look. 'When was he released?' asked Barton.

'He's been released since then, gone back in, and finally back out for some years now. Claire's his probation worker. She doesn't meet him at his house alone because of his profile, but we've had no issues with him at all.'

'What did he do exactly?'

'Nearly thirty years ago there was an incident at a hostel where a female was killed. Deacon did it, but the woman had attacked him and tried to gouge his eyes out first. She was known to the police and was extremely unstable. No one in their right mind would have begun a relationship with her, but he did. However, he broke down during the court case and was declared unfit for trial under the Mental Health Act. Later, schizophrenia and psychosis were diagnosed. They discharged him, apparently cured. This was before my time, but my predecessor said he caused no problems.'

'Cured? Surely once that crazy, forever crazy?' asked Zander.

'We don't use that term now. It's unhelpful. We have a lot of service users with mental-health issues. I assume that with a combination of drugs and psychological assistance they believed he was ready to be released. Unfortunately, some time after that a man armed with a knife burgled him, but it was the thief who died.'

'So again, there were mitigating circumstances.'

'Not so much in that instance. The robber lost possession of his weapon in the struggle and fled, but, as opposed to letting him escape, Deacon caught up with him and strangled him to death.'

'Blimey,' said Barton.

'Exactly. A neighbour backed up the story as he heard the commotion and watched the burglar climb from the window and Deacon then chasing him. Deacon's solicitor tried to claim mental incapacity again, but the judge wasn't having it, and neither were the jury. He received twenty years, and Deacon suspected the judge had considered life. They sent him back to secure settings at Rampton Hospital for a while but on medication he was able to serve out his sentence in normal prison conditions. He was a model prisoner, by all accounts, and they released him not long after the halfway point.'

'Your case worker has no problems with him, then?'

'No. She meets him without fail once a week to make sure he's stable. It's imperative he takes his medicine regularly.'

'Could you ring him?'

'Well, I could try. He didn't want anything to do with modern technology when he first came out, but we insisted on a cheap phone. It's often flat, or he's a while getting back to us. It's not such a huge deal with him being so compliant. We've found that routine is essential to him, and he wants no surprises, which I guess you can understand after what happened. He meets on time every week. Sometimes they arrange to have the next meeting at a café, which is where Claire saw him yesterday.'

'No problem for us to call at his house for a chat?'

'Hmm, in the circumstances, please do, but he might not answer the door. There's an officer from Public Protection who works with Claire. They occasionally go to his flat together to make sure he's not doing anything odd, but they make an appointment. They haven't been for a while, but I'd describe him as harmless nowadays.'

Barton's eye twitched at the words. 'Why do you say nowadays?'

'Well, he has killed two individuals. Most people wouldn't do something like that in the situations he was in. He didn't need to kill them. Anyway, he's over sixty now, so his risk isn't as high for violent crimes.'

'He was in the mental health institute a long time. Did he ever get tried for that first crime?'

'No, he was really unwell. The woman who died also had a history of violence and alcohol abuse. Eventually he'd been in the hospital for as long as he would for a conviction for manslaughter. The Crown decided it wasn't in the public interest to have another trial, especially considering it may have been self-defence.'

'What about relatives?' asked Barton.

'I checked that. None listed. Parents dead. No mention of dependants.'

'How much longer has he got under probation?' asked Zander.

'Only a couple of years. He's said he'll continue to come in regularly afterwards as part of his routine. That in itself shows how committed he is to remaining out of trouble.'

'What was he diagnosed with again? It sounds like it might be paranoid schizophrenia. Are you sure he isn't still a danger?'

'I'm obviously not a doctor, but my experience here has shown me that people with mental-health conditions on our books are generally only a danger to themselves. Some paranoid schizophrenics can be hazardous to those they believe are wronging them, but most display signs of deterioration beforehand and we notice they are struggling to cope.'

'And none of that from Deacon?'

'I had a flick through his notes before you got here. His diagnosis was broad and covers a whole range of symptoms and behaviours. It's why they had such trouble getting the correct dose of drugs. Non-medicated, he sought arguments and had sexual relationships with unsuitable people. I suppose you could call them dangerous liaisons, as he was liable to explode. One doctor described him as a thrill seeker, but instead of abseiling or skydiving, he put himself in perilous situations. Another said he had an innate urge to survive, even if the cost was someone else's life.'

'Not a guy to get on the wrong side of.'

'No, there's a diagnosis of real psychosis when he was hospitalised after both court cases, which is worrying. I haven't had time to study everything, but even though he has been fine with us for years, I should mention some comments to you from when he was first sectioned.'

Barton and Zander exchanged a glance, knowing unwelcome news was coming.

The manager put his glasses on and read from the file.

'This is the doctor's comments when he was committed the second time. He's a changed man, but I think this is worth telling you. "Theodore Deacon has not settled well and we struggle to find the right balance of medication. Provoked, he can rapidly display phenomenal rage. He's a thin man but, riled up, he proves incredibly powerful. Approach with caution at all times, this person is as dangerous as they come."'

45

ACTING DCI BARTON

They took a note of Deacon's address and left the building. Barton was a little more cautious after what happened with The Soul Killer, but Ted Deacon was fairly old and complied with his probation terms. He came in weekly and they'd only seen him yesterday, when he'd been fine. If Zander and Barton couldn't cope with him, then perhaps they were ready for desk jobs.

'You're not allowed to say crazy now?' asked Zander as they approached the address.

'Nope. You must empathise and acknowledge that the person is a person first, not a permanent psychiatric diagnosis.'

Zander nudged Barton and smiled. 'Did you read that today?'

Barton laughed. 'A few days ago. It makes sense, though. Loads of people experience mental distress and it might only be a temporary "problem", not necessarily a chronic illness.'

'I heard about that DI in Norwich who almost got demoted for using the expression "bloody junkies" at a meeting. What's the phrase to use now?'

'A person who injects drugs or a person with addiction.'

'Fat people?'

'I'm not sure.'

'How about a person who likes McDonald's?'

'I like McDonald's.'

Their chuckles tailed off as they surveyed the area. Most of the cars had long since given up their grip on life. A thin trail of smoke seeped from a burned wreck as though it had only recently been put out. Barton felt eyes on him, but the surrounding street appeared empty. Two kids with suspicious-looking roll-ups rose from behind the car, gave them the finger, and ran off laughing.

There was a locked communal door to the block of flats. He pressed Deacon's number. Waiting, they turned round to monitor their vehicle.

'I'll give you five-to-one if it's gone when we get back,' said Zander.

Barton scratched his chin. 'Right, I'll have a pound on that.'

'Last of the big spenders.'

'That way, if it's been nicked, I can spend my winnings towards a taxi.'

'Clever.'

'You, meanwhile, will have to walk.'

After a few attempts at the door, Zander lost his patience and pressed the buzzer on the other five flats. Finally, an old woman popped her head out of a top floor window. Thirty seconds later, she limped towards them without expression. She opened the door a crack.

'Are you two Mormons?'

'No, we're police.'

Judging by the curl of her lip, the latter was worse. Barton put his foot in the door. The lady looked down at it before limping back to her flat and out of sight. A baby was crying in one of the upstairs flats. They could hear a male voice bellowing for it to be quiet. It didn't sound good. Zander was up the stairs in a flash, hammering his fist on the door.

A callow youth opened the door. Barton couldn't quite make out Zander's question, but he could detect the threat in the tone. Zander beckoned Barton up. The lad showed them into the flat where a bonny baby lay on the carpet in just a nappy. The room was tidy, and the baby clean, but it was very unhappy. The detectives approached the child.

Zander crouched and put a hand to the child's forehead. Frowning, he turned back to the lad, who had gone. Barton heard a door slam and looked out of the window to see the lad sprinting across the car park. Barton shook his head at Zander.

The two big men crouched over the tiny child. Barton opened the nappy to reveal what resembled a ploughed field. In unison, they leaned away from the stench.

'Shit,' said Barton.

'Yes, and a remarkable amount from something so small,' said Zander.

The baby girl let out another piercing scream as though her soul were being ripped from her body.

'Do we change her?' asked Barton.

'It might leave us open to all kinds of allegations and complaints.'

'We could ring for a female PC.'

'Hmm, that would probably get us more allegations and complaints.'

The baby whimpered and released an exhausted gasp. Holding their breaths, they cleaned the child up with some wipes they found on the table. Sore nappy rash appeared to be the reason for the baby's cries, but the baby girl had settled now she wasn't dirty and was regarding her visitors with wide-eyed suspicion. Barton stood and stretched his legs. His right knee clicked.

Zander was familiarising himself with a nappy when a scream behind them made them jump. An attractive girl around her late twenties was standing in the doorway with her hand to her mouth. She charged in.

'What the fuck are you doing? And where's Michael?'

'We heard shouting and crying. I assume it was Michael who let us in and ran away. We're detectives,' said Zander as he moved the nappy behind his back. She looked unconvinced until Barton showed his warrant card.

She released a tired breath. 'I'll kill Michael, but I'm not surprised.'

She pulled a pot out of a carrier bag and explained while she got to work. The baby had woken up crying in the morning, and she'd run out of E45 cream. Her brother had agreed to look after the baby, while she ran to her friend's to borrow a tenner and carry on to the chemist, with the father having deserted her long before the birth. Her brother had only left prison a few weeks beforehand, hence no wish for the company of any authorities.

She assured him that he was a good person really, who'd just made a silly mistake. Much like herself, she added with a rueful glance at the baby. The woman was polite and seemed educated. Barton asked if he could use the toilet, and scoped the rest of the flat. It was much cleaner than Zander's place. He had considered ringing social services, but it wouldn't be helpful if she was doing her best. You can't help who your family are, and they can be the only ones left to rely on. It hurts when they let you down, too.

'Would you like a cup of tea?' she asked him when he returned.

'No, we'll leave you to it. We wanted a quick word with the man in number one. Do you know him?'

'Ted? Yeah, he's under me. Good luck getting him to answer the door.'

'Do you know if he's in?'

'He's really quiet. I see him once a month, maybe less. Occasionally, I hear him shouting. I guess at the TV. Irritates me too sometimes. I don't say anything, because nobody does around here. My little girl cries and he doesn't complain.'

'No unusual behaviour?'

She rolled her eyes at Zander. 'Define unusual.'

They spotted a glimpse of the personality that responsibility was keeping repressed. People had hard, lonely lives. They were decent folk hoping for a break that might not come. Barton caught Zander leaving a twenty-pound note on the bookshelf in the hall as they left. Many would frown on that nowadays, too. But it was small things like that that helped keep your humanity intact.

'Are we getting soft?' asked Zander.

'Maybe a little. Perhaps that's progress.'

Zander nodded. 'What did Obama say? The world has changed and we must change with it.'

'Yeah, but he wasn't police. Life is complicated.'

They returned to the bottom flat and a surprisingly modern UPVC door. The flat they'd just been in had the original paint-stained wooden one. There was no bell, so Barton gave it a couple of thumps with his fist.

'Are you getting déjà vu from when we knocked on that last killer's door?' asked Zander.

Barton grinned, even though he'd ended up in hospital.

'Let's look at the facts. This guy is related to the victim. Nothing more. It's highly probable he wasn't present at any of the scenes, especially seeing as he has a perfect alibi for the first crime. All we need to know is the name and address of any living relatives. I was hoping he had a daughter.'

'Can't we check the birth register?'

'Yes, but it's likely we're dealing with people from low socio-economic backgrounds.'

Zander gave the door a meatier whack while raising an eyebrow at Barton.

'You have definitely changed.'

'Senior management love those terms at their weekly meetings.'

'I assume it's DCI speak for feckless men who don't register themselves as the father?'

'I hope so, or I missed the point of that meeting. If he's not on the birth certificate and hasn't mentioned it to anyone, how would we know? It was nearly thirty years ago when he first went away. The file won't be as watertight as they are now.'

'Damn. Look, he isn't answering. I don't fancy our chances with this door either. Twenty years ago, I might have been leaving my telephone number upstairs as opposed to money, and you'd be down here using your boot to make a new cat flap.'

Barton tapped the solid door with his size twelves. 'Come on. We don't have due cause for that, and you're too old for the other. We'll wait. He's expected at the probation office in six days and has never missed an appointment. You can see what he has to say then.'

He handed Zander his losing-bet money after they'd got back in their still-present car. Barton had a last look back. A light flickered in the man's lounge and he wasn't sure whether it had been on when they'd first arrived. His mind whirred as they pulled out of the estate. A lot could happen in six days.

46

THE ICE KILLER

Friday rolls around again. Last night, I had the choice of sex in some new lingerie with what might be my boyfriend, or trawling through old underwear at the charity shop. Brad won. I wore the red wig again as I'd told him I'd coloured my hair. At least it fits nicely. I tensed when he ran his hand through my locks, but he didn't seem to notice. Soon I'll need to explain to him why I wear scarves at work.

Men really are simple creatures. Although, I don't think I'll ever understand relationships because the rougher and wilder I am with him, the gentler and more intense he is with me. The pizza I was cooking ended up burnt, but I enjoyed myself and I'm sure he did, too.

My shift finished at four today. I'm bored and restless back in my flat. At 5 p.m. I decide to act. I choose the blonde wig that Scarlett lent me and black jeans and trainers. A large, warm hoodie I also found at the charity shop will do for cover. Hofstadt lives in walking distance, assuming he's still there. I bought a little penknife during the week and slip it into my pocket, just in case.

The cemetery next to my house closes soon. I ask a man at the gate if the other end is open. He nods, and I wander towards the garden of remembrance where my mother told me Dad's remains were scattered. The graves flick by on the way, slow enough for me to read the names on the headstones. Do the dead have it easy now, or would they give anything to breathe the air again?

I'm not too worried about being locked in here because I know where to climb over the wall so I sit on the bench in the memorial garden and stare at the stone cross in the centre of the small lawn. I used to be able to block out the world on this seat and think of my dad, but now I can hear car beeps, shouts from the road, and a person walking in heels in the distance. Even a tweeting bird distracts me. There's no peace here any more, and I leave thinking of my mother instead.

She lied to me, but I understand the reasoning behind it. I don't think less of her now, or my sister. Once you've told a tale like that, you can't easily take it back later, and they were only trying to protect me.

My feelings for my father are harder to pin down. He seemingly wasted his life and took the lives of others, but how can I judge him if I've done the same? Am I destined to repeat his mistakes? I'm not sure that I would have cared a few weeks ago, but everything's different now. I'm calling the shots in my relationship with Brad. He's waiting on my phone calls, and that's a good feeling. I want it to continue, and losing control is not going to help. There is an itch to see Hofstadt, though. I have to scratch it, but I'll be careful, and no more violence.

There's a rubbish bin at the exit to the cemetery. Removing the knife from my pocket, I slide it through the rotting flowers and hear it clunk at the bottom. I stop next to the praying angel statue and place my hand on her arm. The connection there has gone, too, and so I bid her farewell. She's not me any more. I want to live, not merely survive.

I met Hofstadt not long after I left the private hospital my mother had put me in. You can imagine how delicate I was. I yearned for someone to look after me. They would need to be solid, consistent, balanced and steady. I couldn't cope with volatile. Most of all, they had to be kind. I'd taken a job in a café to boost my benefits, and he popped in one day and read the paper while enjoying a coffee and a cake.

I had to have my hair up at work for hygiene reasons. My mum enjoyed combing it for me and jokingly gave me pigtails, but I left them in. I giggled with all the customers that morning, and he must have picked up on it. He departed with a wink and said there was a tip for a black-haired Barbie. His gratuity was twice the value of his order. A serviette lay under the money with a telephone number on it.

Hofstadt spoiled me rotten at the start, adoring me both in and out of the bedroom. It was fantastic for my self-worth, and I was happy. We discussed kids, and he said he wanted as many as possible. I had concerns due to my mental health. I didn't want to pass on my flaws, but I thought we'd be a good team. He enjoyed spending time with children and often bought ice creams for the kids who played in the street outside.

But as I fell in love, he drifted away. His sexual preferences decayed into weird dressing-up games and role-playing. He wanted my pigtails back and bought a too-small school uniform and a Dorothy dress to go with them. I endured, and still he became distant without any reasonable explanation.

His house is on Vergette Street. I smell the aroma of Wei Fung's as I walk by and remember our first takeaway. His Victorian building looks the same, but on closer inspection isn't. The front garden has been patioed to provide off-road parking. Planters decorate the edges. Glancing up, I see the curtains are yellow and pink. An elderly black woman answers with a huge smile.

'Can I help?'

'I'm looking for Sam Hofstadt. He lived here some time ago.'

Her smile drops, and the door closes showing only half of her face. 'I don't want to know.'

'Has he gone? Do you know where?'

A hard eye dismisses me. 'Speak to next door if you must.'

I step back from the slammed door and look into the window of the next house. An old lady, who looks vaguely familiar, glares at me. I shrug, open her gate and knock. She opens up but doesn't speak.

'Sam Hofstadt. I assume he moved away.'

'Not far enough.' I suspect if she hadn't been in her own house she would have spat on the floor.

'I knew him years ago. I wanted to talk to him.'

'I recognise you from way back. Is he a friend of yours?'

'He was. Then he treated me badly. I suppose you could say I'm here for closure.'

'I'd forget him if I were you. You're well rid of that pervert.'

At my confused expression, she snorts. 'You don't know? He interfered with a child from this very street. Under our noses. It makes me furious just thinking about it.'

'Who was the child? Tell me it wasn't a little girl who often played here. He sometimes invited her in to watch TV.'

Sharp eyes peer over her glasses. 'Long dark hair, around thirteen?' I nod.

'That was the one. It was a girl who was being fostered up the way.'

The energy trickles, then vanishes from my legs. The woman surprises me by gripping my arms hard.

'Are you okay? You've gone awful white.'

I attempt a reassuring grin, but my stomach isn't fooled. Managing to turn my head, I'm sick beside us. She keeps hold of me, despite it splattering our ankles.

'Aye, that's what I did when I found out. Told me that it was his friend's daughter and she had to work a lot. He didn't like the thought of her out on the street at all hours.'

I find a tissue in my coat pocket and wipe my mouth.

'Is he in prison?'

'Not any more, the shite virtually got away with it. The police arrested him for rape after someone made an anonymous complaint. Us neighbours made statements, but the girl disappeared just before the trial. She's not been seen since. He said she stole from him and made up a story, but they still found him guilty of a lesser crime.'

I recover my equilibrium and apologise for the mess. She remains riled up, and continues to vent.

'I saw him a week ago, bold as brass, working in a carpet shop in Millfield opposite Morrisons. I hope he burns in hell.'

'That seems suitable punishment.'

She finally cracks a smile.

'Working in a carpet shop or hell?' she asks.

I give her a little grin. 'Both.'

'Will you be all right, love?'

I bob and shake my head at the same time in my need to get away. I cut through the nearby park where children laugh on the swings. I carry on towards Millfield, knowing I can be opposite Morrisons within an hour.

47

THE ICE KILLER

The day darkens as evening approaches. Sleet has arrived and swirls around me. I'm glad I put a hoodie on even though the flakes are light. I walk up and down the street, spotting only one carpet shop: Windmill Furnishers. The surrounding businesses on the parade clearly struggle for trade. It's a shabby row of buildings, little more than converted houses, opposite the flash multinationals of Marks and Spencer and Morrisons across the dual carriageway. Sam's shop looks empty, although if he works full time, the chances are that he'll be there.

A boom of thunder overhead warns of worsening conditions and, sure enough, heavy rain and sleet fall simultaneously. I step into the phone booth outside Windmill Furnishers and pick up the handset to pretend I'm mid-call. The precipitation hardens and hammers at my glass shell. I don't recall a sleet storm before. I can't see anything, so edge the door open a little and stare past the discount banners stuck to the windows.

Hofstadt appears from a back room and walks towards the front window. It seems as though he's staring right at me, but he looks up at the weather. He frowns at the black clouds and shivers. His hair, once flecked with grey, is almost white now. In my mind, he was in his late forties still, but he can't be far off sixty, and that time would have included hard, anxious, stressful, long days under lock and key. His cheekbones jut from his face as he scowls and retreats into the shop.

He must hate his new career. Before, he was on incredible money as an anaesthetist. He had respect, status and, I realise with a sickening jolt, incredible power. His job was riddled with temptations for a sex offender. Did he steal drugs from work? What foul, depraved offences has he committed on unconscious people? Is there a more vulnerable moment than being sedated for an operation? I shiver as I think of the thousands of children who had been under his care over the years.

It rains solidly for thirty minutes and I'm not disturbed in my phone booth. Few venture out on such a dark, foreboding evening. Just before six, I step from the booth in the expectation that he may finish soon. The dual lanes behind me surge with rush-hour traffic. A trundling cement truck splashes water over my legs as high as my knees. I barely notice because I'm looking at the shop exit and my ex is leaving.

'Sam. Sam Hofstadt.'

He flinches and only cocks his head in my direction. There's a cornered snarl to his top lip. Eyes narrow as he tries to place the blonde lady in wet clothes.

'It's me, Ellen.'

His first reaction is to smile and stride towards me, but concern halts his steps as he, I imagine, remembers the details of our parting.

'Nice to see you again,' he says.

He shuffles away, an old man.

'Wait. I want...'

My mouth closes. What do I want? I came with questions, but I'm not sure I want the answers. This man's life is ruined. Short of physically torturing him, it would be hard for him to suffer further. Yet I need to hear his words, if only to take some control of the past. Maybe to tell me I was worth something.

'Why did you reject me? Why was I so easily discarded?'

He stops and speaks, but the din of roaring cars snatches his words away. I stand in front of him, ears straining. A break in traffic means I only catch the last line.

'You wouldn't understand,' he says.

'Try me.'

'I was protecting you.'

And suddenly, I do understand. He got rid of me just as justice trapped him. They'd charged him already. He knew he would face the truth in court and there'd be no way back. But I don't believe he was trying to protect me. It was because I could confirm the allegations. He wanted me gone. No one else knew my name because I lived a hollow existence where I barely mattered, even when I was with him.

What had he done to that girl? Where did she end up? What was he capable of? Memories breach the walls I've made and the truth pours in. I recall a tired child on his bed under a blanket, and many images of a sleeping girl on the sofa with tousled hair. But maybe not exhausted as I remember, perhaps only drugged.

My face must have been a film of the past as I grimace in revulsion at what he did. I shake my head. 'You sick, sick disgrace.'

The 'meek old man' act is over. He's always known that I'm proof of his lies. He seizes my shoulders and shakes me back and forth, spitting the words into my face.

'Ellen, you're mistaken. And don't think you can tell anyone about it. I'll say you were involved as well.'

My fists clench, then I try to push him away. He shoves me backwards, and a rage floods through me.

48

ACTING DCI BARTON

Barton blinked at the screen and blew out his cheeks because his email box had gone mad again. He wrestled with a myriad messages: filing them in folders and sub-folders, forwarding some, deleting others. It was more like a tedious computer game instead of police work.

He let his mind wander a little as he stared at the pictures of his family surrounding his PC. This was what he wanted, wasn't it? More money and responsibility, and less shoe-wear.

He had thought that as he approached fifty a great maturity would descend on him, but it wasn't like that at all. He still laughed at the same jokes, still took life with a pinch of salt. Maybe he wasn't as fast and fit as he once was, and his energy levels were lower, but nothing major. There was something, though, perhaps best described as a stillness. He didn't react like a youngster any more because his impulses were controlled by years of policing.

That was what this new job required – someone with an ability to process an enormous amount of information and sieve it through the mesh of their experience. He had that skill; to strip situations down to their basic components and build them back up again. But sitting in an office, doing this, he would always be a step away from the action.

Another email came in, this one from Mortis at the mortuary asking Barton to ring him when he got the message.

'Mortuary.'

'Hi, Mortis, it's John.'

'Great to hear I'm not the only one who hasn't gone home yet.'

'Good to hear from you. How are things?'

'Busy, and that's just what I need. I've received the toxicology results back from the PMs we did on those bodies. It confirms the physical signs. That is to say, both men's hearts stopped after massive overdoses. There was both fentanyl and heroin in their systems, but mostly the former.'

'Thanks for that. The investigating team discovered nothing suspicious in their backgrounds either. They were two hopeless individuals with years of addiction and criminality behind them. We also haven't found anyone interested in paying for a funeral for either of them. There were no eyewitnesses to visitors, although a joker rang in saying he'd seen a flaming angel that night. I guess we can put it to bed.'

'I'd say so, but there is one thing. This fentanyl is incredibly dangerous. If it hasn't been cut, it's easily fifty times more powerful than heroin. Just a few grains might be a deadly dose for some people.'

'Yes, it's scary, but we think we have the dealers and the majority of the batch in our possession. Uniform say that the message is getting out there and addicts are thinking twice as they load up their syringes.'

'That's pleasing news, but that's my point. The amount of fentanyl injected into these two men was phenomenal. There's an old saying about a dose like that dropping an elephant, but you could have tranquillised an entire herd with that amount.'

'What are you suggesting?'

'Well, even if they thought they were injecting heroin, it would still have been a considerable quantity.'

'Are you implying someone could have given them a deliberate overdose?'

'It's possible, or they may just have been heavy users. Who knows? It could be a double suicide. Or made to look like one.'

'I can do without any more of those after the last murder case, but it's noted. I'll chat to you soon.'

'Hang on. Have you heard the news?'

'Regarding what?'

'I'm listening to Peterborough Community Radio. There's been an incident on the carriageway near Morrisons on Lincoln Road.'

'What kind of incident?'

'A woman rang the traffic line a few minutes ago as she was just behind an accident. It looks like someone's gone under a double-decker.'

'Dead?'

'The caller said the bus ran straight over the person, so that's usually the outcome.'

'Tell me it wasn't a child.'

'They haven't given further details, except that there's been a collision on the other side of the road.'

'Bloody rubberneckers. When will people ever learn? That'll be a nasty job for uniform and traffic.'

'Sorry, I'm not being clear. They said it wasn't an accident. The person was pushed.'

49

Barton called Control, who confirmed they were already responding to multiple 999 calls. He made for the coat stand. With a wry grin, he peeked into the detectives' room, but couldn't see his sergeants. He returned to his desk and rang Strange.

'Hi, Kelly. Where are you?'

'Stuck in traffic. I finished at six and Malik was driving me to the mechanics on Bourges Boulevard.'

'There's been a civilian run over further along the carriageway outside Morrisons. Can you get there?'

'I doubt that. The traffic isn't moving, and it's his own car. I'd need blues-and-twos to clear a route.'

'Damn. It might be a murder. It's possible the victim was pushed.'

'Okay, no worries. I'm only about five hundred metres away. I'll leave Malik and jog. I'll give you a bell when I know more.'

Barton cut her off, dialled again and caught Zander in the car park. This wasn't the time for training. He explained the situation and gave orders.

'Zander, call Control and find out who's at the RTC. Ring them and make sure no witnesses leave the scene. Then get there as quick as you can. You'll need lights to get through the traffic. Ring me if it was deliberate.'

Barton put the receiver down and stepped out of his office. Ewing and Zelensky were having a full-on row. Luckily for them, they were the only ones in the room.

'That's enough, you two. See if you can get hold of CCTV from the traffic cameras on Lincoln Road outside the business park. It could be the scene of a murder.'

He returned to his desk with his brain churning. Maybe he would like this role after all. Although waiting and not doing anything soon jarred. It didn't take long for his mind to wander to the suspicious incidents of late. He clicked his fingers and made another call to his old boss, DCI Naeem.

'Hi, Nav. How are you?'

'Business or pleasure?'

He could almost see her smile at her end of the line.

'Business. Do you recall a case you worked years ago where the guy, a Mr Ted, or Theodore, Deacon broke down under questioning and was sectioned?'

'Yes, of course. I was in the viewing gallery to watch it. He completely lost the plot and needed to be restrained. They were shocking scenes. Incredibly, it took about five members of court security to restrain him.'

'That's the one. He's been linked to what we think is a rape victim. Do you recall if he had a family? We don't have a record of any.'

'He had an ex-partner and kids. I remember it well as his partner came to the station to talk with me. Due to his behaviour, they'd split up years before, but she still cared for him. They had two daughters, but I don't know for sure if they were biologically his. Funnily enough, I think they named them after characters from *Dallas*.'

'The TV programme?

'Yes.'

'And their names were?'

'Now you're pushing it.'

'Shame. Right, better go. We should catch up soon.'

'Definitely. I must admit I detected a buzz of energy there. It's made me a little jealous.'

Barton laughed. 'Did you miss the action when you became a DCI?'

Naeem had always been astute. 'Ah, the dilemma of the newly promoted. I was much older than you when I got that role. I knew I could make the most contribution as DCI, so I was ready.'

Barton's mobile in his pocket rang. 'Thanks, Nav, let me know if you recall the names.'

'I have kept bits and bobs from the big trials over the years, things like cuttings from newspapers. They're in the loft if you're desperate.'

Barton laughed, but there was more than an inkling of truth in her comment.

'If you could, I'd appreciate it. People's lives may depend on it.'

My sister, Lucy, is parked outside my flat when I return. She jumps in her seat when I crouch next to the driver's side window, as though an alien has appeared beside her.

I last saw Lucy at the funeral, but I didn't really study her. It's easy to get so swept up in your own grief that you don't notice others. She was close to my mother, before she left home. Their relationship was different, more one of equals. Mine always remained that of parent to child. Heavy bags under tired eyes and prominent cheekbones indicate the loss of our mum is weighing heavy on her still.

My reflection in the glass shows someone from another planet. The wig has been pulled to one side and make-up streams down my face. A wild-eyed expression completes the crazed clown ensemble.

Lucy steps out of the vehicle as though approaching an untamed and cornered animal.

'Ellen, what's happened? Come here.'

She pulls me into an embrace despite my soaked clothes. I tremble as tears threaten to fall. The tussle by the roadside already seems years ago, so why do I want to weep? I squeeze Lucy hard in return. It feels good.

'Let's get you inside. You're shivering.'

Trent places his hand on his window as we pass and mouths, 'Are you okay?' I nod.

With the radiators soon filling the small rooms with warm air, I quickly recover. We sit with mugs of hot chocolate at the kitchen table. I don't feel like discussing our father, but she doesn't visit often. She has the answers I need to understand myself. We might as well get started.

'Our dad's not dead, then.'

'No, he's not. But I sometimes wish he had died.'

'Would that make any difference? He'd still have been our father. It's not as though his actions were a reflection on you.'

She finishes her drink and places it gently on the table. 'Mum said never to tell you. She didn't think you'd understand. That comment proves that you don't.'

'I read he killed people, but he was also provoked. What else is there to know?'

'You'll see. It's my decision now Mum's gone, and I'm going to explain what happened. Will you listen until I've finished without interrupting?'

'Yes,' I say with a wobble in my voice, knowing I may never recover from what I'm about to hear.

'Our parents loved each other, but our father was a troubled man. He struggled to cope with normal life. Mum tolerated his strange behaviour and the ridiculous purchases over the years because they were often funny. She said that she knew on some level that they wouldn't stay together long-term, but she could never bring herself to split up with him. He'd lurch from job to job, but we had a house, enough food, and plenty of affection. What more is there?'

'Nothing that matters.'

'Exactly. I'm nearly seven years older than you so I remember the day they brought you home. Dad was between jobs and in the house most of the time. I swear he sickened before my eyes. It was as though the extra responsibility was too much for him to bear. He became possessive, paranoid and aggressive.'

'He hit you?'

'No, but he did others. He'd walk you in the pram, glaring at those he passed. Instead of seeing everyone's normal interest in a baby, he saw danger. People were afraid of him. Mum and I feared his moods.'

'Was he all bad?'

'No, a lot of the time he was quite the opposite. Loving, affectionate, kind and considerate. He was all of those things as long as he didn't feel threatened. And he was so intelligent and loyal. He loved you and wouldn't leave your side. Mum struggled to take you off him.'

'Was I scared?'

'No, you were just like him. You must have heard of the terrible twos and threes. That was nothing compared to your behaviour. Kids lash out, bite wildly, and break random objects. Instead, you fought with a purpose, struck to hurt, and wrecked things of value with a calculated goal. But Dad stuck up for you. There were incidents at playgroups and parties, and the police were even called. Mum couldn't cope and asked for help. Somehow, social services got involved and, to cut a long story short, our father moved out.'

'I don't suppose he liked that.'

'No, but he kept in touch. It might have been all right, but he started drinking and would turn up with this strange look on his face. We tried to get him treatment, but he wasn't interested.'

'Did he still see me?'

Lucy doesn't answer straight away. The guilt is still there. The secrecy was as much her decision as Mum's.

'Yes, until we moved house.'

'And you didn't tell him?'

'No.' Her reply is a whisper, mine is not.

'You threw him out with nothing. He loses his family, all of us, in one go, and then you disappear. No wonder he went mad. Your behaviour was worse than his.'

Her chin is set. 'We discussed it, but they were mum's choices to make, not mine. I was still at school. You said I could finish.'

I sit back in my chair. Deep breaths calm me.

'We didn't plan to keep him out of our lives forever. But without his presence, you settled down. We became a close family. Mum felt remorseful and contacted a charity where they act as intermediaries, so you can communicate without revealing your address, send pictures and letters, but then...'

'He killed someone.'

'Yes.'

'And you cut him off for good.'

'No, not quite. I didn't want anything to do with him, but Mum visited him in the psychiatric hospital. Eventually he got settled on medication and was back to his usual self, which meant we had a dilemma. Should we tell you the truth? We planned to come clean after he was released, but your behaviour changed at school.'

'In what way?'

'You'd been a great student, popular with teachers and the other kids. We had high hopes that you'd go far. I guess puberty brought an unwelcome change.'

'Rubbish. I was never popular. I was more of an outcast.'

Lucy rises from her seat and kneels next to mine. 'That's just not true. Mum was forever driving you to friends' houses and parties.'

'That can't be right. I'd have remembered. And if it was, what the hell went wrong?'

She returns to the kettle, boils it while she gathers her thoughts, and makes us another drink.

'I don't know. Your antics were like a teenager's. Temper tantrums, messy room, your grades fell, you even dropped your best friend, Sally. She was devastated, but we couldn't persuade you to try to make amends. You'd barely communicate with us. You'd stay out late, sometimes all night. You could be so horrible, and we had no idea what to do.'

'Why didn't you take me to the doctor's?'

'And tell them what? Our teenager is behaving like a teenager? We made appointments, but you never went. Besides, it's not unusual to smoke and drink at sixteen. Your behaviour changed, but your exam results still got you into sixth form.'

'But I was friends with Sally in her twenties. She and I were going to go travelling together. We were mates then.'

'That was later, after all the...' she searches for the right word '... incidents.'

There's too much information. It feels as if my head might burst like a watermelon dropped from a height. 'What incidents?'

'The girl who died at school.'

It's one of the things Scarlett and I don't talk about. We were hiding in the common room when we should have been at assembly and heard the head girl's voice approaching. We dropped the incriminating cigarette out of the window, moved back into the room, and tried to look natural. She shouted that she should have us thrown out of school. It was the first time I had the strange flash of light. When I came around, I remained in the same seat, Scarlett was still near the door, and we were alone. It was quiet until the screaming started from outside.

'She fell.'

She holds my gaze for a second and looks away. I can't sit still any more and pace the room. My voice is getting louder, but I struggle to control it.

'Why couldn't you see I had problems? Especially knowing my dad had issues.'

'I'd left by then. Don't you remember?'

I didn't, and try to think back. There are blurred images that won't focus, but she's not finished.

'I craved security and normality and met an older, wealthy man who gave me all of that. We fell in love and I got pregnant. I wanted a new life, so we moved away. We didn't want you near my children. I'm sorry I have to say that, but that was how it was. Mum never told me you disappeared after your A-level exams. I only found out when—'

'Enough! Enough! I know the rest. I had a breakdown, just like my dad. You didn't give a shit and Mum left me rotting in a rubber room. Let me guess, you were embarrassed about me, as you were with Dad.'

I'm shouting now, screaming. My sister picks her car keys from the table and edges towards the door. I throw the little porcelain salt pot at her and miss. It bounces rather than breaks.

'Ellen. Take your medicine. I've seen this before. Please, before you do something you regret.'

'Get out!'

'I'll say one last thing. It wasn't shame that made me behave as I did. It was fear. My husband knows a GP. The chances of developing an illness like schizophrenia is massively increased if one of your parents has it.'

'Why are you discussing my problems without me? And what are you saying, that I was destined to go mad?'

'Not you, me! I was afraid that I was the same. I slammed doors and broke plates too. You wouldn't talk about any of it. I couldn't cope watching it happen to you, and I moved away in a search for peace. I regret that now, so much, and I won't give up on you again. Please, take your tablets, see a doctor. I'll come back and tell you the rest of the story. We'll make you better again.'

The door softly closes, leaving me alone.

51

ACTING DCI BARTON

At 8 p.m., Barton finished a call from Dave Williams, who ran The Wonky Donkey pub. Dave was a drinking buddy of Barton's and Zander's from when they first became detectives. He retired two years ago and had rung to ask Barton to pop into his new place for a beer to catch up. Dave bemoaned how much he missed being a policeman and cautioned Barton to enjoy it, because nothing lasts forever.

Barton watched the last of his team trudging in from the traffic incident earlier and suspected Dave had forgotten the hours and hours of paperwork ahead of them after an incident like this, and it had already been a long day. Barton remembered an inspector at the start of his career doing a day's wrap-up in the beer garden of The Botolph Arms, but those days were distant memories, and a few jars in the pub with the team would have to wait until this was all over.

Barton had received multiple updates from the RTC but little seemed clear-cut. CCTV hadn't helped. He called everyone into the incident room.

'Right, let's sum up today's findings. Strange, you first.'

'It's an odd one. I suspected it would be a disagreement ending in a shove, or someone off their face falling into the traffic. Instead, it was a man and a woman arguing. We have two brilliant witnesses who were leaving a newsagent's further up the street. It looked to them as though the man grabbed the woman first and they struggled. He clearly pushed her towards the road with intent. The witnesses didn't get a chance to consider intervening, because she shrieked like a jaguar – their words – twisted, and physically threw him right in front of a bus.'

'Shrieked like a jaguar?' asked Leicester.

'Yes, he said she sounded like a wild cat.'

'Dead immediately?'

'I'll say. His head was this thick.' Strange put her fingers together. 'He worked in a carpet shop nearby so there was no trouble identifying him. This is where it gets complicated. His name was Sam Hofstadt.' Strange nodded at the blank faces. 'No, I didn't remember him either. He's a sex offender. Went down for the sexual assault of a child.'

Barton groaned. 'Brilliant. That means half of the city could be responsible.'

Strange tutted. 'That's the thing though, isn't it? Responsible for what? Protecting herself?'

'You're right. And I can't see the CPS attempting to convict anyone based on those witnesses' testimonies,' said Barton.

'We need to find her first. You mentioned she was caught on CCTV?' said Zander.

Ewing and Zelensky started talking at the same time. Zelensky gave Ewing a filthy look, and he quickly sat down to let her continue.

'Yes. Multiple witnesses saw her fleeing the scene. Nobody thought to chase her though as they were so shocked at the accident, and she seemed to be the innocent party. One said it was odd because the victim was old, and she was young and pretty. She headed over Rhubarb bridge and into Millfield.'

Barton imagined her running over the pedestrian bridge that passed over the parkway. She must have run towards the streets near where the five deaths occurred. Was it more than coincidence?

'We managed to pick her up again on Eastfield Road next to the park,' he said. 'It's a dark night, and the footage is grainy, but she is tall, fair, thin, wearing black clothes. It's definitely her.'

It was a shame she had blonde hair. Barton had suspected it was the same person from the other incidents, but her hair had been black. What the hell would the connection be, though? He decided to wait and see if anyone else made the same leap.

'Malik, did you have any joy today with the information I gave you about those two daughters?'

Everyone turned to look at Malik.

'I was struggling, but then the old boss, DCI Naeem, rang in. She'd been through some old cuttings. The girlfriend who was at the trial, Pamela Toole, had two kids with Deacon. They were named after characters from *Dallas*. The older daughter who always went with her was called Lucy. She said there was a much younger child, her name was Sue Ellen. She only came to the sentencing, but waited outside with a family friend because she was crying. Intel have found a Lucy Toole and a Sue Ellen Toole at register of births. There's no father named. A search of DVLA records located Lucy. She is now Lucy Breslinski who lives in Harrow, London.'

'They haven't found the other one?'

'No, it's possible she changed her name before she started driving.'

'I liked *Dallas*. It was so bad it was funny,' said Zander.

'You're not the only one,' said Malik with a raised eyebrow. 'I thought it was a seventies porn film, but the lady from Intel used to watch it, which would have been a shock if I was right. She loved it. I've had nothing but professionalism from her over the years, but she sang the entire theme tune down the phone line. It was freaky.'

'Durr, duh, durr, duh, durr, du-du-durr-durr,' sang Zander.

Barton smiled at the bewildered faces of the youngsters. 'Okay, that's our best lead for those murders. I know how you all like overtime. Strange, take Leicester and visit the address in Harrow tomorrow. Don't forget to tell your old friends in the Met we're coming. I was hoping we'd get a local address, so I'm not hopeful, but if she knows nothing, she might at least point us in the direction of her sister. Then we'll be able to eliminate both. Malik, see if you can find any likely matches on the other daughter's date of birth. She might have got married, too. Anyone with any other thoughts?'

Ewing put his hand up. 'Chances are the woman from the bus incident ran home. If she was picked up by CCTV in Eastfield Road and nowhere else, odds are she lives around there. We can blow up an image, ask in shops, maybe knock on doors.'

'There are thousands of houses in that area. That's needle-in-a-haystack time,' said Zelensky, with more venom than necessary.

'Perhaps,' said Barton. 'But think about it. We have a tall, thin, young woman with blonde hair who wears a black hoodie. There can't be too many women like that in Eastfield. We might get lucky and find somebody knows her.'

'It's another unusual event in the same neck of the woods,' said Strange. 'Could it all be linked to the same woman? Those other incidents weren't far away. If so, that's a lot of bad luck she's having.'

'Yes, Kelly!' said Barton. 'I was thinking that. Maybe someone's going around killing their ex-boyfriends.'

Zander laughed. 'She has some varying tastes if one of them was the almost retired assistant manager of a carpet shop and the others were notorious junkies or wannabe rock stars.'

'This woman also had blonde hair. The girl from The Hartley pub that night had dark hair,' said Barton.

'It's not unusual to dye your hair, or even wear a wig,' said Strange.

'True,' said Barton. 'Let's get everything inputted and see what HOLMES comes up with. It's going to be busy for the foreseeable.'

DC Leicester cleared his throat and blushed. 'Actually, I spoke to the bus driver at the hospital as Zander requested. He calmed down when he got away from the scene and stated that he spotted the commotion on the side of the road as he approached. The man was definitely the instigator and shook the woman like a rag doll. The last thing the driver remembered before he drove over the guy was the woman standing next to the kerb with her mouth open. Her hair had fallen down over her eyes.'

'Did he recognise her?' interrupted Barton.

'No, but he was pretty sure she was wearing a wig.'

I've spent the day in bed. The only thing I've managed to do today is ring work and tell them I have the flu. I have a banging headache, muscle soreness and my sweating forehead warns of an approaching fever. When I close my eyes, tyres skid and brakes screech, then there's the heavy silent pause after something terrible has occurred. I was in full flight, splashing through the puddles, when I heard the first scream.

I flinch as someone taps at my door. I open up to Trent's earnest grin.

'You good? I noticed you hadn't gone to work.'

'I rang in sick. I hate Saturdays, anyway.'

'Cool, do you want—?'

Shutting the door in his face makes me feel marginally better. The phone rings.

'Ellen speaking.'

'Hi, Stanground pharmacy here. I'm ringing because you didn't pick up this month's prescription and you will have run out. Are you coming in soon?'

'Sorry, I've been away. I'll come this afternoon.'

'It's early closing today, but our driver is in your area next week. He'll deliver them for you if you'd like.'

After I end the call, I splash cold water over my face in the bathroom. The mirror hides the cabinet where I keep my medication. When did I last look in there? It clicks open, and it's immediately obvious that the foil packets are full. I take them through to the kitchen and place them on the table. Are they the cure or the problem? The first time they put me on tablets was after that girl fell from the window. I can't remember if they helped or not then, either.

Scarlett might know. She'll be drunk by now, but maybe that's the moment to demand an honest chat with her about that day. Back then, it was Scarlett who blurted out the head girl fell. It's been a taboo subject since, with both of us avoiding the topic. I'm not sure why it keeps returning to my mind now, when I haven't thought about it in years.

I pull a woolly hat on to cover my stubble and bald patches, and leave the flat. Leaning against the bannister, I stumble down the steps. It's another bleak day with no wind, which matches my sense of emptiness. I get in my car and drive cautiously with my head only high enough to look over the wheel. The electronic gates open at Scarlett's, and I knock on the door. It would take a lot to jolt me out of my inertia, but she manages it.

'I was hoping not to see anyone.'

She has a nose patch and two deep black eyes. I follow her into the house.

'Drink?' she asks.

'Coffee, please.'

I watch her as she fills the kettle and gets the cups out. She'll speak when she's ready. With two cups in her hands, she beckons me to the lounge. I've only sat in there once before and the high ceilings made the acoustics odd. It's no different today.

'I was thinking about you,' she says.

I wet my lips. 'How come?'

'They named the guy who fell under the bus. I thought, now that's weird, I knew him. There have been some other deaths lately, too. I realised I'd met all of them at one point or another. That's six familiar people who've come to an untimely demise under odd circumstances.'

My face burns, but I say nothing.

'I don't know them as well as you, though, do I?'

I remain silent.

'You're a dangerous person, Ellen. The police released a video of that bus accident, as they called it. I recognised you running away.' She feigns shock and horror. 'Oh, no, the woman was blonde and you don't have that colour hair. Unless you were wearing my wig.'

'He attacked me.' I hand her the bag I'm carrying. In it are her wig and shoes.

'And the other deaths?'

'Accidents.'

She laughs, but it's a quick bark with no warmth. 'Do you remember that girl who fell out of the window at school?'

I nod. Ironic that it's her who brings it up.

'It seems that death surrounds you.'

'That was an accident, too. You said so yourself. Or do you know different?'

'Imagine if the police found out who you were. They may go all the way back to that incident and wonder if it really was so innocent.'

'We're friends. Don't tell them.'

'Of course not, but I need a favour. Nothing major.'

'What is it?'

She shuffles along the sofa and sits right next to me. 'I want to get rid of Tim.'

I break away from her serious stare, but can't say I'm surprised. Nevertheless, I want no part of it. I'm in enough trouble as it is.

'Someone will recognise me from that footage. It's only a matter of time before the police are involved.'

She puts her face next to my ear. 'See what he's done to me,' she whispers, even though Tim's Audi isn't parked outside.

'Go to the police, tell them he beats you. They must have asked what happened at the hospital.'

She stands and walks towards the low glass table. Instead of placing the cup on it, she drops it. The pane smashes into smithereens. I jump, but she spins around with a smile.

'He drove me to A & E and took me inside. Told them in a hushed voice while I was behind a curtain that I'd been drinking and fell down the stairs. He was convincing, I'll give him that. They looked at him with pity and me with revulsion.'

'Leave him, then. You don't need to kill him.'

She swirls her finger around in the air. 'I want all this. I deserve everything after what I've put up with. He has control of the money, the houses are in his name, the businesses are in trust. He needs to go, and you're going to help.'

It's not even a surprise. Scarlett's never been my friend, not really. I've just filled a hole to make her feel better. She'll probably murder Tim whether I help her or not. I wouldn't put it past her to blame it on me after she'd done it, either. A strange acceptance comes over me. Why don't I care that much? Is it because Tim's a bad person, or because I'm a bad person?

She walks behind the sofa and squeezes my shoulders, slightly too hard.

'You know, lately, you've reminded me of how you were back at school. You were a crazy fucker then, and I loved it. In fact, I wanted to be you. We're going to have some fun. Now, how are we going to do it?'

I stare at the bright, dancing flames in the log-burning stove while the world darkens around me.

'We need to make it look like an accident.'

Barton checked himself out in the bedroom mirror. Holly walked in and picked up his towel.

'If you're looking for your bum, it now lives over your belt at the front.'

He frowned. 'I was just thinking my bottom used to look great in suit trousers.'

She came behind him and put her arms around his waist, deliberately leaning back so they couldn't quite touch.

'You'd have thought that gym work would have paid off by now,' she mocked.

He turned her around and whisked her off her feet, cradling her like a toddler.

'Has anyone told you how funny you are?' he asked. 'I've struggled to find the motivation to get going again since I left hospital. The horrors I see at work make me want to spend my spare time with you guys. Despite the fact you're all mad, you keep me sane and happy.'

'That's the sweetest thing you've ever said to me.'

'At least I haven't lost my patter.'

'John, we've discussed this and you know we're in the damage-limitation stage of life, where we try not to get too fat and flabby until our responsibilities lessen. Just think, Luke finishes school in twelve years. Then I can push you around the top deck of a cruise ship to your weakening heart's content.'

Barton dropped her on the bed. 'That's motivational.'

'The only way to stay fit is to get into an exercise routine. Our priority is the children's routine, then we have work commitments, homework, and we need to spend time with each other. If you can find six hours a week to pump iron, it means I'm on my own for six hours pumping an iron over your work shirts. And that's before we fetch your mother today.'

Barton couldn't help grimacing.

'You think this is the right decision?' he asked. 'I quite like her an hour away.'

'How many times did she ring us last week?'

They'd stopped counting when it hit a hundred. It had been a swift descent. Her companion – Barton preferred calling him that as opposed to her boyfriend –had rung a few days ago and said that she wasn't safe to be left on her own. Barton and Holly had spoken again and were picking her up this morning to stay with them until, well, who knew?

Barton stomped down the stairs. He could sense a gloom descending. Cancelling the direct debit to the gym would help. He'd be unfit but at least he'd be richer.

When he arrived at his office downstairs, his face fell. Holly and he had moved his desk out a week ago, but the new single bed they'd ordered must have turned up while he was at work. Holly had put that and the little wardrobe together without mentioning it. She had placed a small night table next to them and left a box of Black Magic chocolates on it – his mother's favourite.

He hoped his mum didn't consider it a prison cell, more a cosy hotel room. He heard Holly arrive and stand behind him. This time her arms easily reached around him.

'We know this might be hard,' she said, 'and there's no saying how it ends, but we are doing the right thing. Without considering the costs of care homes, she'd hate to be in one anyway. We'll look after her here.'

'I'd prefer not to think about what that entails. Are you sure you're happy with it?'

'We'll be fine. Those four nappies you changed when Layla was young should stand you in good stead.' She grinned at his narrowed eyes. He had helped as much as he could back then, but he'd also been out of the house twelve hours a day.

'I did loads of Luke's.'

'Lighten up. Laughter will get us through this, but it won't all be bad. In fact, it'll be fine. Anything involving pads and nappies will hopefully be miles off. She might want a carer to come in for certain things later on, but there are options. And she's mostly still there. She just needs a safe place. Don't focus on the negative, and keep laughing along the way. My friend, Amanda, said when her mum developed dementia, she thought she was a professional singer. Next door told me that her abrupt, distant father lost his inhibitions as the disease progressed. He became like a cheeky, rude, hilarious child.'

She laughed. As she stepped away, he saw her realising something.

'The kids want her here, and it will teach them valuable life lessons, but you'll also want her here. My parents went out like lights. I'd give anything to have had the chance to look after them and tell them what they meant to me.'

Barton gave out a small snort and thanked his lucky stars once again for meeting Holly. He went in search of his laptop and mobile. By the time he got outside, she was waiting in the driver's seat of his Land Rover with the engine running. He clambered in the passenger side with a smile. They drove in companionable silence. It was a superb feeling to have solid support. His phone rang thirty minutes into the journey. It was from Strange, who had driven to Harrow to call on Lucy, the older daughter of Theodore Deacon.

'Morning, boss. Leicester and I have just finished interviewing the older sister.'

'Excellent. How did it go?'

'Good and bad. She confirmed the background story we had of the father. He was a paranoid schizophrenic, but when he reached his thirties, he developed psychosis. It was literally a deadly combo.'

'And he was her biological father.'

'Yep, although she has no dealings with him any more.'

'You think she was telling the truth?'

'Yes, she was convincing. She heavily participates in a whole range of school governor groups, church committees and charities. We'll check her alibis, but my gut says she's definitely not involved in any of the recent deaths; directly or indirectly.'

'That's what we thought. What about her sister? Is she in touch with her?'

'Here's where it gets interesting. She clammed up for a moment and became more cautious. She said there was a sizeable age gap between them and they were never close. Lucy got married pretty young and moved to London, and they lost touch. Their mother used to see Sue Ellen, but the mum died fairly recently. Both were at the funeral but only spoke briefly.'

Barton pondered the information. 'Sisters who only spoke briefly at their mum's funeral, eh?'

'That's what she said.'

'My experience of doing this job is that much older sisters are almost maternal in their affection for their younger siblings.'

'My thoughts precisely. I probed around the topic, but she was convincing. We only talked for an hour, but I got the impression I was dealing with a highly intelligent person. That said, because we surprised her by turning up unannounced, cracks appeared in her story. I asked her why she wasn't friends with her sister.'

'Let me guess – because her sister had problems. They fell out over something.'

'Exactly what I thought, but no. Lucy wouldn't bad-mouth her. She put it down to a bohemian lifestyle. I asked her where Sue Ellen lived, and she was flaky. I finally got out of her that the last she heard she was living in Peterborough still.'

'Did she have a current photo of her?'

'She said not. No phone number either. I asked how they arranged the funeral. She said she organised it, and her sister just arrived.'

'Where did their mother live?'

'Eastfield as well.'

Barton summed up the information in his head. 'It sounds ragged at best. Do you believe her?'

'Hell, no. She's lying through her teeth.'

54

ACTING DCI BARTON

Barton hadn't even been at the interview with Lucy and he didn't believe her either. He was about to list his demands to Strange when he remembered his new role and his promise to give the sergeants some experience.

'What are you thinking, and what's your plan?'

He detected a large inhale and realised Strange knew he was testing her.

'We've parked down her street. She seemed a pleasant woman. I can't imagine her deserting her sister. Therefore, she's protecting her.'

They both kept quiet for a few seconds. Dealing with families was tricky. To many, their loyalty to each other came above the law, even if they were normally law-abiding. Barton was a policeman and suspected under certain conditions even he might ignore the rules to protect his family.

If they threatened Lucy, she could clam up. They had nothing much at this point, but Barton felt something was off balance. This Sue Ellen might not be guilty of anything, but she was involved, of that he was sure. They could seize Lucy's phone. He suspected she was lying about not having her sister's telephone number. Although, if she was as smart as Strange was saying, she'd have deleted the information by now, and possibly got rid of the phone.

If she hadn't, even stupid people knew not to answer the door. Despite what crime dramas often portrayed, doors were rarely kicked in nowadays without a warrant. The law protected the innocent, but it also protected the guilty. It wasn't their patch, either, so even requesting the necessary from a magistrate would be problematic. And what would Lucy be guilty of?

Holly pulled into the road that Barton's mother lived on and drove past an unusual sight. It was a cool day, yet there was a woman stumbling towards them in a semi-jog wearing an ill-fitting men's T-shirt and shorts, and without shoes or socks. Her unkempt grey hair blew around in the breeze. He recognised her as they cruised by. Holly squeezed the brakes.

'Oh, dear,' she said.

Barton spoke into his phone. 'I'll call you back.'

He stepped from the vehicle, incredulous at what he was about to shout.

'Mum, stop running.'

* * *

It took an hour for Barton and Holly to get his mother calm and settled. He stayed with her while Holly packed enough belongings for a long break. He carried the suitcase to the car and returned to the bungalow. His eyes were drawn to the photos in the hallway. They were mostly of Barton and his two sisters. He felt a twinge of annoyance at his siblings' vague offers of involvement. Both had offered to take her for a weekend to give him a rest, but they were still getting off lightly. Barton supposed that he was closest to their prickly mother, seemingly bulletproof to her indiscriminate insults, and his sisters did live a long way away.

He had a sneaky thought of telling them their mum had a proviso in her will that only helpful children would receive any inheritance.

Perhaps they'd take her for a fortnight then, which would give Holly and him a proper break. Barton's kids didn't yet know about the temporary suspension of the skiing holiday. Looked as if they'd be getting another weekend in a north Norfolk caravan.

Holly brought his mother through to the door by the arm. She'd diminished even since he'd seen her less than two weeks ago. Most of her bluster and sharpness had vanished in that time, too.

'We better get going, beat the traffic,' he said.

His mother stared at him with wide eyes. 'Are you leaving me here on my own?'

'No, you're coming, too. Don't you want to come?'

Holly tutted next to her and took over. 'Don't you remember? You wanted a week's break at ours. You were looking forward to spending time with the grandchildren.'

A few minutes later, Holly reversed the car off the drive. Barton stole a final glance at the bungalow. A weak sun lit it up as though for a final moment. Next time he came here, it would be a completely different experience.

He rang Strange's phone when they reached the main road. It was DC Leicester who answered.

'Afternoon, where's DS Strange?'

'She's driving. We're on our way back.'

'Did you have any ideas? It's a tricky one.'

'We thought the same, sir. We stayed outside for a while to see if she did something drastic. She came out and got in a Range Rover. We don't have authorisation to follow her, so we waited ten minutes. We were about to ask Control to track her via number plate recognition, when she returned. DS Strange said that we're meeting her father at his probation office in a few days. We can probably get the information out of him, so we've left it for the moment. Failing that, we attempt a warrant for Lucy's house, or perhaps Lucy will be honest after she's had time to absorb the news. After all, we both want what's best for her sister.'

Barton smiled at that. If only Joe Public were so obliging. Nevertheless, it was what he would have done if he'd had a few moments of peace to think.

'That's great work. Have you notified Control?'

'About what, sir?'

'You're 90 per cent there. This is a clever woman. She might know about tracking phones and not making calls. She'll probably be able to tell if we follow her. If we back off, I'm betting she will get in her car and visit Sue Ellen. Peterborough's two hours away via one of the busiest roads in the country.'

'Got you, sir. I'll ring Control and have Lucy and her husband's cars put into the automatic number plate recognition system. If their vehicles come within fifty miles of Peterborough, we'll know about it.'

Barton rang Zander.

'Afternoon, John. Is your mum okay?'

Barton looked behind him. She was fast asleep.

'Yes, she's good. Have you spoken to Strange?'

'Yeah. I'm up to speed.'

'Is the Millfield operation planned out?'

'Everyone's ready to flood the area over the next few days, knock on doors and see if we can get a hit. Just waiting for your say-so.'

'You've got it.'

Barton closed his eyes for the rest of the journey. He wasn't tired; it was a way of immersing himself in the different cases. There were too many quirks for it to be just a series of coincidences. Someone was up to no good. He'd suspected the girl was the key from the beginning. The fact they hadn't found her was frustrating.

The temperature had plummeted by the time they arrived home. It was lovely to get back to a warm house with the kids. His mum was responding better to Holly, so he left her to deal with getting her moved in. He put the oven on. Holly had removed three packs of sausages from the freezer earlier, so he placed them on two trays. He peeled the potatoes at the rate of about one an hour. Layla came in and smiled at him for a minute while he battled with the small implement.

Chuckling, she took the peeler and potato out of his hands and whispered to him.

'Go and see Granny.'

She'd be a teenager next year, but she was already a mini Holly. He smiled, wiped his hands on a tea towel and strolled to his office. His mother was perched on the edge of the bed with the box of chocolates open on her lap. She gave him a little wave.

'You're spoiling me.'

'You're worth it. Dinner in half an hour?'

'Perfect. John, how long am I staying for?'

He displayed his widest grin, despite his heart breaking.

'You can stay for as long as you like.'

55

It was a struggle to get out of bed before midday. Even ringing in sick again was a massive effort, and I collapsed on the sofa afterwards. My boss is still being reasonable about everything, despite this being the fourth day I've rung in sick, which is a big surprise. I've always thought the management uncaring and cruel. How could I have been so wrong?

Brad rings, and we chat for a while. He's keen and enthusiastic. I empty the washing machine, cursing as the clothes are still soaking wet, while he blathers on. I mouth some obscenities and put it on a quick cycle. He asks if I'm free over the next few days because he misses me at work. Yuck. What is wrong with men? If you're eager, they're as catchable as smoke. Be indifferent, and they turn into Labradors.

I ask Brad why he hasn't invited me to meet his parents yet, in the hope of giving him a coronary. He stumbles over his words and becomes true to form: evasive. It's easy to get rid of him after that. I stare at the TV without watching it, with a thought nagging away. It's not until the light is dwindling outside that my mind clicks into place.

All these years, in the back of my head, there has been the presumption that I pushed that girl out of the school window. I remember the aftermath. Not the shrieks and the weeping, or the accusatory stares and suspicion, but the way my body stopped working. They thought I was in shock. But was it shock at what I saw, or what I did?

Scarlett always said we were miles from that window. She said it was an accident and I've always been so grateful for that. As a friend, she protected me. But have I been naive? Perhaps the reality of our situation is that she is not a friend, and instead she was protecting herself.

How will I ever find out? My past is like a mist-strewn forest. Everything is murky and half concealed. It's difficult to tell which memories are real.

I force myself to relax by slowing my breathing. I send a buzz of energy into every single part of my body, each finger, hand, arm, shoulder and so on, until all I am is my physical form. That's what they taught me in therapy.

In this zen-like state, I travel back to my school days. My sister said I was popular until I made myself unpopular. When the past is so distant and forgotten, it's hard to know if I experienced the laughing children's birthday parties, or if I have created them. Are the images of Lucy and me giggling in the sand on various beach holidays real, or from a movie where I've replaced the characters with my own to bolster my self-esteem?

Images of darkness, confusion and tears filter into those idyllic reminiscences. Yet, there was a theme of light through much of my youth. Her name was Sally. Those memories are hard-wired. They definitely exist. I recall her chocolate breath and high-pitched titter. My fingers flex as once again I feel her small, warm, chubby hands in mine.

When I open my eyes, my body still tingles. To think we called her Fat Sally for all those years. I was joking, but I think I was the only one. Her memories of school must hurt.

A hidden event emerges from the depths of my mind. It's of a mud-splattered Sally in her school running gear, staggering across a field back to the waiting class. She is the last to finish.

'Hippo coming through,' someone shouts.

'Faster. The tuck shop's closing.'

I can hear her hoarse breathing as she staggers towards the relative safety and darkness of the changing rooms. Even the teachers laugh. I'm there, too, watching.

As she passes, her eyes frantically search mine for kindness. I should cheer her on. Congratulate her effort. Support my friend.

'Well done, Sally.'

But I whisper my words to the wind.

Sally never asked me for my friendship. She didn't even tell me to stop calling her Fat Sally. She wanted nothing, and that's what I gave her in return. I chose to be friends with Scarlett instead, who treated me in the same way as I treated Sally. Perhaps that's how it is at that age. Chains of shame run through every school. Yet, I'm such a disgusting person that I also let Sally down as an adult.

I poke the space bar of my laptop and bring it to life. Facebook is somewhere I rarely venture. After various abuses in the past, my privacy means nobody can message me or post on my timeline. I occasionally use it to look at other people's perfect lives when I want to hate myself. It's a favoured form of self-harm.

I have few friends. Fewer after I removed Sally. Each one of her successes highlighted one of my failures. Why did that make me bitter rather than happy for her? What do I say after all this time? It's been years since I even looked at Sally's profile, never mind connected with her. I unblock her and see her page allows messages. She has a green dot on Messenger which shows she's online right now. Sorry is the only word I can think of. Nothing else comes close. I type it and hit send.

Her profile shot is of her sitting on a big hippo at a water park. There's only one large mammal in the picture, and it's the one with the tusks. Sally's smile is carefree. She looks vibrant and healthy. I flick through her photos, noting the only negative aspect of them is the cheese factor – she's been to every Aussie tourism spot in the country.

There's her and her handsome husband grinning on the Harbour Bridge. Her and their two boys in front of a big red rock. The four of them pulling faces next to an enormous banana in a place called Coffs

Harbour. The kids have grown so much. Further back, judging by the balloons, she's had a surprise thirtieth birthday party. She has a family, and a life, even her car beats mine hands down.

Jealousy and being pleased for her battle for supremacy. I smile afterwards. Perhaps I am human, after all. My finger hovers over sending her a friend request. I'm reminded of my second favourite film, *Four Weddings and a Funeral*, and the funeral poem in it – 'nothing now can ever come to any good'. After what I've done, that applies to my life, but I selfishly click on that, too. I wait for a long minute, but there's no reply to the request or the message. I frantically change my settings, so she can message me if she wants.

Ten minutes later, I feel like lobbing my laptop through the window, Scarlett style. Messaging her, though, has given me some peace. I take a quick shower and stare at a fridge without alcohol. Getting pissed won't help my situation, but I don't have lower to go, so what the hell? There's another ping as I pick up my coat to leave for the shops. It's a message from Sally.

My coat slips from my fingers. Grabbing the mouse, I open the message as fast as possible, so as not to let my imagination run wild. Please remember me kindly.

Hi!!! Oh my God!!! Where havé you been?!! So pleased to hear from you!!!

After a few seconds, I laugh aloud. She still overuses exclamation marks.

Hey, Sally,

I type.

Lovely to read your words.

The quiet while she replies makes my mouth dry. With wide eyes, I watch the ellipsis wobbling, which means she's typing.

You too. I've been trying to reach you for ages. I even tried looking for your sister, but she's probably married.

Why? What did you want?

Duh! Stoopid! I want to keep in touch. You were my best friend at school.

My face crumples up in agony. I bare my teeth in an ugly silent cry.

That's lovely of you to say, but I was a terrible friend,

I manage to type through watery vision.

She doesn't reply for over a minute. I rest my head in my hands. It must be true. The ellipsis wobbles again, quivering for a full five minutes. I have time to make a cup of tea for my dry throat before the message comes through.

I can only assume you're talking about what happened in the final years. You were ill then, Ellen. You wouldn't have acted and behaved in that manner if you'd been well. You were much better when they got your medication sorted. We had some fun times. I loved our Friends marathons.

You're just being nice, because you were always a nice person. I even let you down when we were going to go travelling.

You were in love. It was okay for you to want to be happy.

I put myself first. I didn't consider you.

What are you talking about? You came around and we discussed it over and over again. I told you to stay in the end. You were supposed to come to Australia and see me if it didn't work out. I assumed it had, and you were content.

No, I made a mess of it. Fucked up a lot of things and I'm still making stupid choices. I don't seem to have done anything with my life apart from upset other people and myself. I hurt everyone around me.

There's another big wait before she replies.

Are you taking your medication?

Yes.

Make sure you take your tablets, please. You end up in a desperate place without them. And you saved me at school. How can you think you're not amazing?

Eh?

Ellen. From the very first moment at school, everyone wanted to be your friend. You were so tall and cool and beautiful. I was always short and chubby. The kids surrounded me in the playground on my second day. All of them chanting the words, Fat Sally, Fat Sally. You strode through them and linked arms with me. You said, "She's my Fat Sally".

I don't remember that.

How can't you? We had our birthday parties together for years because they were close. You could have been friends with anyone, and you chose me. I'll be grateful until the day I die.

And I was popular?

Well, you were liked. There was always something about you that made people wary. I used to think it was your height and looks, but when you finished puberty, you became what we were wary of.

I don't understand.

You went from wary to scary.

.   .   .

She adds a few joke emojis.

And I hurt people.

It's a statement, not a question.

Yes, a little. You had a really short fuse. A boy from the year below squeezed your bum once. You choked him until the teachers pulled you off.

Was I mean to you?

No, when you changed, I kept out of your way. The others gave me a bit more grief, but they were conscious of the fact we were friends before. If they upset me and you changed your mind about who you hung around with, they'd have feared for their lives.

What?

It's just a turn of phrase. But you did go proper mental.

I hold my breath for a couple of seconds, then type fast.

Can I ask you a question?

Sure, but you'll need to be quick. The kids will be up in a minute and it'll be all go for the school run.

You remember the girl who fell when we were in the sixth form.

Sure.

Do you think I pushed her?

What? Why the hell would you think that?

I spoke to Scarlett recently, and she implied it.

Her response is instant, and would be a shout in person.

Don't listen to a word that witch says. She was the evil one. Stay away from her, you understand. She manipulated and provoked you when you had your troubles. I once heard her spreading those rumours that maybe she was pushed. Scarlett enjoyed the notoriety of it all. If anyone killed that poor girl, it was Scarlett. I'm telling you, she's the psycho.

I close my eyes and concentrate hard. Something inside me screams that she is right, but Scarlett picked on Sally. Maybe Sally *would* say it was her.

Thank you, Sally. For everything.

Don't talk like a ratbag. Look, I've got to go. Let's chat soon, maybe over the weekend, and do not disappear. You have to come and visit. You'd love it out here.

She finishes with approximately a hundred kisses. I smile at her Australianisms and imagine her making the kids Vegemite sandwiches and packing them off in sun hats. They'll have a plunge in the pool later, and bloody barbecued shrimps, and mates over, and all the things that I don't have.

I stare at the puddle of water next to the washing machine. Perfect. I drag the clothes out. Not only are they soaking, they're covered in powder. I leave them on the floor in a big pile. Now I need alcohol. There's a knock at the door, but it's only the pharmacy guy wanting a signature.

After he's gone, I take four deep inhales and four longer exhales to try to clear my mind. Sally has given me good news, saying I wasn't always unpleasant. That's something to be proud of. Then why do I feel ruinous? If I could beat myself with something, I would.

She mentioned the pills though, as did my sister. I'm not supposed to drink too much on them. Right. One night of drunkenness this evening, and I'm back on the drugs tomorrow. I'll punish myself with alcohol. I might even get Brad round. Anything to feel good about myself.

My phone beeps, informing me of two unread messages.

The first is from the nice lady, Millie, at the charity shop.

Missed you for the stock take. Will you come next? I enjoy your company. We'll have a laugh and I could do with the help.

I send her a smiley face. Non-committal, but I'll need her sanity next week as my brain deals with the mood swings the drugs cause as my body gets used to them again. The second text is from Scarlett.

Tonight's the night. I have a plan. Be here at eight.

I grit my teeth and make fists to stop myself smashing my phone into a million pieces on the tiled floor. I'm surprised I don't crack the screen with my reply.

Screw you. Kill him yourself, you bitch.

Stars appear in my vision. I'm losing control as there's another knock at the door.

I'm not sure who I expect at the door, but it's a relief when it's him from downstairs. He's hopping from foot to foot. If I didn't know him better, I'd suspect he needed the toilet.

'Spit it out, Trent.'

'I think the police are looking for you.'

'Why would the police want me?'

God, how could I forget? It's only been a few days. 'Are they asking for me by name?'

'No. They have pictures from the accident where that man fell under the bus. It was on the news again this morning, with grainy footage of someone similar to you running away, but with blonde hair. It's not clear, but I've seen you in the black hoodie you have on in the image they were showing. When I first saw the news clip, I thought it looked a bit like you but dismissed the idea. That was stupid because I've seen your blonde wig. I also know what your run is like. There's not much I don't know about you.'

I frown at that statement. Why would you say that to someone you didn't want to freak out? Nevertheless, I have bigger problems than his stalkerish behaviour.

'Were they just asking if people have seen anyone with blonde hair in those clothes?'

'Yes, they also said tall and mid-thirties.'

'I don't suppose you've got any alcohol in your flat?'

'I could get some?'

His keen little face makes me smile. I'd better not sleep with him again or I'll find him parked on my doorstep every morning with his tongue lolling out.

'Just kidding. I need to pop out anyway. It was self-defence, by the way. That man was a pervert, and he wanted to hurt me.'

'Yes, the policeman said something similar. I'd never doubt you. Seems to me he got what he deserved.'

I stare at his zealous, bulging expression. It's a shame he's such an oddball. Even so, I relax a little knowing I have someone in my corner. Perhaps I should take the pills now and not get drunk. I'll need a straight head when they find me, which I've no doubt they will, and soon. They are closing in.

'How about we watch a film at yours?' I ask.

His eyebrows hit the ceiling. 'Sure, I've got loads of movies. I've downloaded thousands. I bet you enjoy romcoms.'

'You choose. I need to do a couple of things, but I'll be around ten minutes. Put the popcorn on.'

His face falls.

'It was a joke. Just put the kettle on.'

Shaking my head, I usher him out, making sure he doesn't trip over the washing. I trust him not to say anything. I spread my pills on the table and take the doses prescribed. I hate the side effects. One of the earlier ones made my breasts bigger. It was a shame that I wanted to kill myself while I was on them. This current lot steal my appetite and confuse my memory. Are they treating me or just ensuring I'm not a danger? I can't think straight on them. It's no wonder I'm unable to hold down a decent job when I'm so forgetful.

I know I have to keep taking them. When I stopped taking them in the past, my mother would realise. She'd mention it on her daily texts and in most phone calls. Even if I still forgot, she would know. She was more than just Mum; she was also my therapist. Without her, bad Ellen has returned, but part of me loves the drama, and the ruthlessness.

Deep down, I used to think I was attracted to unsuitable men, but I'm not certain that's the complete truth. In reality, I believe I want to find someone like me. Don't birds of a feather flock together? The drugs deaden those urges, but they're still present. Perhaps I was drawn to Brad because he was fairly decent, but without my medication, he doesn't interest me enough. Is that why I spend my time with Scarlett? Am I drawn to instability?

I learnt enough in therapy to know to take the pills though. Otherwise, I self-destruct. I just need to find a new method to remind me now Mum's not here to do it for me.

I step from my flat and consider my predicament. The police will be with me soon. They'll connect the dots. Is it possible to explain everything though? Who have I killed? That girl at school or the strangled man shortly after? There's no getting away from the fact I slaughtered the three men in their house. I can deny any knowledge of the overdoses, but it's possible they'll find DNA to put me in that room. They've seen me shove Hofstadt into the road in self-defence. There are so many deaths; surely too many to explain. When does coincidence exceed reasonable doubt?

I hammer my fist on Trent's door. The thudding sound echoes in the hall. It feels like it's in my head as I try to think straight. Do the things I've done matter to me, apart from my imminent arrest? Is there any regret? I haven't been killing the innocent. The conundrum appeals to my intelligence. Trent opens up, waving a white DVD box at me.

'How about *Four Weddings and a Funeral*? Old but good, and one of your top three.'

I wryly smile and follow him in. Trust him to remember. His bedroom door is slightly open. There's a computer screen with a topless image on it. I'm just moving away with another grin, when I do a double take at the face of the model. I step inside and realise that's because it's me.

58

The next morning, Barton stepped out of the shower and strolled in just a pair of boxer shorts to his bedroom. He received a 'Phwoar!' from Holly and a 'Gross!' from Layla, who paused their argument on the landing as he passed. Layla stomped downstairs, attempting to put her foot through each step. Holly came into the room with a frown. He pulled his suit on and tried to sneak out of the room without getting involved.

'Are you going to have a word with her?'

He stopped in the doorway. 'What about?'

'Her floordrobe.'

'What the hell's one of them?'

'I read it in *Cosmo*. It's when lazy, ungrateful daughters can't be bothered to hang the clothes they don't pay for in their wardrobe. They just drop them on the floor.'

Barton's eyes strayed to the carpet of his bedroom where he tended to leave his clothes. He was tempted to say as adolescent behaviour went, it was neither unusual nor at the terrible end of the scale, but this was dangerous ground. He suspected the argument was about something else. Something he might not understand. Maybe even something he wouldn't ever understand.

A horn outside saved him.

'Kelly's here. I'll talk to Layla when I get home. Love you.'

'Wake Lawrence before you go.'

Holly's scowl deepened as he backed away. He nodded and opened his older son's door. His nose wrinkled at the smell only a young man could produce. It was gone eight o'clock, and the lad remained dead to the world. Barton pushed a lock of hair from a sweaty forehead, causing the eyelids to flicker mid-dream. Barton's dad used to bellow 'wakey wakey' in his ear to wake him up when he was a kid, which was a traumatising start to the day. He gently nudged Lawrence's shoulder.

The lad smiled sleepily until he remembered he was supposed to be a grumpy teen and rolled over with a grunt. Barton sucked his teeth. Time was up.

'Wakey wakey! Come on, son. It's nearly tomorrow.'

Grinning, he stepped down the stairs making the same noise as Layla had. He stared through the lounge window when he was outside his house. His mum was sitting with Luke on her lap. They were laughing at a cartoon.

He got in beside Strange, who pootled along his street. Her driving speed was often a reflection of what was on her mind.

'Morning, boss.'

'Morning. I assume your kind offer of a lift was to save me petrol money, not to bend my ear in a place I can't escape.'

'Of course.'

Strange then proceeded to spend the entire journey discussing her relationship with Sirena. It was a complete info-dump. She turned to him when she'd parked up at the station and raised an eyebrow. Barton couldn't remember there being a question within the previous five minutes. Experience stood him in good stead.

'The important thing is, what do you think?'

She was still talking when they got to the office. Malik passed her a note, which distracted her. While she read it, Barton sneaked into his office and closed the door. His phone rang.

'DCI Barton.'

'But what do you think?'

Barton looked through the window at Strange laughing at him, but she got down to business.

'Right, Ewing, Zelensky and Malik asked around the shops in East-field last night and we're in the right area. Are you still meeting the father at midday?'

'Yes. I could let Zander visit without me, but I have the feeling the case will break and I want to be there.'

Strange rolled her eyes at his inability to leave them to it.

'You have to trust us to do the job.'

He smiled and shrugged at the same time.

'Well, it's up to you to decide the plan this morning,' she said. 'I've got Ewing, Leicester and Malik available. Zelensky is with me for a follow-up chat. She doesn't seem any happier, but her timekeeping is much better. Do the others continue knocking on doors?'

Barton considered his options. He'd tried Deacon's mobile number many times but it was never turned on, so he wasn't confident of a result. Searching might be a waste of time, but a few hours wouldn't hurt. Sometimes people provided information you weren't even looking for.

'Yes, get them out again. We could get nothing from the father at midday. Have intel found a Sue Ellen Deacon elsewhere in the country?'

'Nope, that's a negative. We'll look for Deacons and Tooles in the city and cross-check against the date of birth. It's possible she has a different name. If we get a hit in the area, it would be promising.'

'Good idea. I'll ring you after we're done with the probation meeting. Anything else pending?'

'Nope. We're all focused on this case. I had a chat with Zander, and he feels the same. There is something we don't like about these recent deaths. I asked Leicester about it, but he didn't get what I was saying.'

Barton didn't ask what she meant, because he felt it too. Experience told him there was danger in the air.

59

THE ICE KILLER

I wake up on my sofa. I don't remember coming back from Trent's. A shower helps, but I have a pinprick of darkness in my concentration. There's a whole world out there, but all my mind wants to fixate on is this tiny dim spot. It's the medication. That's what they do. That dot will grow larger until my entire life is dark-grey. It'll take away my energy and drive. What's left will be a poor reflection of myself. No wonder nobody's drawn to me. But I try to focus on knowing this version of Ellen is safer for everyone else.

I'm hungry for a change. With little in my fridge, I venture to the shop. They're searching for a grungy blonde, so a black-haired lady in high boots and a dress steps from my house. I'm almost back at the flats with my purchases when I see Robert Ewing step from the doorway of the nearby terraces.

Most of us have one glorious affair in our lives. It's an electrifying thrill to spend time with a person who puts a thousand-watt light bulb above you. Robert was my mad love. Unfortunately, I wasn't his.

We met over four years ago. He was in uniform then – very sexy. We spent two weeks in bed with the odd break for work. I fell in a way I'd never fallen before. He oozed confidence and had so much to say. Great stories, great looks and great sex. He cut through the fuzz of my medication like no one else. Even his name was perfect. I couldn't wait to be Sue Ellen Ewing. It would have been much better than Ellen Vickerman. We told each other we loved one another, but I struggled to articulate what he meant to me. In the end, I wrote him a letter, pouring out my heart. After that, he changed.

Sex got rougher. He wanted me to do things I didn't want to do. I'm not a prude, but some of them hurt. It was as if normal sex wasn't intense enough for him. He needed it to be dirtier. Better still, degrading. When I looked back afterwards, he knew I was under his spell and he could behave as he wished.

I'd spoken to Scarlett about it. She said if I loved him, I should tolerate his demands. Maybe I'd come to enjoy the deviant things as much as he did. I decided enough was enough in the hope that a show of strength would command his respect. After a further week of my refusing his sadomasochistic requests, he disappeared.

It took a long time for me to forget about him. A couple of months doesn't seem long, but it felt as though my life hadn't started before I met him and ended when he left. Like discovering colour TV, then having to go back to black and white. I let myself down by texting him in desperation. Months later, he texted me again and a new pattern formed. Occasionally, he'd come over. We'd have a few drinks, have sex, and he'd vanish again.

The final time, I said he could do what he wanted, but he told me it was okay. He'd met someone, and they were fulfilling those needs. Who would bring that up while having sex? His work talk was peppered with a woman called Zelensky. I assumed it was her. Finding out there was someone else helped, and I finally managed to move on.

He notices me as I walk towards him.

'Ellen. Is that you?'

'Robert. Long time no see.'

'Wow, you look amazing. Are you going somewhere?'

I'm stunned by the compliment and my mind stills. 'I've been trying a new style. You know, dress fab, feel fab. That sort of thing.'

'I like it. You still live near here?'

'Yes, same flat.'

I realise my error immediately. Taking control of the conversation seems the best distraction.

'Have you left the police?'

'No, I'm a detective now. We're looking for a woman in the area. I don't suppose you've seen her.' He shows me a grainy picture of myself.

'There aren't many women with long blonde hair around here,' I joke.

'Well, it might be a wig.'

He's not concentrating on the photo and a hot flush comes over me. For a moment, I think it's fear, but it isn't. His stare always has this effect on me. His gaze is intense, but then it softens.

'I've got time for a coffee,' he says with hooded eyes.

He gives me the cheeky look that broke my heart all those years ago, and we walk towards my flat. It's a good four hundred metres away, but we're there before I know what's happening. I process the idea of it. Is having sex with him going to matter? Part of me wants it more than anything, and, with the way I am now, that side of me will win.

I'm pleased that Trent isn't leering from his window at me as I pass his flat. Next thing, Ewing and I are kissing in the hallway and up the stairs. Our lips bang against each other's in desperation. He laughs as I manage to get my key in the door. I see the place as a stranger would observe it as we barge inside.

'I like what you've done with the place, Ellen. No problem, though, my tetanus jab is in date.'

The pile of wet clothes doesn't help, or the clutter on the worktops. I watch him take a mobile phone out of each trouser pocket and put them on the table.

'I'll have a quick piss, then we'll get started.'

Did he talk to me like this before? I can't recall. Why would I tolerate being treated in this way? One of the phones lights up. He's clearly got them on silent. Is there anything dodgier than two mobile phones? I wander over and guess that he could have an extra one for work, when I notice the name of the incoming call.

Incredible! Actually, no, understandable. I don't have time to process the betrayal because he returns, having removed his tie. His aloofness irritates me further. But what did I expect was going to happen? My ardour continues to cool as he undresses me. I begin to think I'd rather have a coffee. Soon, I'm naked except for my heels. He drops his trousers, not even bothering to remove them, pushes me over the sink and thrusts inside. It's more brutal than I remember. In my current vacant state, it feels like I'm being assaulted. I turn and look back at him in pain and disgust. That always encouraged him. He slaps my thighs, hard, too hard, then pinches my arse and bares his teeth.

I feel myself detaching from the situation and going to a distant space in my head. Part of me likes the violence and wants to engage, the rest wants nothing to do with it. It's like a spinning roulette wheel, but instead of numbers there are emotions, all of which I recognise. Sadness, lust, despair, joy, loneliness and desire go round and round. The rattling ball stops and settles on rage.

With a howl of pleasure, he comes deep inside me while yanking back my hair. The wig stays attached to my head for a few seconds, then plops off, and he's holding it loose in front of him. His ecstatic laugh shatters my inertia. His face drops as he realises the implications. He couldn't be in a more vulnerable state. I grab the first thing to hand, turn, then it's me that roars.

60

ACTING DCI BARTON

Barton and Zander drove down the slope out of Thorpe Wood Station and were soon onto the A1 heading for Huntingdon probation office. Zander had rediscovered Smooth FM recently and turned it on. He belted out 'Walking in Memphis' as he weaved in and out of the congested roads.

'Not joining in, John? I'd heard your voice could stop traffic.'

'I was thinking how the years fly by.'

'Do you have to?'

'Eh?'

'I was in a good mood. Now what?'

'This morning, before I woke up Lawrence, I watched him dreaming.'

'Creepy.'

'And I realised that when you're that age, your dreams are also your hopes.'

'Please don't depress me, but go on.'

'He could have been dreaming about playing for Man United, dating the hottest girl at school, getting a job he loves, or something else brilliant that might happen in the future.'

'Maybe he was having a nightmare about a scary man in his bedroom.'

'Don't you see? When older people dream it's often about things that have happened, or things that never will. His dreams still might.'

'Speak for yourself. I'm hopeful that United will come calling.'

'They might need you to help with match-day security.'

Zander looked across at Barton. 'You're a real inspiration.'

'Thanks. I feel better now I've shared that. Thank you.'

Zander didn't know the next song, but he put the volume up so it was too loud to talk.

When they arrived at the office, Deacon's offender manager stood waiting for them. She was a lot more youthful than Barton had imagined. Nevertheless, she gave a firm handshake and briskly whisked them to an interview room where a tall, thin man with piercing eyes sat cross-legged in a seat. He appeared all legs and arms. Barton had never met a more cadaverous creature.

'This is Ted Deacon. We've had our offender meeting. He came in early, but I had the time. There are no issues from our end, and he's agreed to answer your questions.'

Barton shook his hand. It was larger than his own, but skeletal.

'I'm Detective Chief Inspector Barton, this is Detective Sergeant Zander. We'll try not to take up too much of your time, but I'd like to discuss your children.'

Deacon didn't reply, but he flinched. Sharp eyes flicked from Barton to Zander and back again. He gave a small nod. Barton continued.

'You have two children, Lucy and Sue Ellen, is that right?'

Again, a slight incline of his head.

'Can you tell me about them?'

'I don't like discussing them.'

Barton considered what leverage he had. There was plenty.

'I've driven all this way for your benefit. If you aren't going to be helpful in this environment, perhaps you'd prefer to come back to Peterborough for a few days to help us.'

The effect was immediate. Any colour in his face leached out. Barton couldn't tell if it was through anxiety or anger.

'Where do your children live?'

'I have no idea. I haven't seen them for decades. Not since I separated from their mother.'

'I'm not inclined to believe you. We're investigating suspicious deaths, possibly even murders. Your younger daughter's safety should be your concern, not trying to impede my investigation by being evasive.'

Deacon's eyes flared.

'What's this got to do with Ellen? Is she in danger?'

Zander seized on the name straight away. 'We haven't been able to locate Ellen. We're worried about her.'

It was definitely fear on the man's face this time.

'Do you have children, detectives?' said Deacon, quietly. 'My crimes meant I had to forgo any involvement in their lives. That's the thing I regret the most.'

Barton considered that titbit. Surely a normal person would regret more that they'd killed. He knew straight away that Deacon wouldn't tell them anything if he thought it was incriminating.

'Did everyone call her Ellen as opposed to Sue Ellen?'

His face lights up at the memory. 'Yes. My wife was annoyed, because she wanted both kids named after that silly programme she loved, but even she eventually called her Ellen, unless she was naughty. Ellen was always my favourite. We were similar, you know. If I'm honest, she's the one I think about the most.'

'Is she still in Peterborough?' asked Zander.

'I assume so. Her mother lived there until she died.'

'That was recently. Were you in touch?'

'Very loosely. I got the odd letter from her.'

Barton's bullshit radar sprang to life. Deacon's answers were measured, and he spoke clearly, but it sounded rehearsed.

'How was the funeral?'

'I didn't go. I told you I hadn't seen her for a long time.'

Barton stood and gestured for Zander to step out of the room.

'I'd just like to chat with my colleague for a minute, Mr Deacon. Bear with me.'

When they were outside, he asked Zander what he was thinking.

'He's lying.'

'I agree, but about what? Hang on.'

Barton rang Strange on his mobile, who answered immediately.

'We believe she's going by the name of Ellen,' he said. 'See if that helps with the searching, but nothing more this end. Anything yours?'

'Brilliant. We could have done with that information earlier, but that confirms what Intel have just told me. They've searched using dates of birth and combinations of names. They found an Ellen Vickerman, lives right in the middle of the target area at Monument Square. It's got to be her, even though she has black hair on her licence. I was picking up the phone to ring you when I received a call from Control. ANPR cameras have picked up the sister's car moving at speed. She's racing up the A1 as we speak.'

'Gotcha.'

'Yep. If she's on her way here, she'll drive past Huntingdon. You'll be able to follow her up the A1. I'll get traffic to monitor her progress when she enters Cambridgeshire.'

'Good idea. Let's see if she's alone.'

'We don't need to worry about that too much. It can only be a sisters' reunion, and we now know where she lives.'

Barton smiled. That was good thinking. 'We're nearly finished here. The father has been as helpful as the sister. We'll drive on ahead and park down the road from Ellen's. I've a suspicion this investigation is going to take a weird turn. Her dad is a peculiar individual, whereas you said the sister was normal.'

'Normal but criminal. She lied to the police by saying she didn't know Ellen's location. At best, that's obstruction. At worst, it's assisting an offender.'

'That's true. We could arrest them both, but we're not sure what Ellen's done, so chances are her sister might not either.'

'Agreed, and we can't afford to make any mistakes with the sister and her husband, seeing as they're solicitors.'

'Fabulous. You kept that quiet.'

'They aren't criminal solicitors, so it didn't seem important before.'

'Get someone to cover the property without being seen.'

'Okay. The team aren't too far away. I'd just sent them on their lunch. I'll ring Ewing and ask him to stand out of sight of the property. If I remember the road right, there's a car park out front and that's the only entrance and exit point. We'll know if she leaves or arrives.'

Barton finished the call and rubbed his temples while he updated Zander.

'Excellent work from Strange. She'd make a good DI,' said Zander.

He looked for sarcasm in Zander's expression, but there wasn't any.

'I want a few more questions with Deacon,' said Barton.

They trudged back in. The offender manager and Deacon were laughing about last night's TV. She smiled at Barton, but Deacon's face dropped to a mask, with only the piercing eyes showing any interest. Barton returned Deacon's stare. Probation wouldn't be happy if he set Deacon off with harsh questioning. The man's gaze was unsettling, to say the least.

'Mr Deacon, I'm going to be blunt because it's important. You killed two people while you were out of your mind. Aren't you worried it'll happen again, and would you even know if you had relapsed?'

Barton often used the disarming qualities of a double question. Deacon looked away as he processed them.

'I haven't killed anyone lately, if that's what you're starting to think. The medication makes me drowsy and disinterested in others' affairs. In fact, I've only left Huntingdon once in the last year and that was to find out why the letters stopped coming from my ex-wife. A neighbour told me she'd died, and I came home. I've paid the price for being ill and then some. It wasn't my fault. I didn't go mad, I was sick. There's a difference, and it begs the question about whether people should be jailed for how they were made. They treated me, and now I'm fine.'

'So you're cured?'

'No, Inspector. People with conditions such as mine generally have them for life. The illness is not fixed, it's managed by a mixture of things, mostly by medication.'

Barton gazed out of the window for a moment and tried to recollect what he'd learned. If these deaths were murders, it would probably be someone not in their right mind.

'What happens if you stop taking the drugs? I understand doing that is common with certain mental-health issues,' he asked.

Hard eyes bored into Barton's, but then Deacon smiled and his face relaxed.

'You're well informed. I have relapsed a couple of times and bad things happened, but I'll never do it again. I'm in control of my life with regular therapy, support groups, my probation visits here and a regime set up to ensure that I don't ever fail. Trust me, taking my pills is never far from my mind. I focus on it all day long.'

The Offender Manager showed them to the door. Deacon said goodbye but didn't rise or smile as Barton and Zander left. They got in the car, and drove to the motorway Lucy would be driving up. Barton rang Control to receive the details of Lucy's vehicle. They informed him she was travelling alone in a red Range Rover and had passed a patrol car as she approached the outskirts of Huntingdon. Barton decided there was no point in waiting. They had an address now. He'd drive there and formulate a plan. He finished the call.

'Right, let's go to Ellen Vickerman's house,' said Barton. 'I'm interested in having a conversation with this woman. She's going to need quite a performance if she hopes to be free after it.'

'I had a twenty-three-stone strongman shout abuse in my face last month, but that guy worried me way more,' said Zander.

'Yes, me too. It's scary that he's out there, potentially a few missed tablets from killing someone. But what's the alternative? He completed his sentence, and they deemed him fit for release. It'd be inhumane to keep him locked up when he's served his time and isn't a threat.'

Zander tutted. 'Not to mention unlawful. It can be a strange world that we operate in. Feels like it's just a matter of when, because who doesn't have wobbles from time to time? I've got extra respect for the probation service. Wait a minute. Did you say Ellen Vickerman? Wasn't that the surname of one of the two guys who overdosed?'

'Shit, you're right. What does that mean?'

'Was she related, or even married to him?'

'My head's spinning,' said Barton. 'I had a feeling she'd be the link to everything. That's seven people dead, and she's the connection. We should be ready for anything.'

'Didn't Mortis say the overdoses might be suspicious?'

'Yes, due to the amount of fentanyl that was used.'

'Ah, maybe someone deliberately gave them too much. Perhaps Ellen did it and killed her own husband.'

61

Robert's eyes focus on mine in disbelief. I daren't break the connection, but I'm aware of the scissor handles protruding from his neck in my peripheral vision. He gargles, and a thin trickle of blood comes out of the side of his mouth. His eyes roll back in his head, and he topples over. I close my eyes for the crash, but there isn't one. He's dropped onto my wet washing with a thump.

It's a shocking moment. I hold the worktop for support, wondering what the hell is wrong with me. I crouch beside his gruesome open-mouthed expression. He's definitely dead, but there's surprisingly little blood with the scissors still in place.

I spot about ten drips, and a big splatter, which probably came from his mouth, and a bit of spray on a cabinet door. I grab the nearest thing to hand in a panic, the knickers he just pulled off me, and clean the tiles. There's a dribble of semen, which must have leaked from me. A benefit of third-floor living is you can hear who's approaching. I'm frantically scrubbing when slow, tentative footsteps come up the stairs.

I freeze, only my eyes rising from my sick task to the handle of my unlocked door. The steps stop outside. I wonder if the sound of the knock will stop my heart, but instead the handle turns.

Scarlett staggers into the room. Her top lip is raised into a ready-for-action snarl.

'Where the bloody hell were you last night?' she says.

It takes a few seconds for her to take in the scene. It's not every day you see your friend naked in high heels mopping up blood beside a dead man with trousers around his ankles.

'Not interrupting anything, am I?' she asks with evident joy.

She steps towards the body. The waft of excessive perfume stings my eyes.

'Jesus, is that Robert Ewing?'

I grab some jeans, fresh underwear, and a jumper, and stand next to her. 'How do you know him, Scarlett?'

She waves her hand dismissively. 'Tim knows him.'

Not a bad lie on the hoof, but she doesn't know that I saw her name flash up on one of Ewing's mobile phones not long before she arrived.

She pauses for a microsecond before grinning at my predicament. 'This will take some explaining.'

'Help me. What should I do?'

I hardly recognise Scarlett as her cold mind runs through her options. Yes, hers, not mine. How can this situation work for her? Even though I'm stunned by what I've done, a piece of the rage responsible remains and it turns its focus towards Scarlett. I realise, without a shadow of doubt, that she'd sacrifice me without a second thought if it helped her cause.

'It's quid pro quo,' she finally says. 'That's something for something, and we know what I need from you.'

Part of me recoils in horror as I understand her price. Robert was morally corrupt, but he didn't deserve to die. Tim is a terrible man, but it still isn't right. Yet, I don't want to go to prison. Should I hold up my hands and admit my mistakes? I yank my clothes on, thinking that as the body count rises my chances of a future crumble.

'Jesus!'

Scarlett and I turn together towards the voice at the doorway. It's Trent with his hand over his mouth.

'What happened?' he asks me in disbelief. 'Are you okay?'

'He attacked me. I defended myself.'

Suspicion passes over his face. But he makes his choice.

'Don't worry, Ellen. I could hear him hurting you. I'm sure he deserved it. What are you going to do?'

'How sweet,' says Scarlett. 'Will you help me with my problem, Ellen?'

'You already owe me.'

'What for?'

'The girl at school. You pushed her out that window. It was no accident.'

Her expression drops long enough for me to guess it's true. She shrugs, then smiles. 'That's the spirit. Show some balls. Yes, I did, and I don't regret it. We got away with it, didn't we?'

'You got away with it. I hadn't done anything. That might have been the incident which made me lose my mind. That guilt weakened me until today. I carried it when you should have.'

I stop shouting and lower my shoulders. There's a look of worry in Scarlett's eyes, then she responds in kind, and her face twists in anger.

'Well. Now we're both killers. I, too, am ruthless. Do you want my help or not?'

I slowly nod.

'Does anyone know he was here?'

I shake my head.

'I wasn't here,' says Trent, backing away.

'Stop, Trent. I need you to help. You always said you'd do anything for me,' I say.

'No, I can't get involved with something like this. Sorry.'

'Wait. I saw a picture of me on your computer last night.'

He stops and looks as guilty as I do.

'That's right. Superimposing your neighbour's face onto hard-porn pictures won't go down well with the police. Shut the door. We need help to get the body out of here. That's all.'

Trent finally nods. I am the most important thing in his life. Scarlett stares at him with disgust. We put three pillowcases over Robert's head and slide his body into a duvet cover. Scarlett wraps an entire roll of Sellotape around it, giving it the look of a mummy. She gives Trent her car keys, and he reverses the Qashqai up to the door. Trent and I struggle downstairs with the body, and place it in the boot. We rush upstairs and shove the blood-stained washing in a bin bag. Trent takes it downstairs.

Strangely, it doesn't feel that weird, more like we're doing a job together. I expect the guilt will come later. Scarlett grabs my arm and laughs into my face.

'Who is that weirdo?'

Alcohol fumes drench me. 'He's my neighbour. He's mad about me.'

I took a photo of the offending image Trent had made of me last night, but didn't mention it. I had no energy for arguing, and it was pretty flattering in a way. The pills haven't completely kicked in because I'm having conflicting thoughts within moments of each other. Surely, I'd be horrified normally. What is clear is that if a person's worth is reflected in their friends, then I'm in deep trouble.

'Can we trust him?' she asks.

I give her a sad smile. 'Absolutely.'

'Does he understand what a dangerous person you are to know?'

'Scarlett, what are we planning to do with Robert?'

She's been thinking about it already because she answers straight away.

'There's a tunnel drain on the next field behind ours. We lost a ball in the stream once and it floated inside. Tim waded in and found it halfway along against some bars next to a rotten dead fox. We'll dump him in the same spot for the time being. You be at mine in a few days when this has calmed down and we'll think of something permanent, after we've discussed your debt to me.'

Scarlett winks at me and steps to the door.

'Don't you want me to come?' I whisper after her.

She shakes her head in disbelief. Then points to a small splatter of blood up the side of the kitchen units. 'You should clear up in here. And what about them?'

My eyes follow her pointed finger and see Robert's two mobile phones on the table. One of them is ringing. The caller ID says 'Strange' on it.

'What do I do?' I ask.

'You're resourceful and you enjoy detective shows. Now's the chance for you to put what you've learnt to use. I'll take the phones. Do I need to turn them off?'

Her voice slurs the last word. I don't relish the thought of relying on her. Trent, on the other hand, I trust.

'Wait until you've driven from here,' I reply. 'It'll look as though he's gone elsewhere. Then throw them down a drain somewhere, but make sure they won't be found. Take the back roads so they can't trace your car with the camera network.'

'This is quite exciting.'

'Should you be driving?'

'That's the least of your concerns.'

She's right. In fact, her crashing the car and dying with Trent would probably be a bonus.

Barton and Zander arrived back in Peterborough and headed towards Eastfield and the younger sister's address. Zander pointed out Malik and Leicester outside a café. They drove a few streets further down and parked in a space fifty metres from the Monument Square flats where they could see who pulled in. If Ewing was nearby, he was out of sight. Barton grabbed his phone.

'There's Zelensky,' said Zander.

Barton frowned as she shuffled towards them. She had a tiny frame, but even so her clothes hung on her narrow shoulders. He poked his head out of the window.

'Afternoon.'

She shivered and merely nodded at him.

'Get in for a minute, please.'

She didn't need asking twice and let out a great exhale as she slumped on the back seat and huddled into her coat. Barton studied her for a moment. It was cold outside, but she still looked really pasty.

'Everything all right?'

'Not particularly.'

Barton wasn't sure what to say to that. 'Did you hear we have an address?'

'Yes, I knew we were in the correct area. An old man I spoke to earlier had seen her over the last few days. Good legs, he said.'

'An unmarked car is behind the sister and she'll be here in a few minutes.'

'Yeah, I've been informed. Strange was looking for Ewing, said he wasn't answering his phone. I told her to ring Malik because he was probably having lunch with him.'

Barton picked up on the tension in her voice. 'Why didn't you eat with the others? We just saw them coming out of the café.'

'I don't want to be anywhere near Ewing.'

Barton sensed Zander tense next to him.

'Have you had another falling out?' asked Barton.

Barton watched in the rear-view mirror as she stared at the back of Zander's head. She decided it didn't matter who heard.

'Thanks for encouraging me to get friendly with Robert, sir. I gave him another chance. He started off telling me how much he loved me, and how great we were together. He has a strange idea of what a loving relationship is, the depraved bastard. We're having a meal at Nando's and I have the impression that people are staring at us. When Robert went to the toilet, a girl came over and told me to steer clear of that creep.'

Her face flushed as she recalled the moment.

'I asked why. The girl, who looked about nineteen, said he'd slept or tried to sleep with loads of her friends while he was with her. She'd seen him in town with another girl only a few days before. It's the same routine for all of us. He's dead keen, and then he gets dirty. Once he's pushed you as far as you'll go, he dumps you and moves on to his next conquest.'

Barton cringed. 'Sorry about that. I thought he was a decent officer.'

'He is, but he's a shit person.'

'Did you tell him you knew?'

'I asked the girl to wait until he came back. His face was a picture when he returned. It would have been funny if he hadn't legged it and left me to pay the bill.'

Zander choked down a strange sound. This was why work relationships were tough. They needed a level of maturity that some people didn't have. Break-ups always led to bad feeling as the locker room tended to split. Sometimes a transfer was the only solution.

'We've got enough bodies on hand if you want to go back to the station.'

'No, I'm staying. What's the plan?'

Barton tutted. 'Well, Strange said she was going to get Leicester and Ewing to park up here, but where is he?'

'He's not picking up,' said Zelensky. 'She left a message for him, but he didn't return the call. She asked me to come instead.'

'Okay, let's see what happens. We'll soon find out if this is the sister's destination. She can't be far away,' said Zander.

Barton's phone lit up with a call from Malik at the shops.

'We're on the way, boss. Red Range Rover just driven by, turning left onto Monument Street.'

'Okay, wait just before the car park. I think I'm going to let the sister go in.'

Barton cut the call as the Range Rover pulled into the car park for the flats. Lucy stepped cautiously from the expensive vehicle. She took some deep breaths and straightened her shoulders. Then she marched to the entrance and pushed open the communal door.

'Those two sisters are coming down the station with us shortly, but I've a mind to let them talk first,' said Barton.

'Why? So they can get their stories straight?' asked Zander.

'I'm not 100 per cent sure Ellen is the enemy, and I'm pretty certain Lucy isn't. Let's look at the facts. There's the strangulation of that man twenty years ago, who had Ellen's skin under his fingernails. She may be tall, but he was a nasty criminal. Would she be capable of that? Those three deaths could be many things, but a lone woman super-killer seems unlikely, even if they did rape her. The overdoses are a little suspicious, but the only thing we really have her for is throwing Hofstadt under a bus. With the eyewitnesses and his history, no jury would convict on that.'

'That showed some strength even if he was an oldish man,' said Zander.

Barton scratched his neck. 'True. Fear makes you stronger.'

'Actually, you're right. It's worth waiting for a bit to see what they do. Anyone normal would be panicking if they're guilty. They might do something incriminating.'

'We get a lot of people who fail to report rapes at the time. What's your feeling?' asked Barton to Zelensky in the back.

'I'm not sure. The public don't have 100 per cent belief in the police getting it right. If you'd killed the perpetrators, you'd worry that it was you who'd end up in prison. Why don't we arrest and charge her?'

Barton nodded at her perceptive reply.

'Remember double jeopardy. The CPS and I don't think we have enough at the moment. If we take her to court and she walks, we don't get to have another go. This is going to be a case where what we think will be unimportant. We must focus on what we can prove.'

'I thought the double jeopardy rules were watered down, so you could try one more time.'

'That's only in extremely rare cases and usually through advances with DNA evidence. That doesn't apply here because we know she was present. She's the last person to know what happened. I fear Ellen's unstable, even though she is intelligent, so she may unravel. Or we'll get the information from her. This is the toughest part of the job. Sometimes we have to let them make a mistake to make sure we get the right verdict at trial.'

'Think of Twelvetrees, that Royal Marine with the postwoman. He's unbalanced and would be safer receiving the right treatment at the right place. Instead, we'll probably see him again at the scene of a crime.' said Zander.

'Let's hope it isn't the scene of a murder.' said Zelensky.

Barton stared at his white knuckles on the steering wheel. Was that what they were waiting for? They'd up surveillance now, but Barton could sense that a resolution was coming. Ellen was also a victim and not a hardened criminal. He would find a way into the truth, as long as she talked to him.

'Let's give them half an hour,' said Barton. 'If we stomp in as soon as she arrives, they'll know we've been tracking Lucy. If we go in guns blazing, she'll tell Ellen to say nothing, which doesn't help our case.'

'What about the mental-health angle?' asked Zander. 'What if she inherited her father's psychotic rage? Who else might she have harmed?'

'What if she did kill the three rapists?' said Zelensky. 'You could argue that she struck out in self-defence. Those men were pretty worthless creatures. Who knows what they did to her? A jury wouldn't convict for murder, no way.'

'The prosecution will have a different view of things if she killed them,' said Barton. 'The law is only on your side in that regard if you have no other options. It's hard to prove you needed to kill someone if you could have run away.'

'Maybe she couldn't have escaped?'

'Three times? I doubt it.'

'Fair enough.' Zelensky clenched her jaw. 'If Ewing turns up, he can go in first. He could do with some summary justice.'

Barton smiled, but his mind was on what was occurring in that top flat. He recalled the warning from Mortis. He needed this Ellen to talk, or they might never know what happened, because dead men don't tell tales.

I remember watching an episode of *Criminal Minds* that had the police looking for signs of blood spillage. I frantically pull out the multitude of cleaning products I seem to have accumulated over the years. There are two types of bleach, good old washing-up liquid, and I even use the steam cleaner afterwards. I sit back on my heels and stare at the rest of the small lounge-diner. The furniture looks unkempt, frayed around the edges and worn. It's like me – unloved. And lonely.

My ears twitch at the sound of a big car pulling up, then I hear someone else climbing the steps. It's a rarity for anyone to lock that communal door at the bottom. Trent leaves it open, or otherwise people tap on his window. The rap at my own door is light and fast. Do the police knock like that? At least it's secured now, so they'll have to kick it in. While I wait for the thin wood to splinter, it finally sinks in what I've done. How have I come to be casually cleaning the surfaces of blood from a man I murdered? Should I be pleased there are people helping me clear up the aftermath, or just horrified?

'Ellen, let me in.'

As soon as I hear her voice, I wrench the door open in relief. Lucy bites her bottom lip as her eyes roam over my haunted face.

'What is it? What happened?' she asks.

I reach for her but my hands freeze and shrink back towards my body. My mouth makes a sound, but it turns into a wail. It's a cry for what I've become. Deep down, there's even a sense it was my destiny. She takes off her handbag, closes the door, and envelops me in a hug.

'Talk to me. I saw what happened to you on TV, but my husband's ill with this flu going around. I came as soon as I could,' she says. 'Why didn't you ring me?'

She looks close to tears. I barely know her husband, Greg, but try to sympathise. I'm tempted to tell her about Robert's drooping eyes as he died, but the intelligent part of my brain is still running in the background. That needs to be my secret. It's time I spoke to a professional and got back on track to where I'm not a danger. In the unlikely event that I get away with everything, that is. I open my mouth, but can't think of where to start. Lucy smiles and sees the sink full of water and the marigolds on the side.

'Come on, let's clean and talk.' She slips off her two-inch heels and pulls on the gloves. 'You dry.'

As we work, I tell her the rest. She knows Vickerman was my boyfriend back then and that I took his name. I mention Wee Jock's death all those years ago and how I think it might have been me who killed him. She frowns, hesitates, then seems to change her mind. She finally talks.

'After you disappeared, we hired someone, and they found you outside an address near the town centre. You'd had some kind of episode. We drove you straight to a doctor that Greg knew from university and he said you needed residential care. We wanted to help you.'

'By putting me in a mental asylum.'

'It was a private hospital, and very expensive. Greg and I paid for it, not Mum.'

'Did you know they found someone dead in the back garden of that address?'

'It was a rough area, any number of people could have done that, and it's time to move on. That was a long time ago and is best forgotten.'

She answers too fast, and it doesn't ring true, but I'm distracted by the revelation of their kindness. If I'd known it was them and not Mum who put up the money for my healthcare, maybe I'd have been nicer to her. But if she wanted to help me, why was she so distant when I recovered? My ongoing care was with the NHS, not someone like BUPA.

'Why did you keep me at arm's length for all these years? I've been so alone.'

She takes a deep breath. 'You were supposed to continue with your appointments. You attended sporadically, at best. We couldn't afford to carry on indefinitely. We registered you with a GP but by then you were displaying the same commitment to taking your medicine as you were the appointments. You turned up at our house once, but luckily we were out.'

'You should have helped me.'

'I had two children. We had to put them first. They were toddlers, and I couldn't cope with anything else.'

I'm ready to argue back, then see how wrong I'd be. I shouldn't be around children. Perhaps I should be alone, just like my dad.

'Didn't you miss us, though, Lucy?'

'Of course, I thought about you and Mum all the time. But we were so busy with the kids and the business. Greg's parents had died and you know Mum rarely went outside, so we had to do everything ourselves.'

That was true. Mum was agoraphobic. I used to believe that meant she was afraid to leave the house, but it's actually a type of anxiety disorder where she feared being in places from which escape was difficult. Home was the only place she felt safe. Once supermarkets started delivering groceries, she rarely set foot outside the front door again. If I wanted to see her, I usually had to go around her house. An alarm bell rings in my head.

'Wait a minute. You said that Mum continued to visit Dad even after he was sent down. How did she manage that with her condition?'

'I challenged her on it. She said our father had a strange hold on her. Even after years had passed, she felt compelled to help and stay in touch with him. That urge to remain part of his life, even in a small way, was strong enough to override her irrational fears. You know there were no more men in her life. Even though in the end they only communicated by letter, she died still loving him.'

It sounds odd to me, but then maybe our entire family is mental. I wonder what's wrong with Lucy, although it would have to be pretty bad to be worse than Dad and me. Cutting your family out is cold, though. I get the impression she doesn't have much of a life of her own.

'Did you know I used to visit where Mum told me that Dad's ashes were scattered in the cemetery to be close to him?' I say. 'I would chat to him about my problems, and it made me feel better. It was as though I had someone who understood me and didn't judge. Like he was a presence in my corner when things were tough.'

Lucy takes my hand. 'I'm so sorry, but I'm back now. My children are at university, with Carrie studying in America, so I can be here for you. We'll get you right. Our practice is doing well and we will pay for whatever needs doing. Please finish your story.'

I stare at my hands. She apologises for the years of hurt and deceit in the same manner as someone who is ten minutes late for a meeting, but I continue with my tale. I tell her that my life was empty, and I hated myself. That I visited The Hartley pub to find answers and ended up back at Quantrill's house. I explain how they attacked me and describe how they died. Her considerate expression drops, so I rush on.

The urge for honesty wavers as I see how deadly my life has become. I say how I headed to Vickerman's place two weeks later, which was only a few houses up from Quantrill's, yet can't bring myself to mention what I did to them. Instead, I pretend they wanted to take this new drug, but I declined and left. She doesn't look overly bothered hearing about their overdose. I finish by telling her how I bumped into Hofstadt in the street, who lost it and tried to kill me. She knows how that ended.

She hugs me again, although not as tight as before. That's a lot of rotten luck for one person, even if she believes what I've said, and I haven't mentioned Robert. I don't hug her as hard in return, either. It's as though my lies have weakened me. I'm sick of the deceit. Her mind struggles to process all she's heard, and she looks out of the window at the cemetery. The lines on her top lip and cheeks are highlighted. They're fine, but it could almost be our mother standing there deep in thought.

'It's only a matter of time before the police find me. What should I tell them?' I say.

My sister is quiet as we move into the bathroom and start cleaning in there. I'm embarrassed by how filthy it is. Then she talks as a solicitor would, and I listen. She makes me repeat what she's said. She questions me and goes over it again. She takes my arm.

'The police came to see me at my house. I told them I didn't know where you were, but I don't think they believed me. My first thought was to come here, but I suspected they were parked down the street and waiting for me to leave. That's why I didn't ring and waited. If they ask, I haven't seen you since we spoke briefly at the funeral.'

I raise my eyebrows. The police can track cars nowadays. If they were suspicious, they may have tracked her today. I get my sister to collect all the cleaning material and put it in a carrier bag, while I walk to the bedroom, the only room we haven't cleaned, and look out from behind a curtain. The street seems normal. I grab the bag from Lucy and open the lounge window. I lean out and swing it back and forth. When it has enough momentum, I let go, and it flies towards the cemetery fence and precariously sits on top of it. With my heart in my mouth, I watch the contents settle and gasp as it slides over the other side.

I decide to go downstairs to see if there's anyone in the car park. If not, I need to get out of here and find time to practise my story. Should I hand myself in if they don't arrive? The car park is clear. I've almost pulled the door closed when I notice two large men, one black, one white, and a small blonde woman leave a car in the distance and march in my direction. As an afterthought, I remove my phone, turn it off, post it through Trent's letter box and run up the stairs.

My sister has the kettle on.

'They're here,' I say.

'Everything will be all right, Ellen. Remember what I said. Our father cursed us with many things, but he gave us intelligence. Together we can get away with this.'

It's another strange phrase, but this time the knock on the door makes it vibrate in its frame.

64

ACTING DCI BARTON

Barton sent Zelensky around the back of the flats to make sure there was no fire escape or another way out. When Zelensky returned to confirm there wasn't, she, Zander, and Barton, went inside and up the stairs. Zander gave the door a firm rap. They weren't expecting Lucy to open the door and ask them to come in. Barton hadn't met either sister, but the family resemblance was obvious.

'Hello, Lucy,' Barton said. 'I see you managed to find your sister after all.'

Lucy stepped forward and put her hand out. He contemplated it for a second and decided manners cost nothing. She raised an eyebrow at him. She had sharp green eyes like her father that spoke of a quick mind. They weren't too far from the level of his. He resisted the urge to look down as he'd heard the click of her high heels.

'This is my sister, Ellen, Inspector Barton. The one you've been looking for.'

The detectives entered and saw a noticeably younger woman in the kitchen. She was also thin and tall, even in trainers. Her expression as she shook their hands was similar to her sister's but harder. The green of her eyes was a lighter, almost unnatural shade that Barton found hard to pull his gaze from.

'We've been searching for you. Didn't you see the TV appeals?'

'I haven't seen any, but that's probably because I haven't been well. The bus attack was traumatic. In fact, there's been a lot of shocking incidents lately, and I've struggled to cope. I have some issues with my mental health, which has even stopped me going to work. We lost our mother recently, too.'

Barton probed for an undercurrent of deceit but couldn't detect one. There was a seriousness around both women that was unsettling. He had a sense of not having the upper hand and so he sought to regain it.

'Let's start with Lucy not informing us of Ellen's whereabouts. That's an offence in itself.'

'I feel it's fair to warn you that I'm a solicitor, Mr Barton,' said Lucy. 'Not a criminal one, but the basics are taught through university, and I am well read. I don't recall your officer ordering me to reveal her location. Even if you did, the police have a terrible reputation for dealing with people with mental-health issues. I'm sure I could find many examples of you locking them in cells with no support or medication. I suspect there have been suicides in such cases.'

Barton didn't know exactly what questions Strange had asked her. To a certain degree it was immaterial. Getting a prosecution for it would be unlikely, especially since Lucy was correct.

'Besides,' she continued, 'Ellen hasn't been charged with a criminal offence, or any offence for that matter. She has a clean record. The newspaper reports of the incident with the bus include eye witnesses that will say it was self-defence.'

'There's been more than one incident,' said Zander. 'I find it hard to believe that Ellen wasn't aware of the deaths of the other people she was acquainted with.'

'She's told you she doesn't watch the news and has been housebound. Do the CPS have a new category of offence called burying your head in the sand? However, she wants to help as much as she can. I was about to give you a ring to see how we could assist your enquiries.'

Zelensky let out a 'hmm' and was silenced by a stern glance from Barton.

'There are many questions we have for both of you,' said Barton.

Lucy gestured to the table with a hand. 'Why don't you take a seat?'

Barton hid his smile by gazing around the room. They were dealing with someone bright and trained in the legal profession. He checked the living area to see if anything looked unusual. Nothing did. It was clean and tidy and smelled fresh. The washing up next to the sink was considerable, as though it had been left to pile up or multiple people had eaten.

'Do you live here alone, Ellen?'

'Yes, she does.'

'I think Ellen can answer for herself.'

Lucy's jaw bunched, but she nodded.

'Yes, I do,' said Ellen.

'These are one-bedroom flats, aren't they? Do you mind if I look around?'

He turned on his heel and had pushed the bedroom door open before they had a chance to reply. There were clothes and shoes all over the floor. He recalled his daughter's bedroom and wondered if Layla was destined to still have a floordrobe when she was Ellen's age. The bathroom was dated but spotless.

'Happy?' asked Lucy, who had followed him.

'Yes. I'm pleased you're being so helpful. We'll drive you down to the police station and take a statement from both of you.'

'Is that necessary? We'd rather do it here in the comfort of my sister's home.'

'I expect you would, but no. The conversation will be recorded there. I'm cautioning you now as what you say may be given in evidence. There's free legal advice at the station for your sister if you have other plans.'

'Very funny. And if we refuse? It's not like we're under arrest.'

Barton respected Lucy's approach. She was searching for information by her open questions, while also trying to appear accommodating. He now knew that Ellen had mental-health issues, which meant he would need to be careful how he progressed. The Twelvetrees case was a good example of the danger of locking individuals up without the correct support.

'You said you wanted to help,' said Barton.

'We do.'

'This is how you do it. If you decline, I'm happy to arrest you both. I probably will do at the station because people have died. Me not cuffing her is based on your cooperation. It's highly likely Ellen will need to appear before the courts to explain what occurred during the Hofstadt incident. At the minimum there will be an inquest by the coroner's office. And that's before we find out what happened in the other situations we know she's involved in.'

He turned to Zelensky. 'You go back with the others. Zander and I will drive these helpful citizens back to the station. Ellen, Lucy, do you have any questions before we leave?'

Ellen shook her head. Lucy grabbed her coat and returned to stand in front of Barton.

'I've spoken to Ellen and told her to tell you everything she's told me. We want to put these terrible events behind us and move on.'

'I'd appreciate that.'

'However, I've told her not to say anything without me present.'

Barton couldn't prevent a flicker of anger from passing over his face, but Ellen stared in his eyes as she walked past and said, 'The truth will shock you.'

65

ACTING DCI BARTON

Barton and Zander shared a glance as they descended the stairs. It was a strange situation. Malik and Leicester had been waiting outside in case of something unexpected. Barton watched as Ellen drew stares from the younger officers. There was a willowy grace to her that he'd rarely encountered.

'Change of plan,' said Barton. 'Leicester and Zelensky, you escort the sisters to Thorpe Wood Station and get them a coffee in one of the interview rooms. We'll follow. Malik, wait for a moment.'

After the sisters were out of earshot, Zander smiled at Barton.

'Did that seem weird to you?' he asked.

'Yes, somewhat. It felt a bit like I was playing a game but didn't know the rules. But they'll be on our turf now.'

'We're going to separate them, right?'

'No, I don't think so. Let's discuss it on the way. Malik, where's Ewing?'

'I've got no idea. He texted me about an hour before lunch, saying something had popped up.'

'You mean cropped up?'

'Who knows what he meant? He was supposed to meet us at the

café and never showed. I've rung him a few times, but it rang out and went to voicemail. He had a test drive booked for a new car this afternoon, so he might have gone there.'

'Great. It sounds like he's sloped off early. If you get hold of him, tell him to return to the station. I want everyone's paperwork done, especially witness statements from those present at the fatal RTC. Then we'll have a meeting after I've spoken to Ellen and Lucy.'

Barton got into Zander's car.

'It sounds as if Ewing is a bit of a Romeo,' said Zander.

'Love toad is a better description. Did you know Strange and I encouraged Zelensky to give him another chance?'

'Ouch.'

'Yes. Right, that can't be helped. I think we interview the sisters together, seeing as they've said they're going to talk, but I'll check with CPS. They've had time to concoct a story if that's what they want to do, but you and me have heard enough lies to spot that.'

'They are smart, but we need to be smarter.'

'Correct. This is where we prove our worth. I think they will be overconfident. We can always interview them individually afterwards. If we split them up now, they'll get the best solicitors, and we might end up with nothing.'

'Good call, especially considering the evidence we have is inconclusive. Besides, Ellen has mental-health issues, so we'd need to provide an appropriate adult anyway. How about getting Strange to do the interview with you? Have a woman's perspective. She's the most recently qualified of us to do interviews at this level, and she might also be immune to Ellen's charms.'

Barton was happy to try any angle, and that seemed a good idea.

'I agree.' Barton grumbled with frustration. 'Bloody hell. This is starting to get to me. Ellen could say what she likes to a certain degree and there's nobody left to give another version of events. Let's hope she tells the truth, because Cox has been gone a while and we've barely solved a thing since I was in charge.'

'That's what happens,' said Zander with a cheeky look. 'You do a great job and keep getting promoted until you finish in a role where you're out of your depth.'

Barton put his foot down on the parkway. He had a sinking feeling this case would define his career.

Before conducting the interview, Barton rang the CPS solicitor to clarify what they'd need before charging. When Barton had finished explaining everything, the solicitor put him on hold. She returned without enthusiasm.

'Apologies for that, I was double-checking with a colleague. I hate to use a cliché, but this is a real can of worms. We could charge her with manslaughter for the bus, but that's not the case we're interested in. People have been killed in those other incidents, and we have no idea what's occurred. We need that woman to tell us what she knows. Sweet-talk her if necessary. You can always come down hard later, but right now we're whistling in the wind.'

Barton frowned as he deciphered the avalanche of clichés but got the message. He cut the call and took the stairs to the interview suite where Strange was waiting. He briefed her, and she was as intrigued as he was. They entered Room Two and pulled up chairs in front of the sisters.

He warned Ellen and Lucy that, while they were not under arrest, they were under caution, which he repeated. He also reminded them that the interview was being recorded and they could request other legal advice at any point. Zander was watching the feed in another room. Barton would tolerate Lucy's presence, because it was Ellen's story he wanted. Besides, it wouldn't be much different from a criminal solicitor being present.

Barton remembered his first murder case where they'd suspected the woman had killed her husband. Barton had wanted to go in guns blazing and beat her down with facts and suppositions, wielded with righteous fury. It had been DCI Naeem who suggested he say nothing and learn.

She said you get one chance at the first interview. If they're happy with no solicitor present, then it's a great opportunity. Best practice is to keep it relaxed, put the subject at ease, and let them tell their version of events. And then you keep them talking and talking, for as long as possible. Few can maintain their performance over many hours. The answers they give may well be the only holes the Crown's prosecutor finds. Strange smiled at Ellen.

'What do you have to tell us?'

Ellen's wide eyes watered. Barton felt a twinge of pity as a tear rolled down her cheek. Lucy put a hand on her sister's.

'Where would you like me to start?' said Ellen.

'Maybe from the beginning.'

After a deep breath, those cool eyes blinked a few times, and she began.

'I slipped off the rails a bit during the last few years at school and started hanging around with the wrong crowd. I think it's important that I tell you I'm attracted to unsuitable men. They seem to be able to pick up on my vulnerabilities and take advantage. A man called Carl Quantrill took my virginity in a brutal manner when I was eighteen. It wasn't rape, but it wasn't far off.'

'This is the same Carl Quantrill who died with his housemates recently,' said Strange.

'That's right. It messed me up further. I ended up in a destructive relationship with an older man called James Vickerman. He got me hooked on class A drugs, regularly hit me, made me steal for him, and finally made me change my name to his when I had no idea what was going on. He was tangled up with all manner of bad types, and I can't remember much for most of that time. I got concussed when he threw me down a flight of stairs in a shopping centre. Even then, he wouldn't let me go to hospital.'

'It sounds like you had a tough start to life,' stated Strange.

Barton noticed that the sisters didn't exchange looks at that point.

'It went horribly wrong when I was attacked by one of those scumbags. Wee Jock dragged me into a back garden. I don't even think he wanted me sexually, just to hurt me. Vickerman somehow found out and managed to free me. I ran and had a complete breakdown. I never knew what happened until years later when they told me that my attacker had been killed.'

'Why didn't you tell the police what you knew?' asked Barton.

'I didn't want to get involved. I was admitted to a private hospital for a lengthy period and had managed to escape Vickerman's jealous rages and my drug addiction. That world, and the people in it, had nothing I wanted.'

'That was a long time ago. Were you cured?' asked Strange.

'No, my condition is not something you can cure. The medication and support you receive afterwards make you well, but it's easy to relapse. I found it easier to live a quiet life. One with few friends and little upheaval. As you can imagine, it's hard for me to form trusting relationships and I don't seem to meet anyone nice. Anyway, the years ticked by without incident until recently.'

'How did you end up at Quantrill's house?' asked Strange.

Barton had agreed earlier that Strange would reveal they knew some parts of the story, but not all.

'My mother died, and I struggled to cope. I don't have much of a support circle. My sister lives quite a long way away, and I had few acquaintances outside work. I was due to meet a friend on that Saturday night, and he never showed. When I walked past The Hartley, I remembered going there when I was young. So, I went for a drink. They were in there, Quantrill, Ash, and a guy I didn't know called Duncan.'

Ellen paused and wiped her eyes. She either didn't want to talk about it, or it was an act. Both seemed possible.

'I take it all four of you returned to his house?' said Strange.

'That's right. We drank a lot in the pub, and stronger alcohol came out at theirs. Things changed, the atmosphere, and I just knew something awful was going to happen. They, they...'

Ellen's face hardened. Her jaw bunched, and she removed her white knuckles from the table and put them underneath.

'You can take a break if you like,' said Barton.

'No, I want to get this over with and go home. They all wanted to have sex with me, against my will. It's a blur, but two of them couldn't manage it. Quantrill did. The big one, Ash, got mad because he couldn't perform. I remember him pulling his arm back to hit me, then I woke up battered and half-naked and tried to sneak out. Ash stopped me leaving, but the others said to leave me alone. They were fighting as I left. They'd told me earlier that Vickerman lived ten houses from them because they sometimes scored drugs from him. I was frightened and couldn't think of where else to go.'

'They were all alive when you left Quantrill's place?' asked Barton.

'Yes, but two of them were really drunk and the muscly one was spoiling for a fight. I could hear bottles smashing. Vickerman and his flatmate, a guy called Quinn, were still up when I knocked. They seemed in a strange mood with bloodshot eyes. I told them I'd been attacked, and they reckoned they'd sort it out for me. I said to leave it, but they ran upstairs to get ready, whatever that meant. The moment they left me alone, I grabbed a long coat near the door and sneaked out.'

'And went home?'

'Yes, I tried to forget. I rarely watch the news and it wasn't until the following Friday that I heard the three of them had died.'

'And yet you still didn't get in touch with the police?'

'I wasn't sure of the dates. Part of me thought they got what they deserved. I visited Vickerman's a few weeks later to find out exactly what had happened. I was scared of him, but felt I had to go. Him and his flatmate, Quinn, reckoned that they just spoke to the three men who raped me, but they didn't look convincing. In the light of day, they had sores and picked at their track marks. Vickerman had a terrible cough, but he wanted me to stay. They said they were getting heroin that night. I think they only let me leave because I said I'd return later that evening, but I didn't bother.'

'How did you know that Vickerman and Quinn had died if you don't watch the news?'

'I heard it on the car radio. But what could I do? Their deaths weren't anything to do with me, and I didn't believe their story about the others. I just wanted to keep my head down from then on.'

Strange leaned back in her seat. 'Can you remember what Quinn and Vickerman wore on the night they headed to Quantrill's place all fired up?'

'No, sorry. It was dark stuff, jeans probably. Dark baseball cap.'

'Black baseball cap?'

'I guess. It could have been dark blue.'

Strange made some notes, then looked up. 'Tell me about Hofstadt.'

Ellen sank into her seat. She seemed more weary than upset.

'I'd walked to Morrisons because I had some vouchers and fancied getting some fresh air. I got caught in heavy rain, so I took shelter in a phone booth. I saw Hofstadt looking out of the window of a carpet shop. We'd dated years beforehand, although he dumped me and vanished really abruptly. I didn't know why at the time. He came outside shortly after, and I approached him because I wanted to understand the reasons. He shouted in my face that I'd told stories to the police and he'd finished up in prison. He said that I ruined his life, but I had nothing to do with it. I got annoyed as it wasn't my fault, so I told him that perhaps I should have a word with the police.'

'Did you know he was a sex offender?'

'No, I read it online afterwards.'

'Then what happened?'

'He went crazy, started shoving me towards the traffic, saying I deserved to die. He'd always had a weak leg from a football injury and stumbled. I was pushing him away and, well, you saw how it ended up.'

'And you still didn't report the incident to the police?' asked Barton.

'I was going to, but when I heard about his criminal record, I thought screw him.'

'And you hadn't spoken to Hofstadt in years?'

'No, I assumed he'd met someone else and chose to be with them.'

'Your hair was blonde that night. Can you explain that?'

'My hair's fallen out. This is a black wig. Stress, I guess. I have a few wigs that I wear, and I try different colours.'

Barton felt another twinge of sympathy. He hadn't been overjoyed when his own hair fell out. Nevertheless, the cynical part of him knew it was also a pretty convenient excuse to be in disguise.

'What colour wigs do you have?'

'Black, blonde and red.'

Barton immediately thought of the telephone call from the drunk about that Saturday night. He claimed to have seen a flaming angel. It was probably Ellen, and it matched her story.

'Can we have a look at your phone, please, Ellen?'

'That won't be possible because she's misplaced it,' interjected Lucy.

'That's okay. I can order phone records without the phone or a warrant. Then I'll check her call history against that of the others involved, in particular those who suffered untimely deaths, to make sure this stacks up. We already have most of their records. In fact, Ellen can give us signed authority for hers now.'

Barton didn't need authorisation, but it was a sneaky way to check for compliancy. He examined the sisters' faces for signs of worry, but neither sister's body language displayed any emotion.

'No problem,' said Lucy. 'We have nothing to hide, but my sister has been through enough for one day, don't you think? That will be all she'll say at this point. She needs to relax and take her medication.'

Barton raised his eyebrows. Regardless, he had a lot to consider.

'Interview terminated. Please give us a moment to consider things.

I'll be back shortly with the authorisation for your mobile records,' he said.

Barton left the room shaking his head. He'd heard plenty, but the lost phone was making him even more suspicious. The truth was in there somewhere, but how much of the rest was lies?

Outside, Barton leaned against the wall with his head down. After a few moments, he looked across at a confused Strange.

'I'm glad I'm only a sergeant,' she said.

For the first time in many years, Barton felt out of his depth. If there was a God, he'd heard Barton earlier boasting about his experience and calmness under pressure. A detention officer asked if everything was all right. Barton arranged for her to ask if the two sisters wanted another drink while they waited. Barton always treated the lowly paid detention staff well because they paid it back at times like this. Then he and Strange joined Zander in the room where he'd been watching the video feed and took seats next to him.

'I don't think I've ever been so unsure concerning something so serious,' said Barton. 'Ellen makes me uneasy, and it's not just her looks or cool demeanour. It's an unusual vulnerability that is making me feel sorry for her, even though there's something inside warning me to stay away.'

'That's how I was feeling when she was speaking in her flat,' said Zander. 'You want to believe her. It's almost like a lure.'

'You mean like with a hypnotist?' said Strange.

'I was thinking more of a cliff edge. You know, when you shouldn't get close, but it's hard to resist.'

'Ellen seems vulnerable to me too,' replied Strange. 'She's been through at least two terrible experiences, whatever she did after them. She reminds me of a colleague I knew in London. She wasn't that pretty, but there was something about her that made you enjoy spending time with her. Loads of men wanted a date, but it was as though she couldn't see her own worth. She'd get tangled up with idiots and they treated her like shit.'

'And we know how that type of man reacts if the woman tries to stand up for herself,' said Zander.

'Violently,' confirmed Strange.

Barton took a deep breath. 'What is Ellen guilty of? Murder? GBH? Poisoning? Nothing? Can we prove anything?' Neither of his sergeants spoke, so he continued. 'I'll run this past the CPS solicitor and see if she wants to charge. Although I'm not even sure if the custody sergeant will authorise keeping Ellen in.'

'Some would give her a reward for ridding Peterborough of its scumbags,' said Zander.

'True. It's far from straightforward with her having mental-health issues and her sister being a solicitor,' said Strange. 'Also, would she have the strength to kill those three men? Ash was huge. I get the impression she's a remote type, as though she struggles to feel strongly about most things. If three men raped her, she gets my vote for just being here and telling us it happened so clearly. I'd have been there for hours if they'd done it to me, chopping them to pieces.'

Zander gave her a firm nod while Barton swore under his breath.

'Shit, I'll ring the CPS, and I'd like to bounce this off someone with more experience,' said Barton.

'Cox,' offered Strange.

'I can't see her swapping her newborn baby for the phone. It wouldn't be fair when she's off, either.'

'The super?'

'I'll need to ring him anyway, but I reckon that he'll tell me to make the decision.' Barton clicked his fingers. 'I'll ring Naeem. She loves a mystery.'

Barton sent Strange off to prepare the statement and a mobile-record authorisation for Ellen to sign, told Zander to get anyone who was around to the detectives' room and returned to his office. After a ten-minute conversation with the CPS, Barton put the phone down and took a deep breath.

He picked it up again and called his old DCI. Pick up, pick up, he pleaded as it rang.

'Nav speaking.'

'John here. Are you busy?'

He spent ten minutes updating her. Afterwards, he could hear her nibbling a biscuit for a while. He could almost see her eyes focusing as she rolled the information around in her head.

'That is a puzzle,' she said.

'Not helping,' he replied, but he knew she'd have more.

'First, relax. If you get uptight, you won't be at your best. We have procedures. What are they?'

'Take statements. CPS will charge if appropriate. Lock up if we need further questioning. When we're confident, get them remanded in court.'

'So, you've taken a statement. If CPS don't want to charge, the rest is easy.'

Barton shook his head even though he was on the phone. 'CPS don't think there is sufficient evidence for a prosecution. There's too much doubt. Even I believe part of Ellen's story, but I'm not sure I believe it all. There's something unbalanced about her. I can't be clearer than that.'

'Don't ignore your gut feelings, but do you have to keep her locked up overnight?'

'I'd like to, but if we get a confession of sorts tomorrow, it's weakened if she says she didn't know what she was saying after no sleep in our cells with her mental health, assuming she can cope with a night behind bars.'

'You need to remember that she's also a victim. That seems to be a fact, and she has no priors. But you have a hunch, and that's important. What makes you think there's more to it? It's credible that she was raped by those men and fled to her ex-partner, Vickerman. He flew into a rage. She left, but Vickerman and Quinn visited the house and attacked the rapists, who ended up dead. They attempted to conceal the evidence by wiping the door handle. They also cleaned the murder weapons of their own prints, but placed them back in the hands of their victims.'

'Possible.'

'The killers were drug addicts. Who knows how they would react during the following week? They could have felt guilty and overdosed deliberately the next weekend as Mortis hinted, but more likely it was just a mistake. You don't have any evidence of her buying drugs and poisoning them, if that's what you were thinking. Take a photo of Ellen, so you can check if any of those we caught with the deadly fentanyl recognise her. They'd jump at the chance for her to take the rap rather than them, but that'll take time and they may lie. As for the paedophile in the road, forget about that. I've seen the footage. She's got away with that one, even if she did it on purpose. It's all plausible. What's stopping you from releasing her?'

Barton looked at the photo of his family on his desk. 'It's her dad. He's a multiple killer, and I suspect she's inherited some of his traits.'

'That's possible, but you can't prove it. Do you think she's likely to commit any more crimes?'

'Not in the next few days, no. The men who died have known her for years. They're historic. But I trust her sister, who seems dependable and solid. If we tell Lucy to bring Ellen back tomorrow, I'm sure she'll do it.'

'Great, that's a plan. It will take a while to collect and sift through phone evidence. If you keep her in, she'll need food, drink, and various support workers. Tell Ellen to return tomorrow, even if it's only for her to check in, and let her go again. Do the same the day after. If she doesn't turn up, we'll know to dig deeper. If she's had any contact with

Hofstadt in the past year, we'll know she was lying about that, too. Same with all the victims. We can't hold her for having a murderous father and if she's an innocent victim, we have a duty to really focus on her well-being.'

Barton finished the call. His old boss was spot on, as always. He recalled talking to others himself in the same way she'd spoken to him. Pressure had made him panic, and he wouldn't make the same mistake again. It was time to put the magnifying glass over Ellen's life. They would look for little holes in her and everyone else's stories. If they were there, Barton would tear them wide apart.

Barton left his office and returned to the detectives' room. Zelensky, Strange, Zander, Leicester and Malik were there. Barton stood in front of the boards displaying the faces of the victims, or killers, depending on what the truth was.

'Here's the plan. I'm releasing Ellen. Her sister, who is a solicitor, will ensure she returns tomorrow at 10 a.m. I suspect she may come back with a brief who specialises in criminal cases and we might get no more out of them, but they've been reasonably helpful so far. Zander, can you sort that?'

'Sure. It's a pity we can't bail her to return, then we could put conditions on it, like her not leaving the property.'

Barton considered everything for a moment.

'No, she's definitely not telling us the complete truth. Zelensky, did you say that there was only one way in and out of that place?'

'Yes, it's a block of six flats with no access to the rear. I knocked on all six doors earlier. Only the bottom two opened up, and they were both weird.'

'Weird in what way?'

'A speccy guy looked me over like he'd ordered a call girl, and the woman opposite told me she knew I was from the council and to stop lying. I'm glad I don't live there. It backs onto a cemetery, too. There's a two-metre iron fence keeping people out of that, so if you left, you'd need to leave through the car park to the main road.'

'Right, when we're ready, drive Lucy and Ellen back. Then wait outside and keep an eye on them. It'd take too long to set up proper surveillance, and it doesn't matter if they see you. I just want to make sure she returns tomorrow. If she wanders out the front, I need to know about it. I'll get some cover later tonight to take over. If they leave, call it in and we'll go from there.'

'Call records?' asked Strange.

'Right. Let's not forget that she probably lied about the where-abouts of her phone. She's with one of the networks where we can get call information fast. We'll see how lost that phone is.'

Barton's mind was whirring now.

'Malik, get her phone records. Check them against all the other victims. If you score a hit, we'll know she's been lying. If she uses her phone, same again. Leicester, where's Ewing?'

'Still no sign, sir. His phone isn't ringing, it's straight to voicemail. He said he was going to drop in on his sister because she's just had a baby. I'll message her on Facebook.'

Barton frowned and caught an uneasy look from Zander, too.

'Was Ewing working near those flats?' asked Zander.

'No, he was quite a few streets away.' Zelensky blinked as she realised what they were implying. 'Ellen can't have done anything like that. We only spoke to him less than an hour before we went to her flat, when he said something had come up.'

'It's a tiny window for getting rid of a body and tidying up the mess,' said Zander.

'Zelensky,' said Barton, 'check that Ewing didn't know Ellen Vick-erman before you drive her back. If she knows him, or you suspect she knows him, tell me. Leicester, pull Ewing's work and personal phone records. Compare them against everyone's, including Ellen's. Get onto the phone companies and ask for locations where both Ellen's and Ewing's phones were last used. Malik, chase Ewing's next of kin to see if they've seen him. Strange, have those statements finished and signed, and we can get the ball rolling.'

Barton tried to consider all the angles. With the new interception laws, they could get most companies' call records online in minutes. Besides, Ewing had a work phone. Who he'd been ringing on that would be easy to determine. Barton needed to know if he'd rung Ellen's number. If he had, she wouldn't be leaving the building.

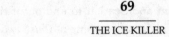

THE ICE KILLER

I sit quietly in the back of the police car on the way to my flat. Lucy is next to me on the phone to the hospital near her house. Greg has been taken in with suspected pneumonia. She has a sheen of sweat on her forehead that wasn't there in the police station and her hands tremble. I relied on my mother to keep me relatively balanced. Whereas it's clear that when the storm raged around my sister, Greg was the mast she lashed herself to.

The clock on the dashboard informs me it's gone 8 p.m. and the night is dark. I feel rather than see the young female detective, Zelensky, glancing back at me.

'So, you don't know a Robert Ewing?' she asks.

'No. I told you that earlier.'

'Good for you.'

She stops then and grimaces. I recall Ewing mentioning her. Looks like another woman that he's abused.

As we approach my home, it dawns on me that it's only a matter of time until the net closes in. They won't link me directly to Ewing, because it's been years since we had any contact, but they will connect Scarlett. After all, she rang him shortly before he got his just deserts. They'll eventually connect her to me.

Repeating my story to the police has changed how I feel about what I've done. The men I killed should have been punished further by society. You could argue that I finally gave them the sentence they deserved. Apart from Ewing, that is, and I will pay the price for that transgression.

I already sense the deadening effects of the drugs, but it seems neither the drugged me nor the crazy me have much compassion.

I need to visit both Trent and Scarlett to find out if they hid the body. It's hard to get my head around a scene of those two dragging a corpse through the fields. Scarlett's reasons for doing so are clear. She lives in a drunken world where she neither feels nor loves, which isn't so different from mine. She is close to the edge, and not a solid prospect to trust with your future.

Trent's reasons for helping are harder to fathom. God knows what the sentence is for hiding bodies, especially those of public servants, but it can't be good. I had better not look it up later, either, when I fetch my phone from him, although I suspect Trent will already have done so. Do I let events play out and hope for the best? Or do I act?

We arrive at the flats, and my sister and I get out of the car. There's a chink in Trent's window, where I can make out enough of his face staring out at me. I nod to him, and he disappears. At the door, I glance back and see Zelensky has parked in one of the spaces and turned off the engine. Lucy's voice is rising behind me as we climb the stairs. Tears stream when she terminates the call.

'How is Greg?' I ask.

'He's in Intensive Care. Pneumonia's been confirmed.'

My sister's a decent person. Life doesn't come with an instruction manual, so the best of us try to do the right thing most of the time, and that includes Lucy. I pull her into a wooden hug and whisper into her ear.

'It's not a problem, you should be with him. He'll need your strength.'

She wipes her eyes. 'But they told us not to leave the flat.'

'I'm not supposed to leave the flat, you can. All you said was that you'd return me to the police station by ten tomorrow morning. Come back first thing if you're able.'

'I can't leave you on your own.'

'Lucy, I've been on my own most of my life. A few more hours won't make any difference.'

It's a low blow but, even though she flinches, it gives her an out. She should be with her husband anyway, just in case. She grabs her things, and I follow her down to the door, where she pauses.

'Take your medication,' she says. 'I'll be back in the morning.'

Her Range Rover burns off in a cloud of smoke and screeching tyres. I watch the detective talking on her phone while she stares at me. I wave and return inside. Alone again, with time to ponder.

In my flat, I spend a few minutes on my make-up, focusing on my eyes. I'm not sure what will happen tonight, but I want to look nice just in case it's the last thing I do. I put the red wig on, and pull on thick jeans and a warm jumper. Dragging a bin liner out, I put everything I can think of that might incriminate me inside it. My diaries go in, any medical notes, and the wigs and clothes I wore at the incidents.

My medication is still on the side. I throw the pills that I was supposed to take and didn't in the sink and turn on the tap, but leave today's dosage in front of me. The angel and demon come out on my shoulders. They're pleading and persuading in equal measure. It's hard to decide. Will steady Ellen win the day, or do I need unpredictable Ellen's strength to pull me through? What should I do?

I trot down the stairs to Trent's place, and he lets me and my bag in. He's all of a jitter.

'Where the hell have you been?' he snarls under his breath.

'I got taken in for questioning, but relax. They don't know anything. There's no link to me from the murder, neither is there one to you. Did you hide the body where Scarlett said?'

'We couldn't. Scarlett drank from a bottle as she sped through the streets. Her driving almost made me forget the body in the boot. When we got back, her husband, Tim, was in the house. He'd returned early from a business trip. It was a nightmare. He started asking questions about who I was, and Scarlett didn't know anything about me. Tim thought I'd gone there to bang his wife.'

I stifle a chuckle at the irony. 'What happened?'

'She called Tim some names and said she'd drive me home. Tim took the keys off her, saying that he'd take me back. I had to sit next to him while he drove me into town. My heart wanted to leap out of my chest. I got him to drop me outside Peterborough Conservative Club on Broadway, so he doesn't know where I live.'

'What did he say on the journey?'

'It was weird. He wasn't rude, but he told me to stay away in a kind of sad manner. Apparently, Scarlett needs help, and he's going to arrange it for her. I spent the whole time imagining that smells from the corpse were filtering into the car. I kept waiting for the body to roll around or some kicking to start from behind us. My God, you owe me.'

'Yes, I understand that, and I appreciate it.'

He surprises me with his speed and grabs my wrist. My body tenses, my teeth grit, and I grab his arm to shove him off, but he easily pulls my hand away. Spinning me around, he holds me tight from behind and snarls into my ear.

'You really, really owe me, and you always will.'

Stunned by my lack of strength compared to his, I relax my shoulders and gradually his breathing slows. I carefully step away from him.

'I have some stuff to do,' I say, 'but I'll return later and we can discuss your payment terms. If I don't calm Scarlett down, we'll all end up inside for a long time. I'm going out of your back window and through the graveyard. Lend me your mobile.'

'No, use your own.' He hands me the phone I pushed through his letter box what seems like fifty years ago.

'They'll be monitoring it, and I'll need to hail a cab. Forget it, I'll use a phone box. While I'm gone, don't do anything or go anywhere. I'll be back.'

I open the window and climb out. My coat catches on his window lock, and Trent has to free me. He passes me the bin liner. The cold tonight penetrates my clothing with ease. I can only assume the polar express, as Scarlett called it, has arrived. I smile at what was a simpler time with my breath puffing out of my mouth in front of me as it would from a small steam train.

Trent shivers and carefully pulls the window shut. There's litter everywhere around the back of the flats, including used nappies, and I even see a needle. I step through it with caution. There are two loose metal panels, which I pull to the side. They screech a little but stay in place. I have to unscrew the one next to them. My already numb fingers make it a frustrating task.

On the other side, I glide the bin liner through after me, taking care not to catch it on any sharp edges. I also grab the bag I threw over yesterday and creep through the cemetery. There's not a cloud in the sky and the moon and stars light everything up as though under a spotlight. The tombstones glitter with ice and the sound of my crunching steps fill the air. There's a trailer filled with bags of rubbish where the paths meet in the centre. My two go on top.

I head to the lowish wall in the far corner from where I've seen the odd tramp leave. I pass the praying angel, but in this light she seems to be judging as opposed to pleading. Ice crystals on her face make her expression more demonic than angelic. Powerful glinting wings now give me the impression that she is not here to plead.

I walk diagonally across the graves to keep off the gravel, imagining faces around me in the undergrowth and bodies underneath attempting to grab at my ankles. But only a fool would be outside in this weather. When I get to the far wall, I peek over and note the drop, but I'm tall and jump down easily, and soon I'm scurrying towards Brad's house. I need to see a friendly face, to remind me that I have things to look forward to. I press the doorbell with a throbbing finger. The door opens.

'Hello, dear,' says a lined face from behind a safety chain.

'Hi, sorry, I thought Brad lived here.'

'He does, dear, but he's playing football on the AstroTurf. Are you his girlfriend?'

'Yes, I suppose so. I was passing and thought I'd stop for a coffee if he was about.'

'Come in, or you'll catch a cold out there.'

I step inside the hall and gasp with pleasure at the warmth. She's not quite as old as I first suspected. Only her face is lined, but her hair looks wonderful. Perhaps it's a wig.

'Will he be back soon?'

'No, probably not. Although it's nice to finally meet you. You must have been seeing each other for nearly a year. Do you want a coffee, Grace? Follow me.'

'Grace?'

She stops at the tone of my voice. Her kind eyes water at the obvious error. She wrings her hands and cringes.

'Not Grace, then?'

'No.' Grace is the manager's secretary. She's only twenty and has a face that pauses conversations as she passes. It seems I'm even more on my own than I imagined.

'It's fine. Brad and I only had one proper date with a bunch of friends. I was hoping for more. I don't suppose you could ring a taxi for me?'

She calls A2B and we sit in the lounge.

'I'm sorry, love.'

'Ah, well. These things happen. I'll be free for Ryan Gosling when he pulls his finger out.'

She perks up at my joke.

'You're better off out of it. Get a normal bloke. He keeps going on and on about football so much that I thought he was hiding something. I wondered whether he was gay. But no, unfortunately it really was football. Silly boy needs to grow up.'

A beep sounds from outside.

'Don't tell Brad I was here, please.'

She rests a hand on my arm.

'Of course not, and be careful. A lot of nutters live around here.'

The taxi driver takes notice of my serious demeanour and, apart from asking me my destination, keeps quiet. While he drives me to Stilton, I consider my options. Scarlett's behaviour will be the key to my actions. The gates are open for a change at her house, and the driver heads straight in. We pass the right-hand gate and I see it's bent in the middle. I pay the man and walk past Scarlett's Qashqai. The bonnet is scratched, and a headlight has a crack in it.

I press the doorbell. The beam from the taxi's headlights highlight Tim's gaunt face as he opens the door.

'She's been ranting about you,' he says. 'But you'll have to come back another time if you want to talk to her.'

I raise an eyebrow, and he gives me a tired shrug. He beckons for me to follow him in.

Scarlett is laid out on the sofa in the lounge. Empty glass in one hand, phone in the other. Her white top is mostly red. Even unconscious, her hatred has made her ugly. I scowl at another bruise on her forehead, but Ewing's body being in her car is more pressing. Tim walks to a small fridge next to the spirit bottles and grabs a can of Diet Coke.

'Do you want a drink?' he asks.

'No. I won't stay. Can I borrow her car to get home? I'll bring it back tomorrow.'

He studies me for a moment. 'Sure.'

I wait for the catch.

'You'll have to find the keys first. She drove it into the gates earlier, which you probably saw. She tried to drive it again later, but I'd disconnected the battery because she was so drunk. In a rage, she threw the keys in the pond. The silly cow had thrown the other set in the same spot last week.'

Anger sparks inside me. 'Why are you so horrible to her?'

To my surprise, he replies with venom. 'Me, horrible to her? You're her friend. Her only friend. You must understand what a drunken bitch she is.'

'I'm not surprised, living with you.'

'What? I'm only ever kind to her. I've tried to get her help, but she refuses—'

He cuts himself off and takes a deep breath before continuing.

'I understand why, but I can't take any more, and I'm leaving her. Do you know what she said she would do to me tonight before she passed out?'

Confused, I shake my head.

'Kill me in my sleep. Crazy cow.'

'But you get drunk and hit her. You say awful things. She's covered in bruises and you stop her leaving the house and don't let her have any money. You're the monster.'

The disbelief on his face is so natural and immediate that my fury leaches away. He plonks himself on the sofa next to Scarlett, who moves slightly and begins a stuttering snore.

'Ellen, I don't drink. I haven't touched any alcohol since I decided I had to deal with the baby dying. Every time I had a hangover after that happened, I was swamped with depression. One of us had to carry on and look after Dwayne, so I got sober. That way I could function. Scarlett already drank too much and chose the alternative route, being rarely sober. Once, I got her dried out in a detox clinic, but all she thought about was our loss, so she resumed her drinking. I suppose she had more guilt to bear.'

It's a lot to take in. 'And you keeping money from her and the bruises?'

'You know she has a black Amex, and I put a thousand pounds a month in Scarlett's current account, which goes on top of her wages. I did hit her once, but only because she was biting me. She is forever falling over things, slipping down the stairs and tripping in the garden. It's amazing she doesn't hurt herself more. I often put her to bed after cleaning her up.'

I try to think back to how he was with me. 'You're creepy with me, and over keen when I arrive here.'

'That once was a mistake. Surely we're all allowed one slip-up. She shows me no love of any kind. Apart from that drunken pass, I've been faithful, which is more than I can say for my wife. I caught her bringing a man here earlier. Scarlett and I haven't had sex for years, not since...' His Adam's apple bobs a couple of times until he steadies himself. 'I was always pleased when you came because Scarlett would lighten up and live a little. I wanted her, us, to be happy, but she's too haunted. You being a friend to her has really helped. That's why I offered to give you some money.'

'What money?'

'Scarlett said she asked you if you wanted it, but she told me you'd been doing escort work to get by.'

'What? She said I was selling myself?'

'Not exactly, just that you were escorting.'

Incredulous, I decide to ask the terrible question. 'What did happen to the baby?'

'She fell asleep with the baby while I was away on business. She found out when she woke up.'

At my horrified face, he continues. 'It does happen, sudden infant death, but I think Scarlett was drunk. It explains why she's never forgiven herself. The loathing she feels is only for herself. It will only end badly and I don't wish to be here when it does. There comes a time in your life when you've had enough, and Scarlett's there now.'

'She does seem particularly out of control at the moment.'

'I'll say. She's the runaway train approaching the end of the line. Anyone else would have left her long ago. Scarlett told me not to tell anyone that Dwayne asked to attend boarding school, because he couldn't stand to live here any longer, and now I need to leave. I'm going to tell her in the morning.'

I stare at Scarlett, who appears to have settled somewhat. She still clutches the phone and glass. I remove them from her hands. I suspect Tim's news will cause her to snap, especially after what she's been threatening to do to him. What he's said though makes sense. She's suffered since the baby died and, without help, she's deteriorating fast. Should I have done more and is she beyond help? We're all so consumed by our own troubles that we can miss others going under.

I have to think of myself first, and I might need Tim on my side, so I stand and walk towards him. Up close, I see his cheeks redden and he looks away first, but then he returns my stare with a shy grin. Has he told me the full truth, or does he have secrets too?

'It's funny you should say that,' I say. 'Scarlett wanted help killing you.'

'What? When?'

I turn Scarlett's phone on and lift her hand. After some gentle poking, her index finger opens it. I flick through a load of raging texts that she sent me today with increasing desperation. I nod slightly, noticing they implicate only her. Eventually I find the one saying she wants me to kill him. I pass him the phone. His eyes flick up with real concern after he's read it. I take his hand and give it a little squeeze. It's clammy.

'Come on. You can drive me home.'

He gives Scarlett a long backwards glance as we walk from the house. His Audi bleeps, and he opens the door for me. We roar through the gravel, out of the gate and down the country roads back to the A1. I smile as

I feel the back-end slide around. Even with all the madness, the thrum of the powerful engine stirs something inside me. You could easily get used to living this way. Tim realises the roads are slick with ice and slows down.

I ask him to drop me at the cemetery, saying I'm nipping to a friend's nearby. We drive past the Conservative club where he dropped Trent. He doesn't say anything, but I wonder if it registers inside somewhere. When we arrive, he pulls up, gets out and pulls me into a hug. It's a few seconds too long. I kiss him on the cheek and start to walk away.

'Ellen!'

I stop. He has a sad smile.

'I knew when I first met Scarlett that I'd love her for the rest of my life. Don't worry, even if I do leave in the morning, I'll find her the help she needs.'

I nod and stride out of sight. There's a concrete marker against the cemetery wall where I came over. I have to strain to pull myself up, but manage it with two attempts. I pass the angel monument with my head down, not wanting to feel her judging eyes upon me. It's so cold that my brain pounds inside my head. Everything around me is white and blue and doesn't feel real. It's impossible to imagine a summer breeze or flowers in bloom while this deathly wind howls through the skeletal trees and bone-china graves.

I stuff the red wig I'm wearing in the trailer as I pass it. My scalp shrinks as soon as it's exposed. I pull on the hat in my coat pocket, but it makes little difference. My chest wheezes from sucking in the frigid, thick air. Events are in motion now. There's no way back from here. What's the phrase? Let the chips fall as they may. It's always been clear to me that everyone looks after number one. We all keep secrets and we all tell lies.

I slide through the gap in the fence with the agility of a wooden horse. I struggle to coax any dexterity from my useless fingers, but finally the screws link, and the metal panels fix into place behind me. I check my watch. Three hours have gone by. I tap on Trent's window, but through the condensation I can see he is already staring out. Has he even moved?

He helps me through the window, and I shiver violently in his lounge. My jeans are stiff through cold, and my teeth chatter. Empty eyes blink at me, but finally he relents and makes a cup of tea and puts a blanket over my shoulders. When I have control of my teeth, I give him the news.

'Scarlett has everything in hand. Her husband is leaving tomorrow, so she'll be able to get rid of the body. I've got to attend the police station in the morning, but I don't think they'll keep me in. It's phone records they'll be checking and mine add ballast to my explanations rather than implicate me. I'll go to Scarlett's after and help her, then we'll be in the clear.'

His blank stare hints at disbelief, but then I realise he isn't listening. He only has one thing on his mind. I stand to leave, although I doubt there's any chance he'll let me go. He steps in my way.

'You know what I want.'

'And if I say no?'

'I'll tell the police.'

'You'll go to prison too.'

'Yes, but for nowhere near as long as you will.'

'I'm freezing cold.'

'I don't care. It'll warm you up.'

I have to buy some time. What he wants is nothing to me, or at least I didn't think so. I don't want to be like this, but I don't know how to change. Crazy Ellen is too much for this world. It's a place she doesn't belong. But medicated Ellen doesn't have a life. She breathes, but she doesn't live. I nod at Trent. He leaves the room and goes to his bedroom. I hear rattling and movement in there. I assume he has gone to get a condom or something weird like a cowboy hat. Instead he returns naked, armed only with a satanic smile.

A rage from the depths of my being urges me to fight him off. I've had enough of being used like an inanimate object, but I stifle it. I need to give him this moment, but I won't make it easy. As he approaches, I lean towards him and spit in his face. He smiles and slaps me with an open hand, then throws me towards the sofa. I'm bent over it and his nails tear at the raw skin on my legs as he yanks my jeans down.

Then he takes me, like a beast. He uses me as all men have. His guttural grunts echo around the walls, but I do not cry. He can't hurt me. No one can.

I wake from a dreamless sleep the next morning and take a warm shower. It still feels as if my insides are frozen, even though the heating has thawed my extremities. I pull back the curtains and look into the car park. There's a man waiting in a Toyota with the engine running. I bet he's had a long watch. When I returned to my room last night, I gave the woman a thumbs up before I turned out the light. She must have been relieved from duty at some point.

I decide on no make-up today, and no wig. My hair seems to be falling out where it wasn't and growing in the bald patches. Perhaps I'm like a snake, and it's all for a fresh start. Put on black jeans, a black shirt and black boots. The wig goes in my handbag. I stare at my pills on the kitchen table. I only have a few seconds' pause, before I grab the ones I didn't take yesterday, put them with the ones I should take today, and throw them in the sink. I'll need ice-cold Ellen if I'm to survive.

My phone rings and I see it's my sister. I answer it.

'Hi, Lucy. Are you on your way?'

'Sorry, Ellen. Greg's still in Intensive Care.'

'I'm on my own, then.'

'Of course not. We're sending Carson. He'll pick you up at nine-thirty and take you in. I've briefed him. He's an old friend of ours. Don't worry, Ellen. You haven't done anything wrong.'

We attempt positive farewells, but I struggle not to focus on her absence. I wish Greg well. That's the thing with partners – you choose them. It's a decision, whereas families just are. It'd be nice to be chosen for once, but I swing between two opposing personalities, and who'd want to be with someone like that?

An enormous saloon car pulls into the car park at half-past nine. I walk downstairs and ignore Trent, who is standing at his door.

'Come around when they let you go,' he orders.

A small man with grey hair and a tailored suit climbs from the vehicle. He looks straight into my eyes, not at my mostly bald head.

'Carson Black. Sit in the front, please. I have a few questions and I'll explain how we will deal with this morning's proceedings.'

I walk around to the passenger door, passing the Asian man in what must be the police observation car. He has the window open and is staring at a moving pile of clothes on the floor next to the exit. It seems we have another vagrant in residence. Word of my free soup must have got out. It's a different one, because the other man was bald, and I can see a head of hair. The other one was also silent. This guy groans as though he's been kicked in the stomach.

'Be a human and see if he's okay,' I tell the officer.

I get in the smooth interior of the Bentley and we pull away. I glance over my shoulder and see we're being followed. Carson speaks to me as though he's giving orders to a valued staff member at his stately home. He looks like a smaller version of George Clooney. It's reassuring, but I've no nerves, even though I could be walking into a prison sentence.

As we near the police station, I open the glovebox and place my phone inside it. Carson watches me do it, but keeps quiet. We park in the car park outside and walk to Reception. We're ten minutes early, but the inspector from yesterday is there already. There are a few other unlucky souls in the waiting area. They stop talking as I pass and stare at my head. Barton opens a door for me.

'Thanks for coming back, Ellen. Let's get to the bottom of this and we'll be able to put these terrible events behind us.'

I give him a bright smile, even though he's wrong. The nightmare for him has just begun.

ACTING DCI BARTON

Barton and Strange guided Ellen and her solicitor into the interview room, completed the legal warnings, and got the tape running. Her new solicitor had a capable air about him.

Despite her involvement in numerous deaths, Ellen hadn't told them any obvious lies, or at least they'd found no evidence to the contrary. Her phone records didn't contain any numbers of the three men who died so violently in their house. The two overdose victims had mobile phones on their persons and Ellen's number wasn't present there either. Hofstadt's phone only had five numbers stored, which didn't include Ellen's. And they also knew she wasn't on Ewing's list of callers because they'd checked last night.

None of the drug dealers recognised a picture of Ellen, and Barton had even sent Leicester back to speak to the man who'd been at the house where the fentanyl tip-off had been wrong to see if he knew her, but there had been no answer. It was a long shot, and Barton's rising concern was the fact Ewing was still missing.

Ewing lived with a flatmate on David's Lane in Werrington, but nobody had answered when Malik knocked. Zander got hold of his sister and she confirmed he was supposed to visit yesterday afternoon and hadn't turned up. She said she never met any of her brother's girl-friends, saying only that she guessed there were many.

Barton decided that he'd speak to Ellen this morning, then they'd get serious about locating Ewing. Hopefully, he'd walk into the station beforehand and be surprised at all the fuss. From what they'd been learning about him, he could easily just be with one of his many women.

Barton had spent quite some time thinking about Ellen the previous evening. There was no reason to suspect Ewing's disappear-ance was connected with the spate of deaths, but Barton still asked Strange to search Ellen and Ewing's social media for connections. There were none and, seeing as they hadn't been in contact on the phone either, there wasn't an obvious link. Uniform were walking the area where he was last seen with a recent photograph and they were now analysing the rest of Ewing's call records.

'Right, Mr Carson. What we want from Ellen today is detailed state-ments around her relationships with the six men who are deceased. I'd like to know when she last saw them, how the relationship was left, and anything else that may be of interest to our investigation into the premature death of these six men. We also need more details on her relationship with another deceased from a long time ago with the nick-name Wee Jock. Ellen's skin was found under his fingernails.'

'I see. Anything else you want?'

'We want to take a look at Ellen's phone.'

'Right, and that's it?'

'I have questions about Ellen's mental health and I'd like access to her medical records.'

'I understand. Now, we're happy to help, but we have a few condi-tions first.'

Barton stared at him. 'We're usually the ones who state the conditions.'

'My client has been more than helpful so far. It seems to me what you're interested in is her incriminating herself. Are you charging her with anything?'

'Not at this point.'

'My client is free to go?'

'Ellen said she'd come back and assist us.'

'Do you seriously expect Ellen to answer these questions when you are looking for evidence to implicate her?'

Barton didn't like the way this was going. Carson was after something, but Barton couldn't work out what it was.

'If she has nothing to hide,' he said, 'surely, she'd prefer to remove herself from the suspect list.'

'It won't matter what she says here today, you would still be suspicious. Am I right?'

Barton sighed. 'What is it you want?'

'Ellen has agreed to do the statements for you, but they will take time. She'd like to do them elsewhere, at home preferably. She'll bring them in tomorrow. I have advised her not to bother doing them. However, she wants to help. She will also be able to bring her phone in for you at the same time, as she thinks she knows where it is. She will then give you permission to view her medical records. Are we in agreement?'

'Why can't she write her statements here?'

'If you keep her here, she'll write nothing at all. You will have to charge her or let her go. You've asked for her records, so you are well aware Ellen has mental-health issues, and you know she's in mourning. Police stations affect the most balanced individuals, never mind those with anxiety. What seems to be the problem?'

Barton decided to lay his cards out.

'Ellen, are you on medication for psychosis?'

Ellen had been looking down at the table. She raised her head and fixed Barton in her stare. The green eyes of yesterday had changed. They were harder now, hawk-like. He had the strange feeling of being prey.

'I'm on a variety of tablets. To save you looking them up, I'll tell you. Some of them are anti-psychotics, others for schizophrenia. They're used for anxiety and depression. Most patients need a balance, so two prescriptions are rarely the same. Are you asking if I'm mad?'

'I was wondering what you'd be like if you stopped taking your medication.'

'I would struggle, but I bet half your staff are on antidepressants.'

'Do you have murderous urges?'

'Do you think I killed all these people?'

'I believe you're more responsible than you're telling us.'

Carson let out a short brittle laugh and interrupted.

'Frankly, Mr Barton, I don't care what you believe. I'm only interested in what you can prove. Which appears to be nothing. You can't arrest her for bad luck.'

Barton leaned back in his seat. 'Fine, I agree to your terms. However, Ellen will have to be somewhere other than her flat, as I'm ordering a full CSI today.'

'Do you have any evidence at all against my client, or are you just fishing?'

'We don't have many people to question apart from Ellen. That's because everyone else is dead.'

Carson smiled. 'It's a pity that dead men don't tell tales, isn't it, Inspector? Our jobs would be much easier.'

Strange had only spoken to caution them at the start of the interview, but now she leaned forward with purpose.

'How do you feel about the deaths, Ellen? These were ex-boyfriends and school friends. Are you sad?'

Ellen's piercing gaze turned to Strange.

'It's a shame.'

Strange waited for Ellen to say something else, but it appeared she had finished.

Half an hour later, Barton watched Ellen and her brief leave the building. It was the link to her father that was playing on Barton's mind. He returned to his desk, knowing just the man for a quick opinion. Mortis picked up after a few rings.

'Are you back at work?' asked Barton.

'Aye,' replied Mortis.

'Everything all right?'

'Ask your question, John.'

'It's around mental health. I know that's an interest of yours. I'm curious as to the likelihood of a parent passing on their illnesses to their offspring.'

'Go on. At one point, I wanted to be a psychiatrist.'

Barton quickly updated Mortis on the case.

'Ah, I see. You're wondering specifically if it's likely that the father's propensity to kill has been transferred to his daughter.'

'Correct.'

'The simple answer to that is maybe. Research is progressing on the subject, but human brains are complicated. No two are the same. I read some research a little while ago that said your lifetime risk of developing schizophrenia was about one in a hundred. If one of your biological parents or a sibling has it that rises to around one in ten. The stats are similar but with a bigger range for SMIs such as bipolar or personality disorders.'

'SMIs?'

'Serious Mental Health Issues. But remember that people with SMIs are rarely dangerous to anyone but themselves, and the chance of them being a murderer is remote. Around 10 per cent of the population will have an SMI in their lifetime. And one in five of us will experience suicidal thoughts at some point. It's incredible that we as a nation are only just waking up to these facts. That's millions of people and we only have around seven hundred murders in England and Wales each year.'

'Right, I agree, they're shocking statistics, but I'm not sure how much help they are to me. What about if both parents had issues with their mental health?'

'Again, there is a lot of variation depending on which research you use, but some reports have stated it could be as high as a one in two chance you'll inherit your parents' conditions.'

Carson drives me back to my flat. He parks a little way down the road, as if he knows that I'm going to sneak into my car and drive away. I'm free as long as I return in the morning, so I can go where I please, but I'd rather not be followed. I take my phone from the glovebox but resist the urge to turn it on. It must hold many desperate messages waiting. Before I get out of the car, I thank Carson for being there for me. I have no idea who he is, or where he's come from, but I suspect he doesn't race to Peterborough at the drop of a hat for anyone.

'I appreciate your help, Carson.'

'No problem. I've represented your mother and father for years.'

I step outside and slam the door but linger. It's a strange turn of phrase that he's used. Why would they both have need of a criminal solicitor? I make a mental note to ask my sister. The passenger window winds down. Carson leans over and looks up at me.

'Don't do those statements, and I'd disappear for a bit if I were you, too. As for your phone, I'd lose it permanently, whatever's on there. The police don't have anything on you at the moment, or they would have arrested and charged you. Eventually their resources will be dragged elsewhere, and the crimes will be forgotten. After all, no one innocent has died. I know a smart detective when I see one, and

Inspector Barton is close to making a decision. We don't want him finding out the truth. Remember, I'm only a phone call away.'

Carson has driven off up the road before it registers that he's told me he knows I've killed people. Does that make him a bad person? Is he motivated by loyalty or money? Suddenly, it feels as if the world is full of corruption. What's the point of our existence if we just do terrible things to each other? Carson said to vanish, but I don't have the funds for that. I also know that my time in Peterborough isn't over.

There's a small Police Scientific Support Unit van parked outside the front door of the flats. A uniformed policeman standing there glares at me as I slip into the driver's side of my car. I accelerate away and join the traffic into town. I'm starving and drive down Oundle Road to Woodston Chippy. It's midday and hard to believe yesterday was so arctic because the sun has melted the frost that froze everything in its spot.

The radio cheerily explains that even though tonight will be cold, the chill will depart tomorrow when a warm front pushes in from the Atlantic. In two days' time, we'll be free of the depths of winter. I park next to the chip shop, enter, and ask for my order to be open. With loads of salt and vinegar on, it smells heavenly. I stand outside, burning my tongue as I shovel fuel into my mouth. Sweet Millie's charity shop is next door to the chip shop.

I'd forgotten about Millie. I can see her eating an enormous bag of crisps. She must feel my eyes on her because she looks up. Her chubby face bursts into a huge grin. It warms me even more than the sun. I push the door open and approach the counter.

'Fancy a chip?'

'No, thanks, love. I had some yesterday. It's deadly working so close. I was thin when I first opened the shop.' She winks at me. 'Well, not really thin.'

I laugh, which makes me wonder when I last did. She talks nineteen to the dozen about a load of stuff I have no interest in, but I relax. It's normal, and wasn't that what I wanted to be? There's no point hiding from my problems, so I turn on my mobile. It erupts with beeps.

'Ooh, you're popular,' says Millie. 'Sometimes I don't receive a message for days and think I've forgotten to turn my phone on, but I haven't.'

'Millie, can I tell you something? It's not good.'

'Sure, get it off your chest.'

I look at her earnest face and shake my head. 'No, it's fine.'

'Ellen, please. A problem shared and all that.'

'I killed a man.'

'So it *was* you that I saw on television. That wasn't your fault.'

'I'm talking about someone else. He wasn't a decent person, but he didn't deserve to die. I think I should confess.'

Millie's eyes widen, but she doesn't say anything for a while, just munches her crisps.

'What will owning up to it achieve? It won't bring him back, but you'll ruin the rest of your life. Do you think you'll get away with it?'

'I don't know, maybe, maybe not. It's all such a mess. I hoped to be happy and have someone special of my own. Surely that shouldn't be too much to ask. Although I've been feeling so up and down of late, and often out of control. Perhaps prison is the best place for me.'

'You know what, if you'd asked me years ago, I'd have said do the right thing and confess. But life has taught me that nice people come last. Don't admit to anything. Be lucky, but learn from it, and live your life with gratitude. Ellen, I know you think you're lonely now, but you aren't, not really. You've so many years left with no responsibility and so many possibilities. Don't throw the opportunity away. You could get a passport and be backpacking around India in a few weeks. I'd even pay for your ticket if that's what you want to do.'

I move around the counter and hug her. Again, I've been so swept up in my own problems with isolation that I haven't considered others who must be going through the same thing. I make a promise to myself that I will see more of Millie, although the future looks grim if my freedom relies on Trent and Scarlett keeping their mouths shut. It's placed me in a weak position.

'What are you saying? Be mean and horrible, and I'll win?' I ask.

Millie wipes her eyes. 'Just look after yourself. No one else will put you first, you have to do it yourself.'

I give her a guilty smile. She doesn't know the half of it.

'I'd better go. I'm going to have a drive. It'll be a chance for me to think about things and make some tough decisions.'

Although, the harsh reality I find myself in already has my full attention. The chilling focus that trickles into my veins shocks me. I attempt a winning smile at Millie, but it reaches nowhere near my eyes. She doesn't seem to notice and gaily replies.

'Okay, don't forget stock check next Thursday.'

'Only prison bars would stop me.'

She laughs and waves me off. Outside, I throw the empty chip wrapper into a bin, get in my car, and look at my phone. There are texts from both Trent and Scarlett along with missed calls from Brad and work. There are four voice messages, one of which is from my sister. Lucy's says to head to her home in Harrow, even though she'll be at the hospital. Brad's message is casual but keen. Clearly his mum didn't tell him that I knew about his other office chum. Trent's call is raging and demanding, whereas Scarlett's is frantic and doesn't make sense. The last text is from her. It reads:

I can't take any more. I'm going to end it all. Tim told me this morning that he was leaving me. Now he's gone, and he'll never come back, and it's all my fault. Please come. I don't want to die alone.

That message could mean a lot of things. More danger for me, or perhaps one of my problems solved. My fingers swiftly type out a reply.

I'm on my way.

75

ACTING DCI BARTON

Barton stared at his inbox. He was getting heat from his supervisors about the mysterious deaths. Ewing still hadn't appeared, although Malik had been back to Ewing's house where a neighbour said she thought she'd seen him last night. If Ewing just had a personal problem, it'd be better off dealt with by Barton. He didn't want to escalate the search unless absolutely necessary. That would involve the national and local news, and it wouldn't look good for the police if they couldn't locate their own people. Especially if he appeared a few hours later.

Barton steepled his fingers and tried to think outside the box. He'd already sent Zelensky out to search for Ewing at the haunts she knew he frequented. His gut was yelling to him that Ellen Vickerman was involved in some way, but there was no evidence.

Barton opened the door to the main office and stared at Strange and Zander, who were chuckling at the water cooler. The disparity between their two sizes made him think of the musclebound Trevor Ash. Could Ellen really have taken him out? He recalled a story where a man had lifted a car off a cyclist. Did superhuman strength exist? An idea leaked into Barton's brain, and he picked up his phone again.

'John,' said Mortis. 'I'm touched by your need to regularly hear my voice, but I do have work to do.'

'How's things?'

'I'm putting the phone down.'

'Last question. I'll never bother you again.'

'Deal, get on with it.'

'I was thinking about who killed the three guys in that house. We imagined it was a strong man, but maybe it was a woman who, in dire need, found great power to kill and escape. But then I recalled you saying that the wine bottle used to beat Duncan wasn't wielded with incredible force. It was more of a pulverising than a pounding.'

Mortis hummed for a few seconds. 'You can be a genius at times, DCI Barton. Are you referring to hysterical strength?'

'Erm, maybe.'

'Hysterical strength is a display of extreme strength by humans, beyond what is believed to be normal. It often occurs when people are in life or death situations.'

'So, in desperation, they become bionic?'

Barton moved the phone away from his ear as Mortis laughed his head off at the end of the line. Mortis finally calmed himself.

'Thanks, John. I needed that. Let me explain it to you.'

Barton took a deep breath and prepared to concentrate.

'Human beings have two basic kinds of physical ability: gross-motor skills using large muscles, like running, thumping, and jumping, and fine-motor skills involving small muscles, like threading a needle, drawing, or tying a shoelace. Fine motor skills decline fast when we're under pressure. Try opening a door with a key when a monster is chasing you. But gross-motor skills come into their own: the closer a lion is roaring at your heels, the faster you'll run.'

'But there must be limits.'

'Yes, you're still restricted to your body's potential, but we are capable of much more than the normal range of power. Usually, your muscles don't work at 100 per cent due to a built-in self-protection mechanism, so you won't overload them and get injured. In extreme cases though, tearing your biceps is a lot less detrimental to your health than being thrown under a bus.'

'In that case, a fit and healthy strong woman could really surprise you?'

'Very much so. Under stress, the body releases powerful analgesics which deaden pain, which overrides the aching feeling we have through effort. Some say that the pain of muscle fatigue is more an emotion than a reflection of the physical state of exerted muscles in question. When we're tired, there's much more in reserve, but few can tap into those reserves on demand. Some athletes can for short periods, like roaring weightlifters, but most of the surprising cases we hear about occur during terrifying events.'

'Thanks,' said Barton. 'I think that was helpful. If Ash had used the wine bottle on Duncan, his head would have been pulp.'

'Correct. One final point. Not everyone will react positively. We don't all have such a strong urge to fight back or a need to survive. It's perfectly possible that you could surprise or disappoint yourself in such a situation, because fear can also make you freeze.'

76

ACTING DCI BARTON

Barton decided he needed fresh air and food. He drove to the Herlington Centre, which had the fastest Subway he could get to without the aggravation of driving into the town centre. While in the queue, he rang Sirena, who was managing the potential crime scene at Ellen's flat.

'Anything?' he asked.

'Potentially. There are blood splatters on the kitchen units.'

'Large or recent?'

'Small, but it's hard to say how long they've been here. I would guess fairly recently, as they show up clearly under luminol.'

'Okay, I'm just refuelling, then I'll be over. Ten minutes max.'

Barton inhaled his Meatball Marinara melt, wishing he'd got two of them, and raced around the parkways. He stepped from his car after parking and strode up the stairs. The weather was definitely heating up as he was sweating when he reached the top floor. He stood in the doorway.

'Do I need shoe covers?'

Sirena came out of the bedroom in a full Tyvek suit. She pulled her mask down.

'No, we only have the bedroom to finish. This is where the blood-stains were.' Sirena pointed to a clean kitchen-unit door.

'Ah, I assume they've been removed with bleach,' he said. 'No DNA?'

'Unlikely, and there weren't loads of splatters, anyway. If someone was stabbed to death here, it'd be a lot worse, but they could have been stunned with a heavy implement. We might struggle to get any DNA from the bathroom too, because that's also been thoroughly cleaned recently. The bedroom, on the other hand, is like a bio swamp.'

The gears in Barton's brain clicked over. When he'd been in Ellen's flat before, it had smelled clean. Had she cleaned it up to hide something? Her sister had been there, though. Surely Lucy hadn't helped her mop up the bloodstains. That didn't seem likely, even to his suspicious mind.

'Anything in the bins, inside or out?'

'Empty inside. The bins outside haven't been collected this week, so we have a technician picking through them now, but they're for six flats.'

'Understood. Look, DC Ewing has gone missing and I'm worried about his safety. It seems he's a bit of a ladies' man. He may have slept with Ellen at some point, so see if there's a picture or anything that might link them, then go over that bedroom with your tweezers, because at the moment I've got nothing.'

'Sure thing. If he's been in this room, we'll know about it when the tests come back.'

Barton frowned, knowing that by the time the results returned, Ewing's fate would be sealed. Sirena stepped towards him with a serious expression on her face.

'I need to tell you something though. We'll be finished today, and then I'm taking an extended leave. I'm hoping to return, but we'll see.'

'What's going on?'

'My father had a bad fall last week outside his apartment in Greece. He lives alone and they won't release him from hospital without someone to look after him. I'm going home to help him recover.'

'I'm sorry to hear that. You should have said before.'

'It's my problem, so I didn't tell anyone. Or should I say it's my privilege, depending on how nice a person you are.' She grinned at him.

'Stay in touch, then. I'm sure it's the right decision.'

Barton smiled back. Looked as if he wasn't the only one making sacrifices for family. He had another thought and decided better out than in.

'Does Kelly know you're going?'

'No, not yet. I only made my mind up a few days ago. I think it will be fine. We aren't the perfect match. I'll miss her, and I'll miss you, John. There's something about you that I find reassuring. It's not easy to say what it is, but you are honest, supportive, and dependable.'

'Handsome, chiselled, daring?'

'Perhaps daring.'

She pulled him into a hug and kissed him on both cheeks.

'When I'm back, you can be my large heterosexual friend – every gay girl needs one. Now, get out of here. I'll ring you when we're finished.'

Barton plodded down the stairs. Life was always changing, but sometimes those changes made you sad. He was feeling melancholy when he got back to Thorpe Wood Police Station. Leicester rose from his seat as Barton traipsed in.

'Sir, I've found a match. The last person to call Ewing's personal phone is a regular number on Ellen's list. I've found the details. The phone is registered to a Scarlett Starr at an address in Stilton.'

Barton's meatball melt gurgled in his stomach. That was a coincidence too far. He wanted Ellen and Scarlett in the station asap, but he had a decision to make. Did he ring the number first, or go to the property? He didn't want to spook Scarlett in some way. You always had to look at the odds. Scarlett Starr was probably just a friend or his current girlfriend. Ewing was missing though, and Scarlett knew Ellen. Was it a love triangle, or maybe women taking their revenge for being treated badly? Tendrils of real dread were tightening around his heart when his mobile phone rang.

'Barton.'

'Good afternoon, Inspector. It's Ellen Vickerman.'

Barton paused. There was something cold and clinical about the way Ellen was speaking. 'How can I help you?'

'I know who has Robert Ewing.'

I'm standing behind one of the stone posts on the road outside Scarlett's house. When I drove up, I gasped in horror. It's as if Scarlett did it for the world to see, especially with the gates being broken. Tim's Audi is outside the house and facing towards the road. He is lying on top of the bonnet, arms stretched out as though sunbathing. Blood has poured down the sides and the front of the car, almost like a macabre artwork. Tim's wearing a light green shirt with a large blackened stain on his chest, where I suspect he's been shot at point-blank range.

So that's what she meant by him never coming back. I searched my feelings for the fear and worry that should have been present, but that Ellen was hiding. It's a good time for this to play out. I've no doubt Scarlett is suicidal. Her life as it was is over now, but she'll also be angry.

She's looking at decades in prison if she goes down one path, and she'd grass me up to align our fates. If she chooses the afterlife, I wouldn't be surprised if she took me along there, too. I never expected to ring the police for back-up, but I find myself telling the inspector the truth that she has Robert.

'Say that again,' says Barton.

'I know who kidnapped Robert Ewing, and I know where she's keeping him.'

'Go on, then.'

'Scarlett Starr told me she'd stabbed him and driven him to her home in Stilton. He's going to die.'

'Where are you?'

'I'm outside her house. I received some texts from her this morning when I retrieved my phone.'

'It's North Street, isn't it?'

Interesting. 'Yes, how did you know?'

'Never you mind. We're on our way. Stay away from the property.'

'I'm sorry, Inspector. But I have to go in. She's at the door now, pointing a shotgun at me, so I have no choice. I think she's gone mad.'

'Wait, she has a gun? Is it loaded?'

'She's just reloaded it. I suspect she has more ammunition, and she belongs to a shooting club.'

'Is he dead?'

I cut him off. Scarlett's not in sight, but she'll be in the house. Perhaps she's already dead, but that's not likely. She's never been the type to leave the stage gracefully. I walk up the drive bathed in bright light. The sun has real strength in it now, but something feels odd. Out here on the edge of farmland, I usually hear birdsong, but it's deadly quiet. I suppose gunshot would warn even the most stupid of birds to flock elsewhere.

Standing next to the car, I put a hand to Tim's cheek. He's cold, sunken, solid and has a decidedly unhuman feeling. I'm about to knock on the door but instead try the handle. It's unlocked, so I push my way in. In their expansive hall, there is a large sideboard. On it sits the weapon that must have done the damage to Tim. He should have hidden that ammunition better. I pick up the shotgun and discover it has indeed been reloaded.

Music starts from further inside the house. I place the gun back where it was and tiptoe towards the sound of Ed Sheeran's 'Castle on the Hill' finishing. The same song starts up again. Scarlett is seated at the kitchen table with her head in her hands. An empty bottle of vodka is on its side next to her. Every window in the room is smashed. It looks like most of the crockery, too.

'Hi, Scarlett.'

Her head slowly rises, and empty eyes stare at me without recognition. It takes her a few tries to focus, then she jumps to her feet. She rubs the back of her forearm over her face and when those troubled eyes are revealed again, they have changed, and she is Scarlett. She attempts a smile. I expect slurred words, but they are fairly clear.

'Thanks for coming. I didn't have anyone else to ring.'

It's the first time I've seen her without make-up for ages, which is a further sign she's given up. She looks more innocent and younger. I'm not sure what to say. An internal war rages over whether to tell her to think again or get on with it. She lurches around the table.

'I can't even get drunk. Fancy that. Half a bottle of vodka and nothing. I don't know what came over me. I've been so spiteful with myself for so long that I started to blame him. Eventually, I fooled myself that he was the problem, not me. Not this.'

She grabs the empty vodka bottle and hurls it at the window. It sails right through a hole that's already there. She giggles a little and staggers towards me. She hugs me and leans on me at the same time. Soon, I'm holding her up, but she keeps talking.

'How do you live with yourself, Ellen? How can you kill and just carry on? I can't cope. No one should be able to if they've taken a life.'

Frowning, I step back so I can look at her face.

'You pushed that girl out of the window, Scarlett, remember? That was years ago, and you carried on.'

She snorts with laughter, and a stream of watery snot flies out of her nose. She chuckles again as she wipes it away.

'I told you that because you wanted to hear it. Did you feel better for a while?'

'Yes, I did, actually.' I don't know whether to believe her, but I don't suppose it matters now she's back to her favourite topic.

'My life is dull and pointless, and it's not going to get any better.

Can you appreciate what it's like to have everything aged ten and then spend the rest of your life watching it slip away? Do you know the terror of all your hopes and dreams turning to dust, or ashes in my case? I died when I killed my daughter. What's followed has just been a horrible dream. It's time for the nightmare to end.'

She slumps back in her seat with her head lolling to one side, seemingly out of it again. I imagine Barton and his team racing here. Do they have guns? They must do. A truncheon's no good if someone's shooting at you. But I don't want to die. How can I get out of here alive? I close my eyes too and run through my life since that girl died at school. Which event was the catalyst for my descent? Or was the seed of ruin planted by my father the day I was conceived? Time slows as I wonder whether this madness was my destiny. It's a draining thought. I slump next to Scarlett, also tired of life.

I could leave and hope Scarlett follows through on her plan before the police arrive and she drops me in it. Barton knew Scarlett's address, so they've linked her to Ewing, and therefore me. Ewing's DNA will turn up at my property. If Scarlett and I told a different story, who would they believe? A minute passes while I consider who I'd believe. Scarlett's credibility is destroyed by having Ewing's body taped up in her car boot, never mind what she's done to her husband. Unless she blames both on me, and I've just touched the shotgun. I realise Scarlett's watching me.

Having left the front door open, I hear the soft distant clunk of a car door being shut. Scarlett's head turns towards the window, then back to me. I cock my head and hear a car cruise past. The engine dies nearby. Seconds tick by while Scarlett and I stare at each other. Scarlett gets up and looks outside.

'I can't see anything.'

I rise and edge towards the front door when a loud voice shatters the silence.

'Scarlett Starr, come out with your hands raised.'

Barton had put the phone down to Ellen very slowly. This was pressure he understood. Lives were in immediate danger. The most important fact was that the assailant was armed with a shotgun. Great for shooting pigeons, deadly and indiscriminate against humans. What would an experienced DCI do? he thought. Probably give it to Barton to resolve.

He rang Control and recognised the voice of a woman called Ronnie who'd been doing her job longer than he'd been on the force. He gave her the bare details; she'd know what to do from her end. He found out who was on duty in the Armed Response Vehicle. It was Jules Cureton, who he had on speed dial.

'Hi, Jules. Where are you?'

'You walked past me about ten minutes ago at the noticeboard, and you didn't return my hello. Could you not see me from your lofty perch?'

'Sorry, we're involved with a confusing case, which is just blowing open now. It's lucky you're here. We have an armed situation less than fifteen minutes away. I'll meet you in the car park in five.'

Barton updated Strange in the office.

'Shotgun? Hang on,' she said.

She turned to her PC and accessed the Firearms Register. Using the address, she found a record for two shotguns registered to a Tim Ovett. The other adult at the address was Scarlett Starr, his wife. Strange printed the information off, which included a photo of him, and passed Barton two copies.

'Nice work,' said Barton. 'Follow with Leicester, I'll take Zelensky.'

Barton booked a car out with blues and twos and personal protection equipment, then found the ARV team in the basement in their 4 x 4. He explained the situation as he saw it to Jules and his partner Al Smith, then gave them the sheet with the firearms details. They were experienced riflemen. It took Cureton three seconds to make a decision.

'We need to call for the Tactical Support Team. It's too dangerous to storm a house when we know there's someone in there with a shotgun, whoever we think is at risk in the building. Our rifles and pistols are outgunned in that kind of scenario. We'll drive there now and contain the scene, but you're going to want a trained sniper and specialists with smoke bombs and shields. If she steps outside and starts shooting, we'll react, but until the others get there, our role will be stopping anyone else getting involved in the scene.'

Barton had suspected that would be the case. Ronnie had told him that the closest specialist unit was over an hour away. He tried Ellen's mobile number one more time to no avail. He got Google Maps up on his phone and found a rally point a hundred metres further up the road from the house in Stilton. He jumped in the passenger seat. Zelensky pulled away, followed the ARV and accelerated out of the car park. Barton grabbed the radio.

'Delta, Delta, control, four, zero, nine, Alpha.'

'Four, zero, nine, Alpha, go ahead.'

'Good afternoon, Delta. Please show me as double-crewed with PPE en route to the incident at North Street, Stilton.'

'Roger, four, zero, nine, that's all noted. Update on arrival, please, Delta, out.'

Barton listened to the radio as the ARV crew updated their movements. Control would do their job and notify the other departments, including the ambulance service. They pulled onto the A1, which thankfully was relatively clear.

'Keep up with the ARV,' said Barton.

Smith and Cureton had their lights on, but no tone. Zelensky looked over at Barton as the ARV accelerated away and disappeared. Barton smiled. It didn't matter if they lost them as the riflemen were very experienced. Barton and Zelensky pulled into the edge of Stilton village and stopped about a hundred metres from the house, out of shotgun range. The huge house was set alone and was surrounded by a white metre-high stone wall. There were vicious railings on it to stop all but the most enthusiastic of burglars. The ARV had driven past the house and was parked further up and out of sight of it, blocking the road in the process. Barton's phone rang. It was Cureton.

'There's a white Audi on the drive with a seemingly crucified body on the bonnet. The front door of the house is open, but there's no movement.'

'Okay, what's the plan?' replied Barton.

'Close both roads off a couple of hundred metres either way. Luckily, they're so rich they don't have any neighbours. Jules and I will secure that front gate. If that's Ewing on top of that sports car, then we're too late.'

'Can you describe him?'

'Can't see his face. Nice clothes, shiny black shoes, dark-brown full head of hair. Thirtyish.'

'Shit.'

'He looks very dead. Stay away. Once we're in position and have that doorway covered, we'll reassess.'

Barton cut off the call and watched Cureton and Smith slip out of their vehicle and go to the rear. They opened the boot. When they closed it again, both had rifles in their hands. Barton had worked with these men before; he trusted them implicitly. Smith took the lead, and the two men moved into position. The riflemen would want to contain the situation until the cavalry arrived, but Barton had lost two officers in the past year. He wasn't going to lose another one for the sake of thirty minutes. He needed to see who the body on the Audi was. Barton hustled towards the scene.

Smith was at one end of the wall with his weapon trained on the door. Cureton was at Barton's end. He gave Barton a filthy look as he approached. Barton cut him off before he could say anything.

'We don't have time for a negotiator to arrive. I need to know if that is Ewing.'

Barton let out the breath he was holding as he realised the dead man on the car was too old and thickset to be Ewing.

'It isn't him,' said Barton. 'Although, he's definitely dead. You know what that means. Ewing might still be alive.'

'You are not going in there. Even here we aren't completely safe. We're fifty metres from the front door, but a shotgun could still do some damage depending on the type of ammunition.'

Barton paused for a moment. Fucking procedures. He looked back and saw another two cars had pulled up behind him. He rang Strange.

'Get Leicester to cruise one of the cars past the ARV and block the road this side of that blue car. Nobody comes down this road. Tell him to get rid of anyone who turns up. You cover that side, same deal. If you hear shooting, do not approach the house until I say so. These guys will have it under control.'

Barton watched the house as the car drove past them. There was definite movement inside. He thought of the incident with Twelvetrees and the postwoman on the day he'd returned to work after his recuperation. It was the same thing – get those in danger out – but this time the stakes were much higher.

'I'm going to shout,' said Barton.

'I'd rather you didn't,' said Cureton. 'But if you do, remember we know there are at least two people in there. See if you can get them to come out showing their hands. If they don't reply after the first call, leave it. Smith can cover that door and I'll have a look at the rear in case anyone sneaks out. When Tactical arrive, they'll decide if and when to storm the building.'

Barton had been the captain on the school rugby team. He didn't need a loudhailer. He nodded to Cureton, who took aim at the front door. Smith also had his gun trained there. It felt strangely quiet. Barton spotted another three cars and an ambulance pulling up in the distance. He heard the door to one of them shut. Barton gritted his teeth to stop him cursing. He filled his lungs while poking his head over the wall.

'Scarlett Starr, come out with your hands raised.'

There isn't much doubt who's outside. Scarlett sobers up fast and sweeps past me, although I'm beginning to wonder if she's had anything to drink at all. Usually, she moves around in a cloud of Chanel with a hint of meths, but I didn't detect that when I hugged her earlier. I follow her to the door, and we look out towards the gates.

'I can't see anyone,' she says.

'Me neither.'

Then the sun glints off something next to one of the stone gateposts. I clearly hear the voice again.

'We can see you both. Please leave the house with your arms raised.'

I pick out the rifle barrel poking through the railings, even though the people behind it are mostly hidden. One of them has a shaven head. It has to be Barton.

I glance across at Scarlett. Her eyes narrow.

'How did they know about this?'

I try to sound nonchalant. 'Maybe a neighbour rang them.'

'We don't have any.'

'Passing car?'

'You told them. Bitch.' She hisses the last word.

'Yes, I didn't know what to expect.'

Scarlett laughs. It sounds surprisingly genuine and happy.

'I'm glad it ends this way,' she says. 'You've been both a thorn and a rose to me ever since we met. The boys wanted to be with you, and the girls were scared of you. I hoped to be the same, but you're more broken than I am. I know why you called the police. You're going to tell them I killed Robert, aren't you? That maggot neighbour of yours will say anything you want. I suppose it's poetic then that I kill you.'

I already had an eye on the shotgun behind her, but she twists and turns much faster than I expect. She has the weapon in her hand and is lowering it when I manage to get my hands on the barrel. We struggle and tug, with the gun jolting between us. Scarlett's teeth gnash with frenzied fury. She's incredibly strong, possessed even. I summon my reserves to haul the gun away from her, but only succeed in pulling her towards me. She keeps shoving and we stagger out of the front door and into the courtyard.

With my back prickling at the imminent arrival of a bullet, I release one hand and thump her as hard as I can in the face. It hurts me, but seemingly not her. Something inside me is telling me not to hurt my friend; my only friend. With a wild shout, Scarlett spins the shotgun and when I'm off balance, she rams the heel of her hand into my chest and knocks me to the floor.

The sun blinds me for a moment, but then it disappears behind a cloud. Scarlett's face is terrible. The thing that stares out from her eyes is merciless. She raises the gun to take aim.

'No, Scarlett, don't!' I scream. 'Please. I don't want to die.'

She pauses, then smiles.

'Fuck you.'

Barton observed the scene in front of him with dismay. As the barrel of the blonde woman's weapon came down to point at Ellen, events were out of his hands. Everything appeared to be happening in slow motion. As the gun levelled, Barton knew it was decision time for Smith and Cureton.

The woman's fingers moved onto the trigger. Two sharp bangs echoed out, filling the air. Scarlett wobbled but made no sound. She staggered to the right and took a few clumsy steps towards them. She shook her head twice and sank to her knees. One of her arms dropped away from the weapon, but the other swung it in their direction. Smith and Cureton fired again, and Scarlett's face and neck exploded with red spray. Her head slumped back, but she remained sitting as she died.

Barton went to stand but Smith put a hand on his shoulder to stop him. With their weapons raised, Smith and Cureton advanced on the two women. Barton stood up as Cureton picked up the shotgun beside Starr's inert body. He opened the weapon and paused. Looking back with a pained expression, he shouted out the devastating news.

'Empty.'

They checked Ellen was unarmed and uninjured, with Smith staying by her side until Cureton returned with the second shotgun that was listed on the licence. Cureton confirmed the house was clear. Barton rang Zander, who he could see next to the ambulance, then made his way to the scene.

Barton shook the hands of the two shooters.

'We'll wait over there,' said Cureton, pointing at a bench on the lawn.

He watched them trudge away, knowing they would replay this afternoon in their minds for the rest of their lives. Authorised Firearms Officers crew were highly trained, but they weren't soldiers, and they weren't killers. They would need support to get them through what they'd done. Ellen, however, stared impassively at them as they left, and then at him. She answered his questions around what happened, and who'd died, without emotion. Zander listened, before moving away to update Control.

'Are you okay?' Barton asked Ellen.

'I'll live.'

'What the hell happened here?'

'I don't really know. Scarlett had been having an affair with Ewing for years. He treated her like shit, though, and she was an unstable alcoholic. Her husband found out and said he was going to leave her. She told Ewing that she was free and he told her that he wasn't interested in a relationship. Last I heard, she was going to discuss it with him. She rang me and said she'd killed Ewing in the heat of an argument. Then she'd returned here and shot her husband as he tried to leave.'

Barton heard crunching in the gravel behind him. It was Zelensky, being followed onto the drive by Leicester and an ambulance. He didn't want Zelensky seeing Ewing and what could only be another dead body.

'Zelensky, take Ellen to the paramedics, please, and get her checked over.'

'Where's Ewing?' asked Zelensky.

Ellen gestured at the cars. 'She said she'd put him in a boot.'

Barton nodded at Zelensky to take Ellen away. Then he walked past the deceased on the bonnet to the rear of the Audi. Flies buzzed around the horrific entry wound in the man's chest. Even in death, it was easy to match the face to the Tim Ovett who owned the shotgun licence. The car and its boot were locked. Strange and Zander stood either side of him.

'Apparently, Starr put Ewing in the boot,' said Barton.

Strange stepped towards the dead body. She glanced down at the groin area and put her hand in the right pocket, pulling out a pair of keys. She pressed the fob, and the boot popped open a few centimetres. Barton yanked it up, eyes wide as he peered in, but it was empty. He swallowed hard, then turned to the Qashqai parked next to it.

The paramedic asks me my name and gives me the once-over, but I tell her I'm fine. She seems more interested in what's going on near the cars, as is the officer who drove me home the other night, Zelensky. She was the one that Ewing hurt and she obviously hasn't got over his behaviour. I've done her a favour but she doesn't know that yet. Her pretty face is tormented. There's concern for a colleague, but I can tell she still loves him. I expect she retained a glimmer of hope that one day he would come back to her.

'Scarlett said she'd put him in the boot of the Qashqai. Perhaps he's still alive,' I say.

Zelensky's features soften. The conflict is evident on her face.

'Go over.' I nod. 'I'm not going anywhere.'

The paramedic picks up on Zelensky's worry.

'Ellen's all right,' the paramedic says to her. 'Just a bit of shock. She'll be okay here.'

Zelensky looks at me, then past the ambulance, as though confirming there is nowhere for me to go. She doesn't linger and swiftly walks back to the murder scene.

I sit on the bed in the ambulance. Raised up, I can watch as Barton uses a baton to smash the driver's side window on the Qashqai. He fiddles inside for a minute, then walks to the rear of the car. The boot rises, followed by audible gasps. The paramedic stands up on the back of the ambulance next to me, straining to see.

'Go. You'll be needed there. I'll just have a lie down.'

He's not been told otherwise. No one has arrested me. I've done nothing wrong here. While he strides over, I slip out of the ambulance and try to leave, but the other paramedic is in my way.

Barton stared down at the tightly taped-up duvet and pillowcases that concealed a body shape. He checked for evidence of a rising diaphragm but knew he was wasting his time. Strange stood next to him and took her penknife out of her pocket. She found an area of loose material and slid the knife into the thick cotton and made a slit. The smell of death enveloped them.

Holding his breath, Barton reached down and ripped the liner open. He soon exposed the rictus grin of Robert Ewing. The deep cut in his neck revealed his fate. His face looked serene, which was strange because it couldn't have been a peaceful end. A howl arose from behind him. Zelensky stared at Ewing with her mouth in a haunted snarl. She sank to her knees.

'No, no, no.'

Barton picked her up and held her to him, moving her so she wasn't looking at the body. He nodded at the paramedic, who dutifully, yet pointlessly, checked Ewing for a pulse. The shock of staring at one of your own was tough to bear, and nobody spoke for a minute. Zelensky lay limp in his grip. He carried her towards the ambulance as though she weighed nothing. As he approached the back and saw it was empty, he frowned as to where Ellen had gone.

The other paramedic was sitting on the rear of the ambulance. He helped Barton lay Zelensky on a stretcher.

'Where did she go?' demanded Barton.

'The girl with the black hair?'

'Yes!'

'She wanted some fresh air and wandered over there. No one said to keep her here, but she can't have gone far.'

Barton ran hard through the gates and looked left and right. Both roadblocks were still in place. The one on the right had a uniformed officer staring straight at him. Barton's stomach lurched as he jogged towards him, shouting as he did.

'Did you see the tall girl?'

'Yes, she'd been out walking and heard gunshots. Her car was parked on the other side of the barrier, so I let her go.'

The look of disgust on Barton's face caused the man to step backwards. Strange had caught up with him by that point.

'Shit,' she said. 'She's gone?'

'Yep.'

'I took her reg,' the officer said. 'Just in case.'

Strange wrote it down and called Control.

'Trace this registration in real time, please. She'll have headed for the A1. Ring me when it's set up.'

For a brief moment, Barton imagined himself leaping into a car and chasing after Ellen, sirens blaring, and speeding up the motorway in hot pursuit. But instead he felt the weight of responsibility on his shoulders and returned to the scene. Three people had tragically lost their lives, and the police were responsible for one of the deaths. Rare events like this had to be dealt with so carefully due to the overwhelming interest from the public.

Cureton and Smith would have to stay at the scene until they were relieved of their weapons. They'd had little choice but to shoot Starr, but that didn't matter at this point. There would be an investigation into the shooting, and they'd probably be on light duties until its conclusion.

As for chasing after Ellen, that wasn't an option either. In a few minutes, she would be on one of the busiest roads in the country. If she realised that the police were pursuing her, she would likely put her foot down. If she had a head-on collision with a family, the police would take part of the blame. It wasn't worth the risk. He was pretty sure he knew her destination, and the road cameras would track her if she kept to the main routes.

At that point, the Tactical Support Team arrived. He called Zander over to him and Strange.

'Kelly, take Malik and drive to Ellen's sister's address in Harrow. I'll brief Tactical and they'll go as well. You can update them fully on the way. They'll take over if Ellen is there. It's the only place I think she'll head for. Call me when you arrive and let the Met know what's happening. Ellen needs to be brought back to the station. Zander and I will still be here. It's going to take CSI days to sort this out.'

Barton and Strange strode to the Tactical van while his mind continued to process recent events. There was still no obvious evidence that Ellen had murdered anyone, but her fleeing had been enough for him. He'd stake his reputation on her being involved. They would catch Ellen Vickerman, then arrest and charge her for murder. His main hope was that the killing was now over.

THE ICE KILLER

I need to see Trent, but I want to speak to my sister first. The police will guess that, so I don't have long. As I screech along the country roads, I wind my window down and throw out the two shotgun cartridges that I removed from the gun when I arrived at Scarlett's house. That must have been a nasty surprise to her, although only for about a second.

I'll miss Scarlett. She was a ruined creature with a warped heart, but she was all I had. It was a quick end for her, and a fortunate one for me. I hammer up the slip road and veer into the traffic on the A1. If they're on the ball, they'll pick me up on the number plate cameras that they used to track my sister. I tear along at nearly 100 mph. Madly, some young lad in a BMW overtakes me.

At Alconbury I ease off and follow the country lanes into Hunting-don. I park in an all-day car park near the railway station. I take my sunglasses from my coat pocket and put them on, while pulling off my wig. A train to King's Cross leaves in five minutes. Soon, I'm on it and start to work out my next move.

There's a Tube map in the carriage. Metropolitan line and then the Bakerloo line will get me to Harrow. They'll think I'm going to my sister's house, not knowing she's at the hospital with her husband, Greg.

Barton shook the hand of Inspector Brown, who was in charge of the Tactical Support Team. He spent five minutes giving the man an update and sent him on his way. Strange took Brown's phone number and agreed to give him as much information as they had en route. Barton rang Control to ask for the Firearms Commander to be updated about the deaths.

They would send a Post Incident Manager to take over the scene and to open a Post Incident Suite where they'd run through the facts over and over again. It was tough on the riflemen who were just doing their job, but the records had to be made while events were still fresh in the mind.

Control informed him that Ellen's car had been picked up by a camera approaching Alconbury. At least Ellen was headed in the right direction. When the scene at the house was secured and taped up, Zander came over to Barton's car.

'What next, boss?'

'For my sanity's sake, let's go through everything from the beginning.'

It took nearly a quarter of an hour for Barton to lay out what they knew.

'That's one unlucky girl, or a murderous one,' said Zander.

'Surely nobody's that unlucky,' replied Barton.

'And we still have no forensic evidence, CCTV, witnesses, or anything like that which is concrete?'

'No. Well, we do, but at the moment it backs up Ellen's side of the story more than any alternative,' said Barton.

Zander blew out a long breath. 'That doesn't help.'

'There's reasonable doubt on all the deaths. Each one would be looked at in isolation and we have to prove it was definitely her. We don't seem to be able to do that. Look at the people she might have killed. What jury is going to judge her harshly when she's been raped at least once and taken a sex offender down who was trying to kill her?'

'What about Ewing?'

'I'm not sure what link, if any, there is from her to him. I've heard stories concerning Ewing and women. Even if we could somehow prove she was involved in his death, a good defence wouldn't struggle to make him look terrible. Besides, it sounds like we've just shot and killed the star witness.'

Barton spent the next five minutes talking to Cureton and Smith. They'd put their guns back in the safe and were making notes on how events had played out. He stepped away when his mobile rang. It was Strange.

'Hi, John. She's not tripped the next two cameras on the A1, so she must have gone onto the smaller roads. She might have headed into Huntingdon. What do you want us to do?'

Barton rubbed his face while he considered the options.

'You're only an hour from Harrow. I still think that's where she's heading. Let's see if we can at least speak to the sister and maybe catch Ellen at the same time. I have a feeling neither sister is as innocent as they pretend.'

'And the Huntingdon angle?'

'Her father lives there, although they haven't spoken for years. I'll send Zander there and I'll get Traffic in Huntingdon to look out for the car. She's a bright woman. It's possible she went to the railway station.'

'Bugger,' said Barton as he disconnected the call.

'More problems?' asked Zander.

'Yep. It's as though I'm battling the whole family.'

85

THE ICE KILLER

After I arrive at King's Cross, I soon skirt around the underground system and get out at Northwick Park, the stop before Harrow on the Hill. It's rush hour now, and I'm swept along with the tide of humanity. It's only a few minutes' stroll to the hospital, where I ask for directions at Reception. I ring the doorbell to the High Dependency Unit. A nurse smiles when I ask for Greg Breslinski. She tells me to wash my hands, and I walk quietly to room four.

My sister is sitting next to the bed with her head resting on the covers. She holds Greg's hand. There are no beeping machines and he looks gaunt, but I can see his lips moving as he breathes.

'Hey,' I say.

'Hey,' she replies, with a tired but relieved grin.

'Good news?' I ask.

'Yes, I hope so. They've said he's over the worst. After a day's rest, they'll let me take him home.'

'I'm pleased.'

She reads the distance in my speech correctly. 'What happened?'

'I want to tell you about the dreadful things I've done.'

'You did.'

'No, that wasn't all of them, and there's been more.'

She nods, but then steels herself.

'Sit down and tell me everything.'

There's a strange look on her face. One of weary acceptance, but also a hint of guilt. I force myself to begin.

'I'm a killer, but that's not the shocking bit. The evil part is that I don't care about the lives I've taken. I know murder is wrong, but it's like I don't particularly feel that way.'

'Go on.'

'I have no restraint. I'm vengeful and violent.'

'Get it all out,' she urges.

And so I do.

I start with the girl from school, and I finish with killing Robert. I even fill the hazy bits in with my imagination. Afterwards, I wait for the recriminations to begin, but she's quiet. She rises and pulls me into what feels like the strangest hug I've ever had, where the other person's need is more than my own. When we break, she has tears streaming down her face.

'What's up?' I try to make light of it. 'No morality lessons?'

'I'd be a hypocrite. It's time I told the truth, too.'

'Should I sit?'

She nods again, and we both take a seat. After blowing her nose and taking a deep breath, she talks as though she's releasing something from deep within.

'I'll start from the beginning too. Mum and Dad met when they were young and fell madly in love. They were very much peas in a pod, but not in a good way. Our mum described their match as hell-sent. It was tempestuous and violent, on both their parts. They exhausted their friends with their bitter splits and inevitable reunions, and then I came along.'

I rise and pour myself a glass of water to prepare myself for what's coming.

'Go on, keep going,' I say.

'They hoped a baby would calm them down, then they could get married and live peacefully, but nothing changed, and they continued to have huge rows. When you arrived, it deteriorated further, and Dad lost control. Eventually, he left while he was still sane enough to make rational choices. Mum retreated from the world, but you, Mum and me got on fine until you started puberty. Sadly, whatever sickness lies in our family, you had it worst of all. It was as if you'd inherited the ruin and fury of both of them.'

'Was that why you left?'

'You and I fought like animals because I wanted to control you. I'm surprised you don't remember. But Mum saw you as someone who needed to be treated like porcelain. That's how she managed her illness, by avoiding tension and conflict. After our dad moved out, she lived her entire life in second gear. No shocks, no drama, no rage. We brought out the worst in each other, so I left for both our benefit.'

'You married an older man and lived a quiet life as well. At least you didn't murder anyone like Dad and I ended up doing.'

Her sad frown tells me that isn't true.

'No, I took a life too, Ellen.'

The glass of water nearly slips from my grasp, but I also seize the truth at that moment.

'Wee Jock?'

She grimaces. 'Yes, we'd hired a detective to look for you. He rang and told me where you were. When I arrived, Wee Jock was there and you'd been fighting. I told you to come with me, but he grabbed your arm and shouted at me to fuck off. He slapped my face, and an irresistible anger came over me, and everything I'd been holding back was released in an instant. Such total, devastating, wrath.'

I should focus on the gruesome crime, but I recognise her words.

'And I bet you know this,' she continues, 'but it's quite liberating to be that angry.'

I can't stop a chuckle sneaking out. 'We are a mad family.'

'Yes, Mum told me at mad Aunt Dora's funeral that Aunt Dora had been sectioned four times in her life.'

'Really?'

'Yes, our genes seem to be off kilter. I felt so powerful and ruthless when I attacked Wee Jock, but, afterwards, I was scared of what I was capable of. I left him on the patio and never looked back.'

'No wonder they didn't find anyone for it.'

'No, but a few years later it happened again when I had an argument with a woman in the park. She was drunk and rode her bike into one of my children. I wanted to kill her. Carson got me off in court, but I swore that I'd never behave like that again. I tried medication, but it thinned my hair and made me drowsy. Luckily, we were wealthy, and I tested different things. Eventually I learned that if I kept myself away from dangerous situations and looked after myself, I could control myself.'

'You trained yourself to be better?'

She smiles. 'Not like in *Kung Fu*, if that's what you're thinking. Just healthy eating, yoga, running, mindfulness. It's a bit hippy, yet it works for me. But I let you down. I left you under Mum's guidance, and that was never going to work for you. The only way the hospital could get you under control was to over-medicate you. I suspect your GP did the same thing.'

'But then I felt like a zombie. A lonely one at that.'

'Perhaps that is our lot in life. The price of everyone else's safety is our isolation, but we should still have each other. I knew you'd stopped taking your medication and I should have done more. Instead I left you again.'

I squeeze her hand, then stand and stretch, strangely relieved and exhausted.

'I feel lighter,' I say. 'As though I understand who I am, and it helps to appreciate that I'm not the only one. You know what, even though we've committed terrible crimes, I don't think there's a worse feeling than thinking you're different from everyone else.'

'I'll give you the keys to our house. You can come back to ours and rest. We'll talk more when Greg's better.'

'I do have a final question. What about your kids? Are they okay?'

'They're both fine. Normal, whatever the hell that is. I had concerns with the terrible twos and threes and the teenage years had me worried too, but they're quiet, studious youngsters. Greg is so incredibly dull that any volatile behaviour from my genes has been doused by his entrenched boringness.'

I can't help a louder laugh. 'Sounds sexy.'

'It's what I need. He's the water to my fire, and the calm to my storm. Although I must admit, he's vague when he talks about his youth.'

It makes sense. Claude and Carrie were always quiet children. Carrie had a bit more bite about her. She once slapped her brother around the face for cheating at cards, but they spent most Christmases with their heads buried in books. I wonder if Brad could be my Greg. We sit quietly in thought for a moment until a question comes to my mind.

'What possessed you to have kids after how we turned out?'

Lucy shrugged. 'I'm not sure. Why does anyone start a family?'

I smile at her, but I'm beginning to think she's madder than me.

'Can I stay here tonight? I'll sleep on the chair. But I should go back and talk to Trent. I have to know if he'll keep quiet. I need to be free.'

'Make sure you come home to us afterwards. I don't want to lose you again. What are you going to do if he doesn't toe the line?'

'It'll be his choice. Funnily enough, I used to read psychology books to try to self-diagnose my problems. Most advise you to fight or face your fears, but a man recommended doing something different with your demons.'

She raises an eyebrow.

'He said to use them to your advantage.'

86

Barton's alarm woke him at five, but he'd barely slept. They'd had no luck in locating Ellen or Lucy. Strange had waited outside Lucy's unlit house for two hours, but there'd been no movement. She'd knocked around the nearest homes, but, typically for people in huge houses, no one had much idea about their neighbours' movements. An older woman who lived in an isolated cottage on the opposite side of the road had said that the Breslinskis were a private couple. They were polite, but never chatted. It was as if the pair of them chose to stay out of others' lives.

Sirena had rung Barton last night when she'd finished at Ellen's flat. She'd said there was nothing immediately incriminating in the bedroom and they'd have to wait for the lab results to come back. The only unusual thing they'd discovered was when they took the sink drain apart, they'd found a lot of tablets at the bottom of the pipe. They had gone for testing.

It was that that had kept Barton up. Could it be that Ellen was a criminal psychopath? Or perhaps she'd stopped taking her meds? Cambridgeshire Police and the Met were on the lookout for the sisters and they were checking CCTV, but it wouldn't be easy if she had a different wig on or had taken it off. Zander had waited at Ellen's father's house in Huntingdon until the young mother they'd helped before had left her flat and told him that she'd seen Ted leaving shortly before Zander arrived.

Barton climbed out of bed, crept downstairs and made a cup of coffee. No one else had stirred, so he let himself out and drove to work to crack on with the massive amounts of paperwork he had to do. He had a meeting with the super later that day, which he wasn't looking forward to.

He waged war with his inbox until Strange arrived at eight with bleary eyes and a huge Costa coffee carton.

'Come on. Let's visit Ellen's father,' said Barton. 'It might be time to kick a door down.'

'You think Ellen's hiding there?'

'No, the police found her car at Huntingdon railway station. She'll be with her sister.'

'But you reckon her father is implicated somehow?'

'I don't think he's directly involved, although it's possible he knows where Ellen is, but he'll know her state of mind. There's murderous psychosis running in that family. I'm sure of it. He's going to answer my questions today.'

'And if he doesn't want to help?'

'I can be persuasive when I'm filling a doorway.'

They arrived at the estate in good time despite it being rush hour. The curtains in Deacon's flat were drawn, but Strange could hear the TV when she pressed her ear against the window. They slipped into the building when someone else was leaving and Barton pummelled the door. No one came.

Barton leaned down to the letter box, opened it, and shouted through.

'I'm coming through the door in ten seconds whether you open it or not.'

Barton counted out loud. When he got to four, Strange bent down and yelled through.

'We're about to arrest your daughter for murder. If you have anything to say, now's the time to say it.'

Four seconds later, they heard bolts sliding across. Deacon peered out at them like an irritable vulture.

'What's happened to Ellen?'

Barton walked through the doorway, giving Deacon little choice other than to back up. Strange followed and closed the door behind them. They both stared at the multitude of locks. The word 'tablets' was on a yellow Post-it note next to the handle in big black felt tip. Barton slid past Deacon and found himself in a small lounge diner. It was strikingly similar to the layout of Ellen's flat. There were differences, though. Deacon had written 'medicine' on pieces of paper and stuck them to the cabinets and walls in large red letters.

Barton knew they had hit the mark when Deacon only stared at them instead of complaining about their uninvited entrance. Barton pointed at the writing.

'I assume this is so you don't forget?'

'That's right. I have other ways to help, too.'

'You take them down if probation visit.'

Deacon nodded.

'What happens if you do forget?'

Deacon's eyes narrowed.

'I won't, because of these methods. I began putting these up years ago, just to be certain.'

'We know what happens when you're ill, Mr Deacon. People die, isn't that right?'

Deacon's expression hardened further. 'I suppose so. Try not to worry, you'll be one of the first to know. What's this got to do with Ellen?'

'She's been involved in multiple deaths. A man was pushed under a bus, others were stabbed or strangled, and she was at a scene with a murdered detective in a car boot.'

'I'm sure there's a rational explanation.'

'You mean like your killings were explainable? I think Ellen has the same problems you have. CSI found drugs that had been thrown away. That dead detective disappeared near your daughter's home.'

'That doesn't mean it was her. Those flats and that area are full of odd people.'

'There was blood on Ellen's kitchen cupboards.'

'I don't want any involvement in this. My hands are clean. Besides, I don't care what she's done. She's my daughter and my loyalty is to her.'

'Obstruction of justice will have you back inside.'

'I've told you. I don't know anything.'

'Where were you yesterday afternoon?'

'I attended an anger management course, which probation had arranged.'

Barton swore under his breath and stormed out. It felt as if he was the one who was out of control, but grieving for a fellow officer would have to wait. Strange drove on the way back to Peterborough while he gathered his thoughts.

'What exactly are you thinking?' asked Strange. 'That Ellen and Scarlett killed Ewing in her flat, then dragged the body to the car, before driving it to Scarlett's house.'

'Something like that.'

'We should speak to all the neighbours around there. Ewing was a solid unit. Two women would struggle to drag him down those stairs. You know how heavy and cumbersome dead bodies are. Perhaps Scarlett's husband was involved. Then they argued when they got back home and she shot him.'

'That's a fair point. It's conceivable someone else helped them. Wait, didn't Zelensky say that she spoke to some weird characters in the downstairs flats? That chimes with what Deacon just said about there being a load of odd people around there. Let's swing by and talk to them, maybe apply a bit of pressure. One of them might have seen something.'

They arrived in Peterborough and drove straight to Eastfield. A uniformed officer, PC Rivendon, was standing next to a sleeping man curled up on a piece of cardboard. There was a framed photograph of a couple and their child next to the wall behind him.

'Everything all right?' asked Barton.

'Yeah. I'm trying to get him to move, but he keeps going back to sleep.'

Barton looked at the matted blond hair and filthy face.

'Leave him be.'

Then the eyes opened and the man pulled himself up into a sitting position. He stared at Barton with recognition and then looked away. Barton did a double take, but it was definitely him: the ex-marine who'd pulled the postwoman into his house.

'Twelvetrees?'

'Yeah, but I'm trying to sleep.'

'What the hell are you doing here?'

'What do you think happened? I lost my house. The police took me to the station but couldn't get me any help with my mental health. They kept me in overnight and released me the next morning with a caution and an appointment at the hospital that morning. I went home first, but it was boarded up with all my stuff inside. There was a number to ring on the door, but no one ever answers. I've been sleeping rough ever since.'

Barton's face flushed.

'God, I'm sorry. I thought they'd make sure you were okay. I'll get your things back for you.'

'There isn't much point. What the hell would I do with it all? I can't drag a dishwasher and fridge around with me.'

They all heard the furious shout from the flats behind them. Barton grabbed Rivendon's arm.

'What's been going on in there?'

'That's the first sound I've heard.'

Barton and Strange exchanged a glance.

'Anyone else been near? No sign of Ellen having returned?'

'No, nothing.'

Barton turned to Twelvetrees.

'Stay here. I know a guy at The New Haven hostel. We'll get you off the streets.'

'Don't worry about it. There are more generous, kind people about than I imagined. To be honest, it's not been too bad, apart from the cold. Apart from the copper here, people leave me alone.'

Another bellow came from the flats.

'I'll get going,' said Twelvetrees. 'Looks like you have your hands full.'

Barton watched him grab his meagre things.

'Wait for a moment,' said Barton. 'This argument in the flats might be nothing. Let me at least take you for a burger and chips around the corner.'

Few men can resist a free burger. Twelvetrees nodded with a slight smile.

'I'll stay for a few minutes.'

'Excellent. Rivendon, ring this in, then cover the entrance to the flats and listen out. It might just be a domestic.'

Barton and Strange were outside the front trying to judge which flat the shouting was coming from, when a pained howl came from the bottom-right flat. It didn't sound like a domestic, it sounded like a war.

My sister drops me at the Tube station and I'm soon heading back out of London. I carry on through Huntingdon, even though my ticket is only to there, and alight at Peterborough. I have a story ready about wanting to buy the extra distance, but the barriers are up and I simply walk through. It's tempting to stop for a bite to eat, but I'm surprised by how nervous I am.

I'm not sure how Trent will react to what I have to say. He's a strange lad, but he's a long way from being stupid. He holds my freedom in his hands. Would it be so bad being his girlfriend? At least he's keen. The problem is that I can be two separate people, depending on my state of mind, and, unfortunately, neither of them wants to be with him.

I'm guessing the police have a person on the front door of the flats still, or at least parked in the car park, so I head to the cemetery. The gates are open, and it seems so different from how it was on that freezing-cold night. The angel stares benignly over me as I pass. Even the drunks on the benches are in good humour. One has a tray of food from a takeaway.

'Fancy a portion, darling?' the filthy individual shouts, waving a sausage at me.

'I'm not hungry, thanks, but I'm happy to slice it up for you.'

They laugh, and I suspect for a moment they're content. Who am I to judge? They choose how to progress through life and I will decide on my path. I reach the fence and fiddle with the screws on the other side. It's tricky not being able to see what I'm doing, but easier than when I had frozen fingers.

Something makes me pause as I'm about to head through. There's light noise all around me. Singing birds, the reassuring hum of a lawn-mower, the warm breeze through the trees seems gentle and friendly, and even the smell in the air hints at new beginnings, perhaps freedom.

With a smile, I slip through the fence and tap my fingers on Trent's back window. As I suspected, he's there in seconds. His ghoulish face stares at me with unconcealed anger.

'Get inside,' he hisses. 'Where the fuck have you been?'

I pull myself in. 'Calm down. What's wrong with you?'

'Are you kidding? There's been police outside my place for days. I'm running out of food. They know.'

Trent is close to losing any semblance of control. We communicate in angry whispers.

'Trent, they know nothing, or they'd have pulled you in.'

'I can't stand it any longer. I'm going to confess.'

'Just sit tight. They'll leave soon, and you can go back to normal.'

'This isn't fucking normal. Stay and help me.'

'I can't stay here. My sister said she'll have me until it blows over. The police will want to question us both but, as long as we say nothing, I don't think they have any concrete proof.'

'No way. You're staying with me.'

'Please, keep your voice down. Look, I can't hide away, or I'll look guilty. Living with you would connect us. It will already seem suspicious that I ran when they shot Scarlett, but I can tell them I panicked.'

I realise my error immediately. Trent can't have seen the news. He does a strange tormented dance and begins to whimper.

'Jesus Christ, Ellen. They'll shoot me too.'

'You idiot, she was waving a shotgun at the police. If they question you, just keep quiet. My sister will get you a brilliant solicitor.'

Nothing's helping calm Trent down. His mind is overloading with the pressure. He's puffed himself up and paces back and forth, gulping in air. His hands rake his hair.

'I've got to leave, Trent. I'll ring you in a few days.'

He stops pacing and murderous eyes bear down on me. He takes two steps to the side and grabs something out of a toolbox. It's some kind of thin, sharp screwdriver, long enough to impale me and stick out the other side of my back if it was jabbed in my direction. He takes two steps backwards and locks the door. Then he bellows, phlegm flying in my direction.

'I did you a favour, so now you're mine. You *will* stay here with me.'

'I can't. Don't blow it now. I'll get everything sorted and you can come and stay wherever I am. Surely you don't want to hurt me.'

He scrunches his eyes repeatedly, causing tears to slide down his cheeks. I edge towards the bedroom, but notice his jaw bunch just in time as he thrusts the screwdriver at me.

'Bitch!'

I catch his hand and manage to push it down. He forces so hard that the point drives deep into the wall between my legs and a lump of plaster drops off.

'Argghh!' he roars.

With his spare hand, he backhands the side of my head, sending lights flashing in my vision.

I cling onto the screwdriver, pulling his arm away from his body, but his free hand searches for my eyes. Sensing the surge of energy before it races through my body, I snarl and stamp on his left foot. With him unbalanced, I place a hand on his right hip and, roaring at full volume, throw him sideways into a big pile of cables, keyboards and computer parts.

He clambers up, shocked by the ferocity of my onslaught. It feels as though my eyes are going to burst from my face. He tries to step away, but his feet tangle in the cables. He knows what I'm capable of, because he carried the evidence. Whatever his hopes were, they are dashed now. Too late, he sees my power. I pick up his weapon. The rage I feel is blinding, then there's a heavy knock.

Even through the thickened storm of anger, I know to freeze. Trent's eyes look to the door, then to his screwdriver in my hand. He sees danger on one side and safety on the other. I put my finger to my lips, and try to whisper 'shh', but it comes out as an evil hiss.

'Help!' he screams.

I step towards him. The door smashes and splinters behind me, and a big foot smashes out the panels. A shaven head and broad shoulders crash through, filling the doorway, hands smashing the wood out of the way. It's Barton. I turn back to Trent.

'Don't move!' demands Barton.

Moments can define a life. Simple decisions change futures, yours and others, and a second is all it takes.

88

ACTING DCI BARTON

Barton had raised his meaty paw to hammer on the door again when a strangely high-pitched cry for help came from the flat. He checked the strength of the wood by rattling the handle, stepped back, lifted his leg and struck the centre of the door with his heel. The cheap material split and his foot knocked a panel out. He pushed his head through the gap, knocking the surrounding pieces out with his shoulders, and climbed through, shouting, 'Don't move,' while he stumbled into the room.

His eyes quickly passed over the scene. It resembled an electronic workshop with paraphernalia over every surface. Red lights bleeped and flashed. Even the kettle seemed futuristic.

A thin man with glasses was against the window with his hands raised in self-defence. Barton recognised the back of Ellen. Her arm pumped backwards and forwards, four, five, six times, and the man collapsed onto her. She let him slide off to the floor. It was Ellen's face that turned to him, but she was different, almost unrecognisable. Strange clambered through the gap in the door and edged towards Ellen.

'He was trying to kill me.' Ellen spoke quietly.

'Drop the weapon,' ordered Strange.

Barton's arms reached out to pull Strange back. Now he understood. The hard-faced killer in front of them would have no mercy and was as deadly as they came. Dispassionate eyes calculated Strange's approach. Ellen dropped the screwdriver and took a step forward.

'No!' Barton roared.

Strange thrust out a fast right, which headed towards her attacker's chin, but Ellen swatted it away. She grabbed Strange by the throat with one hand and her ponytail with the other, yanked her past the sofa, and slammed her forehead into a computer screen on a crammed metal bookcase. Before Barton could move, Ellen had repeated the move, dropped Strange onto the floor, and pulled the bookcase on top of her.

She turned to Barton with cold-hearted purpose and stamped towards him. Barton had never seen such an expression of malice. The strength leaked from his body and out of his legs. Remembering Mortis's words about such a situation, he took a step back to balance himself. He didn't want to hit her in the face, so he hurled a crushing blow from a huge left hand straight into Ellen's stomach. She crumpled to the floor and writhed around in silent, breathless agony.

Barton stepped over her to Strange, reached down and heaved the bookcase and its contents off her back. She gasped and opened an eye.

'Are you okay?'

Strange nodded, but then her eyes widened and she stared behind him. Barton sensed movement behind him. He slowly turned, expecting the screwdriver to arrive in his back.

Ellen had pulled herself to her feet. She stared icily at him as Rivendon arrived in the broken doorway. With a scream, she ran towards Rivendon. With an almighty shove in the chest, she blasted him back through the doorway where he banged into the opposite flat door and crumpled to the floor. Barton scrambled after her as she climbed through the broken door. He ran into the car park feeling out of breath and eased up with a wheeze. He hadn't been out of hospital that long. There was no chance of catching her.

Ellen was fleeing towards the exit, where a figure stood in her way.

'Stop her,' shouted Barton.

Instantly, he recognised the danger in asking a trained killer to confront a psychotic killer. Twelvetrees shrugged the sleeping bag from his shoulders and stepped towards the running figure. Twelvetrees had no qualms about where to hit, and he smashed a fist straight under Ellen's chin, lifting her clean off the ground. She lay motionless at his feet.

89

ACTING DCI BARTON

A week later, Barton leaned back in his groaning chair and flexed his left hand. He'd strained something thumping Ellen, and it still ached. Poor old Strange was signed off with a fractured skull, though, so he'd got off lightly in comparison. Especially considering Trent Anderson's bloody demise. Mortis said that Anderson would have been dead before he hit the ground.

Ellen Vickerman didn't regain complete consciousness until she was cuffed to a stretcher in the back of an ambulance. Barton felt little guilt for her serious concussion considering what she'd done to Strange. After the paramedics had checked her over, he'd charged Ellen with the murder of Anderson and the GBH of Strange. She'd stared dispassionately at him as he'd cautioned her and merely nodded when he'd finished.

He'd wanted to charge Ellen for all the other suspicious deaths, but even knowing she was likely responsible hadn't made it any easier for him to be able to prove anything. And Ellen was the only one left to give an explanation.

Zander had arrived soon after and driven Twelvetrees to the station to make a statement. Twelvetrees had been told about the sleeping spot by another tramp who favoured it because it was out of the wind. As promised, Barton took Twelvetrees for a burger and chips, then found him a place at The New Haven homeless hostel, but the manager rang Barton a few days later to say he'd taken his meagre belongings in the middle of the night and left. Barton wished Twelvetrees well, but without much hope.

The next day, the magistrates had asked Ellen how she pleaded to the charges. She had again been represented by the same solicitor, who had explained she would only answer to confirm her name. The bench hadn't even bothered to confer, and she had been remanded in custody. In the dock, Ellen's face had again displayed no emotion as the door behind her had opened and a security officer had led her away into the dark.

Barton considered himself lucky that he hadn't been suspended over some of his unconventional techniques. Perhaps he should have waited for back-up at Scarlett's house. Maybe he should have arrested Ellen and Lucy sooner. He pushed the thoughts aside. He'd been doing the job long enough to know that not everything in life was clear-cut. You did your best in difficult circumstances, and the police carried the burden of proof. There was no point in being right if the guilty evaded justice.

Barton's supervisors had materialised after there had been a result, but the press had picked up on the confusing elements. Right-wing papers were demanding an inquiry into the police investigation, whereas one left-wing paper had already blamed the authorities for not giving Ellen any support after a multitude of terrible experiences. Barton shook his head. They didn't know the half of it.

There was also a nagging thought at the back of Barton's mind. While the rest of the station was pleased justice would be done for the death of Ewing, the pointless demise of Trent Anderson didn't sit well with Barton. If Ellen had killed the other men, she had done so for a reason. The harsh would say rational ones. The pitiless killing of her neighbour didn't fit that. Barton had suspected Anderson might not be an innocent in all this. After looking around Anderson's flat, he'd called in the experts.

Still, they had Ellen for a senseless murder right in front of their eyes, whatever she said. She wouldn't escape justice for that crime. Barton cracked on with the paperwork. It wasn't easy with the lack of corroborating facts, but he knew that his job was only to present as much evidence as possible to the Crown Prosecution Service. It would be up to them to decide what they would prosecute her for at Crown Court.

A knock came at the door. The force's new IT guru, Barry Tomas, smiled from the doorway.

'Come in, Baz. Was I correct about Trent?'

'You were right, John. You are a clever boy. Sorry, it's taken a while.'

'Did you have trouble bypassing his security?'

'Hell, no. His applications were tight, but it's easy nowadays when you have the hardware. The only worry I had was if he'd set up a "delete all files" command if the firewall was breached.'

'And he didn't?'

'Nope. The stuff on the PC was too important to him. It took ages because of the volume. This guy was very, very sick.'

Barton put his face in his hands. 'Tell me,' he said through his fingers.

'Let's start with the great news. He had CCTV all over his flat, multiple cameras, one looking out of the lounge window, even a concealed one in the toilet, which obviously isn't normal. First thing I checked, of course, was his murder. As I told you in the week, we have a crystal-clear recording of her stabbing him to death.'

'Okay, what's the problem, then?'

'This guy had been on the edge for days. You can see him prowling around in the flat, talking to himself, furiously masturbating at the TV, singing, you name it. Manic behaviour. When Ellen gets there, they clearly have a row. But it's him that makes the first move. He attacks her.'

'Bollocks. Why?'

'Who knows? They struggle and they're going for it. Then you guys turn up and they stop. That's the weird bit. It's like they're both weighing up the odds. You come crashing through, and she stabs the hell out of him.'

Barton considered the evidence. 'We still have a chance of a murder conviction. The police were there, and she was in no danger. She could have stepped away. No one had to die.'

'I agree, 100 per cent. It gives the defence a little wiggle room, though, especially when you combine it with the other... things.'

'I'm not going to like this, am I?'

'I've seen plenty in my time, but this guy took stalking to the next level. He has files and files on Ellen. Most of which were taken by his surveillance cameras, but he's written poems and all sorts. There's sick stuff where he's superimposed her face onto hundreds of porn images. There's so much of it, he categorised it by year and month. But the most damning piece is a recording from a few days before he died. It's of them having sex, but it isn't a leap to say he violently raped her.'

90

It's been a strange six months. Inspector Barton came to the prison to see me. He tried to persuade me to be honest about everything that had happened. Apparently, I owed it to the victims' families. Carson was present. He just shook his head at me. Part of me wanted to come clean, but I don't think anyone would understand.

Carson was shocked when I told him the truth, and he thought he'd heard it all, but he said it was his job to defend me. I asked him why he helped our family, when it was clear we were capable of such violence. He said when he first met my sister, he felt compelled to help her, and that the feeling had never gone. Carson joked that men are defenceless against the combined power of beauty and danger. I'll never ask, but I suspect, from hearing the way he talks about her, that Lucy and he were occasional lovers.

We concocted a story that was close to the truth for the death of Detective Robert Ewing. I said that I bumped into him in the street and took him to my flat. Then Scarlett turned up, and they rowed. I left and thought no more of it, later finding out that she had murdered him, and Trent helped her move the body.

I laid it on thick with Trent's death. The evidence they found on his computer was helpful. I said he'd been abusing me for years. I lost

control for a moment and stabbed him, only to hurt him, after Trent
threatened to say it was me, not him, who helped remove Ewing's body
when Scarlett killed him. Unless I submitted to his sick demands. This
was the big hole in my defence as Carson couldn't prove that Trent and
Scarlett knew each other. They had his email and phone records and
she didn't appear on either. The search history from his computer
helped. He'd checked the maximum sentence for illegally disposing of
a dead body. Apparently, it can be punished by a maximum sentence of
life imprisonment, an unlimited fine or both. No wonder he lost it.

Unfortunately, quite a bit of my evidence sounded lightweight, but
my container of shame was helpful in gaining sympathy. More than
one jury member wept when they heard the details of my foul gang
rape and saw my shredded dress and gruesome injuries. Carson and
his team have thrown everything into it. He skimmed over my mental
health. Obviously, he didn't want them thinking I was a psychopath.
The prosecution went at that hard, even bringing my dad's criminal
and medical history into it. The judge made no apology for hearing
from all witnesses and professionals, however relevant. It would be for
the jury to make a decision.

I was also charged with the murder of Quantrill, Ash and Duncan,
but the judge dropped the cases after Carson made the jury shake their
heads at the inadequacy of the Crown's evidence. As for the other two
charges, Carson said it was in the lap of the Gods. Twelve normal men
and women, people like me, would rule on the rest of my life.

I've just heard that after nearly an entire week of deliberation, the
jury have come to a majority verdict as opposed to a unanimous one.
Carson hoped that was encouraging, as it meant that not everyone
agreed. They've brought me to the dock. A hush settles over the packed
gallery as the court usher sweeps to the front.

'All rise, this court is now in session. The honourable Judge
Arkwright presiding.'

It seems I care about the verdict after all because my knees tremble
as I stand. Tears blur my vision. In a few moments, I'll know if I will
spend the remainder of my days behind bars. Imprisonment has

changed me. They dosed me up to the eyeballs in healthcare when I first arrived, but my case interested the prison psychiatrist. Over the weeks and months, he found a balance that worked. I then took my sister's advice and got healthy.

Ironically, prison suits me. There's no alcohol to self-medicate with. I have a girlfriend, too. She is a boisterous creature whose family hails from Trinidad, but she's eternally upbeat, and I love that. I eat well. Virtually none of the other prisoners eat their salads, so I can have extra. The gym is well equipped, and I feel good. The doctor has dropped my medication further now, and, after sessions of therapy and support from other prisoners, I find being behind bars comfortable and secure. Obviously, no one gives me any shit.

The judge enters from a rear door. I unclench my fists. Is this how real people are: nervous but controlled? I do feel regret and remorse now, but I know not to beat myself up too much either. It's life. Carson asked me to smile more at the start, but I found it hard and unnatural. He later told me to stop because I was scaring him, never mind the jury.

'Would the defendant please remain standing?' says the judge. 'Everyone else may sit.'

The judge talks about the case and the clear verdict he expects to receive. He reiterates that in the forty years since he took his oath, he has never come across anything like it. As he speaks, I catch my sister's eye in the public gallery. She does a little wave, just a few fingers, and I do the same.

She has been my rock. Her visits keep me grounded. I want to get out of jail because I have something to go back to. Halfway through the trial, my father started coming as well. I have found his presence reassuring. He's conquered similar demons, or at least learned to control them.

'Would the foreman please stand?' says the judge.

A sharp-faced woman who must be well into her sixties gets to her feet. She seemed puritanical at the beginning, but I saw her shed tears on many occasions.

'Do you have a majority verdict?'

'We do, Your Honour. Ten of us are in agreement.'

'Very well. In the case of the Crown versus Vickerman, please announce your verdict clearly when asked, so all may hear.'

The foreman swallowed, then raised her chin and nodded.

'To the charge of the murder of Robert Ewing, how do you find?'

'Not guilty.'

'And to a lesser charge of manslaughter?'

'Not guilty.'

The public gallery erupts with anger. Cries of quiet from the usher eventually regain order.

'To the charge of the murder of Trent Anderson?'

'Not guilty.'

An audible gasp fills the courtroom. The judge presses on.

'And the lesser charge of manslaughter?'

'We find the defendant guilty.'

There is more confusion than outrage at the last verdict. I let out the breath I'm holding. Carson told me this was possible, and the judge would ask for pre-sentencing reports. He does just that and announces that, due to the seriousness of the crime, I will be remanded again to appear in a month's time.

The baying crowd have their voice now, and it's a relief to return to the peace and silence of the cells. Carson said the judge has an enormous sentencing range with manslaughter, from a few years to forever. I have a month to wait, but at least I have hope.

It feels as though I haven't slept for a month, but, despite that, the day has come. I can sense the entire court's eyes on me. We get the newspapers in the prison library, and I watch the news. It seems there are many who support me as well as those who have decried the verdict. That said, one red top called me The Ice Killer, due to my cool demeanour under questioning, and it stuck. To be fair, the article was balanced. The judge has a tricky task with much to consider.

Prisons are full of men and women with mental-health problems who've broken the law and damaged other people's lives and possessions. What's the answer? Should they all be punished, even though surely you could argue that some are out of their minds when they commit crimes? Or is the humane thing to give people the support and therapy they need? I can't help my nature. It's the way I was born.

Life's not simple. Robert Ewing's family hoped for answers, and I gave them nothing concrete. They will also want vengeance, and who am I to argue against that?

Lucy and my father sit beside each other. Brad is next to them, too, and Millie next to him. They've all said they'll visit, however long I get. Brad writes often. I thought about mentioning the secretary from work, Grace, but decide it doesn't matter. If he can forgive a little killing, then

I can absolve him of some minor deceit. Typical, just when I find my family, I could be taken away from them forever.

I've had a lot of time to look inward. I like to think I'm a good person, just capable of bad things. But with the right help and support, I can be a valuable and decent member of society. Hopefully, the judge will give me that chance today. I wonder if someone reading my thoughts would agree.

I will accept the judge's decision and move on. I'm balanced now, and I understand the perils of being from a family like mine. I must take my medication religiously because if I don't, I become the worst of them. And, once again, I will be the angel of death.

Barton knocked on DCI Cox's open door.

'Enter,' she said.

'No, it's okay, I just wanted to say we're glad you're back.'

She raised an eyebrow at him.

'Pop in for a minute, will you, John?'

After he'd sat in the chair opposite her, she smiled at him in a way he couldn't recall her doing before.

'I think we've all learned a lot about ourselves in the last six months or so. I've discovered that being a full-time mother is fabulous, but not for me. I missed my job. My partner has happily agreed to be a house-husband. Let's hope he finds it more rewarding than I did, although I suspect he's in for a big surprise.'

'Very much so.'

Cox paused for a moment.

'Do you resent me taking my job back?'

'No, of course not. I bet the management are pleased you've returned.'

Cox snorted. 'Rubbish. The chiefs have worked their way up. They understand what police work entails, and in particular how tough some cases can be. I know they hung you out to dry by saying that a more experienced Chief Inspector would have done a better job, but the public wanted a scapegoat, and you were inexperienced. Did the senior management give you any help during the case?'

'No.'

'Next time you'll learn to ask, then it's their arses on the line. I knew you'd struggle to adapt to what's fundamentally an office role, but who'd have thought such a case would come along? If it means anything, I think you did a great job. I've worked with many detectives of all ranks over the years, and I can honestly say you are the best of the best. I mean that. Don't worry, I won't be doing this job for long. I have a son to support now, and my ambition is endless. I'll drag you in my slipstream.'

Barton stood to leave. 'I hope that's better than it sounds, but do you know what? I don't want your position, not yet. I enjoy being a DI. I'm a man who likes to get in the trenches from time to time.'

Cox reached over and shook his hand.

'Good for you. Now, I hear that Strange, Zander and you are going to Crown Court for sentencing. Take them for a meal or a few drinks afterwards, on me. They did well, too.'

Cox sat down, and her chair gave out a pained croak. Barton received a dirty look.

'God knows what you've done to my chair. It's like an elephant's been using it.'

Barton got back to his desk and found a new mop leaning against it. On the handle was written, 'This is the property of John Barton.' Strange and Zander came and stood next to him.

'We knew you were getting demoted, we weren't sure how far,' said Strange.

'Very funny, but you need to be careful. I'm a master delegator now and someone needs to clean the toilets. I'll buy you both a toothbrush for tomorrow.'

They headed to the basement, and Barton drove them to the car park on Oundle Road near the courts. It was an overcast day with a swirling wind and they were subdued as they were searched as they went into the court building.

There were no seats left, so they strained their necks at the rear of the gallery. Zander found Strange a chair to stand on. Barton listened to the surprisingly short preamble with interest. The judge said he would explain the reason for his sentence afterwards.

Barton thought Ellen Vickerman stood proudly in the dock, even though she had two large members of court security either side of her. She had worn a simple cream suit, and her hair had grown back a couple of inches. It was cut into an elfin style that suited her. Every eye in that room was on her face. An unexpected wave of emotion engulfed Barton. He wondered if she'd suffered enough.

'Ellen Vickerman,' said the judge. 'I sentence you to life imprisonment.'

93

It took nearly ten minutes for the court staff to regain a semblance of control. The threat of removing all spectators finally got the place in order so the judge could return. Barton kept his eye on Ellen. She flinched when she heard the verdict. She searched for her family in the gallery, and then she cried. Barton wiped a stray tear away when her shoulders heaved. Never did he think he'd feel compassion for someone he suspected was a ruthless killer.

The judge cleared his throat and addressed the court.

'This is your final warning, please stay silent. The sentence is life, but I am only imposing a minimum term of ten years. This may seem harsh or lenient depending on your viewpoint, but I suspect we will never see a case such as this again in my court in my lifetime. I pray that we do not. We must remember that people have lost their lives, and their families have lost loved ones, but, as with most things in life, nothing is black or white.

'I bow to the jury for reaching a judgement in a complicated matter. The Crown's case was weak at best in many aspects of these deaths. I'm pleased that a not guilty verdict was returned on the other charges because there was simply not enough proof. Suspicion, hearsay and feelings are not enough to convict for murder in our legal system.

Apart from the defendant, the only people who know exactly what happened in these cases are the deceased, and they do not speak.'

He turned to Ellen.

'That brings me to Ms Vickerman. As a person, you seem cold and unthinking. Your evidence has been unreliable and you are not a credible witness, but you've often been the only witness. There is no doubt, however, that you killed Trent Anderson and assaulted two officers as you tried to escape. Whatever provocation there was is immaterial if the police have arrived. You were safe at that point, and there was no need to do what you did. The courts serve justice, not you.

'Your mental health has been well documented, but personality disorders are not a defence in themselves. You say you don't recall throwing your medication away, but only you can be responsible. Regardless, in this day and age, we should show humility and understanding when others find life tough.'

The judge's glare returned to the public gallery.

'I struggled to come to a decision as to what I should do with the defendant until I stripped down my role to its basics. I am here to protect the public. My main concern is that Ellen Vickerman may be a few missed tablets from being one of the most dangerous people I've met. Anyone who could take a life in the manner you did will always be a danger. Therefore, you need to be monitored for the remainder of your days.

'I think ten years behind bars as a minimum is just for what you did. I pass further decisions on to the mental-health experts, prison staff, and parole service, who will be better placed than I am to decide if after ten years or more you are fit to rejoin society. If they decide not, you will spend the rest of your natural life behind bars.'

94

Barton, Strange and Zander plodded down the steps of the courthouse. They stood in a circle looking at each other.

'It's weird,' said Zander, 'but I felt sorry for her at the end. I've also never considered how tough the judges have it before. I'm still not sure what I would have done if the decision had been mine. I suppose that while she's in jail, the public are safe.'

'Yes. Let's hope if she gets out, we never hear from her again,' said Barton.

'What? You two see a pretty girl and go soft in the head. She probably killed Ewing in cold blood as well as those deadbeats. I'll sleep safer if she spends the rest of her life doing laundry on the lifers' wing at HMP Peterborough.'

Barton nodded. He suspected everyone would have their own view on the case of The Ice Killer.

'You know what, despite what the newspapers say, we still make a brilliant team. I hope we have many years ahead of us,' he said.

Strange grinned. 'I'll drink to that. Come on, I've had enough of killers, let's move on to tequilas.'

'And I can definitely drink to that,' said Zander.

Strange and Zander high-fived each other, and did he detect them hold each other's stare for a moment longer than usual?

'There's a pub opened in Fletton, run by an old custody sergeant. You remember Dave Williams, Zander?' asked Barton.

'Yeah, he was a sound bloke. We can start there, if you like.'

They ambled back to Barton's car, and he drove them down London Road. The Wonky Donkey was one of those new micro pubs that were popping up all over, selling real ale and shunning fruit machines and music for old-fashioned chatting. Barton shook the hand of the landlord, who gave him a big grin.

'Good to see you again, John. Have you lost weight?'

'Very funny, Dave. I hope your beer is better than your jokes.'

'It's a strange coincidence that you turn up just as I put free peanuts on the bar.'

'What beer do you recommend?'

'They're all excellent.'

Smiling, Barton placed the order and helped himself to a big handful of nuts while he waited. The three of them had a sip of their real ales with suspicion as they usually stuck to lager.

'Nice,' said Barton.

Zander, a committed Kronenbourg fan, also nodded in approval.

'Mine tastes like it came out of the washing-up bowl after Sunday lunch,' said Strange.

Barton pondered asking how she knew that, but decided it'd been a long enough day already. Instead, he smiled at the landlord. Dave still had a full head of hair, but it was now flecked with grey. He had some cheek, too, as his shirt was tighter across the waist than it used to be.

'How long have you been retired now, Dave?'

'Two years, mate.'

'Do you miss it?'

Dave nodded. 'Every day.'

'You retired early, didn't you?' asked Zander. 'Why not stay on?'

'It was family. I missed out on a lot over the years and decided I was ready. You never know how long you have left with someone, so spend time with them now.'

They finished their beers and stepped outside. Barton drove them to the car park at the rear of The Yard of Ale pub.

'You can leave the car and collect it tomorrow,' suggested Strange.

'Maybe. I've got to pick up a few things from Asda for Holly,' said Barton.

They gave him a suspicious look. Strange linked arms with Zander as they strolled away and said something that made Zander put his head back and laugh. They would make a good couple, thought Barton.

After he'd been to the shops, he would send a text to his sergeants and tell them he wasn't returning. He reckoned they wouldn't mind too much. The retired detective was right. There was only one place Detective Inspector John Barton wanted to be, and that was home.

EPILOGUE

The thundering of feet across the landing woke Barton. Luke reached the bottom of his parents' bed and burrowed his way under the duvet until he was between them.

'Hey,' whispered Barton. 'That's my spot.'

'Cook the breakfast, Daddy. You promised us bacon sandwiches.'

Barton smiled as his stomach growled. He slipped from the covers, dressed, and wandered downstairs. Once the oven was on and the bacon was in, he looked out of the window at the stunning mackerel sky with the sun just rising. Autumn had arrived in a rush this year. His mouth watered at the thought of thick rashers, real butter, soft white Hovis, and his family around him. It was how he imagined heaven to be. With twenty minutes to waste, he grabbed his trainers and stepped outside to get a newspaper.

He breathed in the air and stretched. It was a relief that The Ice Killer case could now be closed, although it would never be forgotten. Barton nodded to a couple walking their spaniel down Moggswell Lane on the way to the Herlington Centre and relaxed as he admired the gold, scarlet and russet falling leaves. The lad with the pink hair was unlocking the shop door as he arrived. An old guy shook his walking stick in Barton's direction.

'Bloody late, again.'

'Morning,' said Barton, hoping that he wasn't referring to him.

Barton grabbed a copy of *The Sun* newspaper and blinked at the front page, which had nine letters in bold:

WOMANHUNT

He read the article in the queue as the elderly man berated the youth at the counter for not opening up on time.

'Sir?' asked the youth.

Barton hadn't noticed he was next in line because he couldn't believe what he was reading.

Four men had been found stabbed to death in a shared house in Brooklyn, New York. The authorities were looking for the other tenant. The landlord had let himself in after reports of a disturbance and discovered a scene of total carnage.

The FBI confirmed that what exactly happened was unclear, but they desperately wanted to talk to a British student from Harrow, London. There was a picture of the person they were after. Even though Barton hadn't met her, he knew her mother and aunt. Her name was Carrie Breslinski.

AUTHOR'S NOTE

Thank you for reading my DI Barton trilogy. I've really enjoyed writing about John and his family, and that includes his police family. I had a little tear in my eye as I wrote the end. That said, they weren't easy books to write. Even though I was a prison officer for four years, I had minimal dealings with the police. Therefore, I had to do a lot of time-consuming research and count on some current and retired detectives, such as Julian, to read the books and make sure they were procedurally accurate.

My E in A-level biology didn't help much with the post-mortems either, so Google was my friend. I hope DI Barton never looks at my search history, or I might as well hand myself in at HMP Peterborough right now. I had to concentrate hard when I wrote them due to the intricate plots, which was tough with home schooling. My six-year-old boy helped by interrupting me every four minutes to tell me which Pokémon was the most powerful.

I'm going to write a standalone exciting prison book next, but do you miss Barton, Strange, Zander, Mortis, Sirena et al? In a way, you can help me decide on my next novel. I love reading your reviews on Amazon, so please head over there if you enjoyed the series and let me know if you want more.

If you want to connect on social media, please do. Thank you for your support.

MORE FROM ROSS GREENWOOD

We hope you enjoyed reading *The Ice Killer*. If you did, please leave a review.

If you'd like to gift a copy, this book is also available as an ebook, digital audio download and audiobook CD.

Sign up to Ross Greenwood's mailing list for news, competitions and updates on future books.

http://bit.ly/RossGreenwoodNewsletter

Explore the DI Barton series:

  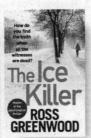 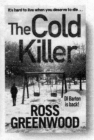

ABOUT THE AUTHOR

Ross Greenwood is the bestselling author of ten crime thrillers. Before becoming a full-time writer he was most recently a prison officer and so worked everyday with murderers, rapists and thieves for four years. He lives in Peterborough.

Follow Ross on social media:

twitter.com/greenwoodross
facebook.com/RossGreenwoodAuthor
bookbub.com/authors/ross-greenwood
instagram.com/rossg555

ABOUT BOLDWOOD BOOKS

Boldwood Books is a fiction publishing company seeking out the best stories from around the world.

Find out more at www.boldwoodbooks.com

Sign up to the Book and Tonic newsletter for news, offers and competitions from Boldwood Books!

http://www.bit.ly/bookandtonic

We'd love to hear from you, follow us on social media:

 facebook.com/BookandTonic
twitter.com/BoldwoodBooks
instagram.com/BookandTonic